PRAISE FOR #1 *NEW YORK TIMES* BESTSELLING AUTHOR
JULIE GARWOOD

"Once again, Garwood delivers another suspenseful, highly entertaining, and romantic story line in *Wired*."
—The Associated Press

"Whoever thinks romantic suspense is dead should read a Julie Garwood book." —*USA Today*

"A trusted brand name in romantic suspense." —*People*

"Julie Garwood creates masterpieces every time she writes a book." —*The Kansas City Star*

"Undoubtedly Garwood is a pro." —*Kirkus Reviews*

MORE TITLES BY JULIE GARWOOD

WIRED

JULIE GARWOOD

BERKLEY
New York

BERKLEY
An imprint of Penguin Random House LLC
375 Hudson Street, New Yyork, New York 10014

Copyright © 2017 by Julie Garwood
Penguin Random House supports copyright. Copyright fuels creativity, encourages
diverse voices, promotes free speech, and creates a vibrant culture. Thank you for buying
an authorized edition of this book and for complying with copyright laws by not
reproducing, scanning, or distributing any part of it in any form without permission.
You are supporting writers and allowing Penguin Random House to continue to
publish books for every reader.

BERKLEY is a registered trademark and the B colophon is a trademark of
Penguin Random House LLC.

ISBN 9780451469489

Berkley hardcover edition / July 2017
Berkley mass market edition / July 2018

Printed in the United States of America
1   3   5   7   9   10   8   6   4   2

Cover photograph of man by Claudio Marinesco
Cover design by Katie Anderson
Book design by Kristen del Rosario

For Jo Ann Cowan, my best friend.

You've gotten me through some harrowing times and have always been there for me.

Thank you . . . thank you . . . thank you.

Do not go where the path may lead.
Go instead where there is no path and leave a trail.

—RALPH WALDO EMERSON

ONE

A FIVE-MINUTE CLIP ON THE EVENING NEWS TURNED ALLISON
Trent into a full-blown criminal. She had wiggled across
the line many times before, but she'd never done anything
so bold or blatant. Within a couple of years she had accu-
mulated more than eighty million dollars. On paper that
would have made her a titan. In reality she was as poor as
a church mouse.

The motivation to commit the first crime came to Allison quite unexpectedly as she was sitting on an overstuffed
sofa in a coffee shop close to the Boston College campus.
She was working on a class project that was due the next
day and was so completely focused on the computer sitting
on her lap that she was oblivious of the activity around her,
not even hearing the news broadcast coming from the television that was suspended from the wall opposite her—that
is, until the words "terrible injustice" broke through her
concentration and drew her eyes up to the screen. The
young male reporter seemed genuinely sympathetic as he
read his story from the teleprompter. The subject was a lo-

cal nursing home called Sunset Gardens, one of twenty homes for the elderly located across the East Coast owned and operated by a corporation out of Philadelphia. The corporate home offices, he explained, kept a database with vital information pertaining to every single one of their clients. They were vigilant in protecting privacy, had all the bells and whistles installed to keep personal data ironclad against bugs and viruses, and had paid a hefty salary to a tech company whose only job was to monitor the system. None of that mattered, though. Their system had been hacked, and the identities of all the residents in all twenty facilities were stolen with one keystroke. And because First National was designated as the official bank for all Sunset Gardens homes and their residents, within minutes its accounts were wiped out as well.

The reporter went on to point out that a large number of the residents had no family to help them, and while the money in First National was FDIC insured, it could take the authorities a good long while to sort through the facts and reimburse every account.

What were the residents supposed to do until then? Allison wondered.

A sense of outrage was growing inside her as she listened to the catastrophic details of the crime, but the tragedy hit home when the reporter played a clip of his interview with one of the elderly residents. Her name was Ella O'Connor. He knelt beside Ella's wheelchair and held her veiny hand as he asked her what the news meant to her.

Ella's watery eyes stared at the reporter for a moment as though she was trying to understand the question. "I don't know," she said. And then a look of despair crossed her face. "I hope they don't make me leave."

Ella was all alone, afraid, and feeling helpless. Allison knew exactly how that felt. Her heart went out to Ella and all the other poor souls. Some of them would die before it was all sorted out, and in their golden years dealing with such stress and fear would be traumatic. What had happened to them was beyond cruel.

An interview with the president of the Sunset Gardens Corporation was played next. With a shrug in his voice, he said, "The authorities told me it was most likely the Russians behind the hacking. Or possibly the Chinese. The truth is, we may never know."

His defeated "Oh well, what can you do?" attitude infuriated Allison. She knew the FBI had experts trying to locate the hackers and shut them down, but it was apparent they hadn't had any luck so far. The invasion of secure systems was becoming epidemic. Just the week before, the news agencies had announced that the Pentagon had been hacked. The FBI was certain the Russians were behind the theft of employee information then as well, but proving it was a huge challenge.

What could she do? Something . . . maybe. It wouldn't hurt to try to find the Sunset Gardens hackers, would it?

Was it her ego or her arrogance that made her think she might succeed? She had always had the ability to solve complex problems. Even at an early age, her thought processes were out of the box. She had been just eight years old when her uncanny ability was first noticed. Her older sister, Charlotte, had bought a five-hundred-piece jigsaw puzzle at a yard sale and placed all the tiny pieces on the floor in their room. When Allison came home from school, Charlotte asked her if she wanted to help put the puzzle together. Allison knelt on the floor and stared at the scattered pieces for no more than a minute or two while her brain studied them. Not only could she tell Charlotte what the picture was, but she knew where the pieces fit. It was as though she was watching each part of the puzzle connect to the next. After separating the tiny cardboard tiles into six piles, she went to work. Charlotte watched in amazement. In less than five minutes, Allison had the perimeter of the square picture put together, and within another twenty, the entire puzzle was completed. Allison didn't think she had accomplished anything unusual, but Charlotte was clearly impressed. She told Allison that most people didn't look at things the way she did.

The nursing home story broke just as Christmas break was coming up. Allison had been a sophomore at Boston College at the time and planned to spend the holiday alone. Charlotte and her husband, Oliver, had moved to Seattle a couple of years ago. They had offered to buy a plane ticket for her to come, but knowing they were saving up to buy a house, Allison declined their generosity. Allison did have three other relatives, but she would rather have slept on the street than spent the holiday with them.

Allison and Charlotte had been very young when Aunt Jane and Uncle Russell became their legal guardians. The couple had one son, Bill, who was two years older than Allison, and the atmosphere of their home was neither warm nor welcoming. An air of constant friction permeated the place, usually stemming from something Bill had done. He never showed any signs of ambition or responsibility, and he hung around with a group of creepy misfits. The only talent he seemed to have was a knack for getting into trouble—or *mischief*, as Uncle Russell called his skirmishes with the police.

To Allison, her aunt and uncle and cousin were her poor excuse for relatives. Charlotte was her only family. When they were children, their aunt had often threatened to split them up if they didn't obey and keep quiet, and the possibility of never seeing her sister again had terrified Allison. She'd felt so helpless. She would have done anything to keep that from happening. Her fear, plus her sense of obligation to them for taking Charlotte and her into their home when they had nowhere else to go, had kept her compliant. However, now that she was an adult and had moved away from their house, she felt a new sense of freedom.

Since Allison was spending the holiday vacation alone, she decided to use the time off to focus her full attention on the hackers. She was confident the vast forces at the FBI would find the culprits eventually, but she wasn't going to leave the task to them. It could take too long.

She didn't get very far in her search during the break, yet she didn't give up. Every moment of spare time she could steal between her classes was spent on her hunt. She was well aware of the chance she was taking, and she knew how careful she had to be. Breaking into protected sites was against the law, and yet she wasn't deterred. She couldn't get the elderly victims out of her mind. Finding their money was becoming an obsession.

A breakthrough came when she gained access to the bank's servers and tracked the thieves' withdrawals to various bank accounts that had been set up in a number of European countries. As she suspected, those had been closed within seconds of the deposits, and the money was routed to other accounts. Ultimately she traced the funds to a consolidated account in Ukraine, and from there it was dispersed once again into smaller bank accounts. With each discovery, she became more and more certain the attack was not carried out by a cyber syndicate, but rather by a small group of hackers or maybe even a lone wolf, someone who had devised an elaborate plan to find a vulnerable target and drain the funds before anyone could detect the theft. Step by step, she unraveled the knots.

After a month of searching she hadn't found the source, but she could feel she was closing in. A long weekend was coming up and she was excited to have the extra time. The minute her classes ended on Friday afternoon, she hurried to her house off campus to resume her quest. Changing into her favorite fleece sweats and fuzzy slippers, she propped pillows against the bed's headboard and leaned back, her laptop on her outstretched legs. Around three in the morning, just as she was about to call it quits for the night, she found the last link . . . and presto, she had them.

Her discovery surprised her. The theft wasn't carried out by the Russians or the Chinese after all. All of the routing and rerouting through foreign banks turned out to be just a clever way of diverting attention. The real source was actually on the West Coast of the United States. The hackers were two seniors and one grad student at Stanford University. Their carefully hidden accounts—all containing some form of their initials, CHF, for their first names, Charles, Harold, and Franklin—had a total of thirty-eight million dollars. Certainly not chump change by any hacker's standards.

Allison was euphoric for a good fifteen minutes before worry set in. The way the three men moved money around was a concern. That thirty-eight million could have been gone by morning, and she would have had to spend God knew how long tracking it down again.

She knew what she needed to do. She just didn't know if she had the courage to do it. If she messed up, she could get thirty years in prison, she thought, even as she realized she couldn't and wouldn't let those three greedy lowlifes take what didn't belong to them.

"Screw it," she whispered. "Let's see how *you* like feeling helpless."

She could imagine how angry they were going to be when they realized they had been hacked, and thinking about it made her smile.

The first thing she did was steal the money. All thirty-eight million. She put it in a secure account she made certain they would never be able to find, then set about gathering the proof to nail them. She carefully retraced each step they'd taken, including each routing number, each transfer number, and each account number. Once that was done and the proof was indisputable, she sent the evidence and the thirty-eight million to the FBI. She, of course, made certain the e-mail she was about to send couldn't be traced back to her.

"This is for you, Ella," she said as she triple-checked her work, then typed the e-mail address for the FBI cyber task force and hit SEND.

Her message for the FBI was to the point. "You're welcome."

TWO

IT WASN'T JUST A POSSIBILITY ANYMORE. HE HATED WHEN A hunch became a reality.

Liam Scott walked through the bar of the beach hotel and spotted his friend and colleague Alec Buchanan sitting outside on the veranda. The stars were so bright in the vast Honolulu sky that the tiny lights strung overhead between the palms were almost redundant.

Alec had changed from his work clothes and was wearing a pair of cargo shorts, worn-out loafers, and an old T-shirt that was so faded the name of the 5K charity race it was promoting was illegible. He was leaning back in his chair with his legs outstretched, holding a beer, and watching the surf's hypnotic ebb and swell. He looked as though he was a tourist on the tail end of a long, relaxing vacation and not an agent who had just completed one of the most intense investigations of his FBI career.

Liam hadn't changed out of his suit yet. When he reached Alec, he took his phone from his pocket and laid it on the table, then removed his jacket and tie and draped them on the back of the rattan chair before unbuttoning his collar.

"I ordered you a Guinness," Alec told him.

Liam dropped into the chair. "Thanks. I could use one."

"Looks like we should have this wrapped up tomorrow. Just as long as Meyer doesn't get cold feet." He tipped his bottle to Liam in salute and said, "I appreciate your coming in on this case. I don't think we could have located Meyer without you and your international connections."

"If Meyer's testimony brings down Dimitri Volkov and his syndicate, that's all the thanks I need."

"I was surprised we got him to turn so quickly. I thought he'd hold out longer."

"He's no spring chicken. I guess the thought of the rest of his life in maximum security was enough of an incentive."

"Where is he now?"

"The team's helping him pack up, and they'll be moving him into a safe house. If they can keep him under wraps long enough, Volkov and his army of lawyers won't be able to line up a defense. They'll never suspect that Meyer is going to testify against his old partner."

A waitress appeared and set a glass of the murky dark brew in front of Liam. She was wearing a yellow bikini. A colorful scarf tied around her waist created a wrap that was so short it barely covered her firm little derriere. She wore no shoes, and Liam eyed her long tan legs appreciatively.

"Is there anything else I can get you?" she asked him.

"No, thank you," Liam answered.

She lingered for a moment and slid her gaze up and down his body. She then gave him a seductive smile and said, "If there's anything I can do . . . anything . . . you just let me know, all right?"

Liam and Alec watched her saunter back to the bar. She took her time to make sure the men got a good look at her attributes.

Alec gave Liam's leg a nudge with his foot. "I think that

was an invitation. You might find Honolulu is a very friendly place after all."

Liam laughed. "I'm leaving early tomorrow. I think a good night's sleep is what I need." He lifted the glass to his lips and took a couple of gulps. "When are you going home?"

"I'll fly back to Chicago on Friday. Regan's birthday is on Saturday. She doesn't expect me home until next week, and I want to surprise her."

"I don't get it. Regan is beautiful and smart and funny and sweet. . . . Why that perfect woman married you, I'll never know."

"You're right. She is perfect. Finding Regan was the best thing that ever happened to me."

"You're a lucky man," Liam said.

Alec nodded. "Yes, I am. What about you? Aren't you about ready to find the right woman and settle down?"

"Settle. Now, that's the operative word. Why would I settle when I see marriages like yours and Regan's? No, I don't have any notions of settling down. Work keeps me moving. Besides, I'm not naive enough to think there's another perfect woman out there."

He let out a heavy sigh, envisioning the days of travel ahead of him. He was off to Brussels in the morning to consult on a smuggling case; then he was expected in Singapore by the end of the week, and finally back to DC before the end of the month. He knew how important the work he did for the FBI was, and he'd never been one who wanted to stay in one place long enough to put down roots, always on the move, going wherever the need arose, but lately there was a restlessness inside him, a feeling he couldn't exactly identify.

He took another swig of the Guinness, slouched down in his chair, and stared up at the vast sky. He was interrupted from his thoughts when his phone rang. Glancing at the screen, he said, "It's the Honolulu office."

Alec watched as Liam listened to the caller. From the frown that darkened Liam's face, Alec surmised that whatever he was hearing wasn't good. At the end of the call, Liam stood and looked around. "We have to find a TV."

Alec followed him into the hotel bar. Liam went directly to the small TV that sat on the back counter, picked up the remote, and turned the channel from the baseball game that was playing. A couple of drinking patrons yelled their protests, but Liam turned up the volume and drowned them out. The news anchor finished telling a story about a local politician's resignation and then moved on to the next report about a breakthrough in a major drug ring investigation.

"Jennifer Dawson is reporting to us live," he said as the screen switched to a woman with a microphone. She was standing outside an apartment building.

"I'm here at the apartment where Herman Meyer has apparently been living under an assumed name for the past two years," the inordinately enthusiastic young woman said. "A yet-to-be-identified source has told Channel 5 News that Meyer has been questioned by the FBI and is now ready to testify against his former partner and the alleged head of one of the largest drug rings in North America, Dimitri Volkov. Mr. Meyer reportedly disappeared from his home in—"

Liam switched the TV back to the baseball game and came around the bar to Alec. "So much for the element of surprise," he said.

Alec was angry. "Only a handful of people were in on the Meyer investigation. There's no way one of them made an announcement to the press."

"This has happened before, and it's no coincidence."

Alec nodded. "Whoever is leaking information . . ."

Liam finished the thought. "It has to be coming from the inside."

THREE

JORDAN CLAYBORNE WAS CONSIDERED TO BE ONE OF THE most brilliant hackers in the business. Allison Trent was a thousand times better.

Although they shared a lot in common, there was one other big difference between the two friends. Jordan never broke the law. Allison did . . . repeatedly.

They first met at a reception for a professor who had just received a prestigious award for his contribution to the world of computer science. It was a great achievement for him and for Boston College, where Jordan was an alum and Allison still a student. Jordan sat down next to Allison at one of the tables and introduced herself, but an introduction really wasn't necessary. Allison knew exactly who Jordan Clayborne was. She was a legend at Boston College, a trailblazer, and in Allison's opinion a genius in the technology field. She had sold her start-up company for millions of dollars and was currently writing a series of programs that would teach beginners basic computer skills and guide them all the way to advanced software engineering. More important to Allison, Jordan had done what many believed impossible. She had put the boys in Silicon Valley on notice. She had done exactly what Allison planned to do as soon as she graduated. How could she not have been a fan?

As soon as Jordan asked Allison what her major focus was, the floodgates opened, and for the next two hours they discussed writing code. They bonded that night, and it didn't take long at all for them to become good friends. Neither could have imagined, though, that their friendship would begin a chain of events that would ultimately change Allison's life.

Despite their busy schedules, the two found time to meet often, usually over coffee or lunch. Other patrons of the coffeehouses or restaurants would see the two women talking excitedly and would assume the conversation was about the latest fashions or some new reality show on television. They never suspected the topic of discussion was computer programming.

Allison didn't meet Jordan's husband, Noah Clayborne, for several weeks. The two women generally spent their time discussing their common interest. They didn't delve deeply into personal matters. Jordan shared the facts that she was married and her husband had a job with the government, but Allison knew little else about him. Then one weekend Jordan invited Allison to her parents' home on Nathan's Bay. It was there that she finally met Noah and found out he was an FBI agent. She liked him immediately. He was charming and funny and obviously very much in love with his wife. Allison saw no reason to keep her guard up.

Jordan's parents, the Buchanans, were warm and welcoming, too, and Allison couldn't help noticing the affection they showed each other, something she had never seen between her aunt and uncle. Over the weekend, two of Jordan's brothers and their wives came for a visit. They treated Allison as if she were part of the family. She loved spending time with this gregarious and loving clan, especially the evenings around the dinner table when Jordan and her brothers told stories about their childhood and the pranks they would play on one another. Allison could only imagine the noise and the laughter when all seven of Jordan's siblings were together. She envied them.

It was at dinner the first night that she discovered most members of the Buchanan family were also involved in some aspect of law enforcement. Three brothers worked for the bureau. One was a federal attorney. Even Jordan's father was a judge. In any other situation, because of her forays into illegal activity, Allison would have made an excuse and gotten out of there as fast as she could, but the Buchanans were so much fun she ignored her vulnerability. In hindsight she realized she should have been more cautious. Yet, in her defense, she hadn't thought anyone would have seen what was coming. All she knew was that it felt good to be with a family who liked one another and wanted to be together, not to mention the fact that she and Jordan had plenty of time to sit and talk about languages and codes, and writing programs, and bugs, and hackers.

As the weeks wore on, Allison's crazy workload kept her from getting together with her friend as much as she would have liked, but an opportunity arose when she learned of an upcoming programming seminar. She signed up immediately. She knew she probably wasn't going to learn anything new—that wasn't arrogance on her part, just fact—but the presenter was Jordan, and she wanted to be supportive.

The day of the seminar arrived, and Allison spent the afternoon in the library working on a paper that was due next week. At five o'clock she closed down her laptop and reached for her coat. Checking her watch, she figured she had plenty of time to rush home and change. Jordan was speaking tonight at seven, and Allison wanted to get to the small auditorium early so she could get a good seat. Over a hundred students were attending the event. If it was like her computer science classes, the vast majority would be men—which Allison found galling. Where were all the women? She was aware that women were entering the technology fields, but the forward strides weren't happening fast enough to suit her. She didn't feel intimidated by the men. She could hold her own when it came to ability. It was just that she would have liked to have more women around her and not be looked at as some sort of oddity.

Her sister, Charlotte, had always seen the analytical side of Allison, but most people who had known her as a child wouldn't have predicted she would one day be a computer geek. They claimed that her talent lay in her looks. From the time she was a toddler, complete strangers would comment on what a pretty child she was. Then, as she grew into her teenage years, she was told her slender figure and long, shapely legs made her the perfect model. One photographer announced she had the perfect face: high cheekbones; gorgeous, brilliant blue eyes; perfect complexion; and full pouting lips. She had been just a junior in high school when, while browsing in a department store with her sister, she was spotted by the store's manager and offered a photo shoot for an ad campaign in a local magazine. She went home and asked her aunt and uncle about it, and their answer was curt and dismissive, which was precisely the reaction Allison expected. In the years she had lived with them, she had never received encouragement for anything.

Allison had been about to reject the store manager's modeling offer when her aunt and uncle had a sudden change of heart. They had just received a large bill from an attorney who represented Bill on a shoplifting charge. Realizing that the extra income she could bring into the family would help alleviate some of their financial worries, they gave their permission.

The magazine layout was a big success, and in the months

that followed, Allison received several offers, which she declined. She wasn't interested in a modeling career. But when
an up-and-coming Boston designer named Giovanni Donato
pleaded with her, insisting that no one could wear his clothes
the way she could, she gave in. He had been so kind to her
during the magazine shoot she couldn't say no. She agreed
to work for him, on a limited basis, just as long as the modeling didn't interfere with school and her long-term goals.

Because she was a minor, her guardians demanded to
receive every dime Allison earned, and each check they
received they immediately spent. When Giovanni got wind
of what they were doing, he opened an account for Allison
at his bank, increased her base salary without telling the
guardians, and deposited the difference. Allison appreciated the modeling jobs and especially the way Giovanni
watched out for her financially, but when a couple of years
had passed and she was ready to enroll in college, she knew
it was time for a change of direction. There was no doubt in
her mind that she had been programmed for something
other than modeling. Her future had been determined the
minute her sister showed her how to turn on a computer.
She couldn't remember how old she had been at the time,
but she could attest that it was love at first keystroke. Back
then she was a shy, quiet girl, and people's behavior didn't
always make sense to her, yet computers did. She couldn't
explain how it happened. Maybe her brain was a computer,
she theorized. It all just clicked inside her. Working on the
computer was also a wonderful escape from her relatives
and the endless turmoil at home. When Allison put on her
headphones, all the noise and chaos were blocked out.

With each year of college that passed, her knowledge
and enthusiasm increased. There wasn't anything she
couldn't do with her laptop. Reading codes was one of her
favorite pastimes. After she'd solved the problem for the

residents of Sunset Gardens, breaking into supposedly impossible sites became a favorite activity. She began to expand her curiosity and her exploration. The lure of a complicated program was too enticing to pass up, and the more intricate, the better. She loved looking for bugs. These small programming errors were passages into some very sophisticated systems. She entered hundreds of sites this way, and yet she made sure no one would ever detect her presence. Aware that the bugs had the potential for making organizations and companies susceptible to destructive attacks, she took great pains to hide her tracks. Allison knew she was breaking the law by visiting protected sites, but in her defense, her intentions were purely innocent. To her, these were giant puzzles, and she was simply studying them to see how the pieces fit. She wasn't doing anything harmful. No, she was actually being helpful. If she discovered an intrusion, she would block the hacker, and many times she removed viruses that could damage or even destroy companies. She had no trouble justifying her activities to herself, but deep down inside there was always a nagging voice warning her. If the authorities ever discovered what she was doing, she could have been in a lot of trouble.

She loved college. It allowed her to move out of her aunt and uncle's home and into a house near the campus. Moving day was as joyful as the Christmas mornings she'd shared with Charlotte and her husband when they had lived in Boston, and it was her fervent hope that she would never have to spend another night with her aunt and uncle. Her freedom meant she could concentrate on what excited her. While most of her classmates were hanging out at local drinking establishments, she was in her room playing with code. She wasn't completely antisocial. She had made a few friends, but most of them were interested in other pursuits and didn't share her passion. It was nice to have a friend like Jordan who understood, and Allison was looking forward to her seminar tonight.

When she stepped out of the library, the air was frigid and damp with flurries that would soon turn into a full-blown snowstorm if the weatherman was correct with his forecast. The temperature was unseasonably low for early November. Fortunately, the house she shared with two other students was only three blocks away from the auditorium. She could cut across campus and be there in five minutes.

The house was empty when she arrived. She rushed upstairs to her bedroom and changed into skinny jeans and a long-sleeve T-shirt, then pulled on a thick cream-colored cable-knit sweater and reached to the back of her closet for her leather knee-high boots. They were well-worn and comfortable and would keep her toes nice and warm. Her long brown hair went up into a ponytail. Typically she wore very little makeup, the exception being when she was on a photo shoot with Giovanni. After a little mascara and lip gloss, she was ready to go. Instead of her heavy winter coat, she put on her light gray down-filled quilted vest. It had so many zipper pockets she didn't have to carry a purse or a backpack. Her keys and pepper spray went into one pocket; her small billfold with her money and ID went into another, tissues and cell phone into a third pocket, and there were still two empty pockets for her gray leather gloves. She wrapped the matching gray scarf around her neck twice, then tied the ends the way Giovanni had shown her. She had a killer wardrobe, thanks to him. Not only had he put money aside for her, but he also insisted she take the clothes she modeled as a bonus for a job well-done.

The stairs of the old house squeaked and groaned as she ran down to the first floor. She was surprised to see her two roommates, Dan and Mark, in the living room. They looked very serious as they huddled over a stack of papers on the coffee table. She smiled as she watched them. She remembered how Charlotte had had a fit when she heard Allison was moving in with male students, but after meeting them, Charlotte realized Allison was probably safer with them watching out for her than she would have been living alone. Besides, both of the guys were in long-term relationships.

Dan Campbell was in charge of house finances. An economics major on a scholarship, he would probably graduate at the top of his class next year. When she had answered the post on the student bulletin board advertising a room for rent, it was Dan's persistence that swayed Mark to let her move in. Dan was built like a linebacker yet didn't play sports. His physique reminded her of a big burly bear, but he was very sweet.

Mark Strausman was a political science major who planned to go to law school. He was outgoing and friendly, and Allison liked him very much. He had just become engaged and was getting married after graduation to a girl who went to a neighboring college. When he wasn't in class, he was participating in student government, and Allison had no doubt that someday she would be voting for him in a state—if not a national—election.

For the first couple of months of this term, they had taken in a fourth student; however, Brett Keaton had never quite fit in with the group. While the others pitched in with chores, he was lazy and refused to pull his own weight. A computer science major, he constantly bragged about his grand plan to start a company and take it global. Someday, he vowed, he would own half of Boston. Unfortunately, there was a major weakness in his plan. His academic performance was, at best, below average. He often solicited Allison's help when he was stuck on a project, and while she was willing to bail him out a few times, she had major doubts about his capabilities. Not to mention his aversion to hard work. The housemates were able to tolerate his rather obnoxious personality for a while, but then Mark found him sneaking into Allison's room and snooping around her computer one night when she was gone. Mark reported the discovery to Dan, and the two decided that this was the last straw. They told Brett to pack his things and get out.

Since the three remaining housemates got along so well, they decided not to fill his room. They had managed until now, and there really wasn't any reason to add another person. Everything quickly settled back into a calm normalcy.

"Al, do you have a minute?" Dan asked when he spotted her at the foot of the stairs.

"Sure. What's going on?" She walked over to the sofa and sat on the arm. Seeing that the papers on the coffee table were bills, she waited for an explanation.

"Everything's covered this month except Mark's portion of the rent."

"I feel like an idiot," Mark said. "Before we threw Brett out, I never thought to check my things. I was so mad at the time I didn't think to look at where I hide my money. He took it all. I can't prove it, though."

"Did you know he snuck back into the house one afternoon and was in your room?" Dan asked Allison.

She nodded. "That's what Mark told me."

When she had heard about Brett's attempt to snoop on her computer, she was concerned, but when she got the news about the second incident, alarm bells went off. She had been working on a program for months that, if successful, could revolutionize computer security. She had told no one about it, not even her housemates, because she had a few details to add and wanted to test it thoroughly first. Had Brett somehow discovered her work? She couldn't help being suspicious. She was usually so cautious, but he had been near her on several occasions when she logged on to her computer.

Had she let her guard down? All it would take would be one stupid lapse on her part for him to learn how to access her work. She had built in precautions, and she reassured herself with the fact that she had backed up everything. Plus, Brett had only a mediocre understanding of code, so even if he found her work, she felt certain he wouldn't understand it. Still, there was a nagging worry. Maybe he was attempting to steal something. Her computer perhaps? She realized she had to be more careful. Her life was on that laptop.

"I'm the one who vouched for him in the beginning," Dan said. He shook his head. "So stupid."

"How much do we need to make rent?" she asked.

"Six hundred," Dan replied.

She pulled out her billfold and took three one-hundred-dollar bills from the hidden fold behind the change slot. She had planned to deposit it in her account in the morning. Instead she put it on the coffee table.

Dan threw in two hundred forty. "We're still short sixty."

"I've got sixty," Mark said.

"Al, where did you get three hundred dollars? You're always cash poor," Dan said.

"Birthday money from Charlotte and Oliver," she answered.

"I'll pay you guys back," Mark vowed. "I promise."

"No, that's not how it works," Dan argued. "Next month it could be Al needing some help . . . or me. We don't keep tabs."

Allison nodded in agreement. "Are we done here? I've got to go."

"Where?" Dan asked.

She quickly explained about the seminar and once again headed to the door.

"Got your pepper spray?" Dan called.

"Yes."

"Keys?"

"Yes."

"Cell phone in case you get in trouble?"

"Yes."

"Switchblade?"

She laughed. "I don't have a switchblade . . . and no, I'm not getting one."

"I was just making sure you were listening to me. Be careful."

As she was closing the door behind her, she could hear him still calling to her, "And don't forget . . . be aware of your surroundings."

Dan was a worrier. He was the loving big brother she never had. She wasn't forgetting about her cousin, Bill. He just didn't qualify. She had grown up with him, and he could have taken on a brotherly role in her life, but that had never happened. The only person he worried about was himself, and he certainly wasn't loving.

She heard someone call her name from the other side of the street, and just as she turned to wave to one of her professors, her phone rang. She was in a great mood until she saw who was calling. It was her aunt, who never called unless there was a problem. Allison didn't want to answer and considered letting it go to voice mail, but from experience she knew her aunt wouldn't give up. She also knew that, with each call, her aunt would become more and more belligerent. Allison decided to get it over with and talk to her now.

"Hello."

"Hello, Allison. How are you?" As usual her aunt's voice was rigid. The only time Allison had ever heard any affection in the woman's tone was when she was talking to her son.

"I'm good," she replied. She reached the end of her block and stopped on the corner to let traffic pass before she crossed the street. The streetlights were just beginning to flicker on as dusk settled over the city.

"Are you keeping warm?"

"Yes."

"You're not eating too much, are you? You know you have to stay away from carbs."

Allison sighed. Her aunt was never going to change. "No, I'm not eating too much."

"We've been told you're the perfect size and weight."

Allison gritted her teeth. It was amazing she hadn't developed an eating disorder. While she was in high school, it was salads every night. Her aunt was constantly counting Allison's calories. The pressure was nerve-racking. "Yes, I know."

"Are you keeping warm? We can't afford for you to get sick."

She'd already asked that question. Her aunt was rattled. Allison could hear the tension in her voice. Trying to rush her to explain the problem never worked, though. God knew, Allison had tried to speed up the process in the past. It just made her aunt more nervous and prolonged the silly chitchat until she finally circled around to the reason for her call.

"Yes, I'm keeping warm," Allison repeated.

"I'm sorry. What were you saying? Your uncle's talking to me at the same time, and I . . ."

"Yes?" Allison stopped there.

"Have you spoken to Giovanni lately?"

"Yes. I talk to him every week. Why?"

"We're going to need you to do a couple more modeling jobs as soon as possible. You'll have to put school on hold for now."

Again? Oh, hell no. "Aunt Jane, it's almost the middle of the semester. I can't just quit again. I only need a few hours to graduate. How many times do you think the Jesuits will take me back? What happened?"

It was Bill, of course. It was always Bill. Allison didn't

dare ask what he had done now, because her aunt would get her back up. When it came to Bill, his mother and father lived in Looney Tune Land. Nothing was ever his fault.

"Bill could go to jail," her aunt blurted, her voice shaking with emotion. "Yes, you heard me. Jail."

"Why?"

"For something he didn't even do," she said. "He didn't steal anything. He was just in the wrong place at the wrong time, and when the police came, he tried to tell them that, but they wouldn't listen to him. Now they want to charge him with resisting arrest, too. He's the victim here, and his attorney will prove he's innocent. But there's an issue with the lawyer's retainer. . . ."

"Aunt Jane, I can't—"

"This is an emergency. Your uncle and I are tapped out."

She heard her uncle say, "Tell her to stop arguing and do what she's told. The decision's been made."

Allison could feel a slow burn coming on. She had reached the sidewalk in front of the auditorium and was now pacing back and forth. Students were passing her on their way into the building. She stopped pacing for a second and noticed a man in a heavy overcoat with the collar turned up standing at the top of the steps. He was watching her. Dan's warning to be aware of her surroundings made her take notice, and she walked away from the steps as she continued to listen to her aunt's argument.

"Your uncle's right. We've made the decision. Just remember, family comes first, and Bill needs you. Don't be ungrateful after all we've done for you and your sister—"

She interrupted. "Aunt Jane, it's okay. I don't need to quit my classes. I've already talked to Giovanni, and I'm doing a shoot during break, which is coming up soon."

She waited while the information was relayed to her uncle.

"Oh, that's wonderful," her aunt said with a huge sigh of

relief. "I'm sure the lawyer will wait, knowing the check will be coming. Your uncle will talk to him."

In their minds the problem had been solved, and Bill would once again get a free pass. They really believed, with the right lawyer and enough money, they could get their son out of anything. And thus far they'd been right. They had somehow convinced themselves that Bill was a victim. All he needed was enough love and support, and everything would be fine. Allison tried to care about her cousin, but she couldn't understand his parents' irrational devotion. They had added so many colors to the truth they had actually painted a new reality.

Allison's statement about talking to Giovanni wasn't a total lie. She had spoken with him just last week, but she didn't have any work scheduled. She could call him tomorrow and grovel, she supposed, unless he really did have something for her. He had become not only her employer, but also what she imagined a father should be. She had gained his complete loyalty when she agreed to work exclusively for him. He called her his muse and often asserted that she was giving up the chance to be a top model by staying in Boston instead of moving to New York. She disagreed. She was neither tall enough nor thin enough, and she was already too old by the fashion world's standards. There was also the fact that she didn't have the extra drive it would take to succeed. Besides, her ambitions were taking her in an entirely different direction.

Allison ended the call and, putting her relatives' problems aside, hurried up the steps. Heavy snow had started to fall, and the chill in the air was biting.

There was a seat on the aisle three rows from the stage. She unzipped her vest, removed her scarf, sat back, and then remembered to turn her phone to mute.

Jordan was standing near the podium talking with the moderator. It would be easy to be envious of her, Allison thought. Jordan seemed to have it all. Not only was she brilliant; she was also very beautiful, with long auburn hair, sparkling eyes, and an infectious laugh. The moderator looked enthralled. Jordan spotted Allison and waved to her.

After a brief introduction, Jordan spoke for thirty minutes about her experience as a software developer and her current project creating programs to simplify computer learning. Allison hung on every word. Then came the questions. Some of the computer science majors were a bit condescending, no doubt trying to impress Jordan with their knowledge. Her answers were given so patiently and with such a sweet smile Allison wondered if any of the questioners realized they had just been taken down by an expert.

When the lecture was officially over, most of the audience began to file out, but a few diehards stayed behind to continue the discussion. After twenty minutes of back-and-forth, a couple of students asked more complex questions that piqued Allison's interest. She listened intently to Jordan's expert answers and was spurred by her own curiosity to raise her hand. Jordan turned and pointed in her direction. "Yes? Your question?"

Allison straightened in her chair and raised her voice. "I was wondering if you ever considered using Cobar to write your code for that particular program."

All eyes were on her now. A few people exchanged puzzled glances. Cobar was an obscure programming language unknown to most of them.

Jordan stopped to think for a minute. "That's a really interesting idea," she answered. "Why would you think it would fit this application?"

Allison explained her reasoning, and before long the two women were engaged in a lively dialogue. At first, the other audience members who had remained behind tried to keep up with the conversation by asking for clarification, but it soon became apparent that most of them were lost. As the questions became more detailed—with Jordan asking Allison most of them—the dwindling audience began to lose interest, and one by one they exited the auditorium, leaving just Jordan, Allison, and a small band of fewer than a dozen students.

Becoming aware that most people had left, Allison glanced around at the empty chairs and spotted someone standing at the back of the auditorium. He was the same man she'd noticed outside on the steps. He was occupied, texting on his phone. He obviously wasn't interested in the discussion, and yet he wasn't leaving. He looked up, and for the briefest of seconds their eyes met. She could have sworn he smiled at her. She was certain she had never seen him before. She definitely would have remembered a man as fine-looking as that.

The moderator finally stopped the question-and-answer period by stepping forward and thanking Jordan for participating in the forum. Those still in the auditorium showed their appreciation with a round of applause. As she waited in her seat for Jordan to say good-bye to the moderator, Allison noticed a message on her phone from Dan. He was at the library and wanted her to text him when she was ready to walk home. He'd walk with her. She smiled when she read it. Dan was such a worrywart, but she was secretly grateful he considered himself her protector.

Allison quickly slipped her phone back into her pocket and made her way to the stage to say hello to Jordan, who was just coming down the steps.

"Was I as boring as I thought I was?" Jordan asked.

The moderator had turned out the stage lights and was locking up the auditorium.

"No, you weren't boring at all. How come some of those computer science boys were so condescending?"

"Beats me," Jordan answered. "You put them to shame tonight," she added, grinning.

Allison texted Dan as they made their way to the exit. She looked around for the mysterious stranger who had been watching from the back of the auditorium, but he had disappeared.

The two friends didn't have much time to catch up while they waited on the steps outside, because Dan appeared almost immediately. He and Allison walked Jordan to her car and then backtracked toward their house. On their walk home she told Dan about her programming discussion with Jordan during the seminar.

"You do realize I'm an econ major, and everything you've just said sounds like gibberish to me."

She laughed. "Sorry. I guess I was getting a little technical, wasn't I?" After a minute she said, "I was showing off tonight. I shouldn't have done that."

"Why not? There's nothing wrong with letting people know how smart you are."

She disagreed. "I don't want to draw attention. It could get me into trouble."

"What kind of trouble could you get into? It's not like you broke the law or anything," he said, and then teasing her with a raised eyebrow and an exaggerated look of suspicion, he added, "Or did you?"

"No, of course not," she laughed, averting her eyes.

If he only knew.

FOUR

OVER SPRING BREAK ALLISON PLANNED TO GET AHEAD OF her classwork, but her aunt and uncle demanded that she take on another modeling assignment because the attorney's bill had grown to staggering heights. She knew she could refuse. She was over eighteen, and they had no legal control over her, but saying no simply wasn't worth the barrage of calls and constant harassment. She wouldn't put it past them to follow her into class and make a scene to get what they wanted. It was always easier—and inevitable—to give in.

Keeping Bill out of jail was becoming more and more difficult. He had been ordered by one judge to attend anger management classes. Allison hoped more than anything that these would help, but she had her doubts.

Fortunately Giovanni was ready to photograph the catalog for his new line and was overjoyed that Allison would be available. The photos were shot along the beautifully rugged coast of Maine, and for two weeks Allison posed, as a team of hairstylists, makeup artists, and dressers hovered around her, primping and preening. On the day she returned home to Boston, Jordan called.

"I'm so glad you're back," Jordan said.

Allison could hear the eagerness in her voice. "What's going on?"

"How would you like to visit the FBI's new office building with me this afternoon?"

Allison immediately declined. The last few weeks had been exhausting and she wanted a day to recuperate, but when Jordan mentioned they would be visiting the new cyber center, she reconsidered.

"Agent Jim Phillips is a friend of Noah's and mine," Jordan explained. "Noah's worked with him in the past, and we've known him a long time. He's head of the cyber task force in Boston. I hear the facility is state-of-the-art, and I'm dying to see it. He just called me and asked if I'd like to come and tour it today. He knew who you were and told me I could bring you along, too. What do you say?"

"How does he know about me?" Allison asked suspiciously.

"Noah, I'm guessing," Jordan answered. "My poor husband has heard us talking codes and viruses and programs for hours on end. He probably mentioned you to Phillips. So, do you want to go or not?"

"Absolutely. I'm in."

She hadn't unpacked from her trip yet and went to her closet to find something to wear. She didn't think her usual uniform, jeans and a T-shirt, would be appropriate, so she chose a skirt and a silk blouse with a pair of nude heels.

When Jordan came to pick her up, Allison's two housemates were shooting hoops in the driveway. They stopped to watch her walk down the sidewalk and whistled in appreciation.

"Where you goin', Al? Must be someplace special for you to put on a skirt in the middle of the afternoon," Mark called out in a singsong tease.

She smiled and waved to them as she got in the car.

The ride took a long while. Jordan's GPS led them onto three different highways before they exited into an old industrial area. Allison wasn't even sure they were still in Boston. They turned a corner and ended up on a long, winding road that seemed to be heading to the middle of nowhere. There weren't any houses or other commercial properties around, just thick trees on either side. The branches draped over them like an umbrella.

"Why would the bureau put an office all the way out here?" Allison asked.

Jordan was just as puzzled. "I don't know. When I told Noah we were going there today, he warned me it was in a remote area. I wish he could have come with us, but he had to leave for Florida this morning."

They pulled up to a gate in a tall chain-link fence, and the GPS announced that they had reached their destination. Beyond the fence was a modern three-story building, all tinted glass and steel. There weren't any signs indicating it was an FBI office.

"Are you sure we're in the right place?" Allison asked. "It looks deserted."

"This is the address Agent Phillips gave me," Jordan said.

The gate suddenly opened.

"I guess they know we're here," Jordan said as she stepped on the accelerator and drove through. She pulled into an empty lot obviously meant for visitors and parked in the slot closest to the front door. "There must be a parking garage on the other side of the building or maybe it's underground."

"There's a guard just inside the door watching us."

Jordan nodded. "I count two cameras on top of the building, and the red eyes are definitely on us."

"This is very weird," Allison said. "But the fact that it's

such a highly protected site makes me all the more excited to see what's inside. I wonder if they have a code room."

"I'm sure they do."

They started for the door. "Don't let me forget to thank Agent Phillips. This is such a cool opportunity," Allison said.

"About Phillips . . . ," Jordan began.

"Yes?"

"You won't like him much at first. He's arrogant and wants things done his way, but he grows on you. He can be a real pain. . . ."

"And he's your friend?"

Jordan nodded. "If you're in the mood, I'd love it if you'd take him down a peg, maybe chip away some of his arrogance."

"You want me to show off for an FBI agent?"

"I kinda do."

"It's not going to happen." Allison began to laugh. "You've got a crazy amount of faith in me. I'm sure the head of the cyber task force won't be interested in anything I have to say."

The guard at the door escorted them to a reception desk where another guard sat behind a bank of computer screens. The young man, with a badge clipped to his blazer pocket identifying him as Tom Pritchard, picked up the phone to notify Phillips of their arrival. While they waited, the door guard leaned against the counter, obviously happy to have a break in the monotony of his job and ready to chat. "We hardly ever get visitors, and today we have three."

"Three?" Jordan asked.

"That's right. You two and an agent, but not with this division. I'm not real sure who he works for," he admitted. "But I do know he's got higher clearance than Agent Phillips. He could shut us down if he wanted to."

"Why would he want to?" Allison wondered.

The guard grinned. "I'm not saying he would. I'm saying he could. He's got the authority."

The elevator doors opened and a man stepped out. He was putting his jacket on as he strode toward the desk. He appeared to be in his mid-forties. His hair was trimmed so close to his head he almost looked bald, and his stocky build and thick neck strained the buttons of his shirt.

"Phillips is younger than I expected," Allison whispered to Jordan.

"That's not Phillips," she replied.

"No, that's Curtis Bale. He was head of our Midwestern division in Detroit," Tom said as he opened a drawer and took out two large envelopes. When Bale reached the counter, he handed them to him. Bale couldn't seem to take his attention away from the women, so the guard quickly introduced him.

"Are you here to see anyone in particular?" Bale asked.

Since the question was directed at her, Allison answered. "Yes, we are."

"Agent Phillips," Jordan supplied.

It was apparent that Bale wanted to know why they wanted to see Phillips, because he waited several seconds for one of them to explain. Neither Jordan nor Allison did.

The guard filled the awkward silence. "I think they're here for a tour or something."

Bale's eyebrow went up. "Phillips is giving tours?" He laughed as though the notion was ludicrous.

"Not exactly," Jordan said. "Agent Phillips is a friend."

"Then the rumor's true. Phillips does have friends." He shook his head, then said, "It was nice meeting you. Enjoy your tour." He checked the time on his watch and hurried down the hall.

Tom noticed the two women were still holding their purses and said, "No cell phones or cameras beyond this point. You can leave your things here, and I'll lock them in the desk."

They were handing over their purses just as the elevator doors opened again and Agent Phillips stepped out. He managed a smile for Jordan. When she introduced him to Allison, he gave her a frown and a curt nod. Allison guessed Phillips was around fifty. His thick hair was streaked gray, and his weathered tan implied he was an outdoorsman. His piercing gaze told her he didn't miss much.

Allison followed Jordan into the elevator. Leaning close, she whispered, "He's a real charmer, isn't he?"

The second floor was just as shiny and uncluttered as the first. There were several sleek desks scattered around the area, but there weren't any employees working at the stations. Aside from the stack of Post-its and pens, there were no other papers or personal effects such as potted plants or photos of family. Maybe they weren't allowed, Allison thought. The wall opposite the elevators was constructed of huge opaque glass panels.

A tall young man in a suit that looked a size too large for his thin frame stood waiting for them as they exited the elevator.

"Ladies, this is Agent Kimble," Phillips said. He then turned to Kimble. "If you'll take Mrs. Clayborne and show her around, I'd like to have a word with Miss Trent before her tour."

Clearly surprised by the unexpected separation, Jordan looked puzzled.

"We'll catch up with you," Phillips assured her.

As Jordan began to follow the agent down the hallway, she glanced back at Allison and gave her a baffled shrug.

Phillips led Allison to his office to the left of the main room. While she waited, bewildered, in the doorway, he went to his desk and picked up a file folder, then came back to her and opened it. Looking at what was inside, he said, "Allison, I see your parents died when you were four years old. Your sister, Charlotte, was ten. The two of you moved in with your aunt and uncle, Jane and Russell Trent—"

Shocked, she interrupted. "Wait . . . You have a file on me?" She could feel her face heating up. "Why would you have a file on me?"

Oh God. What had he found out about her?

"We don't let just anyone in here. We're making an exception for you and Jordan. Jordan has clearance, and we've done a thorough check on you."

"Why did you invite us here?" Allison asked. She could feel panic building inside her, but she was determined not to let it show.

"I didn't. It was decided this morning. The order came from above. We knew that Jordan was your friend, and if we invited you together, you would most likely come. Does my looking at your file upset you?" he asked curtly, as though resentful of the intrusion on his time.

She squared her shoulders and took a step inside his office. Perhaps if she appeared cool and self-assured, he would not detect her anxiety. "It upsets me that you have a file on me. Yes."

Allison suddenly realized she was surrounded by federal agents. She didn't have any idea where they'd come from, and she was beginning to feel claustrophobic. Focusing on Phillips, she asked, "What did you decide this morning?"

"To see what you can do."

"Excuse me?"

"I'd like to show you around our operation and then see what, if anything, you can do," he explained.

What she could do? What was he talking about? When he'd opened the file, she was certain he was going to start listing her crimes, but now she was confused. Maybe he had other intentions. Whatever he wanted, he was certainly smug about it. His condescending inflection affected her like a dentist's drill hitting a nerve.

He went back to her file folder. "I noticed you've been a student at Boston College for a long time now. Adding up your credits, it looks like you're about to graduate. However, it's taken you five full years. Why do you think that is?"

She couldn't resist. If he thought to embarrass her, he was mistaken. She took a step toward him, batted her eyelashes, and said, "I'm not real bright."

Several agents laughed. Phillips didn't react. "Are you ready for your tour?" He walked across the room and paused in the doorway. "Just don't touch anything," he said before disappearing behind the tinted glass.

She looked at the wall of agents behind her. She had had enough of Phillips's patronizing attitude and wanted to get out of there, but it was apparent she wasn't being given a choice in the matter, so she reluctantly followed.

They proceeded down a hallway where the walls were clear glass. There was so much activity she didn't know where to look first. They passed a huge room filled with computers and techs, all men dressed in suits and ties, with their jackets off. Allison stopped to watch. They were typing furiously and watching their screens. Against the far wall facing her was a giant world map. Dots of light appeared with lines curving from relay station to relay station, bouncing off satellites around the globe. It was obvious to Allison that they were trying to pinpoint the exact location where a cyber attack originated, but the person or persons at the source had put up barricades. She stopped to watch. The screen was filling up with more dots, indicating the techs weren't getting anywhere.

When Phillips noticed Allison wasn't behind him, he came back for her. "What are you doing?"

She didn't answer for a couple of minutes. As she watched the lights jump across the screen, she began to recognize the pattern. It was one she had seen before. "Is this a training session?"

"No, of course not. This isn't a training facility. These are all professionals."

"Then why is it taking them so long to . . ." She paused. Trying to be more diplomatic, she revised her question so that it wouldn't sound antagonistic. "How long do you think it will take before one of them pinpoints the location?"

"It could take a day or two, sometimes longer, and sometimes the location disappears before we can locate the point of origin." He stared at her while she continued to study the map, then offered a challenge. "You think you can do better?"

There it was again, that smart-ass attitude in his tone and expression. She decided she wouldn't let him irritate her, until he said, "I didn't think so."

Oh, it was so on. She brushed past him, opened the door, and walked into the room. The air smelled clean but with a hint of aftershave. Every male in the room looked up at her and froze. She smiled, hoping to put them at ease as she walked over to a tech in the back row and said, "Would you mind if I have a try?"

All heads turned in the direction of Phillips, who was still outside the glass. He nodded.

Another tech nearly knocked his chair over when he stood. "Here," he said, "you can use the station next to Stan." He rushed to the back row, inserted his card into a slot, then pulled out the chair. "Here you go. All set."

He introduced himself. Then eleven others followed suit. They wanted to know why she was there. She didn't take time to explain. She sat, adjusted the chair, stared at the screen for several seconds, and started typing. Her mind was so focused on the task at hand that she was no longer aware of her surroundings.

PHILLIPS STAYED OUTSIDE, FEELING ANNOYED. HE HAD A LOT of work to get done, and this exercise with Allison seemed a waste of time to him, but orders were orders, and he would, of course, acquiesce. His instructions were to show her the unit before the evaluation; however, her sudden focus on this cyber problem might just produce the results he expected. If that happened, he could bid Ms. Trent goodbye sooner rather than later.

"Sir, how long do you think it will take before she gives up?" one of the agents asked.

Phillips didn't answer him.

Another agent said, "She doesn't need to know her way around a computer. Not with looks like that."

"Do you realize how sexist you sound, Pierce?" the first agent chided.

Phillips kept checking the time. Fifteen minutes passed before Allison stopped typing. She reached for a small Post-it, picked up a pen, and wrote something. Then she stood and thanked the techs for letting her join them.

"Give up?" Phillips asked what he thought was the obvious question when she came through the door.

Smiling, she slapped the Post-it on the lapel of his jacket, turned, and walked down the hall to find Jordan.

He pulled the piece of paper from his lapel to see what she had written. It was an address in San Francisco, California. "What the . . . ?"

"Sir?" The agent next to him motioned to the map on the wall. Every tech was standing and watching as dot after dot and the connecting lines disappeared. In less than a minute only one dot remained. Above it was an address, the same address Allison had written on the Post-it.

"Did she do that?" the agent asked.

Phillips was frowning as he handed him the Post-it and answered, "Yes."

"How . . . how did she do it?" Pierce wondered.

"I don't know," Phillips admitted.

"Do you think it's the right address?"

"I do. Roberts, call the San Francisco office. Tell them to get a SWAT team out there."

"Yes, sir," Roberts replied, then rushed into the nearest office.

The three remaining agents glanced at one another. "What if we're wrong?" Pierce asked.

"Then we're wrong." Phillips was looking up at the empty screen when he said, "Healy, you'd better go get him. He'll want to see this." *And gloat,* he added silently.

"He was right, wasn't he?" Healy asked.

Phillips sighed. "Apparently so. Go get him," he ordered again. "And, Norton, you bring Miss Trent to my office. Where did she go?"

"She's in the encryption room with Mrs. Clayborne. I'll get her."

Pierce spoke up. "I'll get her."

"No, I've got this," Norton insisted, hurrying away.

He found Jordan and Allison surrounded by men who were all trying to explain what their job was. When Norton told Allison that Phillips wanted to see her, Jordan offered to go with her, but Allison told her to stay.

Phillips was on the phone when she entered his office. He motioned for her to sit, but she continued to stand in front of his desk. The second he disconnected the call, she blurted, "Aren't there any women working here?"

Detecting annoyance in her question, he retorted, "As a matter of fact, there are women working here."

"I haven't seen any," she replied.

"We're just filling positions for this new office, but we already have many women on our support staff. And if you'd gone into other departments, you would have seen a couple of women who are analysts and . . ."

Allison didn't hear the rest of his answer. Out of the corner of her eye, she saw a man walking toward the office. There was something familiar about him. She lost her train of thought, and, although it was rude, she turned her back on Phillips and watched as the man came closer. The gun told her he was an agent. A tall, attractive agent, she corrected, with sandy blond hair and the physique of a Roman gladiator.

He came into the office, his expression serious. He looked at Phillips for a brief second before turning his gaze to her.

"You were on the mark," Phillips told him with a hint of reluctance.

"Yes, I heard," he replied.

Allison looked up at him in amazement and recognition. "It's you," she said. "You were at the seminar when Jordan spoke. You were watching."

"Yes, I was there. That was a while ago." He seemed surprised that she would remember.

"What is this all about? What's going on?" She didn't give him time to answer before adding, "Who are you?"

The agent just smiled and held out his hand. "My name is Liam Scott. And I am very happy to finally meet you, Allison."

FIVE

UH-OH. FINALLY? HE WAS HAPPY TO FINALLY MEET HER?

Allison had a really bad feeling about what was coming, and she suddenly had the insane urge to turn around and run as fast as she could, knowing that one of the agents might tackle her before she reached the elevator. She still wanted to try, though.

Fortunately, before she took a step, she came to her senses and decided to stay composed. Phillips pulled out a chair for her and pointed. She sat and crossed one leg over the other. Because she exposed a bit of thigh from the side split of her pencil skirt, she tugged her skirt down and casually folded her hands in her lap. She hoped her nerves weren't showing despite the fact that her mind was racing to figure out what Agent Scott wanted. She told herself to stay calm and try to act like a law-abiding citizen.

Yeah, right. Law-abiding . . . except for the thirty-eight million dollars she took from the CHF hackers' accounts. Not to mention the millions she recovered in subsequent hacks. She hadn't kept the money, of course. She had simply moved it into accounts so the FBI could retrieve it. Still, in order to find the money, she had visited—she preferred that word to *hacking*—protected systems. She had been so cautious and was certain she had gotten in and out without leaving any footprints the FBI or any other agency could follow. She hadn't stolen anything for herself or changed anything that would cause harm. She was only helping out. That didn't make her a criminal . . . did it?

Who was she kidding? If they knew what she had done, she'd have been on her way to lockup.

Now, as she sat there under the close scrutiny of two FBI agents, she wondered if breaking into one of those sites had been her downfall. She kept reminding herself that she'd been careful—she was always careful—yet there were times when she'd been in a hurry.

The silence as the two men continued to look at her so expectantly was unnerving. One second she was confident she was safe, and the next she was ready to put her hands out for handcuffs. Phillips finally went around his desk and took a seat while Agent Scott, his arms folded across his chest, studied her.

She desperately tried not to look at him, but it was impossible not to notice how attractive he was. She couldn't believe she was thinking about such foolish things now. Focus, she told herself. Focus on the problem at hand. Her ability to concentrate was one of her strongest traits. How many times had the sisters of St. Dominic's High School praised her for that very thing?

Were these men going to arrest her or not? She could feel the panic returning. Was this how Bill felt every time the police knocked on his door? she wondered. Or was he more cavalier about it all?

She took a breath and asked, "Why am I here?"

Agent Scott answered, "I've been wanting to meet you.

I've heard a lot about you, Allison. Your talents are quite impressive."

"Who have you been talking to?"

"A few people."

"In other words, you aren't going to tell me."

He didn't answer her question. He just smiled. The dimple in his cheek when he smiled made him look less intimidating. In fact, in any other situation she would have said it gave him a roguish charm. He had a lovely accent, too. British or Australian, she guessed.

Agent Phillips spoke up. "As you know, this is a new facility, and our work here is very important."

"From the little I've seen, it's impressive." She glanced at Agent Scott and said, "I should get going."

Just as she was getting up, Phillips asked, "How do you feel about taking a lie detector test?"

She sat back down. "I'm sorry. . . . Take a lie detector . . ."

"Yes," Phillips said.

"Why would I want to do that?"

"We would like you to come work for us," he explained. "But you're going to have to pass a lie detector test first."

She couldn't quite grasp what he was saying. "You're offering me a job?" She glanced from one agent to the other. Both were nodding.

Weak with relief because she didn't have to worry about going to prison, she let out the breath she'd been holding in. "Thank you for the offer, but I'm going to have to decline."

"Why?" Phillips asked. "You don't even know what the job is or what your salary would be. How can you say no?"

Time to be blunt, she decided. "I don't want to work here."

Phillips looked astonished. "Why not?" he asked, and before she could answer, he said, "I don't think you understand what a unique opportunity this is."

"We know you want to finish college," Agent Scott said. "We'd work around that."

"She's in her last year," Phillips told him. He looked at Allison as he added, "It's taken her five years."

She smiled sweetly. "That's right, Agent Phillips. It will be five years."

Seeing that she was beginning to get irritated, Scott intervened. "I think you should take some time to think about it before you decide. We haven't explained what you'll be doing here."

"I'm not interested, Agent Scott."

"Call me Liam," he insisted. "How about we talk later? You're going over to Jordan's tonight, right?"

How did he know that? "Yes," she said.

"Good." Turning to Phillips, he said, "Are we done here?"

"For now. I had hoped to test her today," he admitted, "but we can wait."

Allison wanted to get out of there as quickly as possible. She needed time alone to figure out what exactly was going on. She knew there was a hidden agenda. She just didn't know what it was. How had they found out about her "talents"? Whom had they talked to? More important to know, what did they want her to do? If she had considered their offer for even one second, she would have insisted on answers to these questions, but the fact that they had manipulated her into this situation raised red flags she couldn't ignore.

"If you come to work here, you'll only have to answer to me," Phillips offered.

He would be her boss? Did he actually believe that would be an incentive? "As enticing as that is, I'm still going to decline."

Phillips came around the desk. "I hope you'll reconsider."

She shook his hand, then Scott's, while she thanked both

of them for letting her see a little of the cyber unit. There was only one problem with a quick exit: Agent Scott wouldn't let go of her. She tugged; he pulled. "Is there a problem?" It was difficult to tell what was going on behind his smile.

"I was hoping you could answer a couple of questions before you left," he replied. "I guess I could ask them tonight."

Oh no. After this encounter, there was no way she was going to Jordan's tonight. She decided to keep that information to herself and play along. "Yes, you could ask me then. Are you about ready to let go of me, Agent Scott?"

"Liam."

Phillips drew her attention. "There is one thing we need to know before you go."

She turned to him. "Yes?"

"Have you ever hacked into a government agency?"

The question shocked her. She wasn't prepared for it. "No," she answered emphatically. Technically she was telling the truth. She had e-mailed the FBI with sensitive information, but she had never broken into their system.

"FBI? CIA? NSA?"

"You can go through the alphabet if you want. The answer is still no. I haven't hacked into any government agencies. It's against the law."

"Never?"

"Never," she insisted.

"If you had, would you admit it to a federal agent?"

He had her there. "No, I wouldn't."

"Now you understand the need for a lie detector test."

"Sure, I do. I'm still not taking one."

"Because?"

It seemed to her that they were back where they started. "Because I don't want to work here."

"About the government agencies . . . ," Phillips said.

"Yes?"

"You've really never hacked . . ."

How obtuse was the man? "No, I haven't."

"Could you?"

He posed the question just as she skirted past Liam and headed for the door. She turned around and said, "I've never tried."

Liam shook his head. "That's not what he was asking. Could you?"

She decided to be honest, no matter how arrogant she sounded. "Probably." She thought about it another couple of seconds, then added, "Yes, I'm sure I could. Happy now?"

Liam grinned. "You have no idea."

SIX

ALLISON WANTED TO FIND OUT WHY SHE WAS BEING INTER-
rogated, but her curiosity was overridden by her desire to
escape. Liam Scott's piercing green eyes were staring intensely into hers, yet giving nothing away.

"Let me guess. You're not going to explain," she said.

"No, not now," Liam said. He opened the door for her.
"We'll talk tonight, and you can ask as many questions as
you'd like."

"Will you answer them?"

"Yes," he assured her. "I'll pick you up at seven."

Before she could argue and tell him she wasn't going
anywhere with him at seven tonight or any other night,
Agent Phillips spoke up. "Trust me, Allison. I'll find a way
to convince you. I think you'll enjoy working here."

She shook her head to let him know she disagreed, and
when she turned back, Liam was gone.

"Would you like to see the rest of the facility now?"
Phillips offered.

"No, thank you."

She didn't wait for an escort. Quickly exiting Phillips's office, she located Jordan and convinced her it was time to leave. When they were finally alone in the car, Allison began to grill her.

"Why didn't you tell me about Agent Scott?"

"Who's Agent Scott?"

"Liam Scott."

Jordan drove through the gates and onto the road before glancing over at Allison. "I don't know who you're talking about."

"You didn't know they checked up on me and planned this whole visit to get me out here?"

Jordan looked completely befuddled. "What?"

"Liam Scott is coming to your home tonight for dinner, and he thinks he's picking me up at seven and bringing me along."

Since they were driving on a deserted gravel road, Jordan didn't bother to pull over. She stopped the car and turned to her friend. "What do you mean, he's coming over for dinner?"

Before Allison could respond, Jordan said, "Take a breath and tell me what happened. Start at the beginning and try to make sense."

"I'm not sure I can. None of it made sense to me. You really don't know Liam . . . ?"

"No, I don't."

"What about your husband? Maybe Noah invited him. They're both FBI. Maybe they're old friends, and he just never mentioned him to you."

Jordan dug her phone out of her purse and went through her messages. There weren't any from her husband, but there was one from her brother Alec, who was in town from Chicago. He hoped she wouldn't mind the late notice, but he had a friend who wanted to meet her. They were coming over for dinner. Jordan read the message to Allison.

"Alec's FBI, too, isn't he?" Allison asked.

"Yes," Jordan replied. "You still haven't told me what happened."

"Phillips had a file on me. He knew about my family, my years working on my degree—"

"Why?" Jordan asked.

"He was offering me a job. I think there's more to it. If this was only a recruitment opportunity, why wouldn't they have called me for a meeting? Why did they get you involved? And why would they have been so manipulative about us coming out here?"

"I'm sorry, Allison. I didn't know anything about this." Jordan thought for a second. "It's a given they want something from you," she said. "Maybe tonight your date will tell you what it is."

Allison looked appalled, which made Jordan laugh. "Liam Scott is not my date. In fact, I don't think I'll come tonight."

"Yes, you will," Jordan said. "You're curious to know what he wants, aren't you?"

"You could find out and tell me."

"Oh no. You have to be there. Besides, from what you've told me, I don't think Agent Scott will let you decline. FBI agents like to get their way. What's he like?"

Sexy. That was the first word that came to mind, but Allison wasn't about to admit such a foolish thought to Jordan. Instead, she said, "Oh, you know."

"No, I don't know. Tell me."

Allison shrugged. "He's an FBI agent. He smiles, though. Unlike Phillips."

Jordan put the car in drive and took off. "I guess I'll learn more about Liam Scott tonight. I wish Noah could be there, but he won't be back from Miami until next week."

Several minutes passed in silence as Allison replayed

the bizarre encounter in her head. "Phillips sounded so sure of himself," she said.

"How so?"

"He told me he'd find a way to get me to work for him, and I don't think he's one to bluff."

"No, he isn't," Jordan agreed.

"He also said I would have to take a lie detector test, and I can't do that."

"Why not?"

Allison trusted Jordan but hadn't told her about all of her forays on the Internet. "Why do you think?"

"You don't think you would pass."

"I know I wouldn't pass, and I could end up in prison." Allison knew she had never caused any damage to the sites she'd broken into, so she wasn't worried about being prosecuted for vandalizing them, yet the sheer volume of her hacks had to mean something. They could add up to a serious charge.

"You're exaggerating."

"No, I'm not."

Jordan didn't miss a beat. "Okay, so don't take the test. Stand firm. No one can force you."

"Aren't you going to ask me what I did that could send me to prison?"

"You'll tell me when you're ready."

Allison smiled. "You're a very unusual woman. I'd be dying of curiosity, and I would probably nag you until you told me."

"Is that your phone beeping or mine?"

"Mine," Allison said. She saw that there were three voice messages, all from her aunt. The first message was quick and calm. Her aunt asked her to call as soon as possible. There was a problem, she said, but she didn't give any further explanation. The second message was more aggressive. Her aunt's voice had a bite to it. She said she had waited two hours for Allison to call back. Why hadn't she done so? Did she realize how selfish and ungrateful she was? The third message was almost comical. In the middle of a blistering rant, her uncle began to shout at her aunt, and within seconds the two of them were in an all-out fight, screaming at each other. Unfortunately, Allison was used to their loud quarrels. The tirades in *Who's Afraid of Virginia Woolf?* were polite disagreements in comparison to this couple's arguments.

"Are you going to call her back?" Jordan asked.

"You heard?"

"It was impossible not to hear. Your aunt and uncle were shouting."

Allison didn't make any excuses for their behavior. "I'll call when I get back to the house."

Three messages so close together indicated the issue was serious. Was Bill in trouble again? Of course he was. How many times had he promised he would not be so impulsive?

They were almost back to campus when Jordan said, "Has it always been like that? You know . . . the screaming and the anger?"

"Pretty much," she answered. She quickly changed the subject, letting Jordan know she didn't want to discuss her dysfunctional relatives. "What are you going to do about dinner? Your brother knows you can't cook, doesn't he?"

"I've gotten better," Jordan protested.

"So . . . carryout?"

Jordan nodded. "I'm thinking Chinese."

ALLISON PACED AROUND THE LIVING ROOM. SHE DIDN'T WANT to go out tonight, not after the conversation she'd had with her aunt. It seemed that her aunt and uncle had gone over the numbers and were convinced there was a missing payment from Giovanni. The amount was substantial, and they believed Allison had either spent the money or misplaced it. She'd heard that she was ungrateful a good five times during the call, and after her aunt finally wound down and her uncle stopped shouting into the phone, Allison calmly explained that Giovanni hadn't issued the check yet. The payment would come at the end of the month, just like all the others.

There wasn't an apology. Just a brisk "All right, then," before the call ended. Allison felt drained. She wanted to scream just to get rid of her anger and her frustration. Honest to God, she understood why Bill acted out. They didn't yell at him, but being the focus of their constant attention was worse than being ignored. When Allison put her headphones on and immersed herself in her cyber world, she could escape the fighting. Bill couldn't.

It was after her uncle lost his job that the fighting had become intense. Financially, they had been in good shape. They owned their house. There were some savings, and her uncle also received a pension. Then Bill began to drain all their funds. Getting into trouble with the law was expensive.

Her feelings for her cousin were convoluted. She was angry with him most of the time, but she also had great empathy for him. Her feelings for her aunt and uncle were even more confusing. She knew she was supposed to appreciate what they had done for her, yet she couldn't stand to be around them and made every effort to stay away as much as possible. Since she had moved out, she had been back very few times, and each time she did return, she took something that belonged to her. Piece by piece she stripped her bedroom until everything she owned or cared about was now in the house she shared with her two friends. It had become a calm refuge for her, but soon she would be leaving it. Graduation was coming up, and she had plans. She was going to move to California. Just thinking about her future after graduation lifted her spirits.

Usually, as soon as she finished a stressful phone call from her aunt, she would find an hour or two to go to the gym and work out. Running on the treadmill helped her clear her mind. Unfortunately, there wasn't time tonight. It was already half past six, and Liam Scott was going to be at her door at seven. He'd probably be prompt, too.

She wasn't going to get dressed up for him. She changed into her favorite comfortable jeans, a long navy blue wool sweater, and flats. She glanced in the mirror. Her hair needed a trim, she decided. It was well past her shoulders. She swept it away from her face with a hair clip. Since she had a few extra minutes and because she looked pale and stressed out, she put on a little blush.

Her mind wandered back to the cyber center. Why hadn't Liam told her what he wanted then? Why drag it out? Was it his intention to rattle her? If so, it worked. The fact that Phillips had offered her a job meant that she was in the clear, right? But what else was in her file? Liam Scott had looked at her as though he knew all her secrets. What if he was just waiting to charge her? Waiting until he could gather more evidence? Maybe he was using this evening with Jordan as a ploy to catch her when her guard was down? God, she was nervous. Let this be a lesson, she thought. She never wanted to forget this sick feeling in her stomach. She had, in fact, broken the law too many times to count, and even though her transgressions were, in her opinion, perfectly innocent, her motives wouldn't matter in court. She vowed she would never do anything illegal again for the rest of her life.

Her anxiety was getting out of control. By the time Liam

pulled up to the curb, she was picturing herself in orange prison garb. She knew she was overreacting . . . yet what if she wasn't? She wanted to lash out at him for putting her through this agony but decided she would be a perfectly composed lady instead. Cold as ice, but still a lady.

She stood by the window and watched him come up the sidewalk. He'd changed out of his suit into jeans and a white button-down shirt and jacket. She had to admit he didn't look nearly as menacing as he had earlier. If she didn't know who he was and had seen him walking down the street, she would definitely have been attracted. Men like him turned heads. Too bad he was an agent. Allison grabbed her purse and headed outside to meet him halfway.

LIAM STOPPED AS SOON AS SHE CAME DOWN THE STEPS. HE watched her stride toward him and made every effort not to react, but it was nearly impossible. He couldn't explain the pull he'd felt the moment he met her. He just knew he didn't like it one little bit. She was a job. Nothing more, nothing less. A means to an end, he reminded himself. She moved as though she were on a runway—back straight, head held high, her expression giving nothing away—no doubt a pose she'd practiced until she perfected it. Damn, she was one beautiful woman . . . a woman with an attitude.

When she got close to him, she frowned and said, "I really don't want to go out tonight."

In answer, he opened the car door for her to get in. "Sure, you do," he said, closing the door before she could respond.

Once they were on their way, he asked, "Are you hungry?"

"I'm always hungry."

He thought she was joking and laughed, until he glanced

at her and saw that she was serious. She stared straight ahead at the street with no expression on her face.

"This is really a waste of time, you know," she said. "I don't understand what you think you'll accomplish by taking me to Jordan's house."

"I thought you'd be more receptive to my proposal if you were in a friendlier environment." When she looked skeptically at him, he added, "Don't worry. I'm not going to hold you captive."

"Why me? How did all this come about?"

"I've worked with Alec Buchanan a few times, and he told me about his sister, Jordan, and what a computer genius she is. Right now I need a genius."

"Jordan is brilliant. Everyone knows that. You heard her speak at the seminar."

"Yes," he agreed.

"So . . . why didn't Phillips offer her the job?"

"Because you're better."

"You can't know that," she protested.

"Yes, I can. I came to the seminar to hear Jordan, but I also heard you. That's when I began to do some checking. You'd be surprised what you can find out about a person."

The slight grin that turned the corners of his mouth made Allison extremely uneasy. Was he teasing? Or was he smiling because he was so pleased with the incriminating information he'd found on her?

"I still don't understand," she said. "If you wanted to ask me to work for you, why didn't you just arrange a meeting and ask me? Why the deception to get me out to the FBI's cyber center?"

"That was Phillips's idea. He didn't think you'd talk to us. Plus, he didn't believe the reports on your abilities. He had to see for himself."

"I've already given you my answer. You needn't have gone to all this trouble."

Nothing was said for several blocks, and the silence was only making Allison more anxious. She crossed one leg over the other, then uncrossed it and crossed it again . . . and again . . . and again. Her hands were folded loosely on her lap, and she was sure she looked relaxed . . . until Liam reached over and put his hand on top of hers. She realized then how jittery she appeared.

"Are you nervous with me?" he asked. The notion seemed absurd to him.

"Nervous? No, of course not. Why would I be nervous? I have nothing to be nervous about."

"Okay," Liam said. He couldn't imagine what was going on inside her mind, but she appeared to be close to hyperventilating. "Tell me about yourself."

"Why?" Allison could hear the apprehension in her voice and cringed inside.

"I want to get to know you, and you can get to know me," he answered.

"You have a file on me. I would think you'd already know everything." The second the words came out of her mouth, she realized how caustic they sounded. God, she wished she could calm down. "Okay. What would you like to know?"

"You live with two men. Are you involved with either of them?"

"Two students," she corrected, "and no. They're my friends."

"Have you always lived in Boston?"

"No. What about you? Where did you grow up?" she asked in an attempt to divert his attention from her.

"I was born in Philadelphia and lived there with my family until I was three," he explained. "Then my dad was promoted and transferred to Melbourne, Australia. I grew up there but moved back to the States to go to Princeton."

"Do you live in Boston now?"

"No."

She waited for him to continue, and when he didn't, she asked, "Where do you live?"

"Pretty much out of a suitcase these days."

It wasn't much of an answer. She wasn't going to press, though. What did she care where he lived? After tonight she probably would never see him again. "Any brothers or sisters?"

"One younger brother. Okay, now it's your turn. Tell me about your family."

She was certain he knew all about her family. The background check Phillips and he had done had obviously been thorough, but she decided to play along. Better to humor the man than to alienate him.

"My aunt and uncle live in Emerson. It's a small town about two and a half hours away from Boston. I have a sister, Charlotte. She's older, but we're very close."

He didn't say a word. He simply waited for her to tell him more.

"My parents went up in a small plane with a friend. All three of them died in the crash. I was four years old when it happened, and Charlotte was ten. My aunt and uncle took us in. If they hadn't, we would have had to go into foster care and probably be separated. I'm very grateful to them."

It wasn't what she said but how she said it in a flat voice that revealed volumes, as though she'd said it so many times it was now an automatic response.

"I have a cousin," she continued. "His name is Bill. He's two years older than I am, and we aren't close at all. You know that, too, don't you?"

"I do?"

Liam flashed a quick smile that nearly broke her concentration. He really was a sexy devil. She shook away the ridiculous thought and remembered what she wanted to say. "Now you want me to talk about him, don't you?"

"Actually . . ."

"Yes, Bill's been in trouble with the law. More than once, as a matter of fact, and I'll admit he can be really obnoxious, and yes, he does have a terrible temper, but he went to anger management classes and has a counselor to get help with that. Okay, so it wasn't his idea. The court made him go. Still, I'm sure it will make a difference." She sighed then and said almost in a whisper, "No, that's not true. I don't think it will make a difference. Bill has some bad habits. Running with a group of troublemakers is one of them."

"What's another?" he asked.

"He's not willing to work hard to get ahead. He's after easy money and doesn't care how he gets it and who he hurts," she answered. "He can justify anything," she continued. "He's always got a get-rich-quick plan, and of course they all backfire. He's bounced a lot of checks, but his parents always cover them. The truth is, Bill hasn't grown up, and I'm not sure he ever will. He's been spoiled all his life. His parents live to please him. It's disgusting, really—" She stopped abruptly, realizing she was sharing far more than she should. It was just that, once the feelings surfaced, she couldn't stop them from spilling out.

"What about computers?" Liam asked.

"What about them?"

"How good is Bill with computers?"

"He isn't a hacker, if that's what you're wanting to know. Yes, he knows his way around a computer, and he thinks he's good, but he isn't. I'd rate him mediocre."

"Does he know what you can do?"

"I don't think so, but I can't be sure."

Allison stared at the passing streetlights, lost in thought. She had rambled on and on and didn't have any idea what Liam was thinking now. Had she been disloyal to tell him the truth about Bill? The irony was, she'd actually softened the truth. After mulling the question over, she decided she hadn't told him anything he didn't already know. She suddenly noticed she was crossing and uncrossing her legs again and immediately stopped.

"Allison?"

"Yes?"

"Are you always this uptight?"

"No, not always," she replied. "But when I'm with an FBI agent who won't tell me what he wants from me, I do tend to get a little apprehensive."

Everything about this situation was bizarre. Here she was, riding in a car with a man she knew virtually nothing about, other than the fact that he worked for the FBI and held a great deal of authority. That was obvious in the way the agents answered to him. It was also undeniable that he was very attractive and charismatic. He definitely oozed animal magnetism. Women went weak-kneed over mysterious men like him, but not her. She would never allow herself to be so vulnerable. She didn't have time.

Allison was so caught up in her musings she wasn't aware that the car had come to a stop.

While she was sitting there pondering her circumstances, Liam had walked around the car to open her door. He waited a minute and then asked, "Are you about ready to get out?"

Startled, Allison jumped, then looked up to see Liam standing over her with his hand out. She felt like an idiot. How long had she been in the zone? This was so unlike her. The only time she ever lost touch with her surroundings was when she had her headphones on and was staring at a computer screen. She stepped out of the car and led the way to the brick town house half a block away. Climbing the steps to the front door, she rang the bell.

Jordan and Noah had lived in their home for less than two weeks. They had been searching the historic section of Boston for some time, trying to find the perfect place, and when this newly renovated brownstone came on the market, they snatched it up. Even though it had been completely updated, it retained the charm of its past life. The double doors still held their original etched glass, and the antique lanterns on either side, which had long ago been converted to electricity, gave an amber glow.

Jordan opened the door and smiled graciously. "Liam Scott, I presume?" she said, holding out her hand.

Liam let Allison walk in ahead of him, then took Jordan's hand. "Thank you very much for allowing us to barge in on you like this."

"Oh, I'm sure it was all my brother's idea," she said. "I'm afraid our home isn't quite ready for guests yet, so I hope you'll forgive the mess. I've been very busy, and my husband has been away on assignment."

"I've never met him," Liam said. "But I've heard a great deal about him. Noah Clayborne has quite an impressive record in the bureau."

"I hope the two of you will get to meet someday."

They stepped into a wide entry hall with an open staircase that led to the second floor. Boxes were stacked next to the wall. The living room to the right was mostly bare, with only two chairs and a sofa. Two lamps, still in their bubble wrap, sat on the floor. Jordan was leading them to the rear when the doorbell rang.

"That must be Alec," she said. "I called him and asked him to pick up dinner on his way here."

When she opened the door, Allison saw a tall, broad-shouldered man holding half a dozen bags imprinted with Chinese symbols.

"Did you order the entire Bo Ling menu?" he asked Jordan, lifting the bags out for her to see.

"Hi, Alec," she answered as she leaned up, kissed her brother on the cheek, and took a couple of the bags from him.

When Jordan introduced him, Allison could see the similarity between brother and sister. It was in their eyes when they smiled. She could also see the comfortable familiarity between them, and it was obvious that they not only loved each other, but liked each other as well.

Everyone followed Jordan as she walked down the hall to the dining room. A folding table about twice the size of a card table sat in the middle with four folding chairs around it. Paper plates and napkins were set at the places.

"The dining table won't be here for a couple of days," Jordan said apologetically. "And our dishes are still packed away. I hope this will do."

After everyone assured her it was fine, she took the cartons out of the bags and set them in the middle of the table. She then asked for drink preferences, and Allison went with her to the kitchen to get the bottles of water and beers.

Alec waited until the women were out of earshot before he turned to Liam and said, "She's the computer genius? Are you sure?"

"Of course I'm sure."

"She's—I don't know—not what I expected. You told me she was a model, but . . ."

"But what?"

"You have noticed she's beautiful. Right?" Alec asked.

Liam laughed. "No, I hadn't noticed. Thanks for pointing it out. You do realize your sister is a brilliant programmer, and she's also very beautiful?"

"I suppose," Alec admitted with a shrug, as only a brother would acknowledge when assessing his sister. "I guess it's just that a lot of the techie types I've met have been guys with long, stringy hair and stains on their T-shirts."

"Kinda like you," Liam remarked. "Are you going undercover again? Is that the reason for the longer hair and the beard?"

"No, Regan and I have been on vacation. I'm only here for one night, then back to Chicago. Regan's already there. She has a meeting early tomorrow morning."

While the two men were catching up, Jordan and Allison stayed in the kitchen, talking in low voices.

Jordan handed Allison a couple of bottles from the refrigerator and whispered, "You look as though you're about ready to jump out of your skin."

Allison let out a long exhale and said, "I'm afraid they're going to force me to take a lie detector test."

"No one can force you," Jordan assured her.

"What if Liam has some kind of leverage?" Allison said.

"You don't know what he wants yet," Jordan reminded her. "Don't freak out until you have all the information. Besides, I'm on your side, no matter what."

A few minutes later they were seated around the table. The muscular men made the small table and chairs seem minuscule by comparison, but even though they looked uncomfortable, they didn't complain. Alec and Liam kept the conversation light. Jordan wanted to know when Liam and Alec had started collaborating, since Liam had mentioned he traveled all over the world and Alec was assigned to the Chicago office. They answered by telling about a couple of the cases that had brought them together. Liam insisted he was the first to do a favor for Alec, and Alec was just as certain he was the first to help out his friend.

"Liam was with Interpol for a while," Alec told Jordan and Allison.

"A short while," Liam corrected.

"But you work for the FBI now?" Allison wondered.

"Yes."

"Why are you traveling to so many countries? The FBI doesn't handle cases overseas . . . or do they?"

"Sure, we do," Liam answered. "We have agents and personnel in attaché offices around the globe, and we work with the governments in our host countries. Whenever there's a crime or an attack involving an American abroad, we're there to help. We also offer our resources to foreign governments when they need them."

"Weren't you with the FBI Fly Team after the hit in Indonesia?" Alec asked.

"I met them there," Liam answered.

"What's the Fly Team?" Allison asked.

Alec explained. "Counterterrorism unit. When there's an attack, they're deployed within hours. They're the lead operatives in getting the investigation started."

She turned to Liam and waited for him to expound, but he didn't. He remained silent until the conversation turned to another topic. She just then realized the stories he and Alec had been telling were about insignificant matters, mostly about eccentric characters they had worked with and interesting places they had visited. For the most part, they had shared very little about the dangers or the threats they had faced. Liam, especially, gave little away. She wondered what he had seen that he didn't talk about. There was something intriguing about him. He definitely was an enigma. One second he was authoritative and domineering, and the next he was charming and charismatic. As she sat there watching him, she wondered if anyone ever saw the real Liam Scott.

Alec was telling the story of their first meeting. "For a while there I thought Liam was a criminal," he said.

"For a while there I was," Liam countered.

"You don't mind bending the law?" Allison asked. She sounded thrilled.

"Depends," he answered.

Once again Liam didn't explain his meaning, yet his response gave Allison a tiny grain of hope. If he didn't mind bending the law, maybe he would be more understanding about her collection of bugs and the number of sites she had visited illegally.

Maybe . . .

SEVEN

ALLISON WAS TOO NERVOUS TO EAT MUCH AT DINNER. AFTER she'd taken a couple of bites of steamed vegetables, her stomach turned queasy, and she didn't dare eat any more. The tension inside her had eased up slightly while the conversation remained light, but now it was returning in full force, and she worried she was about to have a full-blown panic attack. She'd only had a couple of those in the past five years. They'd been unforgettable. And horrific. She remembered she'd felt frozen. She couldn't talk, couldn't move, couldn't breathe. It was as if an iron fist had wrapped around her and was slowly squeezing the life out of her.

Liam was watching her and could see what was happening. The color had drained from her face, and she looked as though she was about to pass out. What was she hiding that she was so afraid he would discover? He was sure he could get her to tell him—eventually—but it would take time, and he had precious little of that.

He decided to once again put her at ease. "Allison, what did you think of Agent Phillips?"

"What . . . Oh, he's very sweet."

Both Alec and Liam laughed.

"Sweet? That's a new one," Liam said.

She realized she'd given her answer without thinking and rushed to correct it. "I mean, he's pretty hard-nosed. Has he always been like that?" she asked.

"For as long as I've known him, which is five, six years now," Alec said.

"Once you're on his team or working with him, he'll back you a hundred percent," Liam added.

She wasn't sure what he meant by that remark. "I'm not going to be on his team."

"You might change your mind," Liam said. "You never know."

She decided not to argue with him. If he wanted to be optimistic, it was okay with her.

Jordan began to gather up the food cartons. "Allison, if you're finished, why don't you and Liam go into the living room and talk? I know you're anxious to find out what this meeting is about."

Anxious didn't quite describe how she was feeling. She took her plate into the kitchen, got another bottle of water out of the refrigerator, and followed Liam into the living room. He waited until she had taken a seat on the sofa, then pulled up a chair to face her. There was nothing to separate her from the intimidating man who sat in front of her. He focused his attention entirely on her as though he was studying her, getting ready to pounce.

Alec surprised her by joining them. He moved the other chair over next to Liam's. Allison could feel her heart beating in her chest. If the two men intended to unnerve her, they were doing a fine job of it.

Liam leaned forward. "Whatever is said here is confidential. I would appreciate it if you didn't discuss what we're about to tell you with anyone. Okay?"

He expected a quick agreement before he continued and was totally unprepared for her refusal. "I'm sorry. No, I can't do that."

"No?" Alec said, nonplussed.

"I can't promise you that I'll keep this conversation confidential," she explained.

"Why not?" Alec asked.

"I'll tell Jordan." Before they could respond, she continued. "I know this must be an important matter. I'll still tell her, though. She's my friend, and if she asks . . . which she will . . . I'll tell her."

"At least she's honest," Alec said to Liam.

"Yes, she is," Liam agreed. He looked very serious, yet he sounded as though he was about to smile.

Clearly exasperated, Alec asked, "Is there anyone else you know you'll tell besides my sister?"

"No, just Jordan," she said. She thought she should probably offer some sort of explanation, so she added, "I'm assuming whatever you have to say involves my work with computers, and Jordan's an expert. I value her opinion."

"Talking to her won't be a problem," Alec assured her. Liam agreed with a nod.

Allison looked first at Alec and then at Liam, examining each of their faces to see if there was the slightest cause for suspicion. They definitely were intense, and yet they seemed sincere. Her anxiety lessened slightly. Maybe they hadn't brought her here to interrogate her or to accuse her of a crime after all. Maybe they had other intentions. She mulled over her situation for several more seconds. "Okay," she said finally. "What is it you want?"

"We believe someone is leaking information on sensitive case files. We're hoping you can help us find out who it is."

"FBI files?" she asked.

"Yes," Alec answered. "At first, there were minor details of cases getting out, but then some crucial information was released. Recently there was a major leak that all but destroyed a case and an agent's credibility. We believe whoever is doing this has access to our system, but we haven't been able to find the leak."

Liam said. "Have you ever heard of the CSA?"

Allison shook her head.

"It's the federal cyber security agency," Alec continued. "Everyone who works there spends their days monitoring other agencies, including the FBI. They also look for viruses. They're the best in the country."

"Best what?" she asked.

"Hackers," Liam answered.

"The FBI gets weekly reports from the CSA," Alec said. "And those reports show there hasn't been any abnormal activity. In other words, no breaches. We don't know if the leaks are coming from the inside or the outside, and we need someone who's never had a connection to either of these agencies to work on this. My fear is that, if we don't stop them, the leaks could get even bigger. Whoever is behind this could be just testing the waters."

"Who discovered this?" she asked.

Alec answered, "We knew there was a leak when we were on a case in Hawaii. We couldn't prove it, though. There were very few people involved in the investigation, and we checked every one of them thoroughly."

"We couldn't find anything suspicious," Liam interjected.

Alec nodded. "The most recent incident was in Atlanta. A field agent was assigned a case involving bribery of a state official. He was just beginning to collect names of possible witnesses, and before he could even do a thorough investigation, the names of the witnesses were released on the Internet. Within a couple of days, two of them disappeared. The blame for the leak fell directly on him, but there wasn't any proof he had let the information out. We're fairly sure there's one source to these leaks, and it's in our computer system. The problem is, there's absolutely no trace of a hack."

Liam braced his arms on his knees and leaned closer. "Do you think you could get in and out of the FBI and the CSA without being detected?"

She had already guessed they were going to ask her to do just that, yet she was still shocked. First impressions, she decided, were often wrong because, when she first met them, Liam and Alec hadn't seemed the type to break rules. "Do you know how many years I would get if I got caught?"

"None if you worked for us," Alec pointed out.

"Could you do it?" Liam pressed.

She took a deep breath. "You want me to go up against the experts?"

"Yes." Liam's voice was emphatic. "Agent Phillips will know the true reason you're at the cyber headquarters, but no one else. The rest of the staff will think Phillips has brought you in as another security analyst. After seeing what you can do, Phillips has decided he would like to give you some other assignments as well. He's asked that you commit to at least a year."

A year working for Agent Phillips? The possibility gave her shivers. Not going to happen, she thought. "How can you be so sure I can do this? You don't know me."

She was wrong. Liam knew pretty much all there was to know about her . . . the important things, anyway. She was very intelligent and had extraordinary skills. That was a given. His investigation had turned up several impressive accomplishments. He discovered that she had written programs for a number of projects but rarely took credit. Even a couple of her professors admitted they had gone to her for help when they came up against a programming problem they couldn't solve. While the information he had gathered on Allison Trent told him most of what he wanted to know, it was Jordan who was instrumental in convincing him that Allison was up to the task. Jordan didn't realize she was helping, but every time she told her family of Allison's amazing talent, Alec took notice and passed the information along to Liam. Alec called her a human computer, and when Liam watched her at the seminar where Jordan spoke, he was definitely impressed. Then today, hearing how she had systematically and immediately torn through the difficult problem at the cyber unit, he realized what a find Allison was. If she was half as good as that demonstration promised, she could get the job done.

He had discovered a great deal about her personal life as well, even though she was very private and tried to keep her thoughts and her talents hidden. She was not very social, but she was loyal and caring, and her friends were just as loyal to her. He also uncovered the fact that her home life had been hellish and still was, which was why she avoided going home whenever possible. She made up excuses on Thanksgiving and Christmas, preferring to spend those holidays alone or in a peaceful environment, often with her sister and brother-in-law until they'd moved to Seattle. Liam's investigation of her background had been quite thorough, but until tonight his findings had merely been notes in an impartial report. Now that he was getting to know Allison, he could see her vulnerability, and though he didn't understand why, he felt the need to protect her.

"I know a lot about you, Allison," he told her. "What I don't know is why you are afraid to take a lie detector test. You haven't hidden any money."

He would have gone on if she hadn't interrupted. "How . . . ? Did you look at my bank statements?"

"Yes," Alec said.

She was taken aback by the quick admission. "Then you know I'm poor."

"Most college students are," Liam remarked.

"Where does all your modeling money go?" Alec asked.

"Her relatives take it," Liam explained.

Allison could feel her face heating up. She couldn't make up her mind if she was embarrassed or angry that he knew about her god-awful aunt and uncle. Before either of the men could continue his line of questioning, she blurted, "I could have hidden money in a secret account. When you know what you're doing, anything is possible."

"But you didn't." Liam made the statement.

"No, I didn't."

"Why won't you take a lie detector test?" Alec asked.

"If you help us, I'll make sure you have immunity," Liam promised.

"Are you serious?" She stared deeply into his eyes, looking for any sign of deception. "No matter what I tell you, no matter what I confess . . . ?" she asked suspiciously.

"You didn't murder anyone, did you?"

"Of course not."

"Commit treason? Sell nuclear secrets to the enemy?"

She laughed at the absurdity. "No."

"You'll have immunity," he reiterated.

She was so astonished, she didn't know what to say. Should she confess all her sins? Could she trust Liam to keep his word?

"Could you excuse me for one minute?" She didn't wait for permission but got up and hurried to the kitchen. Jordan was stacking the cartons of leftovers in the refrigerator.

"Just one quick question," Allison said.

Jordan stopped what she was doing and looked at her friend. "Okay. What's the question?"

"Can I trust Liam to keep his word? He offered me immunity."

"I can't really vouch for Liam, because I've only just met him, but I can definitely vouch for my brother. If Alec trusts him, you can trust him."

"All right, then." She turned on her heel and returned to the two men in the living room. "Okay, I'll help you."

"Do you think you can do it? Can you get in without being detected?" Alec asked.

"Yes," she answered. There was no conceit in her answer, just confidence.

"I still want to know why you won't take a lie detector test," Alec reminded her.

She knew she was going to have to tell them. After she explained, they would undoubtedly think of her as a criminal—which was, in fact, the truth—and for some reason that bothered her. She shouldn't care what they thought, should she? "I did break a few laws, but only in the interest of helping. And also there was the educational aspect. . . ."

"Be specific," Liam urged.

She decided to start with an instance that wouldn't sound so incriminating. "There was the time I decided to look in on my bank just to make sure there weren't any surprises," she said. "My savings account was there, and I didn't want anything to happen to it. I had expenses coming up—" She stopped abruptly when she realized she was already making excuses for her conduct.

"By looking in on your bank, you mean you hacked," Alec began. "And by surprises you mean viruses, bugs?"

"Yes," she admitted. "And as luck would have it, I found a surprise. It was programmed to wreak havoc on a certain day and time, which turned out to be a couple of weeks away from when I found it. It would have corrupted all the bank files."

"What did you do when you found it?" Liam asked.

"I removed it. It wasn't very interesting, just your run-of-the-mill virus, so I destroyed it."

"Did you notify the bank?" Alec asked her.

She looked appalled by the question. "Of course not."

"Did you get in and out without being detected?"

"Yes, I did." She stood then and headed to the kitchen again.

"We aren't finished here," Alec said.

"I know. I was wondering if there's any lo mein left." She straightened her shoulders as she turned. "I'll be right back."

When she entered the kitchen, her phone was ringing. She pulled it out of her purse, saw who was calling, and quickly pressed DECLINE. It was her aunt's phone number. She wasn't in the mood to deal with her tonight.

A minute later she walked back into the living room, carrying a white carton, chopsticks, and a Diet Coke. "All of a sudden, I'm starving."

"Immunity gave you an appetite?" Alec asked.

"Must have," she said.

The lo mein was still warm. While Liam and Alec discussed some details of the investigation, Allison ate the entire contents of the carton. She loved every bite. She finished the Diet Coke, dropped the chopsticks into the carton, and sat back. For the first time since he'd met her, Liam thought she looked relaxed.

Break was over. It was time for him to find out more of her secrets. "Did you look in on any other banks?" he asked.

"Yes."

"How many?"

"I don't know. At least twenty or thirty," she said. "I'd

look in on them every six months or so. I'd always find
more bugs. It's shocking really, how easy it is to use them
to plant a virus."

"Have you ever planted a virus?" Alec asked.

The question offended her. "No, never."

Alec nodded, appeased.

Then Liam asked, "You didn't just look into banks, did
you?"

"No," she admitted. "I checked a lot of businesses. Most
of the viruses I found couldn't do all that much harm, but I
removed a lot of them anyway. There were others that could
do real damage. They were interesting, so I kept them."

"Why?" Alec asked. "Why would you keep them?"

"I wanted to study them. I'm designing what I hope is an
impenetrable firewall," she explained. "That's my goal,
anyway."

They wanted a list of the systems she had "looked into."
Alec took out a notepad and began recording the names as
she recalled them.

"How many is that now?" he asked Liam, fearing he was
going to run out of paper.

"I counted twenty-two," he said before turning back to
Allison. "Did you keep a record of all of these?"

"No. If you'd like, I could write a list. I think I can be
pretty accurate."

"There couldn't be that many more," Alec commented.

If he only knew. Should she pretend to agree? She decided to keep silent.

"You've never looked in on any federal agency?" Alec
asked, clearly skeptical.

"You've already asked me that. No, never. That would
be breaking the law." She rushed to explain, "I know. I'm
not making any sense. I broke the law every time I entered
a bank's or a credit card company's system, but I felt I was

helping them. Going into the FBI or any other federal agency wouldn't be helping."

"Anything else you want to tell us? Now's your chance. You've got immunity," Liam reminded her.

Should she tell them about the hackers who'd stolen from the nursing home residents? It had happened three years ago. She thought she was safe, but there was always the chance that someone would come along and figure out she was the one who had gone after them. "There are a few other things I've done."

"Be specific."

"Now or never, Allison," Alec said. "What else have you done?"

"When I said I had never taken any money . . . that wasn't exactly true," she admitted.

Alec and Liam leaned forward expectantly.

She took a deep breath, then said, "I stole thirty-eight million dollars and sent an e-mail to the FBI telling them where they could access the funds."

Liam seemed to take the announcement in stride. Did anything faze him? Alec, on the other hand, looked shocked.

"Thirty-eight . . . ," Alec began, then stopped.

"Million," she supplied.

She explained everything, from the nursing home segment on the news to the e-mail she'd sent. Alec said he hadn't heard of the hacking. Liam didn't respond. He seemed to be studying her as he listened to her recount the details.

"Did they get the hackers?" Alec asked.

"Yes," she answered. "It was on the news, but it all happened a long time ago."

"About three years ago," Liam added.

"Then you knew about it?"

"I read a report on it," he answered. "A lot of people tried to take credit for getting that money back. None of them could tell the investigators what was said in the e-mail sent to the director, though."

"Do you remember what it said?" Alec asked Liam.

He nodded. "Yeah, I do. It made me laugh."

"What was so funny?" Allison wanted to know.

"Prove you did it," Alec urged. "Tell us what the e-mail said."

She didn't hesitate. "'You're welcome.'"

Alec looked at Liam, who nodded. "That's right," he confirmed.

"Any other chunks of money you've liberated?" Alec asked.

"Yes, and each time I gave specific instructions on how to locate the hackers. And proof so they would go to prison."

"What about the money?"

"I told the FBI where they could find it."

"I'm curious," Alec said. "How much money—the total?"

"Around eighty million."

They both looked incredulous.

Alec had a good laugh and, shaking his head, said, "You're lucky you have immunity."

Jordan entered the room as Alec was speaking. Hands on her hips, she snapped, "But you did promise her immunity, and you're not going to take it back." When they all turned to look at her, she defended her eavesdropping. "What? You didn't think I wouldn't find out what was going on, did you? The house is still empty. Sound echoes," she protested with indignation.

"Don't get all worked up," Alec said, exasperated. "I was just saying what could happen if she didn't have immunity."

"Stop trying to scare her. What she did might have been

illegal, but not a serious crime. She didn't cause any harm. Nobody goes to jail for looking."

"Does she seem scared to you?" Liam asked.

Jordan frowned. "Okay, she doesn't. Allison, don't let them bully you into doing anything you don't want to do."

"I won't," she assured her. "Alec, there's another way of looking at this situation. If for whatever reason you were to take away immunity and decide to arrest me, what evidence do you really have? I could explain that I was telling you a story. I could say that I made it all up to show off," she added with a nod. "You don't have any proof that I've done anything wrong."

She looked so proud of herself Liam wanted to laugh. "You're forgetting you told us you have a file of viruses you've collected, remember? That's what would nail you."

"Yes, it would," she agreed. "If you could find the file."

"You think we couldn't?"

"I know you couldn't."

Liam appreciated her arrogance.

"You're awfully confident, Allison," Alec remarked.

"None of it matters now, does it? Besides, I've decided to quit. No more looking in on protected sites. I promise."

"Except you're going to help us," Liam reminded her.

Allison didn't respond immediately. "Yes, I'll help you with this problem, but . . . I'm not going to commit to working for the FBI for an entire year. I have plans. As soon as I find your leak, I'm gone. And no one else will know I've done this. Agreed?"

It wasn't the deal they had hoped for, and Phillips wasn't going to like it, but Allison appeared to be resolute in her position. Liam nodded to Alec and then said, "Agreed."

Jordan walked into the living room and sat next to Allison on the sofa. "I'm assuming all the secret talk is over."

"I explained to them that, as soon as I get a chance, I'll tell you everything," Allison said.

"We don't want either one of you to talk about this outside this house. Got that?" Alec warned.

"What about Noah? May I tell him?" Jordan asked.

"You're going to anyway, aren't you?" Allison wondered.

Jordan nodded. "Yes. I just thought it would be nice if I asked."

"For God's sake, Jordan," Alec said, "this is serious."

"I know," she replied. "Neither one of us is going to post this conversation on the Internet, and Allison doesn't need to tell me what the assignment is. I've already guessed the obvious. You want her to catch a hacker, don't you?"

"Something like that," Alec answered.

"Don't leave me out. I want to help."

"No, absolutely not," Allison said. "If anything went wrong, you could get into trouble."

"So could you."

"I don't matter," she blurted, unaware how telling the comment was.

"Of course you matter. The FBI has given you immunity. You can't get into trouble."

"What I meant to say is that, if I were to get into trouble, I'd deserve it. I've broken the law. You haven't. Things have a way of getting messed up. It could be dangerous."

"How?"

"What if the person or people I'm going after find out who I am and come after me? It could happen," she insisted.

Jordan turned to Liam. "Are you running this?"

He nodded slowly. He kept his gaze on Allison and said, "I'm not going to let anything happen to you. You'll be safe."

"I still want to help," Jordan insisted.

"I've got a better chance of searching without being detected. That's all I'm saying," Allison said.

The two of them began to argue in a language Liam had never heard before. It was computer talk on an incomprehensible level.

"What would you do, Jordan, if . . ." was as much as Liam or Alec understood.

As Liam listened to the two women debate the best ways of entering a secure site, he couldn't stop staring at Allison. She was beautiful, yes, but what held his attention was the way her mind worked.

Alec interjected a thought into the discussion. "You know, Allison, there are some people who have sold various bugs and viruses for a lot of money."

"I'd never sell them," she protested.

Allison's phone rang again. She muted it and didn't even bother to see who was calling.

"I'm curious. How many viruses have you collected?" Alec asked.

"Oh, you know."

"No, I don't know. That's why I asked," Alec said.

She started to blush. "I'd like to know, too," Liam said.

"A few?" Alec asked.

It was obvious she was embarrassed. "More than a few."

"How many more than a few?" Liam asked.

"Several?" Alec asked. "Or a bunch?"

Jordan nudged Allison and said, "You've already admitted that you have a file of viruses. You might as well tell them how many. They can't do anything to you."

Eventually they would find out, Allison thought. If she just told them now, she'd save time. "Not including the ones I've destroyed, I'd say there're a hundred seventy or so in the file, give or take twenty or thirty."

"So . . . two hundred," Liam guessed.

She nodded. "Or thereabouts. Maybe a few more."

Alec looked astounded. "How long have you been at this?"

"Not all that long."

She picked up the carton and the can and carried them to the kitchen to get away from their scrutiny for a little while. She didn't like being the center of attention, especially since she was now considered a criminal in their minds. Alec was a nice man, she thought, but he looked at her as if she were a freak. Liam didn't, though. He seemed skeptical, which wasn't as bad, she supposed, yet there was something about the way his eyes focused so intently on hers that unnerved her.

Standing at the window with her arms folded, she stared out into the night and thought about the conversation. Maybe she shouldn't have been so honest. It was too late now, but she felt sick with regret. She never should have started looking in on private sites. It didn't matter if her motives were good or bad. She had broken the law countless times. Never again, she vowed.

In the living room Alec turned to Liam. "If only half of what she says she can do—"

Jordan interrupted. "It's all true. Allison doesn't lie."

"She's that good?" Alec asked.

Jordan nodded. "Yes."

Alec shook his head and let out a long, low whistle. "She's a weapon. In the wrong hands she could be lethal."

EIGHT

ALONE IN JORDAN'S KITCHEN, ALLISON LISTENED TO THE MES-
sage her aunt had left on her phone. She had hoped it would
be about something new, but it was the same old story. Bill
was in trouble.

For the first few years of his life, William Alexander
Trent had been the apple of his daddy's eye. Billy, as he was
affectionately called by his parents then, was the perfect son
they had waited eight long years for. He grew up to be somewhat tall and lean like his father, had the same square jaw
and handsome features, and could upon occasion be charming. But weren't most drunks charming at one time or another? Bill, the name he insisted on once he reached puberty,
didn't just inherit his father's good looks and his seemingly
insatiable thirst for alcohol; he also inherited his belligerent
personality. In high school he played football and helped
lead his team to the state championship. Because of his success on the field, he became a big man at school. All the
guys looked up to him, and all the girls flocked around him.

His senior year was the high point in his life. From then on it was downhill.

Bill expected to be flooded with college scholarship offers but learned that, although he was an above-average quarterback, he wasn't exceptional, and since he cared more about his social standing than about his grades, he was a below-average student. When the recruiters didn't come knocking, he adjusted his expectations and ended up barely getting into a state school. He squeaked by his first two years but flunked out the second semester of his third year. It wasn't a question of not being smart enough to succeed; Bill just didn't want to study. From the time he was a little boy, all he'd had to do was throw a tantrum and his parents would fetch whatever he wanted. He never had to work for anything. No effort was ever involved, and even more important, there were never any consequences.

While his former high school friends were graduating from college and moving on to bigger and better lives, Bill was failing at one job after another. Nothing held his interest long. He gravitated toward people who were like him, and when those relationships went sour—as they inevitably did—he just found a different group of underachievers to hang around. He drank and he fought, and when he wanted something, no matter how expensive, he took it, leaving his parents and the attorney to clean up the mess.

His first arrest had happened shortly after high school. He was caught shoplifting a pair of running shoes from a sporting goods store. After that, there were three more arrests. Each time, his attorney was able to whittle the charges down and keep him out of jail, and each time Bill was arrested, the attorney's fees tripled.

Bill didn't do anything to help his cause. His temper continued to get the better of him.

In his last appearance in court, he'd mouthed off to the

judge, a stupid mistake that had led to a round of anger management classes that didn't take. Now, because of a bar fight that sent two men to the hospital with serious injuries, Bill was facing felony charges that would put him away for five to ten years.

Allison was conflicted by the emotions she felt whenever Bill's name was mentioned. Her initial reaction was usually a mix of anger and resentment, yet deep down there was a hint of sympathy for him. He was the product of his upbringing, after all. His dependency had been ingrained in him since he was a child. But now he was an adult, and it was time for him to take some responsibility. She couldn't understand why he continued to act out and why he refused to learn from his mistakes. To her, his behavior was completely irrational. Although they had grown up in the same house, she realized she actually didn't know him very well. They had nothing in common, and he never really paid much attention to her. His fights were always with his father and mother, but no matter how out of control he became, he never took his anger out on her.

Allison could hear the men talking in low voices in Jordan's living room but tuned them out and played her message again. Leaning against the kitchen counter, she put the phone to her ear and listened to her aunt's demands a second time.

"We have a situation here, and you need to come home as soon as possible. Your uncle says the decision's been made. Now come home. Bill has been . . ." Allison turned the message off without hearing the rest and returned the call. Before she could say a word, her aunt demanded to know where she was.

"I want you home now," she insisted. Along with the anger and impatience that usually permeated her aunt's voice, there was now a hint of desperation.

"Can't this wait until Monday?" Allison asked. It was Friday, and the last thing she wanted to do was to go to her aunt and uncle's house in Emerson. By Saturday night Uncle Russell would be a blithering mass of misery. He didn't believe he had a drinking problem because he drank beer during the week and switched to hard liquor only on the weekends. The wrong word would set him off, and he'd go into a rage. He was predictable; she'd give him that.

"Absolutely not," her aunt snapped.

"Maybe we can figure out a solution over the phone."

No such luck. Her aunt went into a full-blown rant and included the word *ungrateful* three times. God, Allison hated weekends with her relatives. She interrupted her aunt's tirade, said she would see her tomorrow, and disconnected the call.

Liam stood in the doorway watching her. He could tell from her stance and her expression that something had upset her. She looked so disheartened. He doubted she would tell him what was wrong, but he asked anyway.

"What happened?"

"I'm just thinking," she said.

"Yeah? About what?"

"Witness protection."

He didn't miss a beat. "Want to tell me why?"

She shrugged. "It's a way to disappear. That's all." She straightened and brushed past him as she returned to the living room.

For the rest of the evening Allison listened to the details of her assignment and answered about a hundred more questions. Most of them centered on the possible ways she could get into the protected sites without being detected. Even though the sites were constantly being monitored, Allison knew there was always a way around every obstacle. She just had to find the vulnerability. To her it was like a complicated math problem. There was always a solution. Truth be told, she couldn't wait to get started.

It was after midnight when Liam called it quits. The night air had turned cold, and as they walked to his car, Allison folded her arms to ward off the chill. After removing his jacket, Liam placed it on her shoulders and drew her close. He didn't know what perfume she was wearing, but it appealed to him. So did her killer body. Damn shapely for a model. No harm in noticing, he thought, as long as he kept the relationship professional. He wasn't about to make a move. Allison was important to him because she was going to help him solve a problem. Once that was done, he would be on his way to another assignment. Travel had become a way of life for him. Even though he had friends all over the world, there hadn't been time for personal commitments, and he had long ago accepted that as part of his job.

"It's cold for this time of year," Allison remarked as Liam drove her back to her house. He had turned the heat on, but she was still shivering. "I'm tired of cold weather . . . but I love Boston."

"Aren't you planning to move as soon as you graduate?"

"Yes," she answered. "I'm thinking Santa Clara, California. It's beautiful there." Several minutes later she said, "You're the lucky one."

"How's that?"

"You get to travel all over the world."

"Yes, I do, but it can get old."

"Maybe you just need someone to go with you."

They stopped at a red light. Liam turned to her. "Are you applying for the job?"

She had foolishly believed she was beginning to relax with him until he looked into her eyes and smiled. He made her forget her every thought. She tried to be practical and analyze her reaction to him. Maybe it was just that he seemed so much bigger than life. She had done photo shoots with a lot of male models, men with perfect profiles and nearly perfect bodies, but none of them was as ruggedly handsome as Liam. There was a raw sexuality to him. She looked down, and her hands were fisted in her lap. She really had to put a stop to that, she told herself.

She knew he'd noticed. She didn't think he missed much of anything. But then, he was an FBI agent. He should notice the little things.

"How do you want to do this?" Liam asked.

"Do what?"

"What we've been talking about all evening. Getting into the FBI system without being detected." He smiled as though he could tell her mind was going in an entirely different direction.

"Oh," she said, pulling herself together. "I've often thought about how I'd do it."

"You've thought about breaking into the FBI?"

"No, I've thought about *how* I'd do it. That's all. The key is finding a weakness."

"What if there isn't one?"

"There's always a weakness," she insisted. "I just need to find it."

"When are you going to start?"

"I have to drive to Emerson tomorrow, and I won't get back until late. Then Sunday I have to finish a paper on algorithms. We don't have class Monday, so that's when I'll start."

He parked in front of her house and handed her his card. It just had his name and a cell phone number. "You can get hold of me anytime, night or day. I'll pick you up Monday morning at eight."

"Why?"

"To drive you to the cyber unit. Phillips is insisting that you work there."

"But that's crazy. All I need is my laptop."

"You're going to be testing CSA security. He wants you in his unit."

"What does he think I'll do at home? Invite people over to watch me?"

He didn't argue the point. "I'll pick you up at eight."

"Meaning, we're through discussing this."

"That's right."

He walked her to her door and patiently waited by her side while she dug through her purse, looking for her house key. She kept handing him things to hold while she searched, and by the time she finally found the key, he held her billfold, her sunglasses, a striped zipper bag, three pens, and a cell phone. She stuffed them all back in her purse.

"Thanks," she said.

"How long do you think it will take?" he asked.

"No time at all. Once I insert the key and turn it, the door will open." She saw his expression and began to laugh. He looked as though he wanted to shake her. "You don't have a sense of humor, do you?"

"Sure, I do. Now answer the question. How long do you think it will take to get into the CSA?"

"I can work pretty fast," she answered with a wry smile as she walked inside and closed the door.

Liam walked back to the car with the image of her smile still on his mind. Letting out a low whistle, he shook his head. "She's gonna be trouble."

NINE

EMERSON WAS A CHARMING LITTLE TOWN WITH ROLLING HILLS, double-wide streets, and weathered clapboard houses that didn't sit on top of one another. Allison's aunt and uncle lived on Baltimore Street. The two-story house sat on a corner lot with a spectacular view of Summer Park. The huge red elm in the front yard was in desperate need of a good trim. One of the thick branches draped over part of the roof. A disaster waiting to happen, Allison thought as she pulled into the driveway.

The couple had moved into the house right after they were married thirty-some years ago and, except for some repairs now and then, hadn't changed a thing in all that while. The hardwood floors were dull and worn, and the variegated gold shag carpet in the den was threadbare. The kitchen still had the same dark oak cabinets and Formica countertops, and the old linoleum tiles still made a checkerboard on the floor.

Allison could feel her stomach twisting into knots. After she took a couple of deep breaths, she got up the courage to open the car door.

Bill must have spotted her from the window. He stepped out onto the porch and waved to her. Okay, he was in what he must consider his charming mood. Better than angry, she thought. Then she noticed he had a beer in his hand. It wasn't even noon yet, and he was already drinking. She didn't think he was drunk, though, because he wasn't staggering around. Usually when he was drunk he was belligerent, and he didn't appear to be scowling . . . at least not yet. Women found him attractive, but Allison couldn't understand why. Those same women had certainly never seen him go into one of his fits. He wasn't so handsome when he was sneering and screaming and throwing punches because he wasn't getting his way.

Why was he at his parents' house? Had he also been summoned? Or had he been kicked out of the apartment they had rented for him? She walked up the steps to face him. He looked haggard. His eyes were bloodshot, and there were dark circles under his eyes. If he kept up his twisted lifestyle, she expected him to be dead before he turned thirty-five. The thought saddened her. There was still time to turn his life around, if he was willing . . . and if he could get away from his smothering parents.

Up close she could see he'd been drinking for a while. He wasn't tanked, but he was getting there. She wondered when he'd started or if this was just a continuation from partying the night before.

He wasn't much for proper greetings. He took a drink of his beer, wiped his mouth with the back of his hand, and said, "My mother snaps her fingers and you come running."

Allison wasn't offended, and she wasn't going to let him bait her into an argument. "No, Bill. She calls and calls and calls until I give in and do what she wants."

"She makes you feel guilty." He laughed after stating the obvious.

"Yes, she does," she admitted. "Why are you here?"

"I want a new lawyer."

"Then get a new one."

"My lazy-ass lawyer says it won't matter how many lawyers I hire. None of them can get the charges reduced. You know what happened, don't you?"

She shook her head. She knew what he was going to tell her, though. None of what happened was his fault.

"I really got screwed," he said. "I'm the one who was attacked at the bar. I didn't start the fight. I just protected myself. I mean, I should, right? I should be able to protect myself."

He looked at her expectantly, waiting for sympathy. She wouldn't give him any. "Were there witnesses?"

"Yes, but they aren't on my side. If it goes to trial, they'll lie under oath. Just you watch and see."

While Allison didn't know any of the particulars, she guessed this time Bill wasn't going to be able to find a way out. "Do you want it to go to trial?"

"My lawyer says it would be a mistake to take it to trial. He wants me to take the deal they're offering."

His face was turning red, and she could see the anger washing over him. She wasn't sure if she should continue asking him questions for fear of adding fuel to the fire.

"Don't you want to know what was offered?" he asked. Antagonistic now, he glared at her.

"Yes, I do."

"Five to seven years, Allison. I'd get seven years, but with good behavior, I could get out as early as five years."

Good behavior? Then it was going to be seven long years, she thought, because there was no way Bill could keep his temper controlled that long. He didn't know how.

"What happens if you decide to go to trial?"

"According to my useless lawyer, I could get twice as long. Now do you understand why I need a new lawyer?

One of those high-priced big shots who knows how to manipulate the law. That's what I need."

"Do you think a new lawyer could keep you out of prison?"

"Yes, of course I do, if he knows what he's doing. Don't you agree?"

She nodded. She was determined to placate him, no matter what. Debating him would only incite his anger.

"Are you on my side or not?" he asked.

"I don't want you to go to prison," she said, giving him an evasive answer.

Allison wondered if he would ever face reality. She knew there had to be more to the story than he was telling. A bar fight didn't usually bring such harsh charges, did it? Unless someone was seriously injured, or unless the prosecutor could prove that there was an established pattern of behavior. How many fights had Bill started? Probably more than he could remember.

"I guess I'd better go inside and find out why I was summoned," she said as she climbed the steps.

She already knew the reason her aunt had called her, of course. If Bill wanted a new, more expensive lawyer, then, by God, he was getting one, which meant his parents needed help coming up with the money.

On the drive to Emerson, Allison had played out the impending scene with her aunt and uncle in her head. She had witnessed it so many times in the past she could practically recite the dialogue by heart. In the end, her aunt would play the gratitude card and expect her to cave. Something was different this time, though. Maybe it was seeing Bill at the end of his rope. Maybe Allison had reached the end of hers. Regardless of the reason, she knew what she had to do.

Her hand on the doorknob, she paused, then turned back to Bill. "This is the last time I'll be coming back here."

He acted as though he hadn't heard her. "I'm scared," he blurted. "This could be bad. I swear, if I get out of this, I'm going to change. I know I've said that before, but I mean it this time. I want to go back to college and finish. I can't go to prison." A look of panic crossed his face, and there was a pathetic whine in his voice when he said, "I just can't. I wouldn't last a week."

Bill looked so tormented, she almost felt pity for him. Was this finally the wake-up call he needed? Or was she being naive once more? Charlotte had told her again and again not to believe anything Bill said. He was a habitual liar and would do or say anything to get what he wanted. Allison had fought against becoming that cynical. She wanted to believe that people were basically good even though life's lessons wore them down. She also wanted to believe in second chances, but how many chances had Bill already had to turn his life around?

Despite her determination to turn away, she heard herself say, "Bill, you know I'll help you if I can."

"I know."

"You might want to stay out here while I talk to your parents. It's not going to be pleasant." She didn't explain further. She guessed he'd hear his parents bellowing soon enough and get the gist of the conversation. Bracing herself for the inevitable fight ahead of her, she opened the door and went inside.

Her aunt and uncle were sitting across from each other at the dining room table.

They hadn't heard her come in, and as she stood there in the entry hall looking at them, her mind flashed back to that day all those years ago when she and Charlotte sat next to each other, holding hands, at this very table.

It was the week after the worst week of their young lives.

They had been at home with a babysitter when the knock on the door came and they were told their mother and father had been in a terrible accident. Allison didn't remember much about the rest of that week. It was all a blur of people coming and going, neighbors stepping forward to make sure she and Charlotte were not left alone, a huge church full of people wearing black, she and her sister sitting in a big black car in a line of black cars, the whispers *What about the girls? Where will they go?* and Charlotte crying. The clearest memory she had was of Charlotte. No matter how Allison had tried, she couldn't get Charlotte to stop crying. Allison felt sad, but she was too young to comprehend death. She kept waiting for her mother and father to come home.

Reality began to sink in when Aunt Jane and Uncle Russell came to take the girls to their house. Allison knew her aunt and uncle, but not well. She had seen them only a few times. Charlotte later told her it was because her father and her uncle had not gotten along. Allison could understand. Her father was a gregarious and kind man. Uncle Russell seemed sour and detached, and he had married a woman who was domineering and never satisfied. Their son, Bill, was a brat.

Allison and Charlotte hadn't even taken off their coats before Aunt Jane told them to sit down at the dining room table. There were a few things she and Uncle Russell needed to make clear. The first was how lucky the girls were to have an aunt and uncle willing to take them in. If they hadn't stepped up, she said, the girls would have been placed in foster care. Allison didn't know what foster care was, but the way her aunt said the words made her imagine some sort of dark and scary dungeon where they would be chained up and fed scraps of rancid food. The second thing her aunt told them was how much of a burden this was go-

ing to be, not only for her and Uncle Russell, but also for
Bill. They were not a wealthy family, after all, but they
were willing to make a sacrifice for the girls out of love and
respect for their dear dead parents. In return, the girls were
expected to be well behaved and hardworking.

Uncle Russell then showed them to the small room she
and Charlotte were to share. The walls were painted a drab
tan, and there were no curtains, just aluminum blinds cov-
ering the windows. The furnishings were sparse: two twin
beds with a nightstand between them and a tall dresser on
the opposite wall. This was nothing like her pink-and-white
bedroom at home with the matching polka-dot curtains and
bedspread. Charlotte sat down on her bed and began to
weep, but Allison was too relieved to cry. Anything was
better than going to that "foster" place. If Uncle Russell and
Aunt Jane were willing to let them stay here, she would do
her very best to make them happy. She never wanted them
to regret giving her a place to live.

She had been on that mission ever since. Until today.
She had had enough.

Her uncle sat hunched over the table with a notepad in
front of him, and next to it was a tall glass filled with an
amber-colored liquid she knew was his favorite whiskey. He
was using a small calculator to add numbers Aunt Jane was
reading to him. Uncle Russell was much younger than he
looked. Years of alcohol abuse and stress had taken a toll on
him. These days, it seemed to Allison he was angry all the
time. He was mean drunk and mean sober, but as long as
she agreed with whatever he told her to do, there weren't any
arguments or threats. In the past she had always tried to
humor him. It was so much easier to get along and do what
he demanded than to argue. Her aunt had told her that her
uncle lost his job when the company he worked for decided
to downsize, but a couple of years ago she had overheard an

argument and known then she'd been told a lie. Her aunt had been screaming at Allison's uncle, dredging up all his past sins, and in the litany was the reminder that he wouldn't have been fired if he hadn't been drinking on the job. The fight had been a real blowout. Even Allison's headphones couldn't block the noise. She heard her aunt say he was lucky there hadn't been sufficient documentation for firing him so the union could force the company to give him a pension. Allison guessed it was easier to pay him off than to take the matter to court. Easier and cheaper.

Her aunt Jane wasn't a shrinking violet by any means. She drank, but not nearly as much as Uncle Russell, and over the years she had perfected the art of looking trod upon. At home she wore her long-suffering weariness like a wrap around her shoulders; however, when there was a fight, she was the far more aggressive and caustic of the two.

They were a complete contradiction when they were out. If a couple could have a split personality, they were the perfect specimens. It was almost as though they were channeling Dr. Jekyll and Mr. Hyde. In public Uncle Russell was funny and sociable; at home he was belligerent and sullen, the degree depending on the amount of alcohol he'd consumed. To strangers, Aunt Jane was outgoing, even friendly. It was almost incomprehensible how these two could present such a different portrayal of themselves—locked in a horribly dysfunctional marriage and seemingly miserable at home, and yet the life of the party everywhere else.

Had they always been this awful? Allison couldn't remember. Her sister protected her from most of the ugliness until Allison was old enough to fend for herself. She didn't know what she would have done without her. Charlotte had held things together, but several years earlier she finally reached her limit and severed all ties with their relatives. It was Oliver who convinced her to do it.

Charlotte met Oliver on her first day of college. She had been awarded a music scholarship because of her talent with the flute, which she had taken up in high school. She had a natural gift for the instrument, but it had also become her escape. When things became too stressful in the house, Charlotte would retreat to the bedroom she shared with Allison and play her flute. The lilting sound took her to a peaceful and calm place, away from the turmoil outside her door. The flute also gave her a future.

Oliver was working on his law degree and happened on one particular afternoon in September to be passing through the music department building, taking a shortcut to the library, when he heard a beautiful melody coming from a small auditorium. Intrigued, he stopped to look through the open door and saw Charlotte standing on the stage playing the flute in front of a small gathering of students. He was so mesmerized he took a seat in the back row and listened, and when the session was over, he followed her into the hall and introduced himself.

Oliver and Charlotte had been dating only six months when they announced they were getting married. Allison feared she'd said yes to the first man who had asked her just to get away from the constant fighting. She understood her sister's need to break free, but she worried that Charlotte was too young and was behaving rashly. In hindsight, Allison could see that it was the best decision her sister ever made. Oliver was perfect for her. He loved the same things Charlotte did, and more important, he was a good and caring man. After graduation he worked in Boston, and then when Charlotte finished her degree, the two of them moved to Seattle, Oliver's hometown. He took a well-paying job with a prestigious law firm, and Charlotte became a member of the philharmonic. They now lived in a beautiful home in a suburb by the bay and were very happy.

While they were still living in Boston, Charlotte and Oliver had tried to maintain a cordial relationship with her aunt and uncle for Allison's sake, but it was difficult. Each time they visited them, Oliver saw how it affected his wife. They would be in the house for less than a minute and the criticisms would begin. Charlotte would try to be respectful and accommodating, but by the time they were on their way home, she would be so beaten down Oliver barely recognized her.

The breaking point came the day they stopped by to deliver a birthday gift to Aunt Jane. Birthdays were never grand celebrations, at least not for Allison and Charlotte. Bill, on the other hand, was treated like a crown prince on his birthday. And when it came to their aunt and uncle, Charlotte and Allison were expected to show a due amount of appreciation. The only reason Charlotte continued to remember her aunt's and uncle's birthdays after she had moved away was to keep the peace. Allison was still in high school at this point, and Charlotte didn't want to cause any dissension that would make things worse for her sister.

Since she and Oliver didn't have much money, Charlotte had taken great pains to find the prettiest silk scarf she could afford. When her aunt unwrapped the box, she stared at the contents for a second and then said, "Oh, it's a scarf." She didn't take it out of the box. She set it aside and looked at Charlotte expectantly, finally saying, "Is that it?" Charlotte nodded, her face turning crimson. Oliver saw the hurt and anger come across his wife's face and decided he had held his tongue long enough. He went after Aunt Jane with a vengeance, telling her how cruel she was. At first, Jane looked shocked that he would be speaking to her in such a way, but when he called her ungrateful for not appreciating Charlotte's thoughtful gift, she lashed out, again recounting everything she had done for Charlotte and her sister. The shouting match didn't last long. Charlotte and Oliver were quickly out the door. On the way home, Charlotte burst into tears, and all the years of pent-up rage came spilling out. It didn't take much persuasion on Oliver's part to convince her it was time to do something about the poisonous relationship.

Charlotte broke free and begged Allison to do the same. She and Oliver had been asking her to move in with them ever since they were married, and they once again urged her to consider it. Allison loved being with Charlotte and Oliver, but she was preparing to enter Boston College, and they were moving to Seattle soon, so that option was off the table. Besides, the sense of responsibility still had a grip on her, holding her back.

Charlotte called their aunt and uncle toxic, and although Allison wholeheartedly agreed, she hadn't been able to get past the guilt. Every time her aunt called her ungrateful, she was reminding Allison of the sacrifice she had made by taking her and her sister into their home. For years Allison had heard how much money they had spent on the girls' expenses because Uncle Russell knew that was what his older brother would have wanted. Yes, they had spent a fortune on the girls, and what thanks did they get? Precious little, according to Aunt Jane. On and on the lectures continued until Allison was weighed down with guilt because she had been the burden that made her aunt's and uncle's lives less than perfect. Would she ever feel she'd done enough to repay the debt she owed them? She honestly didn't know. What she did know was that for years her aunt and uncle had been using fear and guilt to get Allison to cooperate, and it was time for a change. She finally decided their criticism of her wasn't going to work any longer.

Her aunt looked up from the page she was reading and, seeing Allison, motioned for her to come into the dining room. Allison pulled out a chair at the head of the table so that she wouldn't have to sit next to either one of them. Then she folded her hands in her lap and waited for them to start in on her.

Her aunt held up the paper, which had a list of names with lines crossed through them. "Do you see, Allison? These are the attorneys who have turned us down. They refused to take on Bill's case. They all said the same thing: they couldn't do any better than Bill's current attorney. No matter how much money we offered, they all said no."

"I thought you liked Bill's attorney. What's his name?"

"Stephen . . . Stephen Kelly," she said. "And we did like him. He's done a good job until now."

Her uncle adjusted his glasses and looked up from his notepad. "He's given up on Bill and thinks my boy will have to go to prison this time. That's out of the question, of course. I can't let that happen."

Aunt Jane nodded vigorously. "No, we can't let that happen. Bill is too . . . sensitive. And none of this is his fault." She added, "We were able to get a copy of the video in the bar."

"Kelly got it for us," Uncle Russell interjected.

Her aunt insisted that Allison watch the video and pushed her laptop in front of her. In the beginning of the clip, it looked as though three men did crowd Bill and threaten him, but Bill threw the first punch . . . and the second . . . and the third. It was frightening to watch. When he became angry, he lost all control.

"Bill could have killed one of them," she whispered, shaken by what she'd just seen.

Aunt Jane slapped the laptop shut and snatched it away from Allison. "Bill's the victim here. Get that straight," she snapped.

Always the victim, Allison thought. She was amazed her aunt could look at the same video and come up with that conclusion.

Uncle Russell removed his glasses and pinched the bridge of his nose. "This is going to be very expensive."

"No matter what it costs, we have to keep Bill out of prison," Aunt Jane said. "He couldn't handle it, and neither could we. What would our friends and neighbors think?"

Uncle Russell became incensed. "What do you care what the neighbors think?" He picked up his glass and took a long swallow. "Use your head for once. Keeping Bill out of prison is all you should care about. Just how stupid are you?" He snarled the question. "You're more concerned about yourself than your own son."

Aunt Jane half lifted herself out of her chair. "We have to live in this town," she shouted. "And I always put Bill first. How dare you say that I don't?"

And they were off on another fight. Whenever they started a squabble, Allison was always reminded of a horse race where the announcer talks faster and faster as the horses pound toward the home stretch. She wished she had her headphones now to block out the cacophony.

The argument continued for a good five minutes before it wound down. Allison was even more determined now to tell them she'd had enough. She was actually becoming a bit giddy thinking about never having to come back to this house again. It had never been her home. Never.

Bill walked in and glared at his parents. "I could hear you loud and clear outside."

Ignoring the criticism, his mother asked, "Did you find your passport?"

"Not yet. I'll check the safe."

"Be sure to close it."

Why did Bill need his passport? Was he thinking about running? Allison jumped up from the table and ran after her cousin. He was in the den standing at the bookcase.

She stopped in the doorway and asked, "Why are you looking for your passport?"

"I might be taking a trip."

"You can't run away. They'd find you, and you'd spend years in prison."

He whirled around to face her. "Who said anything about running away?"

She could see the fear in his eyes. There were tears there, too. He really was scared. She was about to respond when her aunt summoned her back into the dining room by bellowing her name. She returned and, standing at the head of the table, in a quiet voice asked, "Yes?"

Her uncle grabbed her arm and squeezed. "You sit down and listen."

"We're going to need you to get more modeling assignments," her aunt said.

Her uncle pulled her into the chair. "Quite a few more," he added with a brusque nod. "And that means you're going to have to branch out."

"Excuse me?"

"You know. Work for other outfits," he said.

Did he think she could just knock on Chanel's door and tell them she would be willing to work for them? Or Armani? They really don't have a clue, she thought.

She took a deep breath and said, "I'm not going to quit school."

"Yes, you are," her aunt snapped. "You do what's needed for this family. Stop being so ungrateful."

There it was, that five-dollar word she threw around all the time. Allison wondered how many times she'd say it again before the conversation was over.

"The decision has been made," her uncle said.

"Who made this decision?" she asked.

"I did."

Here it goes, she thought. She tried to pull away, but her uncle increased his grip on her wrist. It felt as though he was going to snap her bone in half.

"No," she said with firm resolve in her voice.

"No? No what?" her aunt asked.

"No to all of it. I don't care how many decisions you've made, Uncle Russell. I'm not going to help you. I'm done."

Their reaction was almost comical. They looked flabbergasted. Her uncle was the first to recover from his shock. "You are not done here. You're done when I say you're done."

He squeezed her arm again, twisting until it burned. She tried to jerk her arm back, but her uncle held tight until he wanted to refill his glass. He had to let go of her then. Alcohol trumped keeping her captive, she supposed. She watched him pour a generous splash of whiskey and down it in a single gulp, wiping his chin on his sleeve.

She scooted her chair so he couldn't reach her and said, "I wanted to tell you face-to-face so there wouldn't be any misunderstanding."

"Tell us what?" her aunt asked.

"I'm finished."

Her aunt looked up at her, her eyes flashing with hostility. "What do you mean, you're finished?"

"I'm not ever coming back here, and it's my hope that I will never have to see or talk to either one of you again."

She had rendered them speechless. She knew why. She had never defied either of them before, and now she was severing all connections. She stood and headed to the front door before her uncle could get up from his chair.

"Get back here," he roared.

She kept right on walking.

Bill followed her onto the porch. "I found my passport," he said to her. He shoved a legal-size manila envelope at her. "This was in the safe, too," he explained. "It has your dad's name on it. I figured you should have it."

"What is it?"

"Looks like legal papers of some kind," he answered.

"Why are you giving them to me?"

"To piss them off. I heard you tell them you aren't ever coming back here. Did you mean it?"

"Yes, I meant it." She started down the steps, then stopped. "I'll try to help you if I can."

He shrugged and turned to go back inside. He didn't say good-bye.

She heard her uncle yelling her name again and continued on to her car. After taking one last glance at the house she'd grown up in, she drove away and didn't look back.

She felt liberated.

TEN

THE EUPHORIC FEELING DIDN'T LAST LONG.

Allison was anxious to get back to Boston. She glanced down at the envelope on the seat next to her. She was curious but decided to wait until she was at the house and in her room before opening it. A mile out of Emerson, her phone began to ring. She looked at the screen and saw that the caller wasn't identified. It was obvious her aunt had blocked her phone number so that Allison wouldn't know who was calling and would answer. The phone didn't stop ringing, and within twenty minutes there were eleven messages. When she stopped for gas, Allison listened to each one of them and was thoroughly disgusted by her aunt's crude remarks and threats.

By the time she reached Boston, there were twenty-five messages. Allison knew her aunt wasn't going to stop harassing her, so she made a detour to her cell phone store and had her phone number changed. She then called Charlotte and left her new number. She didn't explain why. There would be plenty of time to talk tomorrow.

She also called Giovanni to tell him she had changed her

number. She'd hoped to get his answering machine, but he picked up. He grilled her, of course, and was thrilled when she told him she had cut all ties with her relatives.

"It's about time you got away from those bloodsuckers. And don't worry. I won't give your new number to anyone," he promised.

Allison was smiling when she ended the call, thinking how lucky she was to have Giovanni in her life. She pictured him sitting in his studio surrounded by fabric swatches and sketch pads. On a plaque above his desk was printed his favorite quote by Yves Saint Laurent: "Fashion fades, style is eternal"—words he lived by. Even when he was working, he was dressed to the nines, typically in a vintage pin-striped suit with the collar up and a richly colored scarf draped under the lapel. He was a creative genius, but more important, he was a good and trustworthy man. He was also a kind friend.

She parked in front of her house and went inside. It was empty, but she knew within an hour the Saturday night ritual of her roommates hanging out with their girlfriends would begin, and the house would become loud with laughter and music. She hurried up to her room and closed the door. Sitting in the middle of her bed, she opened the envelope and looked inside. The first paper she pulled out was a piece of stationery with some handwriting on it. Underlined at the top were the words *For the attorney.* She wondered who had jotted the notes. Her mother or her father, perhaps? Under the heading was the name of a private school. She recognized it because it had the reputation as one of the best in the city. There were also the names Suzanne and Peter Hyatt with an address and a phone number.

She put the paper aside and pulled out legal-size pages that were stapled together. At the top was the name of an insurance company. Glancing over the copy, she realized it was a life insurance policy for her father. She quickly scanned it. By the time she reached the signatures on the last page, her hands were shaking. She was both astonished and outraged. The policy was worth five hundred thousand dollars, and she and Charlotte were the beneficiaries. Her father had left them a large sum of money, and yet they had never seen a dime. Where had the money gone? She didn't have to think long for the answer. Her aunt and uncle had somehow gotten their hands on it. Everything was making so much sense to Allison now. It was all about the money. That was the only reason her aunt and uncle had taken them in. They had kept the money a secret all these years. Yet how many times had she and her sister heard they were a financial burden? One big lie.

Allison couldn't help wondering where it went. It certainly wasn't spent on Charlotte and her. Any new clothes or essentials were purchased at a discount store, and once the girls were teenagers, they were expected to find ways to pay their own expenses. They had gone to a public elementary school, and when Allison expressed a wish to go to St. Dominic's for high school, her aunt and uncle refused. She wasn't deterred. She persisted until they gave in, with the stipulation that she would have to pay the tuition on her own. It wasn't easy, but she managed to earn the money by working jobs on nights and weekends. Giovanni helped out her senior year.

Her aunt and uncle hadn't lived a lavish lifestyle. They did, however, like to go out on weekends with their friends. Allison supposed the bars and clubs they frequented had taken a great deal of the money. Pampering Bill probably took the rest. There was nothing he ever wanted that he didn't get.

Allison set the documents aside and picked up the piece of stationery again. Suzanne and Peter Hyatt. The names sounded vaguely familiar, but she couldn't place them. She stared at them for several minutes, trying to recall where she'd heard them before, but eventually she gave up. There was an address in Houston and a phone number. She wondered, after all these years, if these were still accurate. One way to find out, she thought. She pulled out her phone and tapped in the numbers. After five rings she was ready to give up, but suddenly a woman's voice came through.

The woman sounded slightly out of breath, as though she'd rushed to get to the phone. "Hello."

"Is this Suzanne Hyatt?" Allison asked hesitantly.

"Yes."

"My name is Allison Trent, and I—" She stopped when she heard a low gasp. "You know my name?" she asked.

"I do," the woman said.

"How?" she wondered. "How do you know me?"

"Your mother was my dearest friend," Suzanne answered. "And I knew you when you were just a little girl."

Still trying to recall, Allison said, "I'm sorry. I don't remember."

"You and Charlotte were so young, and we only saw you a few times because we lived in Houston and you were in Boston." She paused. "How are you and Charlotte? I can't tell you how many times I've thought of you."

"We're fine," she answered. "I'm calling because I found your name and number on a piece of paper that was with an insurance policy belonging to my father. I was wondering if you knew anything about this."

Suzanne responded curtly with a hint of bitterness in her voice, "I know exactly why my name was there."

"I'd really appreciate it if you could tell me more. My aunt and uncle never mentioned you . . . or the policy, for that matter."

"I'm not surprised," Suzanne said with disgust. "I'm sorry," she added quickly. "It's been a long time, but I still get upset when I think about your parents and what happened."

"What did happen?" Allison asked.

Suzanne took a long, deep breath before letting it out. "I met your mom in college, and we became close friends. When we graduated, we both got jobs in Boston and shared an apartment. Actually I was the one who introduced your dad to your mom. He worked in the office next to mine, and a few of us would go out after work. He was a great guy, and I knew he and your mom would hit it off, so I invited her to join us one afternoon. I was right. They were meant for each other." She paused, and Allison could hear a smile in her voice when she continued. "We had a great time back then. Anyway . . . I eventually met Peter, and we were married. When his company transferred him to Houston, it was really hard for me to leave your mom and dad. They were like family. Your mom and I talked on the phone every other day." She laughed. "Our husbands weren't too happy about the phone bills, but they understood. Whenever possible, we would fly up to Boston or they would come to see us in Houston, but once your mom became pregnant with Charlotte and we had our son, Alex, it became more difficult to get together. Then you were born. Your mother was so happy. Our visits didn't happen as often. Still, we never lost touch."

Suzanne paused again, and this time when she continued she sounded very sad. "One day your mother called and said she wanted to ask me something very important. She said she and your dad were making out a will and wondered if Peter and I would be your legal guardians, should anything ever happen to them. Of course we said yes, we'd be honored. But you really never expect anything like that to happen." Her voice cracked from the emotion she was trying to hold in. "And only a couple of days later, we got the news."

Allison could hear the tears choking her words when she

said, "I couldn't go to the funeral. I was nine months pregnant with our second child, and the doctor said I couldn't travel. I wanted to be there, but I couldn't.

"You and Charlotte lived at home for a while, and a couple of neighbors stayed with you. Just as soon as we could, we came to Boston, but by then your aunt and uncle had petitioned the court for custody. Unfortunately, we had no legal standing because your mother and father's will was never finalized. We fought to take you, but there was nothing we could do. Your aunt and uncle were your closest relatives. They put up a really strong fight, and they won . . . despite your parents' wishes."

Allison was stunned. "My aunt and uncle never told us any of this," she said.

"No, I wouldn't expect them to. When we told them we wanted to remain in your lives, they were outraged. There was quite a battle between us. They said that we would only make the transition more difficult . . . that it was best for you if we let you settle into your new home without interference. I disagreed at first, but then they said if we called or wrote to you, they'd block us. I certainly didn't want to cause you more distress. You'd been through so much. I hope we did the right thing."

Allison was speechless for a moment, and then lied. "Yes, you did the right thing."

"You were still so young, but I guess I hoped Charlotte might remember us at least. Of course we tried to keep you both out of the conflict and she hadn't really spent much time with us. I understand if she has no recollection."

"She never mentioned you. I'm sorry."

"Many times I've thought of trying to find you, just to see how you're doing, but then I worried that I'd be stirring up bad memories."

Allison spent the next few minutes assuring her that she

and Charlotte were healthy and happy, purposely avoiding any mention of their aunt and uncle.

Just before she ended the call, Suzanne said, "I want you to know how much we loved your mother and father, and how much we wanted you."

Allison laid the phone down and sat on her bed, rigid with anger. She couldn't scream for fear of alarming anyone who would hear—but oh, how she wanted to. She knew her aunt and uncle were selfish, angry people, but how could they have been so cruel? She remembered being afraid when she was a little girl. If she didn't behave . . . if she was too loud . . . or if she cried . . . there was always the possibility in her mind that she would be separated from her sister. And all that time there was a loving family who would have taken them.

She was about to explode from the fury building inside her. She couldn't sit still. She stood and paced around her room, hearing Suzanne's words echoing in her head: ". . . *we wanted you.*"

A tear slipped down her cheek and then another. All the years of hurt suddenly erupted, and she fell onto her bed, sobbing uncontrollably. She didn't know how long she'd cried, but she stopped when she heard voices below. Her roommates and their friends were gathering downstairs. She couldn't stay there. She had to get away. Wiping the tears from her face, she went to her closet for her overnight bag and threw a few things in it. She'd drive to Jordan's house and spend the night.

When she came down the stairs, a group was standing in the kitchen talking. Dan peered around the corner. "Hi, Al."

She didn't look at him. If she did, she knew he'd see her swollen, tearstained face. Instead she kept her head down and called, "I'm sleeping at Jordan's. I'll see you tomorrow."

She opened the front door and came to an abrupt halt. Liam was standing there.

One look at her and he could tell something had happened. He pulled the door wider and said, "Let's go." Grabbing her bag, he took her hand and pulled her along.

"How did you know?" She whispered the question and really didn't expect an answer.

"Know what?" he asked, glancing down at her.

That I was in trouble, she thought but didn't say. She shook her head, then said, "That I would be home."

"I didn't." He opened his car door for her, then put her bag in the trunk before getting behind the wheel. "Where are we going?" he asked.

"Just away from here. I don't have a destination in mind."

Liam pulled into the street and was turning the corner when Allison spotted her aunt's car speeding toward them. Allison was certain her aunt hadn't seen her. She quickly dug her phone out of her purse and called Dan to warn him.

"Don't let her come inside," she said. "Just tell her I'm out of town for the weekend. And please don't be polite." She looked over her shoulder in time to see her aunt's car come to a screeching halt in front of her house.

"What was that all about?" Liam asked.

"I don't want to go into it now."

"But you will tell me."

He wasn't asking a question; he was stating a fact, and she knew eventually he would coax it out of her.

"Maybe," she said. She dropped her head back against the seat and closed her eyes. She had no idea where they were going, and she felt too weary to care.

He drove to a restaurant on the water called Jim's Shack. "Have you ever eaten here?" he asked as he parked the car.

"No," she answered.

The exterior of the building looked as though it should have been condemned years ago. The wood was weathered and splintered, but inside it looked brand-new. Bright lights on the pier reflected off the water and gave the dining area a glow. The bar wound halfway around the restaurant. It was crowded, but they didn't have to wait for a table. Turned out, Liam knew the owner, Jim, who personally escorted them to a little alcove overlooking the water.

Allison stared out at the serene view of the gentle waves lapping against the pier, and the tension that had coiled inside her began to unwind. A waiter took their drink orders, and as soon as he left, Allison said, "How do you know the owner?"

Liam shrugged. "Who didn't you want Dan to be polite to?"

Two could play this game, she decided, so she shrugged in answer and smiled at him.

Recognizing her stall tactics, he laughed before answering, "I know the owner of this establishment because I came here with Alec last year, and as it turned out, Alec went to school with him, so, of course, they had to catch up. Jim sat and drank with us. Okay, now it's your turn."

"My aunt. I had an argument with my aunt and uncle today" was all she said.

"These are the people who raised you?"

"No, my sister, Charlotte, raised me. She took care of me and protected me from them."

She gazed out the window again while she gathered her thoughts. She suddenly had this bizarre desire to pour her heart out to him, yet at the same time she didn't want him to know how screwed-up her life had been . . . and how pathetic. His opinion of her mattered, and for the life of her she couldn't understand why. On the other hand, he already knew she was a criminal—she'd admitted breaking the law countless times—what difference did it make if he also knew about her personal problems?

Liam waited for her to explain further. When she remained silent, he sat back and watched her. He was trying to figure out why he was so drawn to her. Yes, she was incredibly sexy and attractive. Yeah, right. Attractive? She was a sight more than simply attractive. She was stunning. Every man's head had turned as she walked to their table. She didn't notice. He sure as certain did. He'd dated a lot of beautiful women, but to him there was something special about Allison, and it had nothing to do with her looks. He liked the fact that she was so damn smart. He didn't like seeing her so vulnerable, though. The overwhelming urge to protect her returned. That wasn't unusual, was it? He was an FBI agent, and wasn't it his job to protect and serve? Damn right it was.

Where did wanting to take her to bed fall under his job description? He really needed to get it together and stop thinking about how good it would be with her. But first, he was going to have to stop staring at her mouth.

"What are you thinking about?" she asked.

He wondered how she would react if he told her the truth. "Why do you ask?"

"You looked so intense. Not so much now, though."

Jim stopped by to say hello again and to find out what they wanted for dinner.

"We're really slammed tonight," he remarked in his thick Boston accent as he pulled out a chair and sat, never taking his eyes off Allison. He reminded her of an old sea captain. There were deep lines in his face from exposure to sun and wind.

Liam made the introductions. Allison smiled and said hello, but Jim appeared to be tongue-tied. He finally found his voice and said hello to her. Then he turned to Liam and said, "She's pretty, isn't she?"

"Yes," Liam agreed, then changed the subject. "What's on the menu tonight?"

"You'll want the chowder."

Allison didn't have much of an appetite, and she would have been fine with a couple of crackers, but she followed Jim's recommendation. As soon as she tasted the chowder, her appetite came back. It was absolutely delicious. She ate every bit of it, and when she was finished, she sipped hot tea while she watched Liam devour a second bowl of chowder. She had never met anyone like him before, and she'd certainly never been this attracted to any other man. She was beginning to feel she didn't have to be on her guard every second.

Though she tried, she couldn't stop thinking of how it would feel if he kissed her. She'd probably melt in his arms. The crazy idea made her smile. She was letting her imagination get out of hand, she decided. So, to take her mind off her silly fantasy, she turned her thoughts back to the serious issues in her life, not the least of which was the fact that she and her sister had been lied to for years.

As though reading her mind, Liam broke into her thoughts. "What happened today?"

His question caught her by surprise. "Why do you think something happened?" she asked.

"The look on your face when you opened the door. You were upset. You said you'd had an argument with your aunt and uncle."

"It was a bad day. That's all."

"Tell me," he said. He started to add, "You'll feel better," but caught himself in time. He had the feeling she'd get her back up. Or bolt. She was already sitting on the edge of her chair.

"Do you have any idea how bossy you are?"

"Yes, I do," he answered with a smile.

The dimple in his cheek was messing with her concentration. She wondered how he would react if she jumped across the table and kissed him. Probably put her in handcuffs and take her to the nearest mental ward.

"It's always stressful whenever I have to go back to Emerson," she told him, her voice hesitant.

"I would imagine so."

Just how much had he dug up researching her background? He sounded so understanding. Maybe it was his sympathetic tone or the tenderness she saw in his eyes that made her want to tell him everything. She paused for a second and then did exactly that. She didn't embellish; she simply explained what life had been like living with her relatives and how she had finally broken ties with them.

Her voice shook when she mentioned the life insurance policy. "Thinking about it makes me so angry." She took a deep breath to calm herself. "What do you do when you're angry and frustrated?"

"I like to hit."

"Hit?"

He nodded. "When I need to get rid of the anger, I look for a rugby game. It can get pretty brutal, which I love. I played a lot of rugby growing up, but if I can't find a game, I go to the nearest batting cages and hit baseballs until I wind down. Frustration is another matter."

"Oh? How do you get rid of frustration?"

The dimple was back. "Sex." He saw the instant blush and had to laugh again. "What do you do when you're frustrated?"

She couldn't bring herself to tell him that when her frustration grew, she wrote code. No, she couldn't tell him that because it was such a nerdy thing to admit.

"Same thing," she said with a straight face. She lowered her eyes and asked, "Tell me, Liam, are you frustrated now?"

He stared at her a long minute before answering, "You're playing with fire. It doesn't matter how frustrated I am. This is work and you're an asset. I don't have sex with assets."

She could feel her cheeks burning. Flirting wasn't her forte, and she should never have tried being coy. "I was not asking you to have sex."

Too late she realized she should have kept her voice low. Half the restaurant had heard her. A rather good-looking man wearing a Celtics T-shirt at the end of the bar yelled, "I'll have sex with you, honey, anytime, anyplace."

She buried her face in her hands. "Oh God," she groaned.

A second man at the bar, pointing to the two on either side of him, chimed in, "Forget these guys. They're amateurs. I'm the man you want, sweet cheeks."

When she raised her head and glanced around the room, a dozen people were looking at her and laughing. She was mortified.

Liam took mercy on her. "Want to change the subject?" he asked.

She blocked out the faces that were staring at her and straightened in her chair, focusing on Liam. "Do you like basketball?" she blurted. "I do. I love the Celtics, and if I were going to stay in Boston, I would get on the list for season tickets. Good ones are hard to come by," she rattled on. "And baseball. I love baseball, too. I go to a lot of the Red Sox home games." She stopped because she had to take a breath.

"I'll have to take you to the batting cages one of these days," Liam remarked. He was trying not to laugh at her, because she was so uncomfortable. Her face was still red. Such an innocent, he thought. There wasn't anything phony or pretentious about her. Yet another reason he was drawn to her. She definitely was unusual compared to the other women he'd known.

But she was an asset and off-limits, he reminded himself once again.

She was finally getting past her embarrassment. "I can go to the batting cages by myself. Besides, you won't be in town long enough to take me. Remember? After I do that little favor for you, you're out of here. Isn't that right?"

He didn't like being reminded that he would be leaving. "Right," he said, his voice clipped.

She suddenly remembered a question she wanted to ask. "Why did you come to my house tonight?"

"I tried to call you, and your number was disconnected. I came to find out what was going on."

"When you saw me leaving with my bag, did you think I was trying to escape?"

"Trust me, Allison. There's no place you could go that I wouldn't find you," he said with a confident smile.

"I was going to Jordan's house. I just needed to get away," she said. "I changed my phone number because of my aunt. On the way back from Emerson, she called at least twenty-five times. I'm not exaggerating," she insisted. "I knew she wouldn't stop harassing me, so I changed my number. I'm only giving it to a few trusted friends, and you, of course," she added hastily. "I'll give you my new number now if you'd like."

"I already have it."

Surprised, she said, "You what? You have it? I only just changed it." She shook her head. "If you want something you just . . . get it?"

"Pretty much." The waiter appeared with the tab, and after paying, Liam stood. "Are you ready to go?"

"Yes," she answered, and even though there had been

awkward, even embarrassing moments, she hated to see her evening with Liam end.

As they crossed the restaurant, he put his arm around her and pulled her into his side.

"What are you doing?" she asked.

"Protecting my asset."

The two men who had shouted at her were whistling, but she ignored them and stared straight ahead.

Once they were in the car, Liam asked, "Do you want me to take you home or drop you at Jordan's?"

"Home," she answered. "I've decided I need a little time alone to think about the documents my cousin, Bill, gave me today, and speaking of Bill . . ."

He glanced over at her. "Yes?"

"I have a favor to ask." She paused, wondering how she should bring up the subject of her irresponsible cousin. After weighing her choices for a few seconds, she decided the direct approach was best. "I'm hoping you can help him stay out of prison. I want him to have one last chance." When he turned to her, she saw the incredulous look on his face.

"You're kidding, right?"

"No, I'm serious. If you can, I'd like you to help him. Why do you look so surprised?"

"I've read his file," he said, his tone hard. "There's no way I'm going to help him. He's had too many chances to change his life."

She didn't say another word. She wanted to let him think it through, and hopefully he would change his mind. She knew he would eventually ask her why she wanted to help Bill, and it was going to be difficult to explain. Did admitting that she felt sorry for him make her a complete fool? His growing-up years had surely been as traumatic as hers, just in a different way. Having such controlling and smothering parents who had watched his every move was much worse than being ignored.

The set of Liam's jaw told her he was going to need more time to consider her request. They pulled up in front of her house, and Liam retrieved her overnight bag from the trunk and then followed her up the sidewalk.

"Looks like the house is empty," he remarked.

"They must have gone out to get something to eat. No worries," she added. "They'll be back."

The porch light was off, and the porch was cast in shadows from the light coming through the living room window. The sheer drapes softened the glare and turned the light a golden hue.

At the door, Allison turned back and took a step closer to him. "May I please e-mail you a video? It shows Bill and the bar fight he was involved in."

"You don't need to e-mail it. I can get it, but tell me, does it prove Bill's innocent?"

Once again she didn't give him a direct answer. "It shows three men pressing in on him. Just watch it, okay?"

"Allison, why do you want to help him?"

She sighed. "I want to believe he can change. Is that so wrong? I don't want to give up on him. He's not all bad," she insisted. "Yes, he has a bad temper, but he's never turned his anger on me, and he always warned me when his friends were coming to the house."

"Why did he warn you?"

"He knew I didn't like them."

"And what did you do when he warned you?"

"I stayed in my room with the door locked. None of them ever bothered me."

"You were afraid of them."

Duh. "Yes."

He shook his head. "I guess that makes him a saint, warning you and all. . . ."

"I'm just pointing out that he isn't all bad."

"How about you read his file?" he suggested.

"Everyone deserves a second chance." She looked up into Liam's beautiful eyes and felt her heartbeat quicken.

"He's had a lot more than two chances."

"Then one more won't hurt, will it? I'm doing a favor for you. Couldn't you do this favor for me?"

"And in return I'm giving you immunity. That was the deal."

She could see she wasn't getting anywhere, and she needed to change her terms. She thought for a second and then said, "Okay, how about this? If you help him, I'll work for Agent Phillips and you for a month. A full month," she stressed.

"You're negotiating—"

"That's thirty-one days." She took a step closer until she was all but touching him and said, "That's a real deal."

"What happens if he gets probation and does something else? Are you going to ask for help again?"

"No," she answered. "It's on him then. He'll have to suffer the consequences."

"He should have suffered the consequences a long time ago." He shook his head. "No."

She wasn't giving up. "How about two months? I'll work for you and Phillips for two full months."

"If I were to do this, it wouldn't be for Bill. I'd do it for you, and two months won't cut it."

Sensing victory, she smiled and said, "How long, then?"

"A year."

"A year? That's crazy. No."

"No deal, then."

The argument continued. She didn't back away from him. After several minutes of bargaining, they came to an agreement. Liam would do what he could for Bill if she worked at the cyber unit for six months. In that time, the FBI would allow her to get the few hours she needed for graduation. Allison thought it was a nice compromise. Liam was more suspicious. Based on what he already knew, he figured Bill would break probation within a month and be hauled off to prison. He didn't share his opinion with Allison, though, knowing she would start arguing again.

"One more thing . . ."

"Now what?" he grumbled.

"I don't want Bill to know I had anything to do with this."

"Yeah, okay."

She was so pleased she kissed him on the cheek. Then she quickly lowered her head and whispered, "I probably shouldn't have done that. It's inappropriate."

The woman was a temptress, and it took all the self-control Liam could muster not to touch her. An internal argument ensued. One kiss wouldn't matter. Yes, it would. And yet if he kissed her, his curiosity would be appeased, and he could move on to more important things. But that would be wrong.

"I don't mess around with assets," he said as he slowly closed the gap between them, his mouth just inches from hers. She was looking deeply into his eyes and he could feel his willpower slipping away. One quick kiss. What was the harm?

It wasn't until that very moment that Allison realized he wanted her. She was stunned. Pleased, too, because she'd wanted to kiss him since she met him.

"I understand," she whispered, pressing her body against his. "Rules are rules. So I certainly shouldn't do this." She put her arms around his neck.

"No, you shouldn't," he protested, yet didn't move.

"Or this," she said, softly brushing her lips over his.

"No . . ." He tried to deepen the kiss, but she pulled back.

This was all new to Allison. She wasn't a flirt, by any means, and she rarely messed around, but she liked teasing Liam. He brought out a side of her she usually kept hidden, and she didn't exactly know why. There was just something about him.

"And it would be against the rules for an asset to do this, don't you suppose?" She leaned up, and her mouth settled on his then in a kiss that was anything but casual or quick. As soon as she opened her mouth for him, he took over. His tongue swept inside to rub against hers, sending shivers down her spine. When he wrapped his strong arms around her, she tightened her hold, her fingers sliding up into his hair as his mouth devoured hers. Passion burned between them, and Allison's last coherent thought was that she never wanted it to stop.

Liam nearly lost all control, the taste of her was so addictive. He felt her tremble and abruptly ended the kiss, then made the mistake of looking at her sexy mouth. He wanted her in his bed. He was burning with his need, but he forced himself to come to his senses and gently pulled her arms from his neck. When he was finally able to let go of her, he had to take several deep breaths to regain control. "Yes, it's against my rules," he said, clearing his throat so he could get the words out.

It took a couple of seconds for her to understand. "Okay," she said softly, frowning.

He could tell the kiss had rattled her. Desire lingered in her eyes, and damn, he wanted to kiss her again. Instead, he took her key and reached around to open the door. Then he gently nudged her inside and slowly closed the door behind her.

ELEVEN

PROMPTLY AT EIGHT O'CLOCK MONDAY MORNING, LIAM WAS at Allison's door. He looked gorgeous—and all business—in his suit and tie. She had made up her mind not to mention the kiss. She was going to act like an adult, not a silly girl in the throes of her first crush.

To appear professional, she had looked beyond her typical casual school attire and had chosen a simple periwinkle blue dress. After changing her shoes several times, she finally opted for her nude heels. She figured the extra height would give her an air of authority. No heels could make her taller than Liam, though.

He waited at the door while she gathered her phone, her identification, and a twenty-dollar bill and put them in a small shoulder bag. When she picked up the black leather case holding her laptop, he stopped her.

"Leave your laptop here," he said.

She shook her head. "I don't like to leave it at home if I can help it. If the house is empty, someone could come in and tamper with it or steal it. My old housemate, Brett, already tried. Whenever it's possible, I carry it with me. The guard can lock it up with my bag."

He didn't argue, and once they were on their way, he said, "Tell me about this Brett."

"He lived with us for a while. He was asked to leave after Mark, one of my other housemates, caught him with my laptop. God knows what he was doing with it. They couldn't tell if he was trying to steal it or just trying to open it. I used it when I was helping him with some of his classes, and I don't know how much he saw. I have some very important work on it, so I'm trying to be very careful."

Recalling a conversation they'd had at the restaurant, he asked, "Did you get your paper finished?"

"You remembered I had a paper to write for my class?"

"Of course."

"Yes, I did finish it despite my lack of sleep. I called Charlotte and she kept me up most of the night. When I told her about my argument with our aunt and uncle, she was upset." Upset didn't quite cover her sister's reaction. Irate was a much better description. Once Allison revealed what was in the envelope Bill had handed her, her sister went into a rage. "She wants to confront them," she told him.

He glanced over at her. "What would that accomplish?"

She shrugged. "It won't change anything. I tried to talk her out of it, and she promised to think about it. She's not a violent person, but I worry she'll punch one of them if she ever sees them again."

Smiling, he said, "I like your sister."

"Why? Because she wants to punch Aunt Jane and Uncle Russell?"

"No, because she protected you when you were young."

It was such a sweet thing to say about Charlotte. Allison felt as though she had just been given a compliment, which didn't make any sense. Charlotte was the hero, not her.

"This new FBI building—," she began.

"It's also the new satellite of the CSA."

"And Phillips is in charge?"

"Yes."

Allison tried not to stare at Liam, but it was nearly impossible. He had such a handsome profile, and every time she looked at him, she thought about his lips on hers. She knew she was being foolish, and she wished she could be more sophisticated about it all. *It* being sex, she admitted. She was such a klutz when it came to physical relationships. Maybe she should have read a couple of books on the subject instead of writing code night and day. Why couldn't she stop thinking about it? Had he thought about the kiss? Probably not, she decided. Men didn't ponder such things, did they? She would ask Dan. He'd be honest with her.

Pull it together, she told herself. Now isn't the time to fantasize about what it would be like to be with Liam. Why think about what would never happen?

"Phillips wants to know if I can break into the government system, right?" she asked.

"Right."

"And he's okay with me searching for the leak?"

"Yes."

"I have a feeling he wants me to fail so he can say, 'I told you so.'"

"I think you might be right," he said with a grin.

"He's in for a disappointment," she said. "I am going to get in, and if the leak is coming from inside, I will find it."

"I like your confidence."

"Thank you," she replied. "Phillips is so sure he's hack-proof."

"And you're sure you won't be detected."

"Of course. Otherwise, what's the point?"

They reached the gate, which opened for them without any notification.

"They've been waiting for you," she said.

Her hands were gripped tightly in her lap, and Liam could see how nervous she was. "They're waiting for you, too," he said.

"Are you going to drop me off?"

Once again the parking lot was deserted. Liam parked close to the door where the guard waited for them. "No, Allison. I'm not leaving you. I'll make sure you get settled in."

"Have you thought more about Bill?" she asked as they made their way to the entrance.

"I've talked to a couple of people," he answered.

"And Phillips? You'll have to talk to him, too, won't you? I wish you didn't have to," she admitted. "The man already thinks he has the upper hand, and doing me a favor will put me at his mercy." Six months, she thought. She could put up with him for six months.

"I've already discussed it with him," he answered.

She didn't have a chance to ask another question. The guard had opened the door and was waiting for them to enter. Allison went to the sign-in counter and handed her laptop and her purse to the other guard on duty.

His smile was genuine when he greeted her. "It's nice to see you again."

He wasn't wearing his identification, but she remembered his name. "How are you, Tom?"

He beamed. "You remembered me."

"Of course."

"I'm doing fine today," he stammered. "How are you doing?"

"Good."

"Are you ready?" Liam asked from behind her. As he took her elbow and steered her toward the elevator, he noticed Tom standing to watch them leave, no doubt to get a look at Allison's legs. Granted, they were mighty fine legs, but Liam didn't like the man ogling her.

As soon as the elevator doors closed, Liam said, "Stop flirting with the employees."

She thought he was joking until she saw his frown. "Saying hello isn't flirting."

"And smiling."

Her hand flew to her throat. "Oh my God, what was I thinking? I smiled and I said hello? Shame on me."

He shook his head. "Okay, I might have overreacted."

"Might have?"

She couldn't say anything more because the doors opened and Agent Phillips stood there, waiting. He wasn't much for greetings, she remembered, and it therefore didn't faze her when he gave her a brusque nod.

She responded by smiling sweetly and saying, "How nice to see you again, Agent Phillips."

She could have sworn he grunted. She had to bite her lip to keep from laughing as she followed him into his office. Liam shut the door, and Phillips turned a chair around, pointing at it to get her to sit. She wondered if he had any idea how rude the gesture was.

"Liam and I are at cross-purposes here," he began. "Liam thinks there might be someone leaking confidential information. He believes it could be someone in the CSA, and I'm just as certain that it isn't."

Liam interjected, "There have been too many instances that point to a leak. If it's not a hacker, then it's someone inside the agency who has access to the information."

"I have employees here whose sole job is to search for hackers. That's all they do all day long," Phillips stressed with a hint of resentment that his competence was in question. "I also find it hard to believe that anyone inside the agency is sabotaging investigations. However, I'm willing to look, and that's where you come in, Miss Trent. Liam has arranged that we forgo some of our typical protocols for new employees and let you get to work right away. I understand that you've agreed to give us your services for six months."

Allison immediately turned to Liam. "Then Bill is getting probation?"

Liam nodded.

Phillips didn't allow time for explanations, resuming his remarks as though any deviation from the topic at hand was against the rules. "I would like to start you off in our basic system security analysis, but Liam has made this leak a priority because he has another case to get to and will be leaving us soon."

She nodded to let him know she understood. He continued on with procedures she should follow, but Allison was having difficulty concentrating. The moment he'd mentioned that Liam would be leaving, an unfamiliar pang gripped her. She'd never felt anything like that before and couldn't put a label on it—sadness, regret? She hardly knew Liam, and she was already aware that his work here was temporary. Why would the thought of him leaving upset her so?

Her attention again went back to Phillips, who was saying, "If anyone should ask, you're looking for viruses. I would rather you didn't interact with any of my employees. We take our jobs seriously, and we don't have time for idle chitchat."

"All right," she said when he looked at her expectantly. What a grim work environment, she thought.

"Where do you want her to work?" Liam asked.

"The office next to the break room on this floor. I don't want to hide her away, because that would raise questions.

There's no one else in there right now, and none of her work will appear on any of the big screens." He turned to Allison and clarified. "This is a brand-new facility, and now that it's officially open, we're deciding to close down the Midwest or the West Coast units and we're moving some of the employees here. Until the transition begins, you will have the room to yourself."

That was why there were so many empty desks and such a large parking area, she thought.

"I'll give you an access code so you can begin looking for a sign of a leak as soon as possible."

"The leak you're certain I won't find."

"Exactly so."

Liam took her to the office she would be using. Like with so many other offices in the building, the side facing the hall was a wall of glass. There were three desks and a large screen on the far wall. No matter which desk she chose, she would have her back to the glass. She didn't want people coming and going behind her, so she went to the desk across the room, pushed it until it was more at an angle with the glass, and sat down. People walking past would see her profile. After adjusting the monitor and her keyboard, she was ready to start.

Liam watched her get settled, and when he looked back over his shoulder, he noticed three men standing on the other side of the glass. Maybe they were just curious about the new recruit. Okay, that was an understatement. The pretty blue dress Allison was wearing wasn't formfitting, but there was no hiding the fact that she had an incredible body. If she had been wearing a tarp, they'd still have noticed. The men scattered as soon as Liam gave them his full attention.

After going over the details of the suspected leaks, he handed her a folder that contained all the pertinent information she would need to get started on her search. He then told her he would check in on her in a couple of hours. As he headed for the door, he turned back and asked, "Is there anything I can get you?"

She didn't answer him. She had already gone into her zone. Her fingers were flying over the keyboard, her eyes locked on her monitor.

With Liam out of the room, Allison was finally able to think. It was too difficult to focus with him next to her. Every nerve in her body reacted when he was near. She couldn't seem to put on her mask of indifference and ignore him. She never should have kissed him. All she wanted to think about was kissing him again, and that just wasn't at all normal. She certainly couldn't concentrate on such matters as the security of a major government agency when he was standing so close.

Starting with the facts in the folder she had been given on the people who had received the sensitive information, she began to work her way backward. She concentrated on the four who seemed to be the most obvious leaks. All of the people had received information through e-mails. As she suspected, the origins of the e-mails were obscure, but she eventually found the source for each one of them. The problem was, each source led to another source, and then another, and another. She completely lost track of time as she tried to navigate the maze.

Liam looked in on her a couple of times, but she was so engrossed in what she was doing he didn't disturb her. When he stopped by to ask her if she'd like to take a break for lunch, she didn't look away from the monitor but stared straight ahead, her fingers still working the keyboard, and said, "No, thanks. I'll catch something later."

Hours later, as employees were filing past her office on their way home for the evening, Liam returned. "How's it going?" he asked.

Her concentration broken, Allison looked up at him and shook her head. "I've never seen anything like this. There must be hundreds of proxies. Whoever sent these e-mails sure knows his stuff. Each e-mail is coming through a different route, but it's pretty obvious to me it's ultimately the same source." She sat back in her chair and stretched her arms over her head to release the tension in her shoulders. "I'm not there yet, but I'm sure I'll figure it out," she assured him.

"It's getting late. You need to stop for the night."

"I'd like to keep going, if that's all right. This guy has created a massive labyrinth, and I just know I can find him." Her eyes lit up at the thrill of the hunt. "I want to try a little longer," she pleaded.

Liam swiveled the back of her chair around and turned her away from the desk. Taking her hand, he gently pulled her to her feet and said, "Come on, Allison. It's time to take you home."

She didn't realize how stiff she was until she walked to the door. She wanted to rub the kinks out of her lower back, but she wasn't about to moan and groan in front of Liam. She wasn't a frail old lady. She was feeling out of shape, and no wonder. It had been over two weeks since she had worked out, and her muscles were protesting her sitting for so long without moving.

During the long day, Allison had downed several bottles of water, but she hadn't been hungry. She'd been too busy—and too excited—working through the massive, convoluted puzzle to think about food. She was thinking about it now, though. As if on cue her stomach grumbled. Did she have a granola bar in her purse? Probably not. She glanced at her watch and was shocked. It was already half past seven. The time really had flown by.

As though reading her mind, Liam asked, "Have you eaten anything at all today?"

"I was busy."

"You're going to get sick," he scolded. "From now on you eat lunch. I don't want you to keel over."

He sounded worried about her, and she couldn't hide her surprise. She wasn't used to anyone showing concern or even noticing when she ate or what she ate . . . except for Aunt Jane when she was monitoring her calorie intake.

"Did I mess up your plans for tonight?" she asked.

"No. You're the priority."

She realized he was still holding her hand when they stepped into the elevator. She didn't feel inclined to pull away.

There was a different guard on duty at the desk. She introduced herself and shook his hand, much to his surprise. As he retrieved her laptop and purse, he told her his name was Lawrence, and he would have given her his life story if Liam hadn't dragged her away.

He had just opened the car door for her when his cell phone rang. He saw who was calling and said, "I've got to take this."

After fastening her seat belt, Allison decided she might as well check her messages while she waited. There were two voice messages. Both were upsetting.

The first was from Giovanni. He had called at ten in the morning to report that her aunt had left word for him that she would be by that afternoon to pick up a check for twelve thousand dollars he owed for work Allison had done.

"Don't worry," Giovanni said. "I won't be giving her any money. I won't even open the door. I do have your check ready, and I'd love it if you could drive up and spend the evening with me. My guest room's always ready for you, but if you can't work it into your schedule, let me know where you want me to mail the check. And, darling, let me say one more time how thrilled I am that you finally got away from those vipers."

The second voice mail was from her housemate Mark. He called at four o'clock to let her know that her uncle was parked in front of the house, obviously waiting to ambush her as soon as she returned home.

Liam finished his call and came around the car. He looked serious as he removed his jacket and placed it in the backseat before getting in. She wondered if his call was good news or bad news. His expression wasn't giving anything away.

"I'm starving," he said. "Let's go to dinner."

She didn't have much of an appetite after listening to the messages, but she knew her uncle was waiting for her and she wasn't in any hurry to go home. "I'm not really hungry now," she said. "If you don't mind dropping me off at the library, I think I'll do some work."

One look at her and Liam knew something was wrong. She was so easy to read, and he liked that about her. She couldn't hide what she was feeling.

He started the engine and drove out of the parking lot. "You have to eat," he urged. "I have just the place in mind. I think you'll like it. What do you say?"

"Thank you for the offer, but it's been a long day and I'm not really in the mood for a crowded restaurant."

"Then I know you'll like this place," he assured her.

"Where is it?" she asked.

"You'll see," he said with a sly grin.

Curious, she relented. "Okay."

She sat back and closed her eyes, letting the day's work fade to the back of her mind. She didn't want to think about it or anything else right now.

A half hour later, Liam turned toward the Charles River and pulled into a small parking lot. Coming around the car, he opened her door, took her hand, and led her down a path to an area shaded by large trees. A green wooden park bench sat before a cluster of tall forsythia bushes, and in front of it a long grassy area sloped down to the river.

Pointing to the bench, he said, "Have a seat and I'll be right back."

Allison was a little puzzled, but she trusted Liam and did what he said. After a few moments of sitting on the bench and watching the river, she felt an increasing calm, as though her worries were flowing away with the current. In the distance she could see people walking and biking along the river path, some exerting themselves for exercise, others simply enjoying an evening stroll. A row team out for practice drifted past in their long, sleek boat, the smooth, rhythmic strokes gliding them across the water. The entire scene was hypnotic, and once she allowed it to take over, the noise and commotion of the city faded into the background.

A few minutes later, Liam appeared carrying two cans of soda in one hand and two hot dogs wrapped in foil in the other. "I hope you like mustard," he said as he handed her a can and a hot dog.

"Of course," she said, smiling. When he had taken his seat beside her and opened the wrapper for a big bite of his hot dog, she remarked, "You were right. I do like this place."

He popped the tab on his soda. "My favorite spot in Boston," he said, taking a big swig.

They sat quietly enjoying the view and eating their hot dogs. When they were finished, Liam stretched his long legs in front of him and folded his hands behind his head. Sitting there with him in this place of perfect tranquillity, Allison felt stress-free for the first time in days. She didn't want to talk about or even think about problems, so she asked Liam to tell her about some of the places he'd been assigned. He began with London and worked his way around the globe. Each city or country he mentioned seemed to have a story attached to it, and each story was either heartwarming or hilariously funny. She couldn't take her eyes off him. When he smiled, she felt a little catch in her pulse. The more he talked, the more she wanted to hear. Contrary to her initial assessment of him, she could see he had a wonderful sense of humor.

She especially liked the fact that he didn't have any trouble making fun of himself. Eventually their conversation turned to other topics, and they discovered a number of mutual interests, everything from baseball to ocean life.

When Liam told her about a near miss with a shark, she rubbed the goose bumps on her arms and asked, "How could you ever get into the water knowing that some of the most dangerous predators are right there, waiting for a snack?"

Liam laughed. "And I'm the snack?"

"Yes. Haven't you ever seen *Shark Week* on television? Guess where some of the most dangerous sharks are."

"Australia."

"That's right."

"I grew up swimming in the ocean."

"Is that how you learned to swim? In the ocean?" She sounded appalled. "I can't imagine . . . with all those waves and undercurrents. It can be very dangerous."

"We had a pool in our backyard, and that's where I learned. My father taught me. I was three or four. How old were you when you learned to swim?"

"Around seventeen, I guess. Giovanni taught me."

"The guy you model for? How did that happen?"

"We were on a photo shoot. It was a beautiful location with this infinity pool that seemed to drop off the side of the world. I was modeling a bathing suit, and Giovanni wanted to get some shots of me coming out of the water." She laughed as she added, "I didn't want to disappoint him."

"So you jumped into the water?"

"And almost drowned. Giovanni had to come in after me. He pushed the photo shoot to the next day, and right then and there he gave me my first lesson."

"You must have shocked the hell out of him."

She laughed again. "Oh yes, I did."

Liam could tell she was having a good time. So was he, he realized.

"Here's a question," he said nonchalantly as he reached for her empty can and wrapper. "Swim in the ocean where you know there's a great white, or walk across a lawn where you know there's a poisonous snake—which do you choose?"

She drummed her fingertips on the park bench while she thought about it. "Swim," she finally said.

"My brother and I played that game all the time. Drove our parents nuts."

"What was it like, growing up in Australia?" she asked.

He described his family and their home on the Australian coast with its aquamarine waters and white sand beaches. It sounded like an idyllic childhood. He clearly was very close to his family, especially his younger brother. The two boys had been daredevils, and from some of the escapades he told her about, she suspected they had given their parents some sleepless nights. Allison was captivated by his stories and the way his eyes crinkled at the corners just before he was about to tell of some mischievous prank. She still couldn't figure him out, but she was definitely intrigued. His sense of adventure and the need to do something that mattered had obviously led him to the work he was doing now. By comparison, she was a boring nerd. While she hid in her room writing code, he was out in the world experiencing life.

When there was a lull in the conversation, she looked around. It was night and the river was dark, the only light coming from the moon's reflection off the water and a distant streetlight on the path. She glanced down at her watch. It was almost eleven. They had been talking for three hours. She had been so caught up in their conversation she had completely lost track of time. She had forgotten about her worries for a while, but unfortunately they came rushing back when, as they were walking back to his car, Liam asked her if she had gotten bad news in the messages she had checked earlier.

"Why would you think . . ."

"You're easy to read," he said. "You checked your messages and you were upset."

"Not upset," she corrected. "Irritated."

He hadn't started the engine yet and turned toward her. "Tell me."

She knew he wouldn't let up until she explained, so she quickly told him about both messages.

He didn't hide his disgust. "Your aunt thought she could sign your name to your check and deposit it in her account?"

"She's done it before."

"But you're not going to let her do it again."

"No, I'm not."

"Why do you think your uncle was sitting in front of your house? The money?"

"I don't know. Maybe to try to get me back under his thumb. He's got a bad temper," she added. "And when he drinks, he can be . . . unreasonable."

Frowning, he asked, "Has he ever hit you?"

"Almost. Once. Bill stopped him and told him to leave me alone," she answered. "From then on I pretty much stayed out of his way. For the most part we ignored each other . . . that is, until he needed the money I could bring in."

"You had a hell of a time growing up, didn't you?"

She stiffened. "Don't feel sorry for me. It wasn't all bad, and I got away with a lot. As long as I didn't bother them and I stayed out of trouble, I could do whatever I wanted. And as long as my sister was around, I was okay."

"What about when she wasn't around?" he asked quietly.

"I was more cautious," she said. "I took care of myself," she added before abruptly changing the subject. "How soon will my aunt and uncle find out that Bill is going to get probation?"

"Tomorrow or the day after. What happens when he screws up again, Allison?"

"You've already asked me that question."

"I'm asking again."

She knew he wanted to make sure she wouldn't waver. "He's on his own if he messes up. I haven't changed my mind. I'm done. I promise."

They were just a couple of blocks from her house when Liam said, "If your uncle is still sitting out front, I'm going to talk to him."

"No, I'll handle him. You don't need to fight my wars for me."

"Yeah, well, I'm talking to him," he insisted. "And if he's behind the wheel and has been drinking, he's going to be spending the night in lockup."

The set of his jaw indicated he was going to be stubborn, and when they turned the corner to her street, she was relieved. Fortunately her uncle had left. She was thankful there wouldn't be a confrontation.

Liam walked her to the door and once again held most of the contents of her purse while she searched for her house key. As soon as she got the key in the lock, he turned to leave.

"I'll pick you up at eight," he said.

"I can drive myself. I have GPS. I won't get lost."

"I'm still picking you up at eight."

Thoroughly confused, she asked, "Why?"

He walked back to her. "Because I want to."

The mood changed the closer he got to her. They stood

in the shadows staring at each other, and Allison wondered if he would kiss her again.

Liam was wondering how he was going to keep away from her. Did she have any idea how seductive she was? He couldn't stop staring at her mouth, remembering how soft her lips were and how sweet she tasted.

"Thank you for dinner," she said without taking her eyes away from his.

"You're welcome." His voice was gruff.

He told himself to turn around and walk away, but he couldn't make himself do it. What was happening to him? He'd never had any problems with women before. Allison was different, though. She was messing with his head, and he doubted she even realized it.

"Are you going to kiss me?"

"No."

His abrupt answer should have embarrassed her, but it didn't. "You looked like you were about to kiss me."

"No."

"Why not?" She sounded disgruntled.

The blunt question made him smile. "I'm trying to keep my distance."

"And I'm making that difficult for you."

"Yes."

"In my defense, you're making it difficult for me, too."

"Yeah? How's that?"

"Mixed signals," she said, nodding. "You say you don't want to get involved, and the next minute you're grabbing me and kissing me crazy."

She had a point there. The last time he had brought her home, he was bouncing back and forth between doing the right thing and acting like a teenager with out-of-control hormones. "You're right. From now on we keep this on a professional level. Understand?"

"Absolutely. And just so you know, I don't usually throw myself at men."

She stared at him expectantly, seeming to need his agreement. "Yeah, okay," he responded.

"What happened before was as much my fault as it was yours," she explained very matter-of-factly. "For as long as I'm your asset, we'll keep a professional relationship. I promise I won't let you kiss me again. I have more self-control than you do."

"You think so, huh?"

"Absolutely."

He leaned down and whispered in her ear, "Wanna bet?"

TWELVE

ALLISON NOW UNDERSTOOD WHAT LUST WAS ALL ABOUT. NO wonder it was such a sin. According to the militant sisters at St. Dominic's High School, it was one of the worst offenses, the burning-in-hell kind. Until Liam came along, she had never felt such a raw physical reaction. With him everything was different. He was masculine and sexy and strong, and oh, did he know how to make her want him! All he had to do was look at her a certain way and she felt she was melting inside. Being with him even topped writing code, and how freaky was that? These feelings were so completely foreign to her she didn't quite know what to do about them . . . except keep them to herself. They had agreed their relationship should be a professional one, and she was determined to prove she could be sensible and focus on the work. Liam certainly didn't seem to have any trouble with it.

Each morning of her first week, he appeared at her door to take her to the cyber unit. Allison had protested that she was perfectly capable of driving there herself, but he insisted on accompanying her, claiming their time in the car would give them a chance to discuss the progress of the case. During the long drive, Liam was all business. Once they reached the cyber unit, he walked her to her office and then disappeared until it was time for her to leave. Their journey back to her house was usually quiet. He would drop her off at her door with a casual good-bye, and each time he drove away she would remind herself that she was simply doing a job. Liam called her an asset, and she had to accept that fact. Once her usefulness to him in solving this case was over, he would be gone without a backward glance. This was a business proposition, nothing more.

Just as Liam had promised, Bill had been given probation, but that didn't stop his mother and father from trying to get hold of Allison. One or both had driven to her house several times now. They took turns banging on the front door, demanding to be let in. There were also a good number of crude threats thrown in, and after the first confrontation her roommates decided not to answer the door. On their third assault, Mark timed the banging just for fun. Allison's aunt didn't let up for five full minutes. He claimed he was actually impressed anyone could pound on a door for that long without stopping.

Allison knew what they wanted. She was their cash cow, and they weren't going to let her go without a fight. Luckily she was away much of the time, either working at the cyber unit or attending a class. Mark and Dan would text her to warn her whenever they showed up. Just the possibility that she might have to see them again and speak to them made her sick to her stomach, and every time she thought about the five-hundred-thousand-dollar insurance policy, the anger inside her grew. The only reason those hateful relatives had taken Charlotte and her into their home was the money. They'd spent years shaming them and accusing them of being a financial burden.

She couldn't believe they were driving the long distance almost every single day just to harass her. They must have been confident they could bring her back into the fold, she thought. Their tactics had worked in the past, but no more. Unlike Charlotte and Oliver, Allison had no desire to confront her aunt and uncle. Her goal was to put them out of her life. In time she hoped she could forget their very existence.

Though Dan and Mark never complained, Allison knew the constant disruption was wearing on them. They both were carrying a full load at school and had a heap of other responsibilities on their plates as well. It wasn't fair to make them deal with her crazy relatives, too. Since she was planning to move out of the house after graduation at the end of May anyway, she decided to push up the date and find an apartment to rent for six months while she worked for Agent Phillips. Mark and Dan tried to convince her to stay, but in the end they agreed the move was a good idea, especially if Allison's aunt and uncle never learned her new address.

Dan came through for her. He knew a guy who knew a guy who was moving to New Orleans and had just packed up all his possessions but hadn't yet found a tenant to sublease his place. Allison pounced on the one-bedroom apartment even though the rent was knee-buckling. Fortunately she was going to be making a very good salary, so she could afford it.

Her new home was on the second floor of an apartment building overlooking the river. There was a doorman and assigned underground parking, which was almost unheard-of in such a sought-after area of Boston proper. Over a weekend she purchased a camel-colored sofa on sale, a matching easy chair and ottoman, and a desk. She also bought a king-size bed with the money from Giovanni. She left her single bed at the house for the next student.

It didn't take any time at all to move in. Dan and Mark brought over her books and clothes while she packed her car with the rest of her meager possessions. One trip to a superstore, and by Sunday night she had everything she needed.

Her final task was to call Liam. At first he seemed concerned that she would make such an abrupt decision, but after she explained her reasons, he agreed she'd done the right thing and told her he would be downstairs at the entrance to her building early the next morning to pick her up.

Without the added distraction of her relatives, the next week fell into a predictable routine. When she wasn't in class, she was working long hours at cyber headquarters. It was taking her longer than she had anticipated to find the source of the original e-mails, and that was a real smack to her ego. Yet the puzzle so fascinated her that she hated stopping each night. Liam had to all but drag her out of the building.

While she was working, she was usually left alone. Phillips would saunter in every now and then to look over her shoulder at the monitor, but he rarely spoke to her. Occasionally she would notice employees walking by her office, and sometimes she would pass them in the hall, yet she never stopped to chat, nor did they try to engage her in conversation. Even though they weren't aware of her purpose for being there, no one expressed curiosity. She wondered if they had been ordered not to ask about the work others were doing.

With each day that passed, she knew she was getting closer to the answer. Finding it was just a matter of time and persistence. By Friday afternoon of the second week, she sensed the end was in sight. She glanced up at the clock on the wall. It was getting late, and she prayed that Liam wouldn't appear at the door to stop her. She was so close.

She narrowed her concentration on the screen and worked furiously, as though all her work would slip away if she lost focus for even one second. Suddenly there it was. Everything came together in one single spot. She found the source. The urge to jump up and shout was nearly overwhelming. She couldn't, of course, so she sat there and cheered silently.

Now what? She could either go to Phillips and report what she had found, or wait for Liam and tell him. A no-brainer. She would wait. Phillips wasn't going to take the news well, no matter who told him. He had insisted it was impossible for her to trace the origin of the leaks back to the FBI—and he hated to be wrong. Besides, she had just seen Curtis Bale, the former head of the Detroit division, heading for Phillips's office. It wouldn't be such a good idea to rush in now and announce that she had identified the exact computer the breach had originated from and that it was located in Detroit.

Impatient, she glanced up at the clock again. Where was Liam?

While she waited, she was curious to look around and see what else she could find. Her fingers hovered over the keys. What would be the harm of checking out a few e-mails? Maybe there were other incriminating messages. She shook her head. As much as she wanted to snoop, she knew she couldn't go any further without permission, no matter how great the temptation. She had made up her mind not to break any more laws, and she meant to keep her promise.

But making certain there weren't any more damning messages would be helping, wouldn't it?

While she was having her moral debate—should she or shouldn't she?—Liam walked in. She nearly jumped out of her chair when she noticed him watching her. She was sure she looked as guilty as she felt. He, on the other hand, looked wonderful, but then, when didn't he? The man certainly knew how to wear a suit. Every time he gave her his full attention, her heart did a little flip. She wished she could make herself not care because she knew she was headed for misery. Thank God she hadn't gotten more involved with him. She could get over a couple of kisses. No big deal . . . right?

"Are you ready to leave? I'd like to get out of here. It's been a long week," he said.

She didn't ease into the news. "I found it."

His smile faded. "You're sure?"

"Yes."

"Show me." He pulled up a chair and sat next to her.

"I can show you the original e-mails, but explaining how I got to the source would take a long time." She didn't add her concern that he probably wouldn't understand what she was trying to explain anyway.

"I don't need to know how you got there," he said. "Phillips and his team will want the step-by-step explanation."

"I know what he's going to do. He'll point to that chair, tell me to sit, and then question me for hours."

More like days, Liam thought, but didn't say. "*That* chair?"

"You know. The one in his office. It's like he's training a dog."

Liam put his arm on her shoulder, leaned toward the screen, and began to read the damning messages, examining each carefully as she scrolled through one and then another. He was so engrossed in what he was seeing he didn't realize he was absentmindedly stroking her upper arm.

"The e-mails came from Detroit," he said.

"Yes."

She couldn't tell what he was thinking. His expression wasn't revealing anything, but when the muscle in his cheek flexed once, then again, she knew he was keeping his temper under control. When he finished reading, he looked at her intensely, which immediately messed with her ability to concentrate. How could one man have such a powerful effect on her?

"You did it, Allison. You got to the source. You should be proud of yourself."

Uncomfortable with praise, probably because she'd gotten so little of it in her life, she immediately downplayed her role. "It took much longer than I had anticipated, and I'm sure others wouldn't have taken as long."

"Don't underrate yourself," he argued. "This was not a job just anyone with computer skills could have done."

"What happens now?"

"Alec and I take it from here." He pushed his chair back and hurried out of the room, saying, "Sit tight while I talk to Phillips. Then I'll take you home."

Allison foolishly thought Phillips would want to wait until Monday to question her, but Phillips, being Phillips, felt compelled to get some answers now. He called her into his office, pointed to the chair, and proceeded to question her for two full hours. Liam was there the entire time, leaning against the wall with his arms folded, watching her.

Phillips didn't care how late the hour was. He wanted to know some of the searches she'd done, and he was having difficulty understanding how she had arrived at what he called point zero so quickly. She gave Liam the "get me out of here" look several times, which he completely ignored. Phillips didn't stop his inquisition until eight o'clock. By then she was ready to pull out her hair . . . and his. Six months working under his thumb was going to be an eternity.

THIRTEEN

BY THE TIME THEY LEFT THE OFFICE, NEITHER LIAM NOR AL-
lison was in the mood to talk. He offered to take her to
dinner, but she declined. She was too tired to eat and only
wanted a hot shower and ten hours of sleep.

What she didn't want was to say good-bye to Liam for
the last time.

Just a couple of blocks away from her apartment, Liam
finally broke the silence. "What are you thinking about?
You look so . . . worried."

She wasn't about to tell him the truth, that she was going
to miss him. Instead she turned to him and said, "You completely ignored my signals."

"What signals?"

"I was giving you the look, letting you know I wanted to
get out of there."

He flashed a smile. "Ah, you mean the glares."

"Okay, the glares," she conceded.

"You shouldn't be frowning now. You should be happy
and damn proud of yourself. You found the proof Alec and
I needed."

"I am happy," she insisted, sounding ridiculously defensive. "Maybe now you and Alec won't think I'm such a horrible person."

"No one thinks you're horrible," he said, his exasperation apparent in his tone. "And why do you care what anyone thinks?"

If she was to give him an honest answer, she would sound pitiful, though at times that was exactly how she felt. The truth was, she had never had a close relationship with anyone but her sister. She had kept most people at a safe distance, and that was the way she liked it. She was an intensely private person. At least, that was her excuse for being so introverted. She didn't want anyone to look too closely into her background, because she was embarrassed and a little ashamed. The less others knew about her, the safer she felt. Every time she stepped outside her comfort zone, she felt vulnerable.

Odd, she was so cautious about her private life and yet she was able to set aside her inhibitions when she modeled for Giovanni. She couldn't really explain the contradiction, but when Giovanni and his team transformed her with their makeup and clothes, it was almost as though she became another person wearing a mask no one could see behind.

She loved and trusted Giovanni with all her heart, and although it had taken time, she had grown to care for and trust her housemate Dan. And yet neither one knew what she could do with a computer. During Phillips's long interrogation, he had actually referred to her as a master criminal. She wondered what Giovanni or Dan would think about that. They probably wouldn't believe him, and if they did, they would have been shocked.

Her friendship with Jordan was different. She knew that Allison was a hacker and had broken several laws, yet she still remained her friend. She also knew a little about how

dysfunctional Allison's home life had been and wasn't deterred. If Allison was ever sent to prison, she wasn't positive Jordan would bring her a cake with a file in it, but she
had a strong feeling Jordan might try.

"I asked you a question," Liam reminded her, bringing
her back from her musings.

"I don't like people thinking I'm a criminal."

Before he could comment, she rushed on. "Oh, I know
what you're going to say. 'You are a criminal.' Okay, yes, I
guess you could look at it that way. That's all in the past,
though. Haven't you ever heard of second chances, for
Pete's sake?"

"Allison—"

She interrupted to finish her thought. "And that's why I
insisted that, along with immunity, you and Alec both give
me your word that only a select few would know what I've
done."

"I remember what I promised."

"You know what would happen if it got out that I took
millions of dollars. Even though I gave it to the FBI, I'd be
added to a list, and every time a government agency was
hacked, I'd be dragged in and interrogated. Being on that
list would follow me for the rest of my life."

"I'm not going to let that happen," he said, his tone emphatic. He pulled up in front of her apartment building, put
the car in park, and turned to her. "Why are you worrying
about this now?"

"Because you'll be leaving, and I wanted to make sure . . ."

"You wanted to make sure I'll keep my word."

She knew she had insulted him. His clenched jaw was a
big indicator. Should she apologize? She'd probably make
it worse if she did. He seemed so serious, as though he had
something troubling on his mind.

"I guess this is the last time you'll be driving me to and

from the cyber unit," she said. "Good luck on your next assignment."

The doorman, a retired car salesman named Stamos, unbolted the glass door from within and opened it wide. Allison smiled at him before turning back to Liam. "You don't need to go up with me." She was involved in a tug-of-war with her tote bag. She was pulling on it, but he wasn't letting go.

Liam finally released his hold on the bag and followed her up the steps and into the foyer without saying a word. Allison couldn't tell what was going through his mind, but the way he was looking at her, as though searching for the answer to some pressing question, was making her feel very uneasy.

She wanted to find out how long he would be staying in Boston without being too intrusive. Subtle, she decided. She would be subtle. "Will you and Alec be leaving to follow up on the leak? I imagine you've already taken another assignment after this one. Or is it too soon? Are you waiting to decide, or are you going to take a few days off? That's what you should do. Take some time to relax." She couldn't seem to slow down. So much for being subtle. Her words were fairly tripping over one another. Why she was suddenly feeling so nervous was beyond her. Perhaps it was because it was doubtful she would ever see him again. Maybe once she was away from him, she would come to her senses and figure it all out. It was impossible to distance herself now.

The doorman gained their attention. "Miss Trent, there was an incident you should know about." Stamos's usually booming voice was hesitant. He kept glancing at Liam.

"Stamos, this is my friend Agent Scott. Tell me about the incident, please." She had a bad feeling she already knew what he was going to say, yet foolishly held out hope it was something else . . . anything else.

"You had some company," he began. "An older man and woman came by. They parked right in front of the door, so I saw what they were driving. It was a year-old Chrysler 300C Platinum with twenty-inch polished cast aluminum wheels, a dual-pane panoramic power sunroof, and HID headlights. It's a nice, smooth ride," he continued. "This one had dents and scratches all over it, like someone had taken a hammer to it or maybe had been driving when he shouldn't . . . if you know what I mean. They ruined that beautiful car."

Liam tried to get him back on track. "You were telling Allison about the man and woman. Who were they? Do you know?"

"Oh yes, of course. They told me they were your aunt and uncle. The woman even pulled out her driver's license and waved it in my face to prove she had the same last name."

Allison felt as though the wind had just been knocked out of her. They had found her. And so soon. Damn. It was inevitable that they would track her down, but she had hoped it would take them longer to figure out she had moved, and even longer to find her new address. No such luck.

"When was this?" she asked.

"They showed up around four this afternoon, maybe four thirty." He scratched his jaw as he continued. "They were . . . difficult."

Difficult? That was putting it mildly. "Did they make a scene?" she asked, knowing full well they did.

"Yes, ma'am, they certainly did. They wanted to wait in your apartment. I refused to let them, of course, and that was when they started shouting at me. The woman told me she had your permission. Don't worry. I would never let anyone inside your home," he rushed to add.

"Did they tell you what they wanted?" Liam asked.

"No, and I didn't ask. They tried to push past me to get to the elevator. I pushed back and explained again that they couldn't go beyond the lobby. They both became quite belligerent and as loud as a couple of broken mufflers. Your uncle threatened me, said he could get me fired. I'm pretty sure he was intoxicated."

Of course he had been intoxicated. He usually started drinking around noon, sometimes a little before. It was just the way it was in the Trent household. Allison wished Liam wasn't hearing about her relatives. It was embarrassing to be related to such vulgar people. She reminded herself that their behavior didn't reflect on her, but she wasn't very convincing. "I'm sure he was drunk or on his way there, and I'm sorry you had to deal with them. I know how difficult they can be."

"Now that you know what they look like, don't ever let them inside, and if they try to force their way in, call the police," Liam ordered.

"I'll alert the other doormen. There're three of us in all," he told Liam. "I lock up at ten each night, and tenants have to use their keys to get inside the front door until six in the morning."

Great. Now outsiders were getting involved in the fiasco. The more Allison tried to avoid her aunt and uncle, the more belligerent they became. "I'm so sorry they were a bother," she apologized.

Liam heard the mortification in Allison's voice and immediately felt his protective instincts rising again. "You aren't responsible," he said, putting his arm around her.

Was he comforting her or feeling sorry for her? Allison couldn't tell. She tried to gently shrug his arm away as she headed toward the elevator, but it didn't budge. Instead, Liam walked into the elevator with her and pushed the button for her floor.

As the elevator ascended, Liam's emotions and his good judgment were in a raging battle. It was killing him not to take charge of her aunt and uncle, to tell Allison he would make certain they left her alone. He could be a real badass when he needed to. Allison wouldn't let him, though. She would think he was interfering, and in fact that was exactly what he would be doing. He knew she could handle herself. The way she stood up to Phillips had proven that she could hold her own, but knowing what she had endured growing up in that whacked-out household made him want to shield her from more heartache. She wouldn't like that, either. So he would let her take the lead, and if he needed to get involved, he would make certain she didn't know about it.

The elevator doors parted, and Liam deliberately slowed the pace as they approached her apartment. A strange feeling was taking over, one he didn't know how to handle. He was always so sure of himself and could make the right call when the situation demanded, but this was different. He had set out to solve a problem for the agency. Mission accomplished, right? On to the next step. That was the way these operations worked. Then what was the reason for his reluctance to end this phase of the job?

The reason was obvious. It was Allison. Something inside him didn't want to let go, and he was intentionally drawing out his time with her. He knew he should treat her like any other asset: thank her for her contribution, wish her well, and walk away. But she wasn't just any asset. The memory of how good she had tasted when he'd kissed her kept gnawing at him.

At her door Allison rummaged through her purse for her house key, but she struggled to concentrate on the task. Liam was standing so close, her whole body tensed and her hands shook.

"I'm assuming I won't be seeing you again. Since I no longer work for you, we're pretty much done. Right? Of course we are," she rambled on with a nod, not daring to look up. "Best of luck to you." Best of luck? She couldn't come up with anything better? She felt like such a nitwit.

"How come you're in such a hurry to get rid of me?" he asked, a smile in his voice.

"I'm not. I'm just trying to keep this relationship professional. I don't want to . . ." She could barely breathe. She knew she should get away from him as soon as possible, before she made a complete fool of herself and ripped his clothes off.

He took the key from her, unlocked the door, and followed her inside. He was waiting for her to finish her thought, and when she didn't, he prodded, "You don't want to what?"

She couldn't admit her lascivious thoughts. "Never mind."

She made the mistake of looking into his eyes. She felt like sighing. Or jumping his bones. He was such a strong, muscular man, and with his sun-streaked blond hair and clear green eyes, he was nearly irresistible. It was impossible to pretend to be immune to his charms any longer.

She had prided herself on her self-control. In fact, she had bragged about it to Liam, but what happened next was beyond her control. At least that was the lie she told herself. She leaned into him, put her hands on his shoulders, and kissed the daylights out of him. The kiss was hot, carnal, demanding a response. She poured her heart into that kiss, and if he pushed her away, she didn't know what she would do. She wanted him to feel the passion she felt and to want her as much as she wanted him. Her mouth was open and her tongue rubbed against his. She heard him growl low in his throat and tried to get even closer to him. Being the aggressor was new to her, but she found she liked it . . . with him. She trusted him—which in her mind was a rare and beautiful thing—and that was why she could throw caution to the wind and go a little crazy.

Every argument running through Liam's head flew out the window. Since the moment he'd met her, he'd wanted her in his arms. Who was he kidding? He wanted more than that. He wanted her in his bed, under him, writhing and begging for release. Keeping their relationship professional had been one of the hardest things he had ever done, but he knew, as long as he was in charge of her assignment, he couldn't act on his feelings. Now, he rationalized, she no longer worked for him. He was neither her boss nor her colleague. She worked for Phillips.

He wrapped his arms around her, cupped her backside, and lifted her up until her pelvis was pressed against his. Her mouth was soft and warm, and he was ravenous for more. He knew things were getting out of hand, yet the passion was escalating so quickly he couldn't make himself let go of her. When he finally lifted his head, he saw her face was flushed and she was breathless. His touch had done that to her, he knew, and he wondered if she was as rattled as he was. God, she was beautiful. She tried to move back into his arms, but he put his hands on her waist and wouldn't let her move.

He stared at her a long minute and then in a raspy voice asked, "Do you want to do this?"

The question jarred her. "Do this? What did you have in mind?"

Allison took a step back. Of course she wanted him, but did attacking him make her a sex-starved maniac? That would be wrong. Then again, what was wrong with having one amazing night with him before he left? Nothing, she decided, and her curiosity would be appeased. Yes, the sisters of St. Dominic's would be horrified by what they would call her lack of morals, and they would no doubt tell her she was going to end up in purgatory for a millennium if she didn't get her mind out of the gutter. If so, she really didn't care. Besides, there wasn't going to be any guilt because he wouldn't be around to remind her. Although she wasn't all that experienced, she had had sex before and didn't think it lived up to all the hype. She hadn't been in any hurry to do it again. Until Liam. Everything was different with him.

"Allison, answer me." Liam knew he would let go of her and leave if that was what she wanted, but he hoped to God she wanted him to stay.

"Yes, I want to do this," she finally answered. "But I prefer to call it making love." When he reacted to her declaration, she poked him in the chest. "Don't you dare laugh at me."

His smile was filled with tenderness. "I prefer to call it what it is. Sex."

"Do you have to be so clinical about it?"

He shrugged. "I don't want there to be any misunderstanding. I lead a chaotic life, and a long-term commitment with any woman isn't possible."

When it came to romance, the man was definitely lacking finesse. But then what did she know? The only romance she'd observed was on television. "Okay, no misunderstandings, no complications, no commitments. Agreed?"

"Agreed." He sounded relieved, which she found a bit galling. Did he think she would demand marriage?

She put her arms around his neck again and rested her cheek against his chest. "Maybe we should put it in writing. Then you won't have to worry."

He hid his smile and said, "Yeah, we should put it in writing."

"And get it notarized."

He laughed. "Are you making fun of me?" He squeezed her backside. "I just want to be clear on expectations."

"Did you go through these expectations of yours with the other women you've taken to bed? I'm assuming there have been one or two." It was odd that she didn't like the idea of Liam with any other woman. She shouldn't care, should she? Yet she did.

"No."

"No, what?"

"No, I've never gone through them with any other woman."

She leaned back so she could look into his eyes. "Why not?" she asked, clearly disgruntled.

"You're different."

"Is that good or bad?"

"Neither," he answered. "Just different."

She sighed. "You sure know how to kill a mood. I think . . ."

She was going to tell him he might as well leave, but that thought got all tangled up in her mind the second his open mouth covered hers. The kiss was hard and blatantly possessive. Oh God, how she loved the way his tongue took possession, and she began the mating ritual, pressing her pelvis against his each time his tongue sank inside.

She was trembling when he lifted his head. They walked into the bedroom and stood at the foot of the bed facing each other as they undressed. While he removed his jacket and tie, she kicked off her heels, then turned around so that he could unzip her dress. She didn't have to tell him what she wanted. She simply lifted her hair and waited.

Liam leaned down and kissed the side of her neck, smiling when he saw the goose bumps he caused. Then he lowered her zipper all the way down to the base of her spine. A night-light from the adjoining bathroom cast shadows on the bed and on her golden body. He marveled at how smooth and perfect her skin was.

Heart pounding, Allison slowly removed her dress, carefully folded it, and placed it on a nearby chair. She was deliberately taking her time, hoping she could get her nerves under control, but she quickly gave up and turned back to him.

Liam had to remind himself to breathe when he saw she was wearing lacy black lingerie. She was the sexiest woman he had ever known, and he had wanted her from the moment he had met her. Within seconds, he removed his gun and badge and put them on the bedside table. She tried to unbutton his shirt for him, but her hands were shaking so much, she couldn't get it done. He took over the task, all the while his gaze locked on her.

The look on his face made Allison feel warm everywhere. She curled her toes into the rug and stared up at him. He really was beautiful, she thought, knowing he wouldn't like it if she told him so. She put her hand on his chest and trailed her fingertips down to the waistband of his pants.

"I'm nervous," she whispered.

"I know," he replied, smiling. She threaded her fingers through her hair and brushed it back in an action he found utterly feminine.

"I don't understand why. I'm used to taking my clothes off in front of men."

That statement got a reaction. He was in the process of unzipping his pants but stopped and said, "There's no way in hell I'm going to believe you're promiscuous."

"What? No, of course not. But if I were?"

He shrugged, indicating that it didn't matter to him. "I'd still want you."

"I'm not," she stated again.

"Okay. You like to take your clothes off . . ."

"In front of men," she finished for him. "It's what I do." Now she was smiling, wondering how long it would take him to figure it out.

Had he not been so distracted by her killer body, he

would have been more clearheaded and known right away what she was saying. When her meaning finally sank in, he laughed. "You're a model."

"Yes."

He pulled her into his arms before she could get nervous again. "We won't do anything you don't want to do," he promised.

He was nuzzling the side of her neck, sending shivers through her. She tugged on his hair to get him to kiss her on the mouth. She was the aggressive one now. Her tongue swept inside and rubbed against his, and when she felt his arms tighten their grip, she knew he liked it, so she did it again. She wanted to make him lose control and suddenly realized she was losing hers.

Liam removed the rest of her clothes and then his own. His mouth never left hers, and she didn't even realize what he'd done until her breasts were pressed against his chest. The feeling was exquisite. She felt the heat and the power radiating from his muscles. Her senses were reeling. Everything about him aroused her. The way he caressed her, the sexy growls he made when she pleased him, and his scent. Oh God, his scent was wonderful. It wasn't aftershave, but maybe body wash and male. Clean and masculine. It was a sexy-as-sin combination and she loved it. When he tried to pull away from her, she retaliated by tugging on his lip with her teeth. She wanted to keep kissing him, and he gave her what she demanded.

Liam was already hard and aching to be inside her. He knew she wasn't ready, and when she moved her hips to cuddle him between her thighs, he groaned and took a deep breath. He wasn't sure how he accomplished it, but he got the covers pulled back before the two of them fell into bed together. She was wrapped in his arms and on top of him.

"Damn, you're so soft."

She lifted her head and looked at him with a mischievous glint in her eyes. "I've got you right where I want you."

"Yeah?" He made a quick spin, and she found herself on her back with Liam looming over her. "Now I've got you."

When he moved, his chest hair tickled her breasts. It felt so good she wanted him to move again.

Liam kissed her passionately, determined to overwhelm her, to make her as crazed as he was. Holding on to his discipline and not going too fast was excruciating.

Restless now, she began to move. Her toes rubbed his legs, and she instinctively arched up against him. He kissed her just below her earlobe and then whispered all the dark, erotic things he was going to do to her. She was so aroused now she thought his voice alone could push her over the edge.

Liam had a lusty appetite and proceeded to kiss every inch of her. Most models were as thin as cardboard, but Allison had curves. Full, lush breasts, a narrow waist, perfect hips, and the longest shapely legs. Her ass was pretty damn near perfect, too.

He kissed the valley between her breasts, and when his tongue glided across one nipple, she almost came off the bed. He took it into his mouth and began to suckle while he caressed her other breast. He moved lower. His tongue circled her navel. His hands were everywhere. He pushed her thighs apart and she thought foreplay was over. But she was wrong. He kissed her stomach, then slid lower. She sucked in her breath when his mouth and tongue began to make love so intimately. It was carnal, so shocking, so wonderful, she could feel herself losing control, and that terrified her. She cried out and tried to push him away, but he wouldn't be deterred. She was quickly consumed with desire. She understood what was happening; she just had never experienced it before.

She came apart. Her orgasm took her by surprise and completely overwhelmed her. Wave after wave of intense pleasure poured over her. She clung to him and called his name.

He knew the second she climaxed, so he moved up her body and kissed her hungrily as he thrust into her. She was wet, hot, and ready for him, and damn, she was tight. Once he was fully embedded, he forced himself to stop and give her time to adjust to him.

"Are you okay?"

Her nails dug into his shoulders. She could already feel the pressure building. "Don't stop," she pleaded. "Please don't stop." She wasn't sure if she shouted the demand or whispered it.

Liam would have laughed if he hadn't been in such agony. "Not a chance," he said. "I won't stop."

He loved the feel of her squeezing him, slowly withdrawing and then thrusting again and again, faster and faster. He kept telling himself to slow down, to savor the moment, but his body wasn't cooperating. Neither was she. She lifted her legs and wrapped them around him, taking him deeper inside, and then she began to moan.

He knew she was close. His hand moved down between their bodies, and he caressed the spot he knew would drive her wild. She cried out, tightened around him, and climaxed again. He was there with her and found his own release.

Allison felt as though she had reached the stars and was floating back to earth. It was the most amazing thing. Frightening, too, for she had lost all control. She realized then she had trusted him completely and was shocked how quickly that had happened. She was still holding on to him and never wanted to let go. As soon as the truth registered in her mind, she forced herself to pull back. Her arms fell to her sides. Her heart was still hammering in her chest, and she was still panting, trying to recover.

Liam was having difficulty accepting what had just happened to him. He had had God knew how many orgasms but never one like this. As soon as she let go of him, he kissed her gently on the lips, then rolled away, got up, and went into the bathroom. He wasn't gone long. Allison was swinging her legs over the side of the bed and just about to stand when he grabbed her around the waist and pulled her down on top of him.

"Now you can be on top," he said, grinning.

She stacked her hands on his chest, rested her chin on them, and stared at his handsome face. It seemed strange to her that she wasn't feeling at all unsure of herself or vulnerable now, and she didn't need praise or words of affection from him. He was rubbing her back and it felt wonderful. She was having trouble believing that she was stark naked and lying on top of a naked man. Not just any man, though, but Liam, who she decided was built like a Greek god, and at the moment was just about the sexiest man in the world. He was just so . . . male.

"What are you thinking?" he asked, brushing a dangling strand of hair from her forehead.

"You have beautiful eyes," she said.

"Yeah?" His hands moved down her spine, and he said, "You've got a great ass."

She rolled her eyes. "Only you would notice my backside."

"Every man you walk past notices, sweetheart."

She laughed. "You can't possibly know that."

His devilish smile was back. "Sure, I can. We discussed it. Everyone agreed. You've got a great ass."

His hand moved to the back of her neck, and he pulled her down to kiss her. His mouth covered hers, and his tongue moved inside to stroke her. "I love the way you taste," he whispered before kissing her again.

He couldn't get enough of her. He was already hard and all he wanted was to make love to her again.

"Do you want to . . . ?" He stopped himself before he asked her if she wanted to go again, realizing that probably wasn't the right way to put it.

She understood. "Oh yes, I do," she whispered. She kissed the soft skin under his ear, then teased his earlobe with her teeth. He tightened his hold on her, which told her he liked what she was doing, and that made her bolder. She moved lower, nudging his hands away so she could kiss his chest, then lower until she was kissing his belly button. The description *rock-hard abs* didn't do him justice. Her long, silky hair brushed over his skin. When she tried to move lower between his thighs, he pulled her back up, shook his head, and said, "If you do that, I won't last."

"But I've never . . . and I wanted to try . . ."

He rolled her onto her back. It was a revelation that she wanted him so quickly after finding satisfaction, and to want him so desperately she was almost frantic with desire. Their lovemaking was wild, uncontrolled, and earth-shattering. She had never had an orgasm before Liam, and now she'd had three. She was spent.

Liam fell back on the bed beside her, and they both stared at the ceiling for several minutes as they tried to catch their breath. When he had summoned enough strength, Liam went into the bathroom, and this time when he returned he began to get dressed. Suddenly feeling vulnerable now, she grabbed her robe and put it on. She tied the belt and sat against the headboard, watching him. Her hair hung down over one side of her face. She impatiently brushed it back over her shoulder while she waited for him to say something to her.

"I should get going," he said as he sat on the side of the bed and reached for his loafers.

By the time he was buttoning his shirt and putting on his holster, she had made the no-brainer assumption that he wanted to leave. In fact, it seemed he couldn't get out of there fast enough.

She went into the galley kitchen and got a bottled water out of the refrigerator. It took her three tries to get the cap twisted off, her hands were shaking so. The aftermath of sex, she surmised. Her legs were shaking, too.

Liam walked in just as she was turning, and she bumped into his chest. She offered him the water. He took a long swallow and then put it on the counter and pulled her into his arms.

"I've got to go," he whispered against her ear.

"I know."

"You'll get to sleep in tomorrow, and you don't start your six months with Phillips until Monday. I'd make the most of the time off if I were you."

"Come Monday, heaven help me. Right?"

He smiled. "Right."

Although she wanted to, she didn't ask him what he would be doing. The search she had done at the cyber unit had given him the proof he needed, but Liam still had work to do. She expected he would track down the culprit who had leaked the information, interrogate him, and then lock him up. Her usefulness to the case was over.

Liam let go of her and stepped back. He reached for the bottle and took another drink as he leaned against the counter and stared down at the floor. It appeared that he was studying the tiles. A few minutes before, she had been convinced he was ready to bolt out of there, but now he didn't seem in any hurry to leave. When Allison leaned closer and studied his face, she could tell from the deep furrow in his brow that he was mulling over something important. She presumed it had to do with his work.

"Have you told Alec what I found?" she asked.

"Yes. When do you graduate?"

The jump in subjects surprised her and made her pause a second before answering, "One month."

He nodded. "What about your aunt and uncle? When are you going to talk to them?"

"I don't know."

"They aren't going to give up."

"I know."

He put his arm around her and walked by her side to the door. His hand was on the doorknob when he said, "I want to be there if you do confront them."

"Why?"

"I just want to."

"I can handle them. I don't need anyone to fight my battles for me."

"I just want to see them in action," he admitted a bit sheepishly.

She shook her head. "I'll film it for you."

He laughed, kissed her, and then left.

She locked the door behind him and leaned against it. She didn't quite know what she had expected, but it certainly wasn't that he would leave without so much as a "thank you" or a "that was great" or even a "have a nice day." She had to remind herself that they had made an agreement. No commitments, no complications. So the fact that he left so quickly after their lovemaking wasn't awkward at all.

Just a little heartbreaking.

FOURTEEN

A LITTLE TOO LATE SHE REALIZED CASUAL SEX OR A HOOKUP or a one-nighter or whatever else it was called was more complicated than she had imagined. Maybe she just wasn't the type for that nonsense. She would much rather write code than have sex anyway.

Even she couldn't buy that lie. Sex with Liam had been mind-blowing. So how come she was feeling miserable now? Was it because she was too emotionally involved?

Duh! Of course it was. She guessed she wasn't a very modern woman, after all. To say she was conflicted was an understatement. What was the matter with her? She didn't want or need a commitment from Liam. Maybe she just wanted the sex to have meant something to him and for him to tell her so. Obviously for him it had just been a couple of enjoyable hours getting rid of tension. He had probably already moved on.

She didn't get to sleep until almost two in the morning, but by then she had figured it all out. Liam had been an impulsive distraction from her goals, and she couldn't allow that to happen again. She had too many other things to concentrate on. When she wasn't working at the cyber unit, she wanted to focus on the program she had built—there was still a bit of tweaking that needed to be done. She couldn't let Liam mess with her head, and the only way to accomplish that was to stay away from him. Thank goodness he was going to make it easy for her. He was probably getting ready to get on a plane to God knew where even then.

She slept until ten, then dressed in jeans and a T-shirt and sat cross-legged on the sofa with her laptop to catch up on her e-mails. It had been well over a week since she'd last checked them.

Scrolling through the dozens of messages, some requiring responses, others nuisance promotions to be deleted, she found two reminders that Father Basher was being honored tonight for his service to the university at a cocktail party given by some of the alumni at the Hamilton Hotel. Only seniors, staff members, and a few close friends of the Jesuit professor were invited. There was also an invitation to a reception for him next week so that everyone at the college could say good-bye to him, and though attendance for both events wasn't mandatory, it was strongly encouraged that everyone attend. She made a note in her calendar about the second event. One simply didn't ignore the Jesuits. Besides, everyone admired Father Basher. He was one of the best in his field, and she hated to see him retire. He had taught her to love the Renaissance painters. After taking a required course from him, she had signed up to take another as an elective but had to wait three semesters for an opening. He was going to be sorely missed at the university, and she was happy to see he was being given the recognition he deserved.

At twelve o'clock Charlotte called. "Sorry I didn't phone any sooner," she began.

"Why are you sorry? I didn't expect you to call."

A long, drawn-out sigh let Allison know how frustrated her sister was. "You didn't read your e-mails, did you?"

"I was just checking them now. It's been a busy week."

"You're always on your laptop. How could you not look at your e-mails?"

Allison set her computer aside as she listened to her sister's complaints. When she unfolded her legs, an aching twinge shot down to her feet and she realized she had been sitting too long in one spot. She got up and stretched before heading to the kitchen. Charlotte was getting testy and obviously needed to vent. Allison let her.

She finally interrupted her sister's lecture on communication. "What's going on with you? Why are you so hyper?" she asked as she rummaged through her cabinets for a snack.

"I'm in Boston."

"What? You're here? What are you doing in Boston?"

"I know I told you that Oliver was attending a conference here. Don't you remember?"

No, she didn't remember, but she wasn't going to admit it and listen to another lecture. "Sure, I do," she said instead. She found a potato chip bag with a few crumbs in the bottom and emptied them into her mouth before scrunching the bag and tossing it into the trash.

"At the last minute I got the time off and decided to come with him. Aren't you happy I'm here?"

"Of course I am. I'm just surprised, that's all. I've missed you," she said, and she meant it. "Do you and Oliver want to stay with me? I'll take the sofa and you two can have my bed."

"No, thanks," Charlotte answered. "The law firm is putting us up at the Four Seasons. It's very fancy."

"I'll stay with you, then," Allison said, laughing.

"You know you could."

"I'm just teasing."

"You don't mind that we aren't staying with you, do you?"

"I'm relieved. I'd have to go to the grocery store and change my sheets." She opened the refrigerator door, peered inside, and moved the water bottles out of the way in search of something more substantial. She found a blueberry yogurt cup in the back and reached for it, checking the expiration date before opening the drawer for a spoon.

"You'd also have to close your laptop and try to talk to us," Charlotte said.

"When will I see you?" Allison asked, ignoring the barb about her social skills.

"Hopefully, tonight. I made dinner reservations at our hotel for eight o'clock."

"How do you know I don't have plans?"

"I just assumed you wouldn't be going out. How long has it been since you've had a date?"

"We're getting off topic here."

"You just don't want to answer the question."

"I haven't had any real dates . . . or at least what you'd call a date," she said in all honesty. She wondered what Charlotte would do if she told her about the sex with Liam. She'd probably applaud, Allison concluded.

"That's a pity," Charlotte consoled.

Allison laughed. "It kinda is. I'm really happy you're here," she blurted. "When do you have to go back to Seattle?"

"Tuesday," she answered.

"About tonight . . ."

"Yes?"

She tucked her cell phone in the crook of her neck and opened the yogurt container, then swallowed a spoonful before answering, "I have to attend a cocktail party for one of my professors. It's at the Hamilton," she added. "It starts at six thirty and I'll probably be there until eight."

"Okay, I'll move our reservation back to eight thirty," Charlotte said. "The Hamilton Hotel is just around the corner from the Four Seasons. It won't take you any time at all to get here."

"Are you sure you wouldn't rather come to my apartment? We'll order pizza."

"No, every time we get together we eat pizza. Getting dressed up and dining out will be fun. You'll have to be dressed for the cocktail party anyway. Are you going to wear makeup? Do you have any? I don't think I've ever seen you wearing lipstick or mascara in real life."

That was probably true, even though Charlotte had seen the pictures from Giovanni's photo shoots. "Yes, I have makeup, and yes, I'll wear makeup."

"It's going to be fun." Charlotte sounded so giddy she practically giggled her response.

Allison smiled at her sister's enthusiasm. "You don't get out much, do you?"

"More than you."

"I want to ask you something."

"What?"

"I hate to ruin your good mood, but have you heard from Aunt Jane or Uncle Russell?"

"No, not since Oliver and I cut them out of our lives. You should have done the same a long time ago."

"You're right," Allison agreed. She rinsed the spoon under the faucet and dropped it in the dishwasher. "I finally severed connections, but they keep harassing me. It's awful."

"We'll talk about it tonight. Oliver and I have something to tell you, and we don't think you're going to like it. I've got to go—"

"Oh no, you don't. You can't say something like that and not tell me now."

"It has to be face-to-face."

"That means it's bad, right? I'm right, aren't I? Are you and Oliver having problems? You're not thinking of divorce, are you? Charlotte, you're never going to find anyone as sweet and patient as he is. Have you tried marriage counseling?" Her imagination was getting away from her. "He's perfect for you, and he's—"

Charlotte cut her off. "No, dummy, we aren't getting divorced."

"Okay, good," Allison said with a sigh of relief. "So now I have to think you're going to try to talk me out of something or into something. I'm right, aren't I?"

"See you tonight."

Charlotte disconnected the call before Allison could coax her into explaining.

Allison absolutely refused to worry about what Charlotte and Oliver wanted to talk to her about, so she did exactly that the rest of the day. She came up with all sorts of horrible things, and by the time she had showered, curled her hair, and applied makeup, she decided either Charlotte or Oliver was dying, or they were moving to some remote country and she would never see them again. She realized how mental she was acting, but she told herself she was just a worrier and not out of her mind.

Time was getting away from her. She needed to hurry if she was going to make it to Father Basher's party on time. She opened her closet door and studied her clothes. Creating outfits was not one of her strengths, but luckily Giovanni had been a good teacher and she channeled his expertise now. She decided to wear one of her favorites, a short fitted dress the color of deep burgundy wine. The sleeves came to her elbows, and the hem of the rather tight skirt didn't quite reach her knees. The slit up one side, though provocative, was necessary so she could walk, but the scoop neckline was modest with only a hint of cleavage. Small hoop earrings and her delicate gold watch, a gift from Charlotte and Oliver, were her only accessories. She tried on two different pairs of heeled sandals before choosing. Standing in front of the full-length mirror, she surveyed her reflection and decided Giovanni would have approved.

Although the weather was unseasonably warm, she knew the temperature would drop tonight. As she was reaching for her lightweight coat from the hall closet, someone knocked on her door. She looked through the peephole and jumped back. Liam was standing right outside. She peeked again; he was still there, looking as devastatingly handsome as usual. Her heart started racing. There were moments like this when she was in awe of him. And she needed to get over that as quickly as possible. She hoped she didn't appear flustered when she opened the door, smiled, and said, "What are you doing here?"

"Is that any way to greet me?" He paused to give her the once-over and said, "You look nice."

"Thank you. You look nice, too. Why are you wearing a suit? Are you on your way somewhere?"

"I've been in a meeting."

"Oh. I thought you might have a date."

"No."

"So I was wrong," she said, trying to quiet the inner voice that was screaming, *Take a breath and stop staring at him.*

"Yes."

"What kind of meeting was it?" she asked. "Or is it confidential?" How lame was that question?

"Yes, I can talk about it with you, but I don't want to just yet."

"All right."

"Where were you going?"

"A cocktail party at the Hamilton and then dinner with my sister and her husband. What's in the envelope?"

"A contract Phillips wants you to sign. I'd like to go over it with you first. I was going to come by Sunday, but I got a call and decided to come over now. Is someone picking you up? Do you have a date?" He was frowning as he asked the questions. Before she could answer he said, "You'd better call him and cancel."

"No . . ."

He took a step toward her. "Yes." Enveloped by her wonderful scent, Liam tried to block the image of her naked body wrapped in his arms. It was a hell of a challenge. "We need to talk about this contract. It could take a while, so you should call him," he repeated.

"I was trying to tell you, no, I don't have a date. I was driving myself, and I am not going to cancel dinner or the cocktail party."

He attempted to reason with her. "I might be leaving Boston tomorrow night, and I want to make any necessary changes to this contract after we discuss it. I don't want Phillips to take advantage of you. I really think you should stay home so we can go over it."

She realized how sweet he was being with his concern for her, but didn't dare tell him so. She knew he would be insulted and assure her he was only doing his job. "That isn't an option," she insisted. "I've made plans."

He shrugged. "Okay, then. I'm going with you."

Liam acted as though this were an inconvenience when, in fact, staying close to her tonight was exactly what he had planned to do. He knew he was being overprotective and probably overreacting. He didn't care. The meeting with Curtis Bale at the cyber unit hadn't gone well, which was an understatement.

Phillips had called Bale into the office for a meeting with Liam that morning. While they were talking to him, a member of his staff in Detroit was being arrested. Allison's search had led them directly to the man. He was a tech for the FBI in Detroit, and he had been using a home computer to wreak havoc on the bureau. It didn't take long for them to come up with a possible motive. After looking through his file, they discovered he had received several reprimands for questionable conduct in the past. His record showed his inability to accept criticism and a tendency to respond with anger. His reputation and his job were in jeopardy, and apparently his burning resentment of the FBI authorities had led him to sabotage several cases.

After Liam laid out the case, Bale became outraged because he had been kept out of the loop and was the last to know what was going on. Assuming any weakness in his division would ultimately come to rest on his head, he let his ego take over. He swore that neither he nor any member of his staff had leaked confidential information, and while he was shouting at Liam and Phillips, he brought up Allison's name. He had noticed she was sequestered in a separate office, and he'd surmised she was working on a sensitive project. Since he was aware of the work being performed by the rest of the staff, he concluded she was the one who'd found what he called the alleged proof. Once his argument homed in on Allison, Bale wouldn't back down. He accused her of being little more than a teenager without any training in the field. She couldn't have known what she was doing.

The solid facts were right in front of Bale, but the longer he ranted, the more furious he became. After several hours of angry discussion, he needed someone to focus his blame on, and the most convenient target was Allison. Not only did he accuse her of creating false evidence in the leak investigation, but he went so far as to insinuate she'd had something to do with the closure of the Detroit office. Phillips got into it with Bale then, yet Bale wouldn't relent. He worked himself into such an agitated state he was no longer rational. The so-called facts, he insisted, must have been planted. Were they really going to let Allison, an outsider, ruin careers?

At the end of questioning, Bale was so out of control he was strongly encouraged to take a leave of absence. In a rage he stormed out of the building.

His hot head had forced the outcome and he needed some time to cool down. Liam didn't believe Bale would physically harm Allison, but in Bale's present state of mind, Liam worried the other agent would want to interrogate her in his own personal style and no doubt scare the hell out of her. Liam wasn't about to let that happen. Phillips assured him Bale would be calm and sensible by morning. Until then, no one was going to get near her.

"I'll drive," he said, stepping out into the hallway.

Allison draped her coat over her arm and followed. "Okay, then," she said.

It seemed the most natural thing in the world for her hand to be in his, but once they reached the car, her self-conscious insecurities took over and she quickly let go. She told him whom the party was for and asked if he needed directions to the Hamilton Hotel.

He smiled. "I know where it is. I'm staying there."

Impressed, she commented, "It's very elegant."

"Yes, it is." He didn't add the fact that Alec's wife and her brothers owned the Hamilton Hotels and that they had insisted that Liam stay there.

In the car, Liam went over some of the points he didn't like in Phillips's contract, and although she tried, Allison found it impossible to pay attention. Her mind kept wandering off in another direction, to fantasies of a more carnal nature. She couldn't stop herself from picturing him naked—she decided she wouldn't be normal if she didn't—and what a glorious memory that was. She remembered touching him and trailing her fingertips across his broad shoulders. She sighed inside, just thinking of his hard-as-steel muscles below his warm skin. She had to admit to herself that she loved touching him.

She was thankful he hadn't mentioned the fact that they had had sex the night before. When he'd shown up at her door, she was shocked and nearly speechless. She was also . . . joyful. A silly word, she decided, but it exactly defined how she felt. She had thought she wouldn't see him again for months or maybe not ever because her work for him was done, and he traveled all over the world putting out fires. She had almost convinced herself that she was fine with that. Lots of people shared a night of passion and then moved on without complications. She could be one of those people. She was sure of it. Or was she? She didn't seem to know her own mind anymore.

"What do you think?"

His question jarred her. "About what?"

Exasperated, he said, "The contract. Haven't you heard a word I've said?"

She saw no reason to bluff her way through. "No, I haven't."

He glanced over at her, saw her smile, and shook his head. "I'm trying to help you."

"I know you are."

"Then maybe you want to pay attention?"

He pulled up to the valet in the circle drive and put the car in park. Two attendants hurried forward to open their doors.

Stepping into the hotel was like entering another world, one that was stately and yet chic. Similar to the other Hamilton Hotels, the design blended old-world charm with contemporary touches here and there. The marble floors gleamed, and a stunning staircase with a mahogany banister curved up like a grand ribbon to the mezzanine overlooking the lobby.

Vases filled with fresh flowers were on every table. All of the Hamilton Hotels were renowned for their sophistication. What separated this hotel from the others was the original artwork depicting scenes from Boston's colorful history on each wall.

Sounding a bit awkward and out of place, Allison whispered as though she were in a church, "It's beautiful, isn't it?"

"Yes, it is," he agreed. "Haven't you been here before?"

"Yes and no," she replied.

They had stopped just inside the entrance. Allison turned to him and tried to explain. "Yes, I have been here before, just once a couple of years ago, but I was working then, and when I work I sort of . . . disappear. The photo shoot was in one of the gardens. As soon as the chaos starts—you know, the different gowns and the makeup and hair—I turn into a mannequin."

He laughed. "A mannequin? You'd never pass for a mannequin. Too many curves," he explained as he took her arm and crossed the lobby. "What does 'sort of disappear' mean?"

She shrugged. "I zone out and work problems, write code."

"In your head."

"Yes. It's like daydreaming, and people do that all the time, so stop looking at me like I'm crazy. Don't you ever daydream?"

"Sure, I do."

He wondered how she would feel if he told her that several times today he'd thought about what he would have liked to do to her and what he would have liked her to do to him with that sexy mouth of hers. He also thought about last night and how good it had been with her. No, better than good. It was damn near perfect.

The party was being held in one of the smaller ball-

rooms on the mezzanine level. It was a beautifully ap-
pointed room. The walls were a soft gray, and there were
floor-to-ceiling windows and French doors leading out to
the garden. Bars had been set up in three corners of the
room, and hors d'oeuvres were being served on silver plat-
ters by smiling, impeccably starched waiters. She and Liam
were a few minutes late, so there was already quite a crowd,
and yet the first person Allison spotted across the room was
Brett Keaton, the jerk who had tried to steal her laptop. He
was dressed like a yacht owner in a navy blue blazer with a
silver emblem on the pocket, light pants, and matching
shoes. The only thing missing was an ascot. He looked as
though he had slept in a tanning bed, and his hair was a
light blond. Had he bleached it? God's gift to women—or
so Brett believed—was pivoting from one female to another. Allison wondered if they were charmed by him.

Liam noticed that a couple of unattached males were
heading toward Allison, so he took her hand and pulled her
into his side. He wasn't real gentle or subtle about it.

"What are you doing?" She looked up at him and saw a
cocky gleam in his eyes, as if he had just won the biggest
prize at the carnival.

"I don't want to lose you in the crowd," he said with a
wide grin.

The two men greeted Allison, and once they introduced
themselves to Liam, his grip on her hand loosened slightly.
Both were professors who taught computer science classes.
As they raved about Allison's talent, testifying that she had
saved them from disaster a time or two, Liam noticed how
uncomfortable she was with any kind of admiration. She
didn't know how to handle it.

After the two men moved on, Allison and Liam strolled
through the guests, stopping to speak to several other pro-

fessors and a few students, many of whom mentioned some computer problem Allison had bailed them out of.

When they finally had a moment alone, Liam leaned down and whispered, "It's remarkable that you don't have a big ego."

"How do you know I don't?"

"Compliments bother you."

Before she had a chance to argue with him, he changed the subject. "Let's find the birthday boy."

She laughed. "It isn't a birthday party. Father Basher is retiring. And you don't call a Jesuit a boy."

Allison located the priest on the other side of the room and led Liam through the crowd to meet him. It was apparent Father Basher had great affection for Allison. He held her hand while he told her how much he was going to miss teaching, and her in particular. Bragging to Liam, he said, "I taught this young lady to love art history, which was no small feat, since she always had her nose in her laptop." He turned back to Allison. "I was just speaking to your friend Brett Keaton." He looked around the room as though searching for Brett in the crowd. "Isn't his news wonderful?"

Allison was immediately skeptical. "What news?"

"Why, the number of software companies that are vying to bid on the security program he's developed."

A chill stiffened Allison's spine. "He's written a security program?"

"I think that's what he called it," the priest answered. "He said it will prevent any kind of hacking. I'm afraid I don't know much about such things, but he seemed very excited."

Allison tried to remain composed as the priest continued to chat, but inside she was stoking a slow burn. Finally,

Father Basher let go of her hand and turned to greet other well-wishers.

Liam saw the change in Allison's demeanor the minute the priest mentioned Brett, and he remembered what she had told him about her former roommate. When she turned around, there was fire in her eyes. She scanned the room and finally zeroed in on a small group standing by the door. In the center, holding court, was a young man in his mid-twenties with styled blond hair the color of sunburned wheat. One hand was holding a drink and the other was slipped casually into the pocket of his blazer. His smile said he was relishing the attention he was getting from his audience.

"Brett Keaton?" he asked.

Allison nodded.

Liam glanced over at him once again, and when he turned back, Allison was gone. She was already weaving through the crowd, heading for Brett. Anticipating a show-down, Liam rushed to catch up with her.

Brett had turned his back to the room and was just about to greet a friend who wanted to congratulate him when Allison tapped on his shoulder. Brett swung around, his palm still outstretched to shake a hand, but the second he saw Allison, his smile disappeared.

"I hear you're trying to sell my work," Allison said.

Liam stood a few feet behind her. He knew she must be seething inside, yet her voice was very calm. He was impressed.

"Hi, Allison," Brett said, his phony smile back in place as he tried to hide the fact that he had been taken off guard. "How are you?"

"I'm perfectly fine," she answered in as pleasant a tone as she could muster. "I've just heard about the program you've designed, and it sounds very much like mine."

Brett immediately glanced around at his small group of admirers before striking a pose that made him look both bewildered and offended at the same time. "I don't know what you're talking about, Allison. I've been working on this for months."

"Funny," Allison said, "I don't remember ever seeing you work on a security program—or even hearing you mention one, for that matter—when I was helping you with your classwork. I, on the other hand, have spent countless hours perfecting my program. Don't you think that's odd?"

Liam watched as Brett's body language changed. His hands were now fisted at his sides and his legs were braced apart for a fight. What did he suppose Allison was going to do? Karate-chop him? Liam's instincts told him to step forward and protect her, but Allison was so calm and seemingly unfazed by the threat that he held back.

"You can't prove anything," Brett snarled. "You may think you're the only one who knows anything about computers or software, but you're wrong. I've put my blood, sweat, and tears into this program, and it's finally going to pay off. You'll be wanting to congratulate me pretty soon, unless your pride gets in your way. I'll be in negotiations soon to sell my program," he said, stressing the word *my*, "to several different companies bidding for it. They're coming here for my presentation."

She patted his arm and sounded very sincere when she said, "Well, then, I wish you good luck and hope you get exactly what you deserve."

As she walked away she heard his final smug remark. "I will."

"You think he stole your program and is passing it off as his own?" Liam asked her when they were alone again.

"Absolutely," she responded. "I know what Brett can do, and it would have been impossible for him to have written a program in the time he's been gone. He saw me working on mine."

"You're a better person than I am. If someone stole my work, I'd want to coldcock him. You don't seem too bent out of shape over it."

She laughed. "I'm not."

"How come?"

"I always build a safeguard into my design."

"Yeah?"

"If Brett has my work, he won't be able to sell it."

"You're certain?"

"Oh yes."

He didn't know what was going on behind her mysterious smile, but he could tell she was no longer upset. In fact, she seemed almost amused.

FIFTEEN

ALLISON AND LIAM LEFT THE RECEPTION EARLY AND HEADED for the Four Seasons. The temperature had dropped considerably, but fortunately Liam's car was parked in the circle drive. She grabbed her coat from the backseat and put it on while Liam reached into the glove compartment to get the envelope. They were soon on their way with the heater blasting.

Allison suddenly realized how comfortable she was with him now. When she had opened the door for him tonight, her nerves went crazy and her hands actually shook. Her mind raced with questions. Was he going to say anything about last night? Or was he going to pretend having hot, sweaty, mind-blowing sex with her hadn't happened? Maybe it hadn't been like that for him. She decided to let all of that go and just enjoy the moment.

Liam was quiet as they pulled into traffic. He was picturing the look in Keaton's eyes. Finally he said what was on his mind. "You know what? Keaton's a piece of . . ." He stopped before he said the crude word he was thinking of.

"A piece of work?" she suggested.

He laughed. "Sure. That's what I was going to say."

It took all of five minutes to reach the Four Seasons Hotel. The lobby wasn't as grand in scale as the Hamilton's, but it was just as elegant with its gleaming black marble floors divided into huge squares by creamy marble bands. The furnishings, small groupings of upholstered chairs at the perimeter, were understated, yet they fit perfectly into the refined atmosphere of the hotel.

Since they were early, Allison and Liam went into the bar to wait. The wood-paneled room was softly lit, and candles in tall glass cylinders on each table added to the warm ambience. Most of the tables were occupied. Liam led her to one at the back of the room and pulled out the plush leather club chair for her before he took his seat. Within seconds a waiter appeared. Allison ordered a Diet Coke, and when Liam asked for a club soda with lime, she was surprised. She had a beer on a rare occasion, but nothing else because she'd seen over and over again how it impaired judgment. She wouldn't have known what to order anyway. The last time she had gone to dinner with Charlotte and Oliver, the waiter handed her a wine menu, and after staring at it for five minutes or so, she told Charlotte it might as well have been written in gibberish. She didn't know what wine went with what food, and she didn't really care. Liam, however, was a man of the world. He obviously had no objection to worldly pleasures. She finally concluded that he wasn't drinking alcohol because he was on duty . . . or was he?

Liam opened the envelope and pulled out two sheets of paper. "I had thought to send this contract to your laptop but changed my mind because, as you'll see, I've written notes all over it. It's still readable."

He handed the first sheet of paper to Allison and sat back while she read through it.

"What it boils down to—," he began.

"He'd like to own me for six months, and he has the option to add another month or two or three, should he feel I'm needed."

"That's about right."

"I'm not signing this."

She'd sounded so outraged he couldn't help smiling. "I'm not suggesting that you do. Let's go through it line by line and change what you want changed. I'll have the new one typed up tomorrow and you can sign it."

"Do I need a lawyer?" she asked, and before he could answer her question, she said, "I probably need a lawyer."

"I'm a lawyer. I'll look out for you."

"You're a lawyer?" She sounded suspicious.

"Yes."

He didn't give her any more information. Frowning, she said, "Okay, you're a lawyer. But you work for him."

"Him?"

"Phillips."

"No, I don't work for him. Alec and I brought you in, and we won't let him take advantage of you. Do you trust me?"

"Yes."

He pulled her chair closer, handed her a pen, and said, "Let's get started."

Allison held the pages close to the candle as she pored over the document, crossing out a phrase here, changing a word there. The candlelight cast a beautiful glow on her perfect features, and Liam was finding it difficult to focus. He tried not to be distracted, but damn, it was difficult. Her scent, a blend of flowers and sunshine, was messing with his concentration.

"What did you say?" His voice was gruff.

She looked up at him. "I didn't say anything."

Liam's mouth was just inches from hers, and he thought it might be a good idea to kiss her.

She had the same idea. Her gaze never left his mouth as she inched closer and closed her eyes. She could feel his breath on her lips, and she parted her own in anticipation. Her heart pounded in her chest, just as—

"A Diet Coke and a club soda."

Allison's eyes snapped open to see the waiter set the tall glasses on cocktail napkins. His eyes were downcast as though he had just witnessed something he shouldn't have. She gave him a weak smile before he pivoted and hurried back to the bar. Feeling the blood rush to her face, she picked up her glass and downed every bit of her drink.

"You're kind of flustered, aren't you?" Liam asked with an impish grin. He was obviously enjoying her mortification.

"No, I'm not. Not at all."

"You just drank my club soda."

She looked at the empty glass in front of her. She didn't think her face could have felt any hotter, and she put her hand to her cheek to see if it was burning. Liam's smile wasn't helping any. After a deep breath, she said, "Shall we get back to this?"

She finished making changes to the first page and, after setting it aside, began on the second. Liam's arm was on the back of her chair, and as he examined the contract with her, he stroked her neck. She couldn't tell if it was a sign of affection or an absentminded gesture. All she was sure of was that he was making her task extremely difficult, but it felt too good to make him stop.

She finally handed him the pen and the pages. "Did Phillips really think I would sign this?"

"I'm sure he knew it was a long shot." He put the contract back in the envelope. "I'll have this retyped and you can sign it when you start Monday."

"No, that would give Phillips time to sneak in a few surprises I might not notice. It will only take a few minutes to revise it on my laptop and print it out. I'd like you to give him a signed contract so it's a done deal before I start."

"Are we interrupting?"

Allison jumped when she heard her sister's voice and then immediately felt guilty. She hadn't done anything wrong, and she was being foolish acting as though she had. She was simply sitting in a bar with a man, a very attractive man. Okay, she had had sex with him the night before . . . lots of sex . . . but Charlotte didn't know that. Allison hugged her sister and kissed Oliver on his cheek, then quickly introduced Liam.

When he stood to shake Oliver's hand, he towered over him. Oliver was stocky but solid in build, and his sturdy handshake was accompanied by a genuine smile. Behind his wire-rimmed glasses were eyes that revealed a keen intelligence and an affable nature.

"They'll come get us when our table is ready," Oliver said. "We're early." He pulled out a chair for his wife.

Liam could see the resemblance between the sisters. They had the same high cheekbones and blue eyes. Their smiles were almost identical, too. But there were a couple of distinct differences. Charlotte had light brown hair and Allison's was a deep, lush sable. Charlotte was the scrubbed girl next door, pretty, with freckles on her cheeks, while Allison was a stunning beauty with flawless skin. There was only one other big difference. Charlotte didn't turn him on the way Allison did.

Charlotte hadn't said anything yet. When she finally stopped staring at Liam, she turned toward Allison with wide, questioning eyes. Obviously astonished to see her sister with a man, she interrogated her with one look. Allison read the signals loud and clear. She knew Charlotte was dying to find out about him. There was little that Allison had ever done in her life that surprised her sister, and she loved watching the expressions that were skipping across Charlotte's face now.

Oliver drew his wife's attention. While they discussed what they wanted to drink, Allison picked up the glass she'd emptied and frowned. Then she looked at Liam.

"What happened to the ice?" she whispered.

"You swallowed it."

He didn't look as though he was joking. Okay, so she was flustered and hadn't been paying attention to what she was doing. "I was thirsty," she rationalized in a flimsy excuse to hide her embarrassment.

Charlotte couldn't hold her curiosity any longer. She looked at Liam, then back at Allison. "How did you two meet?"

"I did some computer work for him."

"And you've known each other long?" Charlotte asked.

"Not long," Allison answered. The sisters had never had any secrets between them, and Allison sensed Charlotte's irritation at not being told about Liam.

There was one other secret that Allison was keeping. Charlotte persisted with one question after another, but Allison was evasive with her answers because she didn't want her sister to know about the deal she had struck to keep their cousin out of prison. If Charlotte knew, she'd have thrown a fit. Unlike Allison, she had absolutely no sympathy for Bill. Her attitude was set. He had made his bed and he should have to wallow in it.

Oliver changed the subject. "Allison, when are you moving? Maybe we can fly down and help you get settled."

"She's moving to Santa Clara right after graduation," Charlotte explained. "Allison, I'm so sorry we can't be there to see you graduate. If we could change our schedules . . ."

"It's all right. It's no big deal. Honest," she said. "And, Oliver, I'm putting off the move for another six months. I'm going to do some work for the government."

"Do it from California. All you need is your laptop."

"No, I have to work here."

"Why?" Charlotte asked.

Allison felt like groaning. Her sister wasn't going to give up. "Because I gave my word, and I'm going to sign a contract."

More questions resulted from that bit of honesty, and Liam watched Allison bob and weave like a pro, sometimes giving only half answers. After five more questions were asked and partially answered, he decided Charlotte could work for the CIA. She was tenacious with her inquisition.

A break came when the waiter reappeared. While Oliver and Charlotte talked to him, Liam leaned down and whispered, "I'm getting the idea you don't want your sister to know you helped your cousin."

"You promised not to say a word," Allison whispered back with a warning glance.

"Promise what?" Charlotte asked.

She didn't just have the persistence of a honey badger; she had the hearing of a bat, too. Allison decided she was tired of being the center of attention and was determined to get the upper hand. Liam ordered another club soda, and she said she'd like one, too. Then she sat back, smiled at her sister, and said, "Liam's from Australia." She waved her hand in the air. "Discuss."

Allison was sure Charlotte would have a hundred questions. She didn't have a single one. Still determined to find out every detail in Allison's contract, she persevered.

"Will you please let it go?" Allison pleaded in exasperation.

"Just help me understand why you would want to sign a contract. Have you forgotten your plan to move to California?"

Oliver's cell phone interrupted. "I've got to take this," he said. "I'll be right back."

Allison waited until he'd left the bar, then said, "Oliver

looks rested." She was hoping to turn Charlotte's attention yet again. "He must like his job."

It didn't work. "I can't understand why you would waste six months working here when you could start your career and be closer to Oliver and me."

The argument ceased while the waiter placed the drinks on the table, but as soon as he stepped away, Allison said, "You make me want to bang my head against a wall, Charlotte. How about I put you on the defensive and question your every decision?"

It was a great plan without a follow-through. She couldn't think of anything to ask, and while Charlotte dug through her purse looking for only God knew what, Allison whispered to Liam, "Could you put her on the defensive for me?"

He shook his head and tried not to laugh. He was fascinated by the way the sisters argued with each other. Their squabble was intense but never mean or angry, the way only two siblings who loved each other could fight. They were so comfortable with each other, there was no hint of hurt feelings. Despite their bickering, their deep affection and unbreakable bond were apparent. Oliver hurried back to the table, apologized profusely for having to take the call, and sat.

"Liam, you work for a computer company or the government?" Oliver asked, trying to understand his relationship to Allison.

Before Liam could answer, Charlotte blurted, "Maybe Oliver and I should look over the contract."

Allison let out a frustrated sigh. "Will you please let it go, you maniac?"

Liam did laugh then. So did Oliver. "Liam works for the FBI," Allison said. "Want to discuss that, Charlotte, or do you want to continue to obsess about the contract?"

Charlotte put her hands up. "Okay, I'll stop nagging you."

Allison couldn't have been happier. She reached for her drink and saw that it was empty. She held the glass up. "Did I . . . ?"

Liam nodded. "You didn't swallow the ice this time," he said cheerfully.

Oliver stopped his wife from continuing to grill Liam when he said, "Sweetheart, why don't you share your news with Allison now before dinner? That way she can think about it, and if she has any questions, there's still time to discuss it."

Charlotte nodded. "I guess I should probably fill Liam in, since he's here and he's apparently Allison's boyfriend . . . which I might add, she didn't tell us about. . . ."

"Oh my God, will you stop?" Allison demanded. She glanced over at Liam, who offered no denial. Instead he sat calmly smiling at her sister without comment, and she wondered what was going through his head. Probably wondering if lunacy ran in her family, she thought.

Ignoring Allison, Charlotte turned to Liam and said, "Our father took out a five-hundred-thousand-dollar life insurance policy, and Allison and I were the beneficiaries. When he and our mother died, our aunt Jane and uncle Russell found out about the money and crawled out of the woodwork like roaches and petitioned the court to become our guardians. The judge agreed but with stipulations."

"What stipulations?" Allison asked.

"Once a year they were required to list the expenses and the money they spent on us."

"They only sent in one report," Oliver interjected.

"And it was bogus," Charlotte added.

"How so?" Allison asked.

"They had a huge expense listed for tuition at Vuillard Academy. It's the most expensive school in Boston," Oliver explained.

"We didn't go to Vuillard Academy," Charlotte told Liam.

"They must have asked around and found the highest tuition," Oliver said.

"And no one checked? No one looked. . . ." Allison stopped. It was silly to get upset about something that was far in the past, she thought. Why waste the energy? "That happened years ago. You can't do anything about it now. Besides, the money's all gone."

"We know that," Charlotte said. "But Oliver still wanted to look into it."

"I can't believe no one noticed they weren't sending in reports," Allison said.

"Slipped through the cracks," Oliver said. "I talked to a sympathetic clerk who found the file. That in itself is remarkable, and when he showed it to me, I told him neither of you went to Vuillard Academy. I hope you don't mind, Allison, but I also told him a little of what your life was like living with those people. I said that—"

Allison interrupted. In a rush, she blurted, "You don't need to tell me what you said." She didn't want Liam to hear any of the horror from her childhood. He already knew quite enough. She thought about apologizing to him for making him sit through this, then changed her mind. He could always have gotten up and left.

Seeing that he was entering uncomfortable territory and not wanting to cause Allison further embarrassment, Oliver halted his condemnation of her aunt and uncle. "The clerk I talked to was in foster care, and boy, did he sympathize! He took the folder and all the legal papers to a young, new judge, and the clerk is sure he'll sign the order."

Allison grabbed Liam's glass and took a drink. "What order?"

"Our aunt and uncle will have to account for the five hundred thousand dollars," Charlotte answered. "We know where three hundred thousand went. It took some digging, but we found what we were looking for."

"'We'?" Allison asked.

Charlotte glanced at her husband before answering, "Okay, I found what I was looking for. I won't tell you how I found out, because it might not be legal and there's an FBI agent sitting at the table."

"What did you find out?"

"They didn't own that house. They rented, and as soon as they got the insurance money, they purchased it. Uncle Russell paid off all their other debts, too. They owed almost a hundred thousand dollars to credit card companies and department stores. They even had a tab running at the neighborhood liquor store. I'm guessing the rest went to whatever Bill wanted. And lawyer fees, of course. They sure didn't spend a penny on either one of us."

Allison wasn't impressed by the threat of a court order. "They won't tell where the money went. They'll make up stuff."

"With receipts. They have to prove each expense with receipts," Oliver explained.

It was completely unrealistic, Allison decided. A good attorney was all her aunt and uncle needed to make it go away. When she voiced her reservation, another debate ensued, and it continued until the hostess came to collect them for their table.

Oliver and Charlotte led the way to the dining room, but Allison hung back and lowered her voice for Liam. "I'll understand if you want to take off. You could maybe stop by tomorrow, and I'll make the changes in the contract then."

His response to her suggestion was to take her hand and pull her along.

"I'm not at all hungry," she said then.

"The six club sodas fill you up?"

"I didn't . . ." She stopped and gave him a quizzical look. "Did I?"

He nodded.

"I was distracted."

"I know."

Ever since they were little girls, Charlotte had possessed a strong sense of right and wrong, and she had been willing to act on it. Allison loved that about her, but this time her sister's need for justice had consequences, and Allison wondered if she truly understood what she had done.

"I just wish Charlotte would leave it alone," she whispered.

Her sister heard her, of course, and once they were seated offered her take on the situation. "You're such a peacemaker, Allison, but sometimes you have to take a stand. I won't feel bad for doing the right thing."

"Good for you, Charlotte," Allison retorted. "When are these legal papers going to be sent?"

Charlotte looked at Oliver, who answered, "The court will have to investigate, and knowing how these things work, I expect it could take some time. Maybe weeks. Maybe months."

Allison leaned back in her chair and folded her arms defiantly, fixing her gaze on Charlotte. "Then I have one question for you."

"What's that?"

"Where will you be when our aunt and uncle receive the notice?"

"In Seattle, I assume," Charlotte answered with a slight shrug at stating the obvious.

"Exactly. And where will I be?" she asked.

"Here in Boston," her sister said.

Allison paused to give her sister time to comprehend the implications of what she was saying and then asked, "So, who do you think they'll come after?"

SIXTEEN

DINNER WAS A TRIAL OF ENDURANCE FOR ALLISON, BUT LIAM seemed to be having a good time. He and Oliver talked football, and both men couldn't have been more enthusiastic about the sport.

Allison pushed her fish around on her plate, and although it was quite tasty, she could eat only a couple of bites. Her stomach wouldn't settle, and it didn't help that Charlotte kept bringing up the relatives from hell.

"Do you know what Oliver found out about Bill?" Charlotte asked. She took a bite of her pasta and waited for Allison to answer.

"Can we please not talk about any of them?"

"Okay, but you have to hear this."

Allison gave up. "What did you find out, Oliver?"

"Bill's going to get probation."

"Can you believe it?" Charlotte asked. She took another bite of pasta and said, "Oliver, you have to taste this. It's delicious."

There were a few seconds there when Allison thought her sister had moved on, but she was wrong. Charlotte wasn't ready to change the subject. Turning her attention to Liam, she said, "Our court system is all messed up. Bill should have gotten five or ten years, and what happened? He got probation. Unbelievable, right? Oh, wait. You probably don't know about Bill, do you? I know Allison wouldn't have told you."

"How do you know that?" Allison asked, presuming she'd just been insulted.

"Because you never tell anyone anything. You keep it all bottled up inside, so I'll explain Bill."

"Charlotte, stop. Liam doesn't need or want to hear about our cousin."

Her sister ignored her demand and launched into Bill's history. A few minutes later Allison once again wanted to bang her head into the nearest wall. By the time Charlotte wound down, Allison was groaning. Liam handed her his glass of water, which she immediately chugged, and she was handing the glass back to him before she realized what she had done.

Liam leaned close and whispered, "Remind me never to drink alcohol when I'm with you."

Allison laughed. Charlotte immediately took exception. "How can you think this is funny? And why are you so laid-back about Bill getting probation?"

"I don't think it's funny," she said, irritated that Charlotte had so easily put her on the defensive.

"Okay, then," her sister said, and then continued with her colorful bio of Bill. Once she had said all she wanted to say about their cousin—or the degenerate, as Charlotte called him—Allison was able to get her to talk about something else. Unfortunately, that something was Liam.

"What exactly do you do, Liam?" Charlotte asked.

"He's an FBI agent," Allison said.

"Yes, I know, but I was asking what exactly he does for the FBI."

Allison couldn't come up with a quick answer, so she improvised. "He travels all over the world, solving . . . computer problems."

Liam was giving her the look, the "are you out of your mind?" look she'd already seen several times tonight.

"Allison, I was talking to Liam," Charlotte said, clearly exasperated.

"He also shoots people who ask too many questions."

There was that look again.

"What is wrong with you?" Charlotte asked. "Let the man talk."

Allison gave up and sat back. She decided to stop worrying that Liam might say something about computer hacking . . . and her.

Oliver was looking from Liam to Allison to Liam again. "How long have you two been dating?"

"We aren't dating," Allison said.

"A while now," Liam answered at the same time.

Turning to Liam, she said, "A while now?"

He just grinned at her. Then he patiently answered Charlotte's questions about his background and the places he'd been to. When it came to questions about his work, he was just as evasive as Allison had been and with even more finesse.

"Have any trips on your schedule?" Oliver asked.

Liam nodded. "I'm headed to London Monday."

"Then back to Boston?" Charlotte asked.

"I'm not sure yet."

"I rarely see him," Allison said cheerfully. "That's why this relationship works. Now, can we please be finished with the interrogation segment of this dinner and talk about something else?"

No one argued with her, and the ordeal was finally over.

Since Allison wouldn't be seeing Charlotte or Oliver before they returned to Seattle, she hugged both good-bye and promised to call more often. She took hold of Liam's hand, making sure her sister noticed, and smiled at him as they walked down the hallway. She had decided that acting as though they were dating was better than telling Charlotte she was working for Liam. She couldn't even imagine the number of questions her sister would have then. Truth, she decided, wasn't all it was cracked up to be.

As soon as Charlotte and Oliver turned in the opposite direction, Allison tried to pull her hand away. Liam wasn't letting go. He had a devilish sparkle in his eyes, too. If she didn't know better, she would have thought he'd actually had a good time.

As if reading her mind, he said, "That was fun."

"No, it wasn't."

He laughed. "You were worried I was going to say something about your special computer skills, weren't you?"

"I wasn't worried. I was . . . concerned," she replied. "Why didn't you tell me you were going to London Monday?" There was absolutely no reason he should have told her, but it still bothered her that he hadn't.

"It never came up."

"So I probably won't be seeing you again."

"Sure, you will." He sounded as though he meant it.

"Are you going to miss me?"

Bad question to ask, she decided, because it made her sound clingy. She really needed to get away from him, and the sooner, the better because he was messing with her ability to think about anything other than him.

"Of course."

She waited a minute and finally said, "How come you haven't asked me if I'll miss you?"

"I already know the answer."

God, he was arrogant. "And what might that be?"

"You'll miss me."

She shrugged. "Maybe," she said, and before his ego could swell, she added, "Then again, maybe not."

SEVENTEEN

THE RIDE BACK TO HER APARTMENT WAS BLISSFULLY STRESS-
free. Until visions of his naked body flashed once again
across her mind. Then calm went flying out the window.
She could feel herself blushing and hoped to heaven he
didn't notice.

No such luck. "What's going on with you?"

She brushed her hair over her shoulder and tried to act
nonchalant. "Nothing's going on with me. Why would you
think something's going on?"

"Your face is red."

"I'm not blushing." Her voice cracked and she sounded
as though she was freaking out. He must have thought she'd
lost her mind, and he might have been right. "Thank you
for putting up with Charlotte tonight. When she gets on a
rant, there's no stopping her. It's best to sit back and wait
until she winds down."

"I like her and I like Oliver."

"What's not to like? They're so . . ."

"So what?" he asked when she hesitated.

"Normal."

It was such an odd thing to say. "And you're not?"

"No, I'm not."

He decided not to press for an explanation. "I was wondering . . ."

"Yes?"

"What are you going to do when your sister finds out you bailed your cousin out?"

"Hide."

His smile suggested he thought she was teasing. She wasn't so sure. If Charlotte found out, she would definitely go ballistic and lecture Allison for at least a year. She pictured it and shuddered. Nonstop speeches. She couldn't think of anything worse.

"She would be upset with me if she found out I helped Bill, but it would crush her heart if she knew I was breaking into computer systems illegally, no matter what my reasons were. She wouldn't understand."

She didn't say what she was really thinking. There were very few people whose opinions mattered to Allison, but Charlotte was at the top of her list. She didn't want to disappoint her.

"I'm worrying about something that will never happen," she said, and hoped to God she was right.

She was happy to be home. Liam unlocked her door for her and followed her into the apartment. She pointed to her laptop, which was sitting on the desk in front of the windows, and said, "Have at it."

Hungry now, she put her coat away and then went into the kitchen to make herself a bowl of Cheerios, calling out her password to him so that he could access the Internet. By the time she returned to him, he had pulled up the contract on the screen. She stood behind him eating her cereal and watching over his shoulder as he made the corrections. He couldn't have looked any more relaxed. He'd taken off his jacket and tie and unbuttoned the top two buttons of his shirt. He'd also rolled up his sleeves. She had the insane urge to sit on his lap, put her arms around him, and kiss him over and over again until he never wanted her to stop. She wondered how he would have reacted to her boldness.

She wasn't about to find out. While he worked, she cleaned up the kitchen, then went into the bedroom to put her jewelry away. She put her shoes in her closet, washed her face, and brushed her teeth. She was trying to keep busy and stay away from him because she knew if she sat next to him she wouldn't have been able to stop staring at him, and how creepy would that have been?

What was going on with him? Did he regret what had happened the night before? Or did he even remember? Maybe this was all part of being a hookup, she thought, still not clear exactly what that entailed. What were the rules? She decided she should ask Google to define it for her, or maybe Jordan could explain the nuances for her. Allison felt completely inept and finally admitted she had been hiding in her computer far too long. Maybe it was time for her to start living life instead of reading about it.

First, she needed to get through tonight. She didn't want saying good-bye to be awkward. She sat on the side of the bed, trying to figure out the protocol. After several minutes thinking about it without coming up with any answers, she decided she didn't care. Now all she had to do was believe it.

"Allison, I can't get the printer to work."

He was standing in the doorway, watching her. She jumped at the sound of his voice.

"What are you doing?" he asked her.

She stood, smoothed her skirt, and walked toward him. "I'll fix the printer." She tried to walk past him, but he put his hands on her shoulders and stopped her.

"What's the matter?"

"Nothing," she answered, and tried to veer around him. He didn't let go.

"You looked like you were a thousand miles away."

"I was just thinking about . . ."

"About what?"

"You."

They were inches apart. She stared into his eyes. He stared at her mouth. He tilted her chin up, leaned down, and kissed her. It was a nice, undemanding kiss that was over with before she had time to respond.

It wasn't enough for Liam. His mouth came down on hers again, but this time the kiss was altogether different. It was consuming.

He made her want more. When he lifted his head she realized her arms were around his neck. How had that happened? She was also plastered against him. Did he want another hookup? Should she ask him?

"I was wondering . . ."

"Yes?"

"Never mind," she whispered. "You'd better kiss me again."

"Yeah, okay." He was smiling as she tugged on his hair to get him to do what she wanted.

She became the aggressor. Her mouth was open and her tongue stroked his. She heard him groan and felt him tighten his arms around her. She knew she was pleasing him, because he told her so in between wild kisses. She desperately wanted him. He was leaving in two days and she didn't have any idea when she would see him again. Was it wrong to want one more night with him? One glorious night.

He gave her the shivers, kissing the side of her neck. His breath was so warm and sweet against her skin.

"Do you know what I want to do?" he whispered, his lips tickling her ear. He lifted his head and waited.

She didn't know how to be coy. "Have sex? Because that's what I want to do."

"Take your clothes off, Allison."

Liam had to pull her arms from around his neck and tell her again before she reacted. She turned around then and lifted her hair away from the neckline of her dress. He noticed her hands shook.

"Unzip me, please," she said.

Although she was extremely nervous, she wasn't at all shy with him. In fact, she couldn't wait to get her clothes off and throw herself into his arms. She loved the heat from his skin against hers, the strength that radiated from his muscles. She had never been drawn to any other man the way she was drawn to him. Most of all, she loved the way he touched her. He was rough yet gentle at the same time. How was it possible to be so tender while driving her to the very edge of all control?

He kissed the nape of her neck as he slid the dress from her shoulders and let it drop to the floor. She stepped out of it and turned to face him in her pink bra and panties while she waited for him to remove his clothes. Her toes curled into the carpet, her hands were fisted at her sides, and she had to tell herself over and over again that she wasn't embarrassed. She wasn't sophisticated, either. She could feel her face getting warm. The fire in his eyes made her heart race. She knew he wanted her, and yet he wasn't reaching for her.

"Liam, did you change your mind? Would you rather not do this?" She looked around for her robe, mortified now.

Had he not be so aroused, Liam would have laughed. His hand moved to the back of her neck and he jerked her forward as his mouth came down on hers. The kiss went on and on, his tongue stroking hers in love play. He moved her toward the bed while he stripped off the rest of his clothes and then hers, and as they fell onto the bed, he kept telling himself to make it last. He was ravenous for her, but she wasn't ready for him yet. He pushed her onto her back, then slowly kissed a path down her body. His tongue brushed across her breasts. She nearly came off the bed. The erotic sounds she made told him how much she liked what he was doing. He moved lower between her thighs and used his fingers and his tongue to drive her out of her mind.

Allison wasn't passive by any means. She caressed him, clinging to him as she kissed his neck and his shoulders. She wanted to know all of him, but he wouldn't let her move, so she retaliated by biting his earlobe. He grunted and tightened his hold on her.

His voice was little more than a gruff whisper. "Put your legs around me. I can't wait any longer."

He lifted her thighs, thinking to slowly enter her, but that thought was lost when she pushed against him. With one powerful thrust, he was surrounded by her liquid heat. She was so tight, so perfect. He dropped his head on her shoulder, took deep, shuddering breaths, and tried to slow down, wanting it to be perfect for her.

She didn't want him to stop. She bit his shoulder and whispered, "Don't torment me."

He let out a low groan of pleasure and began to move, slowly at first, until she became more demanding. He was mindless to everything but her. He had never been this out of control before or this desperate to make her belong to him, even if it was for only one night. Sex had always been entertainment for him and a way to relieve tension, but with Allison it was so much more.

He felt her tighten around him as she cried out his name. He found release at the same time, and damn, it nearly killed him.

"Holy . . . ," she whispered

She sounded shell-shocked, and Liam smiled, gratified. He still couldn't move away from her, so he held her tight as he rolled onto his back.

Allison didn't move. She wanted to remember how this felt to be held by him and loved.

"Are you all right?" he asked breathlessly.

She panted her reply. "Oh yes."

As much as she wanted to linger, she forced herself to roll away from him and get out of bed. She found her robe and put it on, threaded her fingers through her hair to give it some kind of order, and walked barefoot out of the room.

What the hell? "Where are you going?" Liam asked. Did she already regret what had just happened? He hoped not. He sure as certain didn't. He'd wanted her from the minute she opened the door tonight.

"To fix the printer."

Liam was floored. This was a first for him. He was typically the one who would ease his way out without hurting feelings. There was always the time after sex when the woman he was with wanted affirmation that it had been wonderful for him, even though it usually wasn't. It wasn't bad, either. It was just sex.

Until Allison.

Bewildered by what he was feeling, he decided he wasn't going to waste another minute thinking about it. Taking her lead, he got dressed. When he joined her, she was printing the second copy of the contract. Liam once again read it over, and only when he was sure everything was the way he wanted did he offer her a pen. She signed it and handed it back.

"Phillips is going to have a fit when he reads this," she said.

Liam smiled. "Yes, he will."

"I guess this is it, then," she said. "And you're off to London."

He put his suit jacket on and walked to the door. "Okay, then. You're going to be all right."

"Yes, I know."

They both put their hands on the doorknob at the same time. Allison let go and stepped back. He turned to say good-bye, changed his mind, and pulled her into his arms. He kissed her long and hard and walked out the door.

And he was gone. It took another hour for Allison to admit the truth. She felt abandoned. That didn't make any sense to her, but then, having sex with Liam and pretending it hadn't meant anything didn't make any sense, either. Didn't he know? Didn't he have a glimmer of a notion that he was more than a casual fling to her? Apparently not.

She really couldn't blame him, because she had only just figured it out. Trying to be a with-it modern woman wasn't working for her. She had no one to blame but herself. She should have known she wasn't cut out for games. She didn't have the nerves or the disposition to be coy or clever. No wonder she hid in her computer. It couldn't hurt her.

EIGHTEEN

EIGHT WEEKS, THREE DAYS, AND NOT A WORD FROM LIAM. Not that she cared, because she didn't. Swamped with work and classes, she had barely thought about him. She accepted the fact that he had moved on, just as she had. She told herself that lie so many times she was almost beginning to believe it.

Exams were finally over. She turned in the last paper she was ever going to write for persnickety Dr. Bracey's class, and she was officially finished. Now that she thought about it, senior year hadn't been all that difficult, just time-consuming.

Her job, on the other hand, was making her crazy. She was getting sick and tired of being dragged out of her apartment by the FBI. There were always two agents—never one or three—banging at her door at the most inconvenient times. Every once in a while, if they were in a "let's prank the employee" mood, one of them would dangle handcuffs in front of her face to get her to hurry. They thought it was funny, but their little stunt wasn't humorous in Starbucks or

the gym. Their ferocious expressions could scare the bejesus out of an ordinary person. The scare tactics were wasted
on her. The agents were having fun, she supposed, and fun
was hard to come by in their line of work, so she let them
torment her.

Her days at the cyber unit were intense. Because Phillips
assigned her only the most complex cases, he kept her isolated in her own office. The other employees passing by
looked through the glass wall and saw her working. When
she glanced their way, they returned her smile, and when she
passed them in the hall, they nodded and said hello, but there
was no other interaction or camaraderie. She didn't take time
to form relationships with coworkers. They most likely assumed she was antisocial. To them she looked as though she
had it all together because she had had years of practice perfecting her laid-back attitude. On the outside she appeared to
be calm, cool, and in control, but on the inside she was a
mess of nerves, and she was mentally counting the days until
she would once again be free to pursue her own dreams.

The FBI owned her now, and in the eight weeks she'd
worked for them, they had managed to turn her life upside
down. She was all theirs for six full months. On paper it
didn't look all that long, but on a day-to-day basis it was an
eternity. Two months down, four to go.

She hated that others controlled her every action, and on
the days when the stress and tension threatened to overwhelm
her, she would put on her Bose headphones, close her eyes for
a few minutes, and think about something pleasant, like
walking along a white sand beach or, better yet, punching her
immediate supervisor, Special Agent Jim Phillips. She bet
that would remove his perpetually smug expression. Allison
didn't consider herself a violent person. She had never hit
anyone, not even her irresponsible cousin, Bill, yet the thought
of smacking her boss did lighten her mood.

Agent Phillips seemed to know what buttons to push, and Allison came close to completely losing her composure one afternoon. He called her into his office for another one of his famous pep talks about the bureau. Then came the suggestions. The latest proposal was a doozy. He wanted her to wear a thin silver bracelet that had a built-in tracking device. She wouldn't have to worry about losing it because, once it was snapped into place, it was impossible to remove. The man was actually enthusiastic about his outrageous plan, and it took every ounce of her willpower to sit quietly and listen. After gritting her teeth, she insisted for the hundredth time that he simply call her cell phone if and when he needed her after hours. He countered that there were times when she couldn't be reached by phone, most likely suspecting she had turned it off. She had to admit there had been a few instances when she had silenced her phone just to have a couple hours of peace.

As much as she hated the job, she loved the work, and how strange was that? The real irony was that she was making a good salary, and it was all hers. Her aunt and uncle couldn't take it from her as they had with her previous earnings.

She was a paid employee of the federal government—an employee who wasn't allowed to quit—with official credentials and benefits up the wazoo. She had been told that the six-month job she'd agreed to would be only from eight to five Monday through Friday. There was a caveat attached, though: if there was ever an urgent situation, she would be required to come in after hours. Thus far, there had been an average of three urgent situations each workweek and one almost every weekend. Agents had pulled her out of bed in the middle of the night too many times to count, had ruined innumerable dinners, and had barged into half the movie theaters in the city looking for her. She became so skittish she even imagined they were trying to interrupt her gradu-

ation. She had been chosen to represent her department and
had just stepped onto the stage to collect her diploma when
she glanced at the crowd and spotted two men in suits hurrying down the aisle toward her. They looked determined.
In the hope of avoiding a tug-of-war, she rushed across the
stage, snatched the diploma out of the president's hands, all
but fist-bumped him in lieu of a handshake, and ran down
the steps, just as the two men reached the front row, turned,
and sat down next to their families.

After the ceremony, she was congratulated by Jordan and
Noah, who promised to celebrate with her on Nathan's Bay
the following weekend. There was a big party scheduled.
Allison had just said good-bye to them when Dan and his
girlfriend made their way to her. Mark and his fiancée were
also there. She had discouraged them from subjecting themselves to the never-ending proceedings, but they insisted on
attending because they were her friends. She surmised they
felt sorry for her because Charlotte and Oliver couldn't come
and she wouldn't have family at her big event, but even if
they came out of pity, she was happy to see all of them. It was
while Dan was giving her a big bear hug that she looked up
into the stands . . . and saw him . . . there, standing in the
middle of a crowd of people who were slowly making their
way to the exits. He was there only as long as a blink, and
then he was gone.

Had she really seen Liam, or was her imagination playing
tricks on her? She'd been thinking about him almost every
day. She couldn't seem to stop. She had told herself again and
again he wasn't worth it, and yet the constant reminder didn't
seem to matter.

Not a single phone call. He couldn't take the time to pick
up the phone and call her just to see how she was doing?
With each passing day it had become abundantly clear she
meant nothing to him. He had moved on without so much

as a backward glance. Liam Scott, she decided, was insensitive and rude, and once again she reminded herself that she was happy to be rid of him.

Her friends took her to dinner to celebrate her graduation. Then Dan drove her home. As soon as she locked the door behind her, she started thinking about Liam again. He really had forgotten about her, hadn't he? He couldn't even be bothered to send her a text or an e-mail. No, she definitely hadn't seen him at graduation. He was in some far-off country, and the man she saw was simply a figment of her imagination. She went to sleep that night calling upon every happy image she could think of, anything to block images of him.

The following week was grueling, and she was glad of it because she didn't have time for thoughts of Liam. She didn't get home before nine or ten every night. Friday finally came, and fortunately there weren't any after-work emergencies. She arrived home at a decent time, packed her overnight bag, and drove to Jordan and Noah's house. Her friends were taking her to Nathan's Bay for the weekend to celebrate her graduation. She'd been there several times with Jordan. She loved her large family and the tiny island. It was magical. And isolated. A bridge arching over a narrow channel was the only way in and out, and the sprawling two-story house was the only one on the island. Judge Buchanan owned the island and constantly fought off eager developers who wanted a slice of paradise. Allison was happy he kept refusing.

She was looking forward to seeing the Buchanans again. They were so kind to her, and time with them was always relaxed and fun. As she drove to Jordan's house, she toyed with the idea of telling her about Liam but decided against it because she planned to erase him from her memory. As if that were possible. Damn it all, she wanted to move on. She hadn't wanted to get involved with any man, because he would interfere with her plans for the future. What had happened to her?

She was in quite a state by the time she parked the car and ran up the steps to the town house.

Jordan opened the door. Allison's greeting wasn't what her friend had expected.

"Men suck."

Too late, Allison saw Noah step out from behind the door. She hoped he hadn't heard what she'd said . . . but of course he'd heard. He was trying not to laugh.

"I'm a man," he reminded her.

How could she forget? Like with Liam, testosterone oozed from every pore in Noah's body.

"You're the exception."

"What about *them*?" he asked with a tilt of his head. "Are they the exception, too?"

Allison froze. "Them?"

Jordan had to pull her out of the way so that Noah could get the door closed. Before she could ask who else was there, Jordan said, "You're in an odd mood tonight. Is Agent Phillips making you nuts?"

That was as good an excuse as any for her lame behavior, she supposed. "He's certainly not making my life easier," she replied.

She walked into the living room, stopped to rave about the new furniture, then turned to go into the dining room, and there, leaning against the new table, was the bane of her existence, Liam "What-a-Hunk" Scott. He wasn't alone. Alec stood on the other side of the table with a green trash bag in one hand and a bottle of beer in the other.

It was almost impossible to stifle her reaction. Liam looked as though he'd been in a fight. There were a couple of bruises on his jaw and cheek and a cut above his right eyebrow. Were they from a rugby game? Or a fistfight? Maybe one of his assignments had turned violent. She told herself she didn't care enough to find out.

Did he have to look so good? He wore old worn-out jeans that hung low on his hips and a T-shirt that was molded to his chest and upper arms, outlining his muscles. The T-shirt had seen better days. There was a faint logo of a sports team on it, she thought, but she couldn't make out what it was. Although Liam's stance was relaxed, his gaze was intense and it locked on her.

She broke the silence. "Hi," she said, and before he could respond, she smiled at Alec and greeted him. She noticed his eyes kept bouncing back and forth between Liam and her. Great. Now he was suspicious and was going to ask questions.

"Why are you holding a trash bag?" she asked, trying her best to ignore Liam.

Jordan answered, "It's your graduation present. I know how you love puzzles, so I got you a dozen. One has ten thousand pieces, and there's even a 3-D one in there. Actually there are only eleven in the bag. I was telling the guys how amazing you are, and I don't think they believed me." She pointed to the table, which was covered in tiny jigsaw pieces. "All the pieces are faceup, so it shouldn't take much time to put it together. It's a thousand pieces, I think."

"I'm not going to show off for you," Allison whispered.

Jordan took pity. "Don't worry. You can put it together when we get back Sunday. I just thought, knowing how puzzles are a great stress reliever for you, and given the circumstances . . ."

Allison could have sworn she gave an almost imperceptible nod toward Liam. "Given what circumstances?" she asked.

Jordan didn't answer her. Noah had come up behind his wife and wrapped his arms around her waist. Allison envied how affectionate they were with each other. Their love was evident in every look, every action.

"She really is amazing," Noah said to Alec and Liam.

Noah had firsthand knowledge. He had been at Nathan's Bay when Jordan's mother complained to her husband about a puzzle that was spread out on the dining table. According to Mrs. Buchanan, the judge had put it there over a month ago. Believing her husband would never finish it, she ordered that the puzzle be put back in the box. Then Allison happened to walk past. She stopped as soon as she saw the puzzle, stared at it a minute, and then began to put the pieces together at a dazzling speed. Noah stood in the doorway watching her and was soon joined by Jordan and her parents. He was certain Allison set some sort of record. Once she was finished, she sighed, turned around, and walked out into the sunroom, leaving her audience speechless.

Alec set the bag on a chair. "You wrapped her gift in a trash bag?" he asked Jordan. "That's kind of lazy, isn't it?"

Jordan laughed as she defended herself. "All the boxes are different sizes. How else do you wrap them?"

The two began a silly debate about gift wrap, but Allison wasn't paying attention. She had suddenly guessed why Liam and Alec were there. She took a step back and shook her head. "Oh no, you don't."

Liam noticed how pale her face had become. "Oh no, what?"

"What's going on?" Alec asked.

"You want me to do something else illegal for you, don't you? Did Agent Phillips send you? Does he know about this?"

Jordan was outraged on her behalf. "You are not going to make her do anything more."

Alec put his hands up. "Hey, we're on her side."

"Ha," Allison scoffed.

"What does 'ha' mean?" Liam wanted to know.

She wouldn't look at him when she said, "It means I'm not so sure you are on my side."

Liam decided Allison had ignored him long enough. She was obviously in a strange mood, and he couldn't figure out why. He was contemplating grabbing her and asking her what the hell was wrong with her when she finally turned her attention to him. She walked over to him, poked him in the chest, and said, "I've been following the contract, and I've been more than compliant, Liam. Way more."

"Way more, huh?" Liam repeated, and dared to smile.

"I've been trying to get along with the man. He wore me down, and I finally agreed to this." She lifted her arm to show off her new bracelet. "But that's it. I'm not doing anything more to keep him happy. I'm already working eighty-hour weeks. And I just found out he programmed his phone number in my cell phone. All I have to do is push the number one and he'll answer. Why he thinks I would want to call him is beyond me," she added. "I'm trying to get along, and Agent Phillips has absolutely nothing to complain about."

Jordan tried to calm her friend. "I think it's sweet that Phillips gave you a graduation present. That's a pretty bracelet."

"It's a tracking device."

"A what?" Alec asked. "Did you say a tracking—"

"Yes, I did. Liam, this isn't funny, so stop laughing."

Alec had more discipline. He just smiled. "If you don't like the bracelet, take it off," he suggested. It sounded logical to him, and Noah's nod indicated he agreed.

She slapped her forehead. "Why didn't I think of that?"

"I'm assuming that means 'What a dumb question,'" Alec said.

She nodded. "I can't take it off. It has to be cut off with a special tool I don't believe has been invented yet."

"Why did you agree to let him put it on you?" Jordan asked.

"Like I said, he wore me down," Allison admitted. "Want to know one of his other numerous suggestions? He was real enthusiastic about this one. He thought it would be a good idea to put a tiny chip under my skin. That way he could always know where I was. Don't they do that to dogs?"

The entire time Allison had been ranting, her eyes were taking quick glances at the table. She moved closer and stared at the puzzle. She simply couldn't help herself. It was a quirk of hers, she supposed, although Charlotte called it a compulsion. She once asked Allison if the house were on fire but there was an unfinished puzzle, would she feel compelled to finish it before she left? Allison remembered she'd told her it was a ridiculous question. Of course she'd get out right away, but deep down she wasn't so sure. She might have been tempted to take the puzzle with her.

Now that she'd seen it, she had to put the damn thing together. It didn't take her more than a few seconds to see the picture taking shape in her mind. And then she went to work, snapping the pieces together.

She was incredibly fast. Jordan watched the three men. They looked mesmerized.

"Faster than a speeding bullet, right?" she whispered to her husband.

Noah nodded. "Her brain's a computer, isn't it?"

"I swear she's wired differently than the rest of us."

"I can hear you," Allison said. "So stop making fun."

"How can you talk and do that at the same time?" Alec asked.

"I can also walk and talk at the same time."

"No need to be sarcastic, sweetheart." Liam made the comment.

"Liam, talk to Agent Phillips," Jordan said. "Tell him to let up on Allison."

Allison was exasperated. She didn't look up when she said, "Do not talk to him. I can take care of myself."

"How come he wants to track you?" Jordan asked.

"He thinks I could be dangerous. At least that's what he keeps telling me. He makes it sound like I have an affliction."

"He's right," Liam said. "You are dangerous."

Allison continued snapping the pieces together. After the first few minutes the others pulled out chairs and sat down to watch in awe, as though they were spectators at some phenomenal sporting event. When the last piece had been inserted, she stepped back and surveyed her work, then turned around.

"Wow" was all Alec could say.

"When my contract is up, I'm not doing anything more for the FBI," she blurted, finishing her argument. "I know that's why you're here, and I'm not—"

Liam didn't let her finish. He took her by the hand and led her toward the French doors that opened to the patio.

"What are you doing?" she asked. Two months without a single phone call, and now he was being domineering? No way was she going to let him get away with it.

She was about to resist when he said, "We have to talk."

Glancing over her shoulder, she wondered why Alec wasn't following them. After they stepped onto the patio and Liam closed the doors behind them, she pulled her hand away. With a bite in her voice, she asked, "More hacker talk?"

"No," he replied. He walked over to the short brick wall that surrounded the patio and leaned against it.

She took a seat next to him. "Then why are you and Alec here?"

"We're going fishing with Noah."

"So you're going to Nathan's Bay?"

"Yes."

She couldn't make up her mind if she was happy or irritated that he would be with her that weekend. Two months without a word and now he was acting as though he'd only just seen her yesterday. Irritated, she decided. She was irritated. She had already been thinking like a clingy rejected woman, and that was simply unacceptable. If she let that attitude continue, she would soon be singing those stupid melancholy songs. "Why do you have bruises on your face? Were you in a fight?"

"Yes."

"Where?"

"London."

"Are you going to tell me what happened?"

"No."

She didn't know if he couldn't tell her or wouldn't tell her, and she once again pretended she didn't care. "You've been in London all this while?"

"No," he answered. "I had to go back last week."

She wanted to ask where he had been for the last two months besides London, but she repressed the urge to pursue the subject. Where he had been or what he had been doing—or whom he had been doing it with—wasn't any of her business. Right?

"Okay, then." She started to get up, but he put his hand on her shoulder and stopped her.

"I have something to tell you."

"What is it?"

He didn't ease into the news. "There's a warrant out for your cousin's arrest."

She braced herself. "What happened?"

"Bill's girlfriend, Mary Lou Something-or-other, went to the movie with another man. Bill found out about the date and waited in the parking lot for them to come outside. According to the police report, Bill was pretty drunk when he jumped the guy. There were dozens of phone cameras filming your cousin beating him to a bloody pulp. He put him in the hospital."

She thought she might be sick. "How bad was the man hurt?"

"He's stable now, but still in ICU."

"Is he going to be okay?"

"Yes," he answered. "I gotta say, Mary Lou sure set the bar low for boyfriends. The guy in the hospital is younger than Bill, but he's already a felon with a record that goes way back. I wouldn't waste any tears on him, Allison, because as soon as he's released from the hospital he's going to be locked up. Turns out, the police have been looking for him. He was involved in an armed robbery a couple of months ago."

He stood over her with his arms folded across his chest. "This is a clear-cut case against Bill. The DA will add charges. Your cousin is going away for a long time."

"If there's a warrant, that means he's not in jail?"

"He ran before the police got there. He hasn't been found yet."

"This is all my fault," she whispered, her voice shaking with emotion. "That man is in the hospital because of me. Bill could have killed him. If I hadn't pleaded for probation, this wouldn't have happened."

"Yeah, it would have," he said. "It just wouldn't have happened this soon. Your cousin isn't going to change. He's got a lot of rage inside. He should be locked up."

She put her head down and covered her face with her

hands. "I'm responsible. Why didn't I think he was capable of such violence? Why didn't—"

Liam wouldn't let her continue to berate herself. "You thought you were giving him one last chance to change his life."

"I was a fool."

"No, you were naive. There's enough blame to go around. Phillips or I could have refused to get probation for him. But what's done is done. He's going to try to get you to help him."

"He doesn't know I helped him get probation, does he?"

"No."

"Then why would he come to me for help?"

"Because you've always helped his family in the past. Hell, you supported all of them. Your cousin has been running with some bad people. One of them might show up at your door. If Bill or one of his friends tries to contact you, I want you to call me."

"What if you're out of the country?"

"You call me."

He wasn't going to let up until she agreed. "Yes, I'll call you."

"Give me your cell phone."

She pulled it from her back pocket and watched as he programmed his number in and added it to speed dial.

"All right, then," he answered with finality.

Allison waited for him to say something else, but Liam stood in front of her, silent and unmoving. The only sound was the chirping of crickets in the darkness. The longer he stood there, the more uncomfortable she became. Just being alone with him was enough to make her heart beat faster, but the way he was looking at her now almost brought her heart to a stop.

She broke the silence. "Was there anything else you wanted to talk about?"

His answer was brusque. "No."

"Then we should go in."

Liam took her hands to pull her to her feet, but when she was standing bare inches away, the willpower he had been relying on all evening evaporated into thin air. From the moment she walked through the door, he'd wanted her. For the past two months, he had looked for every excuse to return to Boston. He had told himself the memory of their time together would fade, but that hadn't happened. And then, when he saw her again tonight, he knew he was in real trouble.

"Allison . . . ," he began.

She waited for him to continue, but he only held her hands more tightly. His eyes searched hers as though he was seeking something intangible.

"Are you going to let go of me anytime soon?" she whispered, hoping he couldn't feel her trembling.

"No, not yet."

She peeked around him to see if anyone was watching. The light from inside poured through the French doors. Thankfully, the dining room was empty. She wasn't worried about Alec and Noah noticing. They wouldn't say anything, but Jordan was another story. She'd have at least a hundred questions, and Allison knew she wouldn't be able to answer a single one. How could she, when she didn't know what was happening herself? The only thing she was sure of was that she had been miserable for months, and Liam was the cause. To avoid a future of misery, she had to keep her distance from him.

She freed her hands and said, "You should leave me alone."

He nodded. "You're right. I should leave you alone." He stepped even closer so that she had to tilt her head up to look at him. She could feel the warmth of his chest against hers and wondered if he could hear the breath that caught in her throat.

He lowered his head, and as though she had no control over her reactions, her fingers slid into his soft hair. "This is all wrong. I can't—"

"Yeah, it's definitely all wrong," he said as his mouth brushed over hers.

And then he kissed her exactly how she wanted him to, and oh, how he made her want more. She heard a low groan, then realized she was the one making the sound. He overwhelmed her, and when he finally ended the kiss her arms were clasped around his neck. She was slow to get her wits back. When she finally found her strength, she pushed against him. Unfortunately, he didn't budge.

"You can't just waltz back into my life and think you can kiss me."

There was that heart-stopping smile again, messing with her concentration. "I don't waltz," he said. "And I already kissed you. Did you forget? How about I show you what I did?"

He kissed her again. She was ready to push harder this time. She absolutely was, until his mouth settled on top of hers. Then she was all in, her tongue rubbing against his, clinging to him while he robbed her of every thought but one. Lordy, did he know how to kiss! She was so swept away in the moment she didn't hear the door opening.

Jordan called out to her, "We'll take two cars. Alec will ride with Noah and me, and you can ride with—" She stopped abruptly when she saw them. "You two seem to be getting along."

Allison could hear the laughter in her voice. Liam finally let go of her.

"You're blushing," he whispered, loud enough, she thought, for the neighbors to hear.

"You like embarrassing me, don't you?"

"Yeah, I kinda do."

She stepped away from him. "Jordan, I should drive myself in case I get called in."

"If you get called in, I'll drive you back," Liam said.

Just then her phone rang, and for the first time since she'd started working for Agent Phillips, she hoped he was on the line. She knew she was acting like a wimp by trying to get out of spending the weekend with Liam, yet her reason made perfect sense to her. She was afraid of being alone with him. She was vulnerable with him, and she hated that feeling because she didn't know how to protect herself.

The call was from Dan. "Are you going to be available Monday evening around seven?"

"Should I be?" she asked.

"You absolutely should be."

She turned away from Liam and walked to the side of the patio overlooking the garden while she waited for Dan to explain. He'd sounded concerned and almost frazzled, which was totally out of character for him.

"What has you so upset?" she asked when he didn't immediately tell her what was wrong.

"I'm not upset. I'm angry. Brett is doing a presentation of your program to potential buyers. There's a group of important company execs coming in, and Brett reserved one of the banquet rooms at the Adams Harbor Hotel. After the way you reacted at Basher's party, I'm guessing he's keeping the time and place real hush-hush. He doesn't want you to find out until it's too late."

"How did you find out?"

"He came by the house, walked in like he owned the place, and asked if Mark or I had found his iPad. We told him no, and then he said he wanted to catch up. We knew he was up to something," he said, adding, "He's such an ass. Anyway, he kept bringing the conversation back to you. Twice he asked where you were and what you were doing.

Neither one of us answered the first time. Then Brett circled around to you again and said he wanted to talk to you and find out if you knew where his iPad was."

"What did you tell him?"

"I lied and said you were in Seattle visiting your sister and wouldn't be back for two more weeks. He was out of there lickety-split. Looked relieved, too."

"How did you find out when this presentation is taking place?"

"Like I said, I knew he was up to something, so I called a friend, and he called a friend who put some feelers out, and I finally got the information I was after. It's on Monday night at seven. Please tell me you're going to crash the party."

She laughed. "I wouldn't miss it."

"Be careful. No telling what Brett's capable of. If he thinks this deal is worth millions, I'll bet he'll have a couple of bouncers with your photo standing at the doors. I'd take some heat with you."

"I don't need an armed guard to crash the party," she protested.

"I don't know about that. Maybe take the armed FBI agent you've been seeing."

"I'll be fine on my own. Don't worry about me."

"Brett doesn't have any money. Someone has to be bankrolling him. The party is open bar with lots of food, and that hotel is expensive. I'll bet his money backer expects a big profit from the sale, too. Listen, I'm reevaluating. Maybe you shouldn't go," he added worriedly.

"Oh, I'm going."

"Then how about I go with you?"

"Dan, if he sees you, I won't be able to sneak in."

"You're not going to be able to sneak in anyway," he argued. "You're a knockout. Men are going to notice you."

"I'll get in," she said, ignoring the comment about her appearance. "And stop worrying. I can take care of myself."

A minute later she ended the call. When she turned around she found Liam watching her. He wasn't the only one. Alec, Jordan, and Noah were also watching.

"What?"

Liam walked closer. "What's Dan worrying about?"

"Dan's the old roommate, right?" Noah asked.

Liam answered, "Yes. He watched out for Allison while she lived with him and another guy."

Allison asked, "Were all of you listening in on my phone conversation?"

"I was on the phone with my wife, so I only caught a little of it," Alec said.

"Yes, we listened," Jordan said. "As soon as I heard you say hello, I decided to eavesdrop."

"You shouldn't—," Allison began.

"Of course we shouldn't. It's rude," Jordan said. "So, what did Dan say?"

"What's he worried about?" Noah wanted to know.

"Nothing, really. Dan tends to overreact."

Liam wouldn't let her evade the question. "Allison, what's he worried about?"

"You're starting to irritate me, Liam."

"Answer me." There was a sharp edge to his voice this time.

She knew he wouldn't stop. He was determined to get his way, and she wasn't in the mood to fight, especially in front of the others. She repeated the conversation she'd had with Dan, and the second she finished, Liam said, "I'm going with you."

"I'd like to come along, too," Noah said. "Maybe I can move some things around."

Alec nodded. "I wish I could be there. I'd like to watch the presentation."

"No, you wouldn't," Allison argued.

Alec grinned. "I really would, but I'll be back in Chicago."

"I have to be in Dallas Monday, so I can't go," Jordan said. "I wish I could be there. Since you've been working on this program for so long, I'm guessing you've built in a way to stop someone from stealing your work. You have, haven't you?"

Allison nodded. "The software isn't complete. Brett isn't smart enough to know that. I'm sure he thinks he has it all figured out, but he doesn't. It isn't possible until I add more code. It's intricate." She could have answered in more detail, but the only one who would have understood was Jordan, so she spared the men a long explanation.

Allison appreciated their support, but she didn't want to discuss her retaliation against Brett just yet, so before they could ask anything more, she said, "I have to move my car. I thought I was driving to Nathan's Bay, so I parked in a one-hour-only spot."

"Your apartment is close. Drive home and I'll follow you," Liam offered.

Deciding his was a sensible alternative, she acquiesced. After he transferred her overnight bag to his car, they were on their way. As usual, traffic was horrible, but Allison had figured out various side streets to take that cut her drive time in half. She parked in her slot in the underground garage, made sure the car doors were locked, and then got into Liam's car. They didn't talk much on their way out of town because Liam kept getting one call after another, all work related. His voice was tense. Something he didn't like was going on, and she wondered if he ever truly broke free from his work and his responsibilities. There was no doubt he was a workaholic. She recognized this in him because she was one herself. Both of their jobs were important, but his sent him around the world on missions that had a powerful impact on people's lives. She could sense the heavy burden it placed on his shoulders.

The bridge to Nathan's Bay was in front of them, and just as Allison was beginning to think she would make the best of the awkward situation and try to enjoy the weekend, she got a call from Not-So-Special Agent Phillips. He told her it was an emergency but promised it wouldn't take long. She translated that to mean she would be at the cyber unit until the middle of the night.

"I hate to ruin your evening," she said to Liam. "I'll make Phillips send someone to drive me home."

"No, I'll come in." He slowed the car to turn around.

"What about fishing?"

"What about it?"

Her phone rang again. Assuming it was Phillips, she didn't bother to look at the caller ID. "Yes," she answered, trying her best to sound pleasant, not surly.

Aunt Jane was on the line. Allison cringed when she heard her caustic voice.

"You listen to me. We need money, and after all we've done for—"

Allison stopped her. "How did you get this number?"

"I know people who— Never mind. I expect you to co-operate."

"Leave me the hell alone," she shouted. She disconnected the call, and let out a sigh of satisfaction. It felt good to shout.

"Which one was it?" he asked. "Your aunt or your uncle?"

"My aunt."

Her aunt called again and again. Allison put the phone on mute, but that didn't stop the woman. Not only did she call; she also texted insults, all starting with the word *un-grateful*.

Where were her computer and her headphones when she needed them? She wanted to escape into her laptop and forget about all her worries. She included Liam on that list. She wanted him to either stay or leave, but not do both. Bouncing back and forth was making her nuts. She still hadn't recovered from not seeing him for months, and then, boom, there he was. Did she want him to stay? She closed her eyes and leaned back against the headrest while she thought about it. Three seconds later she had her answer. Of course she wanted him to stay. If anyone was going to leave, it should be her, not him. Maybe then it wouldn't hurt so much. Liam had the power to crush her . . . and all because she was hopelessly in love with him.

What could she do about it? She didn't have a clue. She worried for the rest of the drive to the cyber unit.

Phillips looked relieved to see them. He followed Allison to her office, gave her the task he wanted completed—another breach of a government facility—then left her alone. Allison glanced over her shoulder and saw Liam waiting for him outside the glass wall. The two immediately fell into a deep discussion, and whatever the topic was had both of them frowning. Every once in a while, one or the other would turn to look at her. Allison was curious but turned her concentration back to the screen and went to work. Finally, around one in the morning she found what Phillips was looking for. Because the hacker was unsophisticated and easy to pinpoint, her task was a rather simple one. Any of the other techs could have done the job, and she wondered why she had been called in. She wouldn't have been surprised if Phillips was simply asserting his control over her.

After e-mailing her report to him, she went to Phillips's office to check out. He and Liam were in a serious conversation that stopped when she knocked on the door. Phillips motioned for her to come in. He didn't require a long explanation of her findings. In fact, he was rather abrupt when he told her he would read her report in the morning and ordered her to go home and get some rest. If she didn't know better, she might have thought he actually was concerned about her well-being.

Liam drove her back to her apartment and parked underground next to her car, then carried her overnight bag and his gym bag up to her apartment, which she didn't notice until he'd unlocked her door and followed her inside.

"Did you text Jordan and tell her . . . ?" she began.

"Yes, she knows. I can drive you out there tomorrow if you'd like."

She shook her head. "No, thanks. I'm going to stay home."

She put her laptop on the desk and hooked it up to its charger. The cell phone had to be close to her at all times—according to Phillips—so she went into the bedroom and plugged it into the charger on the bedside table. Finished with the mundane tasks, she returned to the living room to get her overnight bag. Liam's bag was sitting next to hers, and he was sitting on the sofa, checking messages on his phone.

"Liam, why did you bring your gym bag in?"

He didn't look up from the screen when he answered, "I'm spending the night."

She was so surprised by his casual and blunt announcement she didn't know what to say. She felt a burst of joy, which she quickly squelched. "That's pretty presumptuous, isn't it? Shouldn't you have asked me?"

He put his phone down and smiled at her with that crazy dimple that only appeared when he was up to something. Loosening his tie, he stood and walked into her bedroom, stopping to pick up his bag on the way.

She followed him. "Are you going to answer me?"

"Yeah, I probably should ask, but even if you say no, I'm still staying."

"Why?"

"Why what?" He was being deliberately obtuse.

"Why are you spending the night?"

He took off his jacket and hung it in her closet. "I want to stick close to you for a little while."

She put her hands on her hips. "This has something to do with Phillips, doesn't it? I saw you talking to him, and you and he both looked so serious. Something happened, didn't it?"

He wasn't at all reluctant to explain. "Phillips has been talking to Bale. The guy has a grudge against you."

"Why? What did I do to him?"

"You didn't do anything to him," he assured her. "When you found the leak in his Detroit office, you embarrassed him. Somehow he thought you manipulated information to implicate people who worked for him. He was in charge of the operation there, but he didn't want to take responsibility for the lack of security. He had to blame someone. In his warped mind you're the reason people lost their jobs."

"But that's ridiculous . . . isn't it?"

"Yes, it is," he answered quietly. "Bale wasn't being rational, so Phillips told him to take leave for a couple of months. He came back this morning, and he's still pretty hot under the collar. Phillips hasn't decided what to do about him yet, but his career might be over. Until this gets sorted out, I thought I'd stick around."

He unzipped his bag and took out his shaving kit and a pair of faded boxers. While she stood watching, he stripped out of his clothes and disappeared into the bathroom. She tried not to stare at his bronzed muscular back. A minute later she heard the shower running.

Every thought running through her head only added to her confusion. She knew she had to keep her distance from him. It was the only way she could protect herself. But every time she got close to him, she wanted to throw herself into his arms. Sleeping together certainly wouldn't help her move forward. Yet she still wanted to. She didn't seem to know her own mind anymore.

She forced herself to stop worrying, undressed, and put on a short pink silk nightgown. It had thin spaghetti straps and was low cut into a deep V. Was she wearing it to entice him? Of course she was. And that was the very thing she had vowed not to do. Realizing the mistake she was making, she came to her senses and decided to change into an old T-shirt. Unfortunately, before she could do that, the door opened and there he stood, staring at her. He seemed frozen.

When he finally took a step forward, she walked around him and went into the bathroom. She washed her face and brushed her teeth, and tried to think of anything that would take her mind off him. Her thoughts rambled and she was suddenly wondering about Bale again. Had she gotten people fired? What had she done wrong? Liam and Phillips had seemed so intense back at the office, so they must have thought Bale posed a real danger. Why else would Liam be staying close?

She opened the door and came to a quick stop. Liam was in her bed. He'd stretched out on his back with his hands stacked on his chest and his eyes closed. His gun and badge were on the table next to her cell phone. The lights were out in the living room. She checked to make sure the door was locked with the dead bolt in place, and as she turned back, she looked at the sofa and shook her head. She should have placed a pillow and blanket on it so he would know that was where he was supposed to sleep.

She considered the sofa for herself but quickly rejected the idea. It was her bed and she was going to sleep in it. Decision made, she grabbed her body lotion from the dresser and walked to the other side of the bed. Sitting with her back propped against the headboard, she opened the bottle and squeezed a couple of drops into her hand.

"Liam?" She whispered his name the first time, shouted it the second time.

"Yes?"

"Are you asleep?"

The light coming from the bathroom was dim, but she could see his smile. "I was," he said.

She rubbed the lotion on her arms while she studied him. He was one fine-looking man, she thought for about the hundredth time. That shouldn't have mattered because it was a superficial reason for liking someone. Did she like him? Of course she did. She not only liked him; she loved him.

Allison put more lotion on her legs, and when she was finally finished, she smelled like a gardenia. "How many people worked in the Detroit office?"

"I'm not sure. Why?"

"Did I get them all fired?"

He didn't open his eyes when he answered, "No."

"You said Bale thinks I'm the reason people were fired. He isn't wrong. I am the reason."

He could hear the anxiety in her voice. He rolled onto his side and pulled her down next to him. "You shouldn't be worrying about this."

"Did I get them fired?"

"A few people were fired, but there have been problems with the Detroit office for a while, and it was going to close at some point anyway. Most of the employees are being transferred to other locations. What you did was find the source of a serious leak. The man they arrested put countless lives in danger. He insisted that Bale knew about it and encouraged him. We haven't found any proof of that, but Bale's pissed that it all happened under his watch and he feels backed into a corner."

"But I was the one who—"

He wouldn't let her continue. "Bale doesn't want to accept any of the blame, and that's why he's blaming you." He yawned. "You've had a long day. You should get some sleep."

She didn't know if she should address the fact that he was in her bed and shouldn't be, or if she should just let it go.

Liam rolled onto his back, but this time brought her with him and held her cuddled up against his side. "Allison, I'll keep you safe."

"I know, but what if he—"

She raised her head and he gently pushed it back down on his shoulder and kissed her forehead before closing his eyes again. "If he tries to hurt you, I'll kill him."

NINETEEN

ALLISON SLEPT UNTIL LATE MORNING. LIAM WAS ALREADY dressed in jeans and a button-down shirt. His ever-present gun was on his hip. He looked relaxed. He'd rolled up his sleeves and was in the kitchen talking on the phone.

She put on her pink robe and headed to the refrigerator for a glass of orange juice, but as she tried to pass him he turned and saw her. His phone conversation stopped in midsentence. Putting his phone on mute, he took a step toward her and pinned her against the counter. Then, with his hand behind her neck, he pulled her to him and kissed her. She felt as though she were melting on the spot. He didn't seem to be affected at all. As soon as he ended the kiss, he went right back to talking on the phone. She didn't move for several seconds, waiting until she was sure her legs would support her. When she finally had the strength, she opened the refrigerator, took out a gallon of milk, and walked out of the kitchen. She made it to her bedroom door before she realized what she was carrying. Without a word she turned around and took the milk back. To his credit he didn't laugh, but she knew he wanted to.

What had just happened? He had kissed her as though it was the most natural thing in the world and didn't affect him in the least, and yet it had made her weak-kneed. Might as well face it, she told herself. Liam was a sophisticated and worldly man, and she was inexperienced and naive about such things as sex and romance. What meant everything to her was just sex to him. It wasn't as though he hadn't spelled it all out for her from the very beginning so there wouldn't be any misunderstanding. Sex was just sex, he'd told her, and because he led such an unpredictable life, a long-term commitment to any woman wasn't possible. The fact was, he didn't like the notion of being tied down anyway. Her eyes were finally open, and as painful as it was, she had to deal with reality.

After she showered and dressed, she returned to the kitchen. Liam was still on the phone. She drank a glass of orange juice and took a bite out of a granola bar that was as hard as nails and smelled like gerbil food. After tossing the rest of the bar into the trash, she waited for Liam to end his call. Then she wanted to know why he thought she needed protection. She personally thought it was ridiculous that Bale, a federal agent, would hold a grudge against her. If he were a child, perhaps it would make sense, but the man was an adult. Didn't he have anything better to do than stew over his bad luck?

Liam patiently listened as she ranted, and as soon as she wound down he told her that Phillips would be talking to Bale later today. Until then Allison was stuck with him. He would be sure to tell Phillips to ask why Bale was acting like a child. Would that satisfy her?

She didn't care that he was humoring her. "Yes, thank you."

Liam turned to make another call.

"I've got to get out of here," she whispered to herself. She rushed into her bedroom, checked her overnight bag to make sure she had everything she needed, zipped it closed, and headed to the door. Liam was still on the phone. She dropped the bag on the floor just as she thought she heard Liam call someone "darling." Shifting from one foot to the other, she waited until he finished his conversation, then said, "I've decided to drive out to Nathan's Bay. I'll spend the night there and come back tomorrow afternoon. Why are you shaking your head at me? I wasn't asking permission, Liam. I was informing you of my plans because—"

He stopped her. "If you go anywhere I'm going with you. Understand?" His voice was unbending.

"Yes," she said to placate him. She had already made up her mind that, with or without him, she was leaving.

"That was Phillips I was talking to—"

"You call Phillips your darling?"

"I . . . What?"

"I heard you say 'darling.'"

He shook his head. "I don't know what you heard, but I didn't call anyone darling, and if I did, it sure as hell wouldn't be Phillips."

She realized her imagination was playing tricks on her, so she didn't pursue the subject. If she asked any more questions, Liam might have thought she cared. She wasn't in the mood to argue. She wanted to leave.

"You're going to cooperate, aren't you?" It wasn't a question so much as a statement. He expected her to cooperate.

"Yes, of course. It's got to get better. I'm staying optimistic. Even though I was informed that Bale is coming after me because I tattled on him. Let's get going to Nathan's Bay." She reached for her bag.

Liam put his hands up and stopped her. "Not so fast." There was no way he could put a positive spin on the situation, so he was blunt with his announcement. "Phillips wants you at the cyber unit."

"No," she groaned.

"It shouldn't take long." He managed a smile. Nothing with Phillips was quick. To her credit she took the news in stride. He came to that conclusion when she didn't start crying. She also didn't move. "I guess you could try to hide," he suggested with a straight face.

Allison thought he was serious and shook her head. "No, he'll make a ruckus if I don't go in right away."

"A ruckus?" He put his arms around her and gave her a quick hug. "I like that word. Want to make a ruckus in the bedroom?" he asked with a laugh.

Of course she did. "Absolutely not." Her voice lacked conviction.

He opened the door for her. "Come on. Let's get going."

Usually when Phillips pulled her in on weekends, she took the time to change to her work clothes, but not today. Today she was taking a stand. She was wearing worn-out snug jeans, a cotton shirt, and sneakers. She wasn't going to change. If he didn't like her casual attire, too bad.

Liam left their bags in the apartment and drove her to the office. Rain was coming in. Black clouds rolled overhead as they turned onto the isolated stretch of road, and strong winds battered the tree branches. A clap of thunder shook the car, and Allison flinched. Even though she knew it was illogical, storms frightened her. She wasn't nervous today, though, because she was with Liam. Nothing much ever fazed him, and that was a comfort.

Fortunately they reached the unit and walked inside a scant minute before the downpour. As usual, Phillips was waiting for her outside his office. "London needs your special talent," he told her. "There's a small glitch in their system, and they'd like an outsider to look at it." Then he turned to Liam. "I just got a call." He gave a tilt of his head in Allison's direction and said, "He's coming in. You might want to talk to him."

Liam nodded. As soon as Phillips went into his office, Liam walked by her side to her office.

"Does Phillips live here?" she asked.

He laughed. "No, he lives with his wife."

"He's married?" She sounded shocked.

"Yes, he is."

"Who would marry that man? He's a classic type A personality, and he's obsessive-compulsive. He's—" She suddenly stopped. Wait a minute. She had just described herself.

"I've met her. She's nice."

"Who?"

Exasperated, he said, "Phillips's wife. They've been married a long time."

"I know why their marriage works. He's never home."

He pulled the chair out for her, and as he turned to leave, she said, "I heard Phillips tell you someone is coming in. Who is it? Is it Bale?"

He didn't answer her. He simply walked away.

"You're becoming as rude as Phillips," she called after him.

He obviously didn't understand she was trying to be insulting or he wouldn't have laughed.

The little glitch turned out to be a whopper, and it took her the entire day to straighten it out. She also found and removed two bugs. Her hope of spending a relaxing weekend on Nathan's Bay had been crushed. Maybe another time, she thought, trying to stay optimistic.

She closed down her station and headed toward Phillips's office. She didn't have any idea when she'd be able to leave. She knew he would want her to explain what she'd found in the London office. With an ordinary person that might take twenty minutes, but with Phillips it could take half the night.

She had just rounded the corner in the hallway when she came face-to-face with Curtis Bale. He looked surprised; then his expression quickly turned to anger. Allison tried to maneuver around him, but he blocked her path.

"I know what you did," he said, sneering.

Allison was shocked at first and then took offense to his accusatory tone. "Tell me. What did I do?"

"You made yourself look good. You couldn't find what Scott and Phillips wanted, so you manufactured it. I had nothing to do with those leaks, and yet you did whatever it took to make me and my department look bad. Tell me, Miss Trent, was this all just a game to you, or did you deliberately set out to destroy me?"

"I don't even know you, Mr. Bale. Why would I do that?"

"Don't play innocent with me. Are you aware of how many lives you've ruined?"

He was becoming more agitated, and Allison could see there was no reasoning with the man. She took a quick step to the side and passed him. As she walked away, he shouted after her, "Gloat while you can. This isn't over."

Her heart was still pounding from her encounter with Bale when she reached Phillips's office and found it empty. She looked up and down the hall, and there was no sign of him or Liam. Checking the time, she realized it was already night. She needed to calm down, and because she hadn't had anything to eat since the disgusting granola bar that morning, she took the steps to the cafeteria. Even though it was Saturday, she knew it would be stocked with meals for the weekend techs. The dining room was empty except for a table of four men, who were having an animated discussion as they munched on their sandwiches and chips. They stopped talking and turned in her direction when she walked in. Feeling a bit self-conscious, she smiled as she passed their table and walked over to the refrigerated case. She took out a salad with chicken. When she turned around and started for an empty table, one of the men waved to her.

"Come join us," he called. He stood and pulled up another chair to the table as the other men scooted theirs aside to make room. Once she was seated, he introduced himself. "I'm Sean," he said, and extended his hand. He pointed to each of the others, saying, "And this is Jeff, Paul, and Andy."

They greeted her with smiles, and then Andy said, "We've seen you around. You must be doing something pretty important to have that office all to yourself."

Allison's answer was deliberately vague. "I've been given specific assignments. I'm under contract for only a few months."

Paul spoke up. "I'll bet they're complicated assignments. I was in the security room when you came in and found that breach a couple of months ago. I have to tell you, I've never seen anybody get to a source that fast, especially one that intricate. You were amazing."

Embarrassed by his comment, she said, "I had seen something very similar before, so I just used what I knew."

"Still, that was mighty impressive work," Paul said.

"Where did you go to school?" Andy asked.

"I just graduated from Boston College," she answered. When she told them she had lived in the Boston area her whole life, the conversation turned to more personal topics, everything from which restaurant served the best chowder to who was their favorite Red Sox player. At one point Sean pulled out his wallet and showed her a picture of his one-year-old son dressed in an infant Red Sox uniform.

"I'm definitely going to miss Boston," she admitted.

"Where are you going?" Jeff wondered.

"I plan to move to California when my contract is up," she answered. "I'd like to start my own software company."

"That's a shame," he responded. "We could sure use your talents around here."

While the men around her continued to talk, her thoughts began to wander toward her future. She had planned everything so carefully. Just as soon as she could, she would move to California and start her company. No more long hours under Phillips's thumb. No more interruptions to her life by FBI agents. In California, she would be her own boss. It was exactly what she wanted, wasn't it?

On the other hand, she loved Boston. This was her home and she had good friends here. Why did she have to go to Silicon Valley to take on the boys? She could do that here . . . anywhere, actually, as long as she had a computer. As surprising as it was to admit, the idea of staying was appealing. Who knew she was going to like the work at the cyber unit so much? Certainly not her. She did like it, though—very much, as a matter of fact. Who wouldn't have loved solving problems all day? The men at the table were friendly and intelligent and interesting. Working alongside them would be fun.

Jordan had asked to be part of the new venture, and to-gether they could build a great company. Both of them could continue to write code and design software. Jordan could also fine-tune what Allison had already created. The two of them had other commitments, so it would be a slow-growing company, but that didn't bother Allison. If she stayed in Boston, she'd be able to continue her work at the cyber unit, though she would have to renegotiate the terms of her employment. She absolutely was not going to con-tinue to work eighty-hour weeks. The more she thought about the possibilities, the more excited she became. She felt as though a weight had just been lifted, and she couldn't wait to tell Jordan.

The topic at the table turned to new and innovative software that was being developed. When the talk became even more technical with a discussion about coding, Allison realized not only was she having a wonderful time, but she was where she belonged.

Liam found her surrounded by the four men. They were all smiling like simpletons and hanging on her every word. He grabbed a couple of sandwiches from the refrigerator, pulled out a chair from another table, and pushed it next to hers, then sat. He knew he was being territorial, but that didn't stop him. He draped his arm around her shoulders and gave her admirers the "get the hell out of here" look. They got the message and one by one left the table.

"I think you scared them," she said, frowning over the possibility.

"Thanks. It's nice you noticed."

"I wasn't complimenting you," she replied.

"Sure sounded like it." He tore into the sandwiches, drank a bottle of water, and was ready to go.

On the way back to her apartment, he asked her what she would like on her pizza.

"You're still hungry?" she asked, and before he could answer, she said, "Do you know how many . . ." She suddenly stopped.

"Do I know what?"

She felt silly telling him. "Calories. Pizza has a lot of calories. I'm used to eating salads and snacking on carrot sticks. I'm slowly turning into a rabbit." Embarrassed now, she shyly admitted, "Old habits die hard."

He called a pizza place he knew and liked, put in his order, and swung by on their way. There was a liquor store next door. "You've got beer, right?"

"Yes."

"The real stuff, not the light stuff."

"Light beer is the same as the real stuff."

He scoffed at the notion, and after they picked up what Allison believed was a ten-pound pizza, they went into the liquor store to purchase beer and Diet Coke.

They'd just gotten home when Giovanni called. "Is this a good time?"

Allison was glad to hear his voice. "It is," she said. "How are you?"

He filled her in on his hectic life and finally got around to the reason he had called. "I know you're retired, sweetie, but Maureen, one of my models who is your height and weight, broke her ankle and won't be able to work for quite a while. It's a huge event at the Hamilton. I have four models ready, but I need you, too. Just three designers are invited. It's quite an honor." He thought to add, "And it's all for an important charity."

"Of course I'll do it. When is it?"

"I'll e-mail you the particulars, and, Allison, bless you for helping me."

Liam was standing close enough to hear the entire conversation. He opened a bottle of beer, leaned against the kitchen counter, and said, "That's quite a schedule you're filling. You've got the Brett thing coming up soon. Now you've added a runway show."

"At the Hamilton," she volunteered.

He nodded. "And in between those two engagements you're going to be working your pretty little backside off for Phillips. Anything else you have planned?"

Inside her head, a voice said, "Tonight I've penciled in a shower and sex. Tomorrow, I'll want to hit something, so I'll plead with you to take me to the batting cages. Then, when I arrive back home, sex again." Every part of her wanted those words to come out, but she couldn't let them. In the back of her mind, there was the aching hope that he would want to go to bed with her. She thought he'd liked being intimate with her, yet now she had to reevaluate. He sure wasn't in any hurry to touch her, which in her mind meant he hadn't been very impressed. And that, she decided, was mortifying.

It wasn't her fault, was it? He had far more experience than she did. He'd probably slept with at least twenty women, maybe more, who knew what they were doing. She'd only slept with one other man, and it had been a disaster. She couldn't think about the god-awful experience without shuddering.

She didn't respond to Liam's question. She went into her bathroom, showered, and put on a short white sleeveless cotton nightgown that just reached her knees. Although it was a bit low-cut, she couldn't see through the material, and she thought it was modest enough. There was no way she was going to make herself vulnerable again. She hated feeling so awkward around him. She wanted to hide, so she opened her laptop and did exactly that.

Liam was on the phone for over an hour putting out one fire after another. By the time he finished work, he just wanted to crash. He opened the bedroom door and stood there, smiling at Allison. She was sitting propped up with pillows against the headboard. Her long, gorgeous legs were stretched out, and her computer sat open on her lap. Her head was dropped down, but he could see her eyes were closed. She looked as sweet and innocent as an angel.

He got ready for bed, and when he walked into the bedroom, she was in the same position. She hadn't moved all the while he'd been making a racket in the bathroom. He picked up the laptop and noticed what was on the screen. There were three names with a little information about each, and he could tell she had been doing a search for Bill's friends. He was surprised Bill had any friends at all.

He read the names again so he could check them out, then closed the laptop and put it on the dresser.

Allison was exhausted. There were deep circles under her eyes. And no wonder. She'd been putting in such long hours at the office with no end in sight. He pulled the covers back and tucked her in. She needed the rest. He didn't trust himself to sleep in her bed again, so he grabbed a pillow with the intent of sleeping on the sofa. He made it to the bedroom door before he stopped, turned around, and went back to the bed.

I've got to be out of my mind, he thought, being so close to her. After moving the covers out of the way, he stretched out as far away from her as possible. Fifteen minutes later, he was finally drifting off to sleep when Allison rolled over and snuggled up against him. Her warm body pressed to his was driving him crazy. He wanted nothing more than to have her wake up and reach for him, but that was being selfish. She was exhausted, he reminded himself. He was not going to have sex with her. He repeated the declaration a good five times to fortify his resolve, but it didn't make his struggle any easier.

Oh yeah, he was definitely out of his mind.

TWENTY

ALLISON HAD SEVERAL IDEAS WHERE BILL MIGHT BE HIDING. She remembered the names of a few of the low-life degenerates he had hung out with in high school. Three in particular stuck in her mind. They were always in trouble with the law. When they had been around, she had hidden in her room. She wasn't sure if Bill still kept in touch with any of them, but finding out was worth a try. They were all long shots. Getting Liam to cooperate without calling in the troops was going to be tricky.

Liam was carrying his gym bag to the door when she walked out of the bedroom. "Going somewhere?"

She was dressed for the day in a short skirt and a T-shirt with an image of Tweety Bird on the front. Liam had to take the time to appreciate her long legs and promptly lost his train of thought.

"What did you say?" He quickly recovered. "Yes, I have to leave. However, there will be—"

She interrupted. "How about you take me out to breakfast first?"

"I just ate breakfast."

"Okay, then how about taking a drive before you leave? It's a beautiful day."

He studied her. "Want to tell me what you're up to?"

"Nothing." She made the lie blacker by adding, "Honest."

Allison could see in his eyes that he knew she was lying. She smiled sweetly and said, "I'll be happy to drive."

"Does this drive have anything to do with your search on your laptop last night?"

She was shocked. "You looked at my screen? That's private . . . That's . . ." She stopped when she realized she was sputtering.

"Yes, I did look. The screen was open."

"Oh . . . okay, then. Should I drive or do you want to?"

"I'll drive. Will I need my gun on this scenic drive?"

"You always wear a gun. I'm assuming you'll do so today."

"Allison?"

"Yes?"

"Am I gonna have to shoot someone?"

"I hope not." She walked past him and reached for the door. "Are you coming with me?"

"Sure. I've got a little time before my replacement arrives."

"What replacement?"

"Another agent."

"Why do I need an agent?"

"To go over the rules," he explained patiently.

"What rules?"

He reached around her, pulled the door open, and waited for her to move. "Are we going or not?"

Frustrated, she put her hands on her hips and said, "What rules?"

"The rules in place until we catch Bill and know that Bale has come to his senses."

"Do you really think I'm in danger from either one of them?"

"Just follow the rules," he reiterated.

Allison figured she could go to Phillips for answers, but then realized that wouldn't get her anywhere. He liked to lecture and wasn't one to share information. Ever.

She followed Liam to the elevator. He was putting her in a mood, she decided. It was odd that he hadn't asked her where she wanted to go on their drive. She didn't think Liam liked surprises in his line of work.

She was right. Liam didn't like surprises, and he would have forced Allison to tell him exactly what her destination was if he didn't already know. She'd had three names on her computer screen, and he ran all of them. One had joined the army and was overseas—he'd obviously turned his life around before it spun out of control. The second was doing hard time for an armed robbery. And the third was living in LA with his sister and her husband. He was currently trying to get disability for a bogus back injury.

Allison used the map on her phone and gave directions. They stopped in front of a single-story dilapidated house with a battered and faded FOR SALE sign in the front yard. It was partially obscured by trash and weeds. The place looked deserted. Liam put the car in park and Allison stared past him, trying to see if there was movement in one of the windows.

"Liam, I have something to tell you, and I'd like you to try to be reasonable."

"Reasonable about what?"

She took a breath and, knowing he was about to be extremely unreasonable, said, "This is a house where one of Bill's friends lived. Bill could be inside."

Before she could explain her plan, he said, "He isn't. Agents checked for me. Went through the house, room by room. It's empty, and no one's been there for a long time. See? I can be reasonable." He smiled after making the statement of fact.

"How did you . . . ?"

"The names were on your screen, and I checked them out."

She shrugged. "It was a long shot. Bill knew them years ago when he was in high school. I remembered them because they were really mean, and they scared me. They were the kind of guys who would easily become violent."

"What were you hoping to accomplish here?"

"I thought one of them might be hiding Bill. If I can find him and get him to surrender peacefully, Phillips assured me the court would take that into consideration."

His patience was quickly vanishing. "Are you still hell-bent on helping him?"

"I don't want him to die in a hail of bullets."

"A hail of bullets? You watch too much television."

"If he has the opportunity to surrender, then that's what I'm hoping he'll want to do."

He looked at her for a long, silent moment and then said, "Do you know anywhere else he could be?"

"No," she said. She was emphatic. "And if I did know, I would tell you."

Convinced, he nodded. "Okay, then. Is our scenic drive over?"

"Yes." She thought he looked relieved. "I'm beginning to get the feeling you can't wait to get rid of me."

He laughed, but she noticed he didn't contradict her. They didn't talk much on the way back to her apartment, each lost in thought. She was dying to ask him where he was going or if he would be back, and her determination not to was making her crazy.

His farewell didn't warm her heart. He grabbed her, gave her a quick kiss, and said, "See you later."

She wanted to hit something. She finally understood what Liam had meant when he said frustration and pressure built up. Hitting was a good release, he'd told her. She was about to find out for herself.

She called Dan. An hour later she was being destroyed on a racquetball court at the gym. The only time she hit the ball was during practice before they started a game. Dan was proud—and loud—announcing to anyone who would listen that he had wiped the floor with her. He couldn't just say he'd won?

Even though she had been humiliated on the court with at least twenty men watching, after all was said and done, she did feel better. Liam had been right. Hitting something— or in her case, trying to hit something—helped get rid of tension and stress.

Dan, still gloating from his victory, walked her to her car. "Have you been aware of your surroundings?" he asked, now reverting to his brother mode.

"Yes," she answered.

"Then you know you're being followed?"

"Yes, I do know. He's an agent temporarily assigned to watch over me."

"Why?" he asked, his concern obvious.

She didn't want to go into a lengthy explanation about Bill or even the trouble over Bale's resentment, so she simply said, "I'm an asset as long as I work at the cyber unit."

He nodded, accepting her half-given explanation. "Where's the guy you're usually with?"

She shrugged. "I don't know."

"Are you going to see him again?"

"I don't know." She sounded disheartened and knew he noticed.

Dan opened her car door for her. "You fell for him, didn't you?" Her silence told him everything he needed to know. As pragmatic as ever, he said, "Maybe it's a good thing you're going to California pretty soon. A new start," he suggested. "I personally wish you weren't going, but I—"

She interrupted. "I'm not going. I want to start my company here in Boston. I can take on the Silicon boys from here." She smiled as she added, "And annihilate them."

Dan couldn't have been happier and wanted to celebrate. "What are you doing tonight?"

"I have absolutely nothing planned."

That wasn't exactly true. If she followed past Saturday and Sunday night rituals, she would have eaten a salad and worked on her laptop until the early hours of the morning. Six months ago that routine would have sounded pleasant to her, almost fun, but now she realized how dismal her life had been . . . and maybe still was. Everything had changed, she realized, when she met Liam. He had opened her eyes to the world around her. He'd also opened her heart, and she wasn't at all happy about that.

"I'll pick you up at seven, and we'll get a beer. Mark will probably come, too. Our womenfolk are out of town this weekend."

"'Womenfolk'?" she repeated, laughing.

"I've got a stack of mail for you. Mostly catalogs. I'll bring it all tonight."

She didn't want to go out. She wanted to stay home and wallow in misery. As soon as she realized that sad fact, she told Dan she was looking forward to going out.

"It'll be fun," she said cheerfully.

Her statement turned out to be true. She ended up spending the evening at the Dead End Bar and Grille with Dan and Mark and two other seniors she'd helped out a couple of times in their computer classes. She drank a little and laughed a lot.

Dan was the designated driver. He drove Allison home, handed her the mail he'd collected, and cuffed her shoulder as a sign of affection before she got out of the car. If she had any doubt that he considered her one of the guys, his good-bye clinched it.

TWENTY-ONE

THE DAY OF BRETT'S ARMAGEDDON FINALLY ARRIVED.

Monday morning Allison was happy to be back at the cyber unit. She was going to bury herself in work and then go to the Adams Harbor Hotel and bury Brett. She left work early and went home to change clothes. Black seemed to fit the occasion. She slipped into a pair of slim ankle pants, a black silk blouse, and a pair of black flats. She transferred a few of her things into a black cross-body bag and was ready to go.

She really didn't need to be there to watch Brett's downfall. The computer program would take care of that. She knew she wasn't being very charitable and would even say it was wrong to deliberately humiliate him. Maybe she was being vindictive, but after everything Brett had done, she wanted to watch him crash and burn. She could be contrite tomorrow . . . maybe even go to confession.

Someone was knocking on her door. She looked through the peephole and took a hasty step back. Liam was there . . . again. He had said he wanted to go to Brett's presentation, but she hadn't expected him to be in Boston. She opened the door and moved aside to let him in. She wanted to say hello, and she would do that just as soon as her brain started working again. She was so surprised, and yet so happy, to see him.

"Are you ready to go?" he asked.

"Go where?"

His smile widened. "The Adams Harbor Hotel."

"Yes, of course I'm ready. Don't I look ready? I think I look fine. Just fine," she rattled on.

He slowly looked her up and down. "You look a whole lot better than fine."

Great. Now he was giving her goose bumps. It was his voice. It had turned husky and very sexy.

As she brushed past him, Liam got a whiff of her perfume and whispered, "Ah, come on." Her scent was light and subtle, but to him it was an aphrodisiac that wreaked havoc with his vow to keep his distance . . . a vow he, thus far, hadn't been able to keep.

He couldn't get her out of his mind, and he knew both of them were getting in too deep. What he thought he wanted to be a casual affair had quickly turned into much, much more. Who was he kidding? It had never been casual, and he didn't know what he could do about it.

"I'm driving," she said.

"Okay, sure."

The moment Allison stepped out of the elevator in the garage, she understood why Liam had been so accommodating. His car was blocking hers. He opened the passenger door and waited. His grin was telling. He liked getting his way.

She slid into the seat. "Maybe you should drive," she suggested.

They made the short drive to the hotel. An hour ago Allison had been so sure of herself, but now her nerves began to surface and she questioned whether it was a good idea to confront Brett. She knew she had to stop him from selling her program, but there was no way to predict what the aftermath would be. Fortunately her feeling of self-doubt lasted only a minute, and then she got her gumption back. One look at Liam and she realized she was acting like a wuss. She didn't want him to watch her crumble, if in fact that was what she was going to do. It was time to take action. She was, as Jordan told her, now ready to kick some ass.

Feeling stronger and more determined than ever, she decided she should do this on her own. She didn't need anyone at her side.

"Why are you coming with me? You don't need to," she insisted.

"Yes, I do need to."

"Why?"

"I protect what belongs to me." It wasn't until the words were out of his mouth that Liam realized what he was saying, and he grimaced inside.

She nodded. "I understand. Because I'm the asset. Phillips keeps telling me that." She sighed. "He says I can be dangerous with a computer."

"Yeah, sure. You're the bureau's asset. That's why." The woman was clueless, and he was thankful for that. Otherwise, he'd have to explain what he'd meant, and he wasn't ready to do that. He didn't know his own mind anymore. He was thinking one thing and doing another. He couldn't stay away from her, and the thought of any other man touching her infuriated him. He wanted her to belong to him and only him. Liam knew he was acting like a caveman, but that didn't matter.

Damn, he really needed to get it together.

Allison leaned forward and took a good look at Liam's

face. "Are you all right? You're frowning. Are you worried about tonight? Do you think Brett will cause trouble? Do you—"

He stopped her before she could get more worked up. "It'll be fine."

"You can't possibly know that."

"Sure, I can," he replied. "Noah's meeting us at the hotel. He promised Jordan and Alec he'd see that there was a recording of the presentation so he could e-mail it to them. He's already checked with security to make sure their cameras are working. He even checked out the ballroom. It's not a real big space. A platform has been set up at the far end of the room and serves as a stage. A large screen covers the wall behind it, and there are folding chairs facing the platform with a podium in the center. Brett must have a little educational film for us to see on the screen."

"On what? How to steal and get away with it?" Her voice was filled with hostility.

"But he isn't going to get away with it, is he?"

He sounded a little too reasonable to suit Allison. "No, he isn't."

"And when you prove he's stolen your property, you aren't going to cheer or gloat, are you? At least not there."

"Oh, all right," she agreed grudgingly.

"No fighting, no tackling him to the floor, no biting . . ."

"I can't promise no tackling."

Liam flashed a smile. He couldn't imagine her hurting anyone. She was so soft and feminine. And gentle and kind. Too kind for her own good. The longer he'd known her, the more he'd learned about the little things she'd done to help others get through school. She was even trying to help that worthless cousin of hers. "Just behave yourself."

"My sister raised me to be a lady," she said.

"You had just started sixth grade when Charlotte left for college. You were on your own from then on, weren't you?"

She shrugged. "Lots of people are on their own."

"When they're twelve?"

"I'd rather not discuss my home life now." *Or ever,* she added silently.

He agreed with a nod. "Like I said, behave yourself tonight."

"What exactly do you think I'm going to do? Don't worry. I won't punch him in his phony tan face. I may want to, but I won't."

He laughed. "That's my girl."

He pulled into the hotel's circle drive and parked to the side. The attendant came running, but when Liam waved him off, he turned around and hurried to assist another driver.

"The ballrooms are on the lower level," Liam said as they stepped out of the revolving glass door and into the lobby.

"I know. I pulled up the schematic."

He wasn't surprised. Allison liked to be prepared. "You didn't hack into the hotel's private server, did you?"

"No, of course not. I didn't need to." She hastily added, "And I don't do that anymore."

Noah was waiting for them in a hallway off the lobby. His attire was casual. Nothing in his appearance said *FBI agent*. He smiled as they approached. "Are you ready for this?"

"She's ready," Liam said.

They turned and walked toward a service elevator. Allison led the way and the two men followed.

In a low voice Noah said to Liam, "I thought you were supposed to be on your way to San Antonio."

"I gave the assignment to someone else," Liam answered.

"How come?"

Liam didn't respond.

Allison pretended she wasn't listening to the conversation, but she wanted Liam to tell why he was still here. He didn't seem to have an answer for Noah. Would he get into trouble for turning down an assignment? Probably not, she decided. He was too important.

Noah pushed the button for the elevator. "They expect trouble," he told them. "There's a guard at the double doors. He doesn't work for the hotel. Brett must have hired him."

Allison was shocked, but Liam wasn't surprised. "There's a lot of money at stake."

"He's going to extremes," Allison said. "What must his guests think?"

"Brett's hoping they'll think he's important," Noah suggested.

"You can watch the presentation from the security room," Liam said to her.

She shook her head. "No, I want to walk into the ballroom. I want him to see me."

The doors opened and they stepped inside. Allison assumed they had agreed with her plan to confront Brett, and it wasn't until Noah pressed the UP button that she realized they were ignoring her wishes.

"The ballrooms are on the lower level," she reminded him.

"Security is just above reception," Noah explained. As they ascended, he remarked, "We have to be cautious. We don't yet know who's involved with his scheme. I understand your wanting to be there to stop him from profiting from your work—"

She interrupted. "Oh, he won't be successful."

"You said the program wasn't complete, but couldn't he have finished it on his own?" Liam asked.

"No," she replied. She thought for a second to come up with an analogy that was simple to understand. "Think of it like a giant jigsaw puzzle made up of thousands of tiny pieces," she said. "When you put the puzzle together you have a picture of a beautiful flower garden. Anyone who looks at it sees the entire picture, but you know one of the many pieces that make up a petal on a rose has no backing underneath it. Since you're the one who removed the backing, only you know where it is and how to replace it. Even if someone studies the puzzle with a magnifying glass, the garden will look complete and perfect, but that weak piece will disintegrate very quickly."

"Couldn't someone with enough time and knowledge figure out how to add what's missing?" Noah wondered.

She shook her head. "Not likely," she answered. "They won't be able to find it."

"Why not?"

"Because it isn't on the computer." She smiled and tapped her finger on her head. "It's here." The doors parted, and she stepped into the hallway. "Besides, it won't get to that point."

"How do you know?" Liam asked.

"Let's just say it's possible that my computer recently made a visit to his computer."

"How recently?" he asked as he followed close behind.

She shrugged and increased her pace.

"Then you did in fact hack into—," he began.

"You should have more faith in me. Don't you know me at all?"

Liam caught up with her at the door to the security room. "Yeah, that's the problem. I do know you."

Ordinarily guests wouldn't have access to the security center, but Noah had notified the manager. He hadn't asked for clearance. He'd simply told him they were coming.

Allison felt as though she had just walked into one of the rooms at the cyber unit. There were monitors along two walls with security personnel watching each area of the hotel.

"I want to confront Brett," she reiterated. "I want him to see me."

"That's not a good idea," Noah said.

Liam wasn't as diplomatic. "You're not going in there. Don't even think about it."

"I am thinking about it," she insisted.

She saw Noah smile, and that irritated her almost as much as Liam's high-handed tactics. Don't even think about it? She let Liam know she wasn't happy they were ignoring her plan. Her frown was hot enough to scorch him. He didn't seem bothered. He winked at her.

Standing between the two tall and powerful men, Allison had to concede she was grateful for their support. She had always thought of herself as someone who was strong and independent, who never relied on anyone else. Now, with Liam at her side, she understood how it felt to be protected. She had come to rely on him, and that was galling to admit. Very nice, though.

Noah pointed to two monitors that covered the small ballroom where Brett was to make his pitch. Allison moved closer to get a good look. The audience of twenty to thirty people sat in the folding chairs facing the stage as they waited for the presentation to begin. She recognized a few of them. They were millionaires and billionaires, yet no one would guess that fact based on their attire. Some were dressed in business suits, but the majority wore the uniform of most of the tech people she knew: jeans or khakis with T-shirts or sweaters. Several appeared to be acquainted and chatted amiably. At the side of the room a long table draped with a white tablecloth was loaded with a lavish spread of food on silver trays, everything from shrimp cocktail to caviar. Next to it stood a bartender behind a counter. He was ready to offer any drink the guests could want, but no one seemed interested. Allison noticed several of the guests glancing impatiently at their phones or watches as though there were more important uses of their time than listening to one more pie-in-the-sky dreamer who was convinced he had developed the next revolution for the computer world.

"Do you know any of them?" Noah asked.

"A few but just by reputation. I've never met any of them."

The side door to the meeting room opened, and in walked Brett. He was followed by a man who scanned the crowd as he took a step up on the platform and stood next to Brett. The man was older than Brett by about twenty years and heavier by thirty pounds. He wore a tailored black suit and a crisp white shirt with cuff links. His power red tie said he expected to be taken seriously. His hair was dark and thick and he wore it short, spiked up with hair gel. When he folded his arms, one couldn't help noticing the huge ring, set with a cluster of diamonds, and the large gold Rolex watch. The message was clear. He had money, and he wanted everyone to know it.

Brett didn't need a microphone, but he used one anyway.

"Most of you know me or have heard of me. For those who haven't, my name is Brett Keaton, and standing next to me is Fred Stiles. Once I finished the design for this software, I took it to him and he immediately got on board. He'll take care of the financial on the sale. Whoever buys this is going to set the world on fire."

Liam continued to watch the screen, and then he said, "I'm going to run his name."

"I'll do it," Noah said. "I've got a feeling we aren't going to like what we find."

As it turned out, he was right. One phone call was all it took to know that Fred Stiles was a sleazebag. He had been involved in one shady deal after another. He'd made a lot of money fleecing the unsuspecting. Like a shark who smelled blood in the water, Stiles could sense vulnerability. He'd sweep into a distressed company, drain it of every dollar, then walk away. And all of it was legal. There had been countless complaints filed against him, but nothing ever stuck.

"Sounds like a real nice guy," Liam commented.

"That's not all," Noah said. "He's been investigated several times for his connection to organized crime. They haven't been able to pin anything on him yet, but they're pretty sure he had something to do with a couple of mob executions." After giving his report on Stiles, Noah added, "He's evidently got quite a temper."

"I'd sure love to help him lose it," Liam said.

Allison's eyes narrowed on the jerk who had stolen her work and was now bragging about it. When Liam took hold of one of her hands, she thought he was offering her comfort and appreciated the gesture, until it dawned on her that he was holding on to her in case she tried to bolt.

The lights behind the podium dimmed as Brett continued to boast. "My software will take care of every security threat out there and some you may not even know about yet. No longer will you have to update your firewalls or your antivirus and antispyware software. Identities and passwords will be protected from hackers like never before." He picked up a remote control from the podium and turned to the screen. "Now I'll give you a peek at the product and then answer your questions."

He pushed a button, and a video appeared on the screen. Earth as seen from outer space came into view, and the shot grew closer and closer until it settled on a busy urban street with cars and people rushing about helter-skelter. An unseen announcer with a deep baritone voice said, "The world is a hectic place, and the speed at which it's changing is increasing exponentially. Information is king. Protecting that information, whether it be personal or business, has become one of the major challenges of our lifetime." The voice continued, and after a few of the security problems of the digital world were described, Brett paused the video and turned to his audience. With a self-assured and rather arrogant air, he said, "I now introduce you to the solution for every security problem you will ever face."

Some of Brett's guests leaned forward with interest. Others looked at the screen with obvious skepticism.

Brett pushed the button again. The screen came to life and what appeared to be the name of the software material- ized in letters too small to read. As they moved forward, they became bigger. When the word was almost legible, the video suddenly stopped. The screen went blank. Brett pushed the button again, and then again. Nothing happened. He glanced around at the faces staring up at him and could feel the perspiration on his hands. He turned back to the screen and gave the button another stab. This time the video started again, but it wasn't exactly what Brett was expecting.

In big bold letters a message scrolled down the screen: Brett Keaton, did you really think you could steal my work and get away with it? For those of you watching, my name is Allison Trent, and I'm the creator of this program. There's a vital piece missing, but Brett isn't smart enough to know it. You're a thief, Brett, a thief and a liar and a cheat.

While the audience watched, the words on the screen and the program began to disintegrate and fade away. Now only four words appeared: Brett is a thief.

At first, the audience was stunned, and then there was a mixture of reactions. Some laughed because it was all so absurd. Some were angry because their time had been wasted. And all were united in their disgust with Brett Keaton, even letting it spill over to his associate, Fred Stiles, who also looked furious.

"Man, oh man," Noah said, and began to laugh. "Look at Brett. His face is bloodred. What's he doing?"

"He's trying to stop the message," Liam guessed.

"He can't stop it," Allison said. On the surface she was as calm and cool as a summer breeze, but inside she was boiling. She tried to pull away from Liam, determined to give Brett a piece of her mind, but he held tight. She wasn't going anywhere until he let her.

Brett's audience couldn't get out of there fast enough.

"She's lying," Brett shouted. "She's a jealous bitch and she's lying. Wait. Let me explain. She must have hacked into my program. . . . Wait. . . ." To say that Brett was frantic was an understatement.

His partner didn't move at all until he and Brett were alone in the room. Then he attacked. He grabbed Brett by his shoulders and shook him. "You told me she wouldn't make trouble," he screamed.

"She . . . she can't," he stammered. "I made sure the program was finished before I took it. It wasn't copyrighted yet. I never saw her show it to anybody." He was panicked, and as Stiles tightened his grip, he rushed on. "She wasn't supposed to find out until it was too late. Once we sold the program, we could keep it out of court for years while she fought us. Even then it would be impossible for her to prove. And she doesn't have the money for a legal fight." He took a deep breath and added, "She's going to be sorry she did this to me."

"To us," Stiles said as he loosened his hold and gave Brett a shove away from him. "I want to know if you think she was telling the truth. Is there a missing part?"

Brett didn't have to think about it long. "Yes, I believe her."

"Why didn't you know that? You did look at the software, didn't you?"

"Yes, of course I did. I tested it over and over again, and it looked complete."

"You should have known," Stiles muttered. "We have to get the missing part. It has to be buried somewhere in her computer. There's too much money involved to let this go. We've got to get it," he repeated. "No matter what it takes."

Brett was still irate, but there was a tinge of self-pity in his voice when he said, "She ruined my reputation. I was humiliated and embarrassed."

Stiles agreed. "She shouldn't be able to get away with this."

"No, she shouldn't."

The two men continued to talk as they walked out of the room together.

"I'm guessing they forgot the mikes were still on," Noah suggested.

"Or they didn't care," Liam said.

"In their minds I've become the villain. Brett steals my work and then blames me when I ruin his plans? He's beyond contemptible," Allison railed.

"What do you want to do about this?" Noah directed his question to Liam.

"Excuse me." Allison finally got her hand away from Liam's and stepped back. "I'll decide what's to be done. This is my problem, not yours."

"Ordinarily I would agree with you." Liam told the lie without cracking a smile. "But you're Phillips's asset, so he has to know about this and handle it. I will, of course, offer to help."

Hands on her hips, Allison responded, "How come I'm your asset when it's convenient for you and Phillips's asset when it isn't?"

"It's a quandary," Liam answered.

"I'd call it a dilemma," Noah remarked.

"They're pretty much the same thing," Liam said.

"Yeah, I guess you're right."

They were having a fine time teasing her. "Know what I think?" she asked.

"That you should let us do our jobs?" Liam asked. He evaded an argument by placing his hands on her shoulders and turning her toward the door. She was as stiff as starch.

"I'm still going to tell you what I think whenever I want to," she grumbled.

He smiled. "I figured you would."

When they reached the main floor, Noah said his good-byes and left. Allison and Liam continued to walk across the lobby. When they reached the entrance, Allison suddenly stopped. "Is that Brett waiting for his car? It is, isn't it? If you'll excuse me, I'm going to have a few words with him." Her voice was shaking when she got the last sentence out.

Liam grabbed her arm before she could take off. Exasperated, he said, "Didn't we decide that was a bad idea?"

"No, you and Noah decided it was a bad idea. I didn't."

There was a small alcove near the bell captain's desk, and without any explanation, Liam pulled her toward it and told her to stay put.

"What do you mean, 'stay put'? And will you stop dragging me around!" She was about to go into a full-blown lecture on the merits of good manners and suggest he might want to get some until she noticed he wasn't paying any attention to her. Standing directly in front of her, he was looking across the lobby as he unbuttoned his jacket and unsnapped the leather holster securing his gun.

Liam knew Brett hadn't seen them, but Fred Stiles and the guard hired to protect the door from unwanted guests during their presentation had seen them. They were coming at them, and coming fast. The thick-shouldered guard with squinty eyes reached them first. Standing just a foot away, he looked up at Liam and said, "You don't intimidate me. Get out of my way. I want to talk to that bitch hiding behind you."

Liam didn't move. In a voice Allison had never heard before, he said, "Get the hell out of here."

"That troublemaker cost me a lot of money tonight. I was supposed to get a bonus if everything went smooth. She's the reason it all fell apart, so she owes me." He tried to push Liam out of his way, but Liam didn't budge. Then the man tried to shove him in his chest next. Liam had had enough of pretending to be a nice guy. He grabbed the man's hand and twisted his fingers back as he turned him and half lifted him, slamming him into the wall.

Stiles looked appalled by the guard's behavior. Liam knew his outrage was all a pretense.

People coming and going through the doors of the hotel didn't notice the guard, who had dropped to the floor inside the alcove. When he slowly sat up and rubbed the side of his head, he looked dazed.

Allison was amazed by Liam's strength. She knew he was muscular. She should have known, for she had kissed and caressed every part of him. Still, to twist a man's fingers, lift him, and slam his head into the wall took remarkable strength. And a temper. She was shocked by that revelation. Liam had always been so calm and easygoing with everyone . . . until now.

Unfortunately, the confrontation didn't end with the guard. Stiles tried to walk around Liam to get to Allison, but Liam wasn't about to let that happen, either. He quickly blocked Stiles.

"I want to talk to her," Stiles protested.

"No," Liam said. "Now get out of here."

"I guess I'll have to get my attorneys involved, then," he

threatened, glaring at her before abruptly turning and storming away. The guard, finally regaining his feet, staggered behind him.

Allison had been silent long enough. "I'd love it if you did," she called after them.

She'd sounded so thrilled by the possibility Liam laughed. It took all the discipline he possessed not to pull her into his arms and kiss her the way he'd been thinking about all day. It suddenly occurred to him he'd been fighting an impossible war. He couldn't stay away from her. Then again, he didn't want to.

"Are you ready to get out of here?" His voice was gruff.

Allison waited until they were back in her apartment to lecture him. "You didn't need to use such force with that guard. You could have—"

He cut her off. "He called you a bitch. I didn't like it."

"You can't go around slamming heads into walls just because you don't like the names they call me."

"Apparently, I can," he replied. "Because I just did."

She kicked off her shoes and picked them up. She stopped at her bedroom door and turned. Frowning, she asked, "Is this a pattern? Do you punch all men who insult your assets?"

"No, just the ones who insult you."

She opened her mouth to say something, then closed it. He was walking toward the door, and she couldn't let him leave without answering a question for her. She'd wanted to ask him for days and so far hadn't been able to get up the courage. Now or never, she thought.

"Liam, wait. I want to ask you something, and I want you to be completely honest with me. I need to know . . . if this makes you uncomfortable . . ." Her voice was whisper soft and apologetic.

He couldn't imagine what was going on inside that brilliant but decidedly confused mind of hers. He had a feeling he wasn't going to like the question and told himself that, no matter what she asked, he would not get angry. Unless, of course, she wanted another favor for Bill. Then he'd probably end up yelling at her.

Bracing himself, he said, "Go ahead and ask."

"Do you think I'm sexy?"

"Do I . . . what?"

"Do you think I'm sexy?"

To say he was taken by surprise was an understatement. Had she not looked so serious, he would have laughed.

Allison waited. Liam stood there a full minute without saying a word. Was he trying to think of something diplomatic to say that wouldn't hurt her feelings? She felt so foolish then and wished she hadn't asked. Then he removed his jacket and loosened his tie as he walked over to her with that slow, easy smile of his.

"Yeah, I find you sexy."

Liam pulled her to him, stared into her eyes, and waited. She dropped her shoes, and the second her arms went around his neck, his mouth covered hers. All he had to do was touch her, and his entire body reacted. How could she not know that? No woman had ever made him burn with desire the way Allison did. Every time she looked at him he wanted to take her into his arms. He wanted to cover her with his body and make love to her. He wanted to be inside her. He wanted to hear the sexy sounds she made, to feel her nails digging into his shoulders, to wrap himself in her warmth and her feminine scent. To be overwhelmed by her.

He backed away long enough to ask, "Do you . . ."

"Yes," she whispered. There was no playing hard to get, no hesitation. "Assuming you want to take me to bed."

"Yes." He kissed her again. Her lips were so soft. He loved the way she gave herself so freely. He loved the low purr she made in the back of her throat when she was aroused. Hell, there wasn't anything he didn't love about her.

He led her to the bedroom, leaving a trail of their clothes on the floor, and they fell onto the bed, wrapped up in each other. He couldn't slow down. She didn't want him to. He was mindless to everything but finding a release from the tension building for both of them. It seemed to him they became one then. She arched against him, cried out his name, and tightened around him, her grip strong on his shoulders.

"Let go," he whispered. "I've got you."

When the intensity of their lovemaking was over, Liam rolled onto his back and closed his eyes, exhausted. He didn't want to think about the complications. He tried to sleep, but there was a war raging inside him. His conscience was on the offensive, and it was time he came to grips with what he was doing here. His actions in the last couple of months had been impulsive and definitely out of character for him. He was accustomed to a life on the move, never getting too close to anyone or setting down roots. That was what he had signed up for. Lately, however, something had changed. He'd rearranged some assignments just so he could return to Boston. He'd told himself he needed to stay close to Allison because there were threats against her, and he felt responsible. At one point he'd even been on his way to the airport and turned around so that he could make sure she was okay. And every time he was near her, he couldn't seem to control himself. Granted, she had been a willing partner and had agreed there were no commitments or expectations. The sex had been amazing, but was that all it was? Sex? At some point he would have to face reality and get back to his job and his life on the move. What would happen then?

Since he had met her, he hadn't wanted any other

woman. He'd had the opportunity, just not the desire. He only wanted Allison. He knew exactly when she had gotten to him, too. She had been staring at him while she timidly confessed stealing all that money from hackers, and there was something in her eyes that had captivated him. She was vulnerable, yes, but also gutsy. There was no denying her courage. Even more important, underneath the audacity was a kind heart and a sense of fairness. He'd never met anyone like her.

He just wanted to be with her. No, that wasn't exactly true. He needed to be with her. The truth he had been afraid to admit couldn't be avoided anymore. Damn if he hadn't fallen in love with the woman.

TWENTY-TWO

HE DID IT AGAIN. ALLISON WAS JUST DRIFTING OFF TO SLEEP when Liam leaned over her, kissed her on her forehead, and left. He didn't even say, "See you later," this time.

She should have been angry or at the very least frustrated, but she wasn't. She was beginning to take it all in stride, which, all things considered, was extremely odd. And since she hadn't told Jordan or anyone else that she was in love with Liam, she couldn't complain about his bizarre behavior.

Bill inadvertently took her mind off Liam by scaring the bejesus out of her. She took the morning off and didn't even get dressed until eleven. She had a blistering headache and needed to buy some ibuprofen. The pharmacy was just three blocks away, two if she cut through an alley, and since it was a beautiful day, she decided to walk. The rule was that she could drive to and from work or anywhere else, for that matter, but she wasn't supposed to walk anywhere alone. She assumed the reason was that Bale had not calmed down, yet when she put the question to Phillips, he didn't confirm or deny. He simply told her she could walk anywhere she wanted as long as she had people with her. She had complied with his wishes up to now. Today she figured a quick trip to the pharmacy wasn't a big deal, especially if no one found out.

She had just reached the alley between two buildings when she noticed a man hurrying toward her. His head was down and he was wearing a baseball cap low on his forehead. Even before he reached her, she knew it was Bill.

He grabbed her arm. "It's me, Bill. Don't be afraid. I need to talk to you."

She tugged her arm free. "Have you been out here waiting for me?"

"No, I was on my way to your garage. I was going to wait until you came down. Then I saw you on the sidewalk and I . . . Let's go in the alley and talk."

She declined and told him they would talk right where they were standing. He looked around. The street was all but deserted.

"My attorney told me you got me probation, that you made some kind of deal with the prosecutor? Is that true?"

She was furious. No one was supposed to know about her part in his release. "How did your attorney find out?"

"I don't know. Is it true?" he repeated. "Did you do that for me?"

No reason to deny it now. "Yes."

He sounded desperate when he asked, "Can you get me out of this?" He grabbed her arm again and pleaded. "You have to get me out of this."

Allison inhaled sharply. Not because Bill had hold of her arm, but because she glanced over his shoulder and saw Liam walking toward them. He wasn't wearing a suit jacket, and his hand was on the butt of his gun. He looked as though he wanted to kill someone. Where in God's name

had he come from this time? The street had been empty just
seconds ago, and all of a sudden there he was. If she looked
away, she half expected him to vanish again.

In a rush, she whispered, "Bill, do you have any weapons on you? Like a gun or a knife?"

"No. Why would I?"

She put her hand up as a signal for Liam to stay back,
which he completely ignored. When he was just a couple
of feet behind Bill, he stopped. He was so close she was surprised Bill couldn't feel Liam's breath on the back of his neck.

"Bill, listen to me," she said. "You have to surrender right
now. Surrender to me," she blurted, and even after she said
it, she knew it didn't make any sense. "Okay? If you turn
yourself in, maybe that will count in court and you won't
have to face a longer sentence. Please. Do the right thing,
and I'll help you."

Bill wasn't listening to reason. "Maybe I could get to
Canada and hide there," he said. "No one would ever—"

She stopped him. "You can't hide forever. I don't want to
see you in prison for the rest of your life or, worse, gunned
down."

"You're so naive, Allison," he scoffed. "To you the world
is rosy, and people like me can get a fair shake. You think
all I have to do is walk up to some cop and surrender and
everything will be okay."

"You have to surrender, Bill."

Antagonistic now, he said, "What happens if I don't?"

"Then the FBI agent behind you is going to slam you up
against the building, handcuff you, and take you in. Please.
I don't want you to get hurt."

Bill's head snapped around. Liam was standing there
with his hand on his gun. Like a caged animal, Bill turned
in all directions, trying to find an escape.

"Don't even think about running," Liam warned.

Bill's shoulders slouched. Realizing there wasn't any way out, he gave a long, defeated sigh, as though all the fight that was in him was being expelled at that very moment. His voice sullen now, he said, "I surrender."

Liam quickly patted him down to make certain there weren't any weapons on him while he called the police to come pick him up. Within seconds they heard the sirens approaching from a few blocks away.

Bill turned to Allison and started to beg. "Allison, please, you have to—"

Liam wouldn't let him continue. "Stop right there. Do you have any idea how much your cousin has done for you? The lengths she has gone to?"

When Bill turned once again in her direction, Liam snapped, "Keep your arms folded in front of you and look only at me." Bill complied immediately, and Liam continued. "Now you're going to do your part. It's time you take responsibility."

Allison watched silently as Liam continued to give Bill a piece of his mind, letting him know how furious he was for the way Bill had treated her. By the time the police car pulled up and two officers got out, Bill was cowering and seemed about to cry. She knew she shouldn't interfere, but she couldn't stop herself. She called to the officers, "Bill surrendered to Special Agent Scott, and you can see he's cooperating."

Liam gave her a look that suggested she not say another word. He didn't contradict her, though, and she took that as a win.

"Will you go with me?" Bill asked her. He was practically shaking with fear now.

Liam didn't give her time to answer. "No," he said emphatically. Turning to the policemen, he showed his identification and ordered, "Cuff him. Then read him his rights and get him in the car."

"Yes, sir," both officers said at the same time.

As they led Bill away, one of them turned back and asked, "Anything else we can do?"

Liam nodded. "Keep him in holding awhile. I might have some questions for him."

Bill looked terrified at the prospect of being interrogated by Liam, and as the officers put him in the back of the squad car, he once again looked back at Allison with pleading eyes.

She watched the car drive away before she turned to Liam. He was frowning, which didn't surprise her. She tried to deflect his anger before he started lecturing her.

"Thank you," she said.

"Thank you for what?"

"Not putting handcuffs on him."

"Allison, I don't have any handcuffs with me, and that is why I didn't put them on him."

"You could have just said, 'You're welcome.'" Before he could give her an argument, she asked, "What are you doing here? And how did you know Bill would be here?"

"I didn't. That's my car parked across the street. I was on my way to pick you up when I noticed you walking. Understand me, Allison. You are not going to help Bill." He took her arm and headed to his car. She was all but running to keep up with him.

"Why are you in such a hurry?"

"There's a problem at work, and Phillips hopes you can solve it. I offered to pick you up and drive you out there. He'll have someone bring you home."

"When isn't there a problem?"

"You don't sound too upset about it."

She smiled. "I'm not. I like problems. That's why I hang out with you."

He caught himself before he smiled back. "We're going

to talk about Bill. I want you to promise me—and I mean it, damn it—you will not help him."

"I feel sorry for him," she admitted.

"Tell you what. Let's drive over to the hospital. The man Bill almost beat to death is still in the ICU. You can take a good look at him and then tell me you feel sorry for Bill."

"I understand, and you're right. I can't help him anymore. He's got to be accountable."

"Oh," he said, surprised that she was conceding so easily. "Okay, then."

"Are you disappointed you can't scold me anymore?" she asked as sweetly as she could.

"I never scold people." He paused to think about it and admitted, "Okay, maybe you, but no one else."

When they reached the cyber unit, Liam walked her into the building and stopped at the front desk to say good-bye.

"Where are you off to now?" she asked.

"Berlin."

A bomb had gone off in a shopping center in Berlin the day before. Several Americans had been killed in the blast. It was all over the news. Was that why he was going? Knowing his answer would be evasive, she didn't ask. She handed the guard her purse and headed to the stairs. When she glanced back over her shoulder, Liam was standing in the same spot, watching her walk away.

"Be safe," she said.

TWO AGENTS FROM THE UNIT DROVE HER HOME. ALLISON AS- sumed she wouldn't be seeing Liam for some time if, in fact, he did fly to Berlin. Then again, he could drop out of the sky and land in front of her at any second. She wouldn't have put it past him. With Liam anything was possible.

Bill made the news for having surrendered to the authorities. He couldn't hurt anyone now, and as much as she hated to admit it, he did deserve to be behind bars. She didn't think he would ever get rid of his temper, though. She said a prayer for him and stopped worrying.

Except for the daily scream call from Aunt Jane, Allison could finally relax, which she planned to do just as soon as she figured out how. She went back to working out twice a week, sometimes more often, not because she wanted to stay in shape but because it made her feel better. She had dinner with Jordan and Noah a couple of times. Jordan couldn't stop talking about Brett's presentation, and each time she brought it up, she laughed about the pompous egotism it took for Brett to think he could get away with such a scheme.

Besides her workouts, Allison also played racquetball with Dan and his girlfriend, Margo, a few times. She thought she was getting better. Neither Dan nor Margo agreed, though Margo was more diplomatic. Dan just laughed and shook his head. Over beers late one night he told Allison the latest gossip about Brett. Rumor had it that everyone in Silicon Valley and beyond had heard what he'd done. Even though he was holding on to his story about the computer program being his and blaming Allison for the underhanded "trick" she had played to destroy him and all his hard work, no one believed him. Still, he wasn't going away quietly. Somehow he had gotten it into his head that he had enough of the program in his possession, and he could find a buyer. With each attempt that crashed and burned, he became more and more incensed. He'd gotten hold of her phone number and called several times just to let her know how much he hated her. If he had planned to scare her, he failed. Brett was a blowhard and so inconsequential she didn't mention his drunken calls to anyone but Jordan.

Two full weeks passed and not a word from Liam. No surprise there. She was trying to accept the possibility that she might never see him again. It wasn't as if he had deceived her. He'd been real up front about their relationship. Sex and only sex. No tender words of love. She didn't want to cry over him or sink to self-pity. No, she was more in the mood to give him a good smack. It wasn't a very ladylike thing to do, and she would never give in to the urge, but she certainly was tempted.

It was time to get the upper hand in this nonrelationship. She was determined that, if she saw Liam again, she would tell him she didn't want him in her life. No more mind-blowing sex and then taking off. She'd better tell him over the phone, she decided, because she knew the minute she saw him her best intentions would go flying out the window and she'd want to tear his clothes off and attack him.

It didn't matter that she loved him or that he might feel something more than just affection for the woman he occasionally had sex with. He might even love her a little, but that didn't matter, either, because he would never do anything about it. His job came above all else. She saw how it was draining him. No one could keep up the frantic pace without paying a price. The stress alone would kill an ordinary man, and contrary to what he might believe, he wasn't superhuman.

Not so long ago she would have believed that spending time coding was all she ever wanted or needed. Not any longer, though. She wanted it all. She wanted marriage and eventually babies to love and cherish. She accepted there wasn't any future with Liam. Now all she had to do was find the courage to move on without him.

TWENTY-THREE

THE DOORBELL RANG IN EMERSON, AND AUNT JANE OPENED it to find a young man standing there with a large envelope in his hand.

"Jane Trent?" he asked.

"Yes," she answered cautiously.

He handed the envelope to her. "Have a nice day," he said as he turned and headed back to his car.

Uncle Russell walked into the front hall. "What is that?" he asked, ripping the envelope out of her hands. He tore the envelope open, pulled out a letter, and read silently.

"Well?" she barked.

"Those ungrateful . . ." Beads of perspiration formed on his forehead. "It says here we have thirty days to account for the money we spent on the girls or give it back."

Jane slumped into a nearby chair. "They found out."

TWENTY-FOUR

WORK HELPED ALLISON TAKE HER MIND OFF HER PERSONAL problems. On one of her more challenging days, she had a particularly difficult puzzle to solve, and she enjoyed every frustrating minute of it. Once she finally found the source she was looking for, she sent it on to Phillips with her report and sat back to enjoy her accomplishment. There was such satisfaction and contentment to be had after a hard day's work. As astonishing as it was to admit, she really loved this job. She had even softened in her attitude toward Phillips.

She finished work at five thirty, then went to a yoga class, and didn't leave the gym until eight. Traffic was a mess as usual. She parked in her spot in the garage and was walking to the elevator with her backpack slung over her shoulder when she noticed the camera that faced the entrance was broken. It was hanging by a couple of wires. She made a mental note to tell the super and went on upstairs.

Stamos was waiting outside her door with a policeman. The doorman was fretting while the policeman was filling out a report.

"What's going on?" she asked.

Stamos rushed to explain. "Someone broke into your apartment."

Officer Jay Watts asked Allison to walk through each room and let him know what, if anything, was missing.

Allison was shocked when she entered the apartment. The living room had been ransacked, and the desk drawers had been dumped on the floor. Drawers in the bedroom were also open and the contents spilled on the floor.

"If you have any valuables, you might want to check and see if they're here," Officer Watts said.

The only thing of value that Allison could think of was her laptop and the program she had been working on. Her computer was still in the bag she was carrying, so it was safe. She rushed to her closet to check the cubby where she hid her backup drive. It was exactly where she'd left it. Her clothes and shoes didn't appear to have been disturbed.

"I told Officer Watts it was those people who did this," Stamos told her when she returned to the living room. "Your aunt and uncle. I knew they were trouble the second I saw how they treated their Chrysler. They were here causing another fit downstairs. I had to let them in the lobby because the woman was banging on the glass, and I was worried she was going to break it. I had to help 3A with her packages, but I made sure those relatives of yours had left the premises before I got on the elevator. I'm betting they came back in with another tenant and went on up. I'm sure it was them who did this," he insisted to the officer.

"If it was your relatives, what were they looking for?" the officer asked Allison.

"Money," she answered, "or uncashed checks. That's all they would be interested in."

Officer Watts finished making notes and then said he would inspect the building for any other break-ins. He'd get back to her if he needed any other information.

Before Stamos left he told her the manager had been alerted and promised the damaged lock on her door would be replaced within the hour.

Allison needed a shower, but she wasn't going to take one until she had a new lock. While she waited she heated a frozen Hungry-Man dinner and ate a banana and blueberries. An hour later the lock had been repaired, and she was showered and dressed. She was ready to curl up on her sofa and read her e-mails.

Unfortunately, she didn't have time to relax because she got another dreaded call from the unit. This time one of the assistants called and insisted the matter was urgent, but then it always was, wasn't it? She was also told it wouldn't take long, which made her laugh. Her laptop and purse went into her backpack, phone and keys in her hand, and she was on her way. She had just pulled onto the highway when a car came barreling up behind her. Had she not floored the engine and gotten out of his way, he would have rear-ended her. Traffic was congested as usual, and it wasn't until she turned onto another highway that she noticed the car again. She couldn't tell what the make or model was. It looked like a dark-colored SUV with tinted windows. The highway was four lanes, and there was plenty of room for him, but she still moved to the far lane to get away from him. She glanced in the rearview mirror several times and couldn't see him and assumed he had sped on.

Suddenly he was there, right behind her, riding her bumper, and as she was turning onto the exit ramp, he tapped the side of her car. She barely had time to react before he hit her again, harder this time. Why was this happening? Was it road rage? And, if so, how had she incited the driver? As she swerved to avoid a third hit, her phone flew across the car seat. She grabbed it and pushed speed dial to get Phillips. Careering on two wheels, her car turned onto the gravel road leading to the cyber unit. The crazy car was still right behind her.

Phillips answered on the first ring, and she could tell from the echo he had it on speaker. He sounded as impatient as ever.

"It's Allison. I need help. Someone's trying to run me off the road. He's hit me twice . . . no, three times now."

"Where are you?" Liam asked the question.

She was so shocked to hear his voice, she didn't answer.

"Where are you?" he demanded again.

"About a mile and a half out. I just turned onto the gravel road." It was the perfect place for a carjacking, scrub trees on both sides of the road, not a house in sight. She was all alone. "Oh God, here he comes again."

"Try to stay ahead of him," Phillips said.

"Liam . . ."

"He's on his way to you," Phillips told her. "Keep your head low. Don't be a target. Help is coming." His voice was calming, and that freaked her out almost as much as being hit.

Don't be a target? Did he think the maniac driver might have a gun? She didn't have a chance to ask him what he meant. She got hit again, and this time it was spot-on. The angle was perfect. She lost control of her car and started spinning around and around. She couldn't get the car to stop and made the mistake of hitting the brakes hard. That error sent her flying down a hill. The dead bushes didn't impede her fall. The fat tree stump did. It was only a couple of feet high, but the car hit it full on and flipped over again and again. She felt as though she were in a barrel, rolling down a hill. Her backpack landed on her chest just a second before her airbag deployed. It took most of the impact and protected her.

She became a firm believer in miracles at that very moment. The car landed upright. Both sides were caved in; glass from the shattered windshield was all over the bucket seats; the tires were blown . . . and she didn't have a scratch on her. Her laptop had fallen out of the bag and, crushed by the imploding car door, lay in pieces on the floor. She thought she might be dead and just didn't know it yet. She whispered a prayer and tried to calm her racing heartbeat. She realized then she was perfectly fine except for one little thing. She couldn't seem to let go of the steering wheel.

When she looked up through the broken windshield, she could see headlights on the hill. They quickly retreated and she could hear the car zoom away. The sky went black, and it was eerily quiet. Then suddenly there were spotlights shining down on her. She heard Liam calling her name. He sounded frantic. If she hadn't heard his voice, she would have panicked. She was already thinking about the gas tank blowing up. That usually happened in movies with car chases, didn't it? Of course the driver was usually killed, and here she sat, as fit as ever.

The seat belt was jammed, and the window wouldn't open, but Liam got her out. He had to break the side glass and cut the belt. He also had to peel her hands away from the steering wheel. His expression was grim, and yet he was being so gentle with her as he lifted her through the window. Phillips was there, too, and he looked almost as worried as Liam. How had they gotten there so fast?

Liam didn't let go of her. He held her tight against him. She could feel him shaking when he asked, "Are you all right? Are you bleeding anywhere?"

"I'm fine," she said, surprised she could raise her voice to little more than a whisper.

"Whoever did this to you . . ."

Hoping to calm him, she motioned for him to put her down. She brushed herself off and said, "All right, then. I'm going to need a ride."

Phillips actually smiled, a first for him, but Liam still looked as though he wanted to go to war. He wrapped his arm around her shoulders for support and said, "You're going to the hospital. You could have internal bleeding . . . a brain injury . . . or a—"

"I am not going to the hospital," she argued. "I didn't hit my head, and my backpack protected me from the airbag." It wasn't until she got a good look at her car that she started shaking. Then she spotted the remains of her laptop. "My computer . . . ," she began.

"We'll take care of that for you," Phillips assured her.

It really was a miracle she survived without a single injury. "I'm fine, Liam," she protested. "And I most assuredly am not bleeding internally."

"Unless you have X-ray vision, you can't know if you're bleeding or not."

She was going to have to put her foot down. "I'm not going to the hospital. Understand?"

He took her to the hospital. All of her protests were completely ignored, and that didn't surprise her. He never listened to her. She told him just that as the nurse was pushing her into a wheelchair in the emergency room. She was poked and prodded, x-rayed and scanned, and finally declared perfectly fit. The physician in charge lingered by the side of her bed after giving her the good news.

"Was there something more?" Allison asked. "Have you thought of yet another test you'd like to run?"

He smiled. "No, you're good to go. I was just thinking . . ."

"Yes?" she asked, wondering why he was hesitating.

"Would you like to go out with me sometime?" He handed

her a card with his cell phone number on it. "Call me. Anytime."

She didn't know what to say. She took the card, thanked him for taking care of her, and decided to get Liam out of there as quickly as possible. He was staring at the doctor and looking quite incredulous.

"I'm standing right here," he announced with a good deal of irritation as the doctor walked out of the cubicle.

"He saw you, Agent Scott," Allison said.

Liam sat on the side of the bed and draped his arm around her to pull her toward him. Had the doctor still been there, he would have kissed Allison, just to let him know she wasn't available.

He guessed he should let Allison know it first. "We need to talk," he said.

"When did you get back from Berlin?" she asked at the very same time.

He didn't answer, because the nurse came to discharge her at that moment. Allison insisted that he take her to the office. She knew Phillips would have a hundred questions and she wanted to get the interrogation over as quickly as possible. She waited until they were alone and sitting in Phillips's office to ask Liam what he had wanted to talk about.

"You and me," he said.

She shook her head. "No, we aren't. There is no you and me. We're in a nonrelationship, and that's over."

He leaned against the desk and smiled. "If we're in a nonrelationship, how can it be over?"

He *would* use logic. She shrugged. "I don't know. It just is." She sat down. "I'm through talking about this."

"I'm not."

Phillips entered the office and interrupted. She braced herself for the inquisition.

"How are you feeling?" he asked.

She was shocked by the sympathy she heard in his voice. She didn't want him to be kind to her. She liked him just the way he usually was. Maybe she had hit her head after all, because she wasn't making much sense. She started to answer that she was perfectly fine, but when she looked down, she noticed her hands were shaking almost violently. "It's been quite an evening," she began.

"Of course it has," Phillips agreed. "Flying down that hill—"

"I wish that was all that happened to me today," she sighed.

Liam stood and with a worried frown asked, "What else?"

"When I got home from the gym, the doorman was waiting with a police officer. Someone had broken into my apartment."

Liam's jaw clenched. Not a good sign, she decided. She didn't have to guess why he was out of sorts.

"And you're just now mentioning this?" he asked.

She didn't care for his condescending tone. "Yes, I'm just now mentioning this."

"Do you think the home invasion and your road incident might be related?" Phillips asked. Like Liam's, his voice was also strained.

Allison was getting the feeling both of them wanted to yell at her. She tried to justify her actions. "Yes, I know I'm supposed to call you, Agent Phillips, if there are ever any problems, but nothing was taken from my apartment, and there was already a policeman taking a report, so I didn't think it was necessary to bother you. I'm pretty certain I know who it was. My aunt and uncle."

Her new announcement led to another round of questions, and by the time Liam finished with her, she felt like an imbecile. Just because Stamos guessed her aunt and uncle were responsible didn't make it so.

Liam rubbed his brow as if trying to wipe away a headache. "So you've figured it was your aunt and uncle at your apartment."

Feeling backed into a corner, she said, "Yes."

He nodded, then asked, "What reason do you have for being run off the road?"

"I was thinking it was probably road rage."

"Road rage." Phillips repeated her words and dropped into his chair. "What could you have done to make the driver come after you like that?" Frowning, he asked, "Were you texting?"

Was he blaming her? "Of course I was texting," she countered. "I always text while I drive. Oh, and I was putting on lipstick and mascara, so I had to adjust the mirror. . . ." She couldn't think of anything else outrageous to tell him.

Phillips didn't look amused. "This is a serious matter."

"Yes, it is," she agreed.

"I've taken care of the police report on your car," he said then.

"Thank you."

"It wasn't road rage," Liam said.

She stared at him for several seconds, letting the events of the last few hours sink in. "They're related, aren't they? But how? Do you have any theories?"

"Several, as a matter of fact," he said. "We'll find who did this," he added with a granite voice. "And when we do . . ."

Afraid he would say something crazy in front of Phillips, she stood and said, "We're finished, right? Do you want me to work or go home? I should go home." And before Phillips could answer, she said, "I'm going home. I need to go home."

She was beginning to feel a delayed reaction to the effects of her near miss. Her hands were still shaking so much she knew she wouldn't be able to type, and she felt weak. Liam saw how pale she'd become and grabbed her before she could fall.

She was walking out the door with Liam holding her arm when she turned back. "Where's my laptop?"

"The techs have it," Phillips said. "It was pretty banged up. They'll see what they can salvage."

"Thank you," she said.

THE FIRST SHE NOTICED THAT LIAM HAD HER BACKPACK AND phone was when he opened her apartment door for her. He must have gotten them out of the car, she thought, or maybe she'd held them when he pulled her through the window. She was too tired to figure it out now.

Liam led her to her bed and pulled the covers back. Within seconds of laying her head on the pillow, she was sound asleep.

When she opened her eyes again, she looked at her alarm clock and saw that several hours had passed. She could hear Liam's voice in the living room. He was on the phone. He was always on his phone, it seemed. His job didn't let up. She couldn't tell whom he was talking to, but she caught snippets of his conversation. She heard part of a question about an underground cell and another about an informer. He kept his voice low and she couldn't make out anything else. The minute he ended one call, another came in. She honestly didn't know how he could keep up with it all. She knew he was in a high-pressure job, one that was very important, but she also knew it was impossible for one person to handle so many responsibilities. Even Liam. He sounded tired. No matter how much stamina he had, he would eventually crash. Allison got scared thinking about it.

She got out of bed and stood in the doorway until he

noticed her. "Liam, when did you get back from Berlin?" she asked.

His phone rang and he quickly answered it with "I'll be right there" before giving her his full attention. She could see the weariness in his eyes.

"Allison, I'm afraid our talk is going to have to wait," he said.

"Answer my question. When did you get back from Berlin?"

"A week ago."

TWENTY-FIVE

A WEEK? HE'D BEEN BACK IN BOSTON SEVEN DAYS AND NIGHTS and hadn't bothered to call her? What was the matter with him? Didn't he have any idea how much he was hurting her? No, of course not. How could he know? He was an idiot.

Any other woman would have thrown her hands up and moved on. She had tried, but, fortunately or unfortunately, she wasn't any other woman. It was time for her to find some courage and confront him, and that wasn't going to be easy. If he didn't like what she had to say, would she be able to walk away? What if he rejected her? She thought about that possibility for a few minutes and then decided, yes, it would be devastating, but then at least she would know, and she could then figure out a way to put him out of her life.

Her mind was cluttered with worries while she showered and got ready for bed. Every time she thought about barreling down the hill in her car, she felt sick to her stomach. Time to lose herself in her laptop, she concluded. It was the only way she knew to disappear from the world. And then she remembered her laptop had been destroyed, and she was going to have to buy a new one. Thankfully, she had external backups of all her work.

She walked into the living room and came to a quick stop. Liam was still there. He was standing at the window, staring out into the night. He seemed to be deep in thought. His phone was in his hand, and every once in a while he glanced down at it.

"I thought you'd left."

He didn't look at her when he answered, "No." He was staring at his phone again and shaking his head. "Know what I'm looking at?" He walked over to her and handed her his phone.

She looked at the photo and cringed. It was her car, or rather the remains of her car, at the bottom of that hill.

"You could have broken your neck." He sounded angry, but his hands were gentle when he took her by the shoulders. "You should have bruises all over your body."

"But I don't," she assured him. "I'm fine."

He didn't let go of her. His hands slid down her shoulders and rested on the buttons of her silk pajamas. Then he kissed the side of her neck. As his kisses slowly made their way down to her breasts, he unbuttoned her top.

When she let out a low gasp, he swept her up in his arms and carried her to the bed. They were ravenous for each other, and there was no slowing down once the passion between them was ignited.

"Am I hurting you?" he panted. "I'll stop if I'm hurting you."

"No, no. Don't stop," she demanded, and then she bit his earlobe, and he was lost.

They reached climax at the same time. She squeezed him tight and cried out. Liam groaned before collapsing on top of her. His head dropped to her shoulder as he took deep breaths, trying to recover.

"Are you okay, sweetheart?" He was breathing hard.

She was still reeling. "Yes," she said with a sigh.

He finally found enough energy to move before he crushed her. He rolled to his back but kept her locked in his arms. He couldn't seem to make himself let go of her.

"I've never lost control the way I do with you," he confessed.

"You make that sound like a bad thing."

He shrugged. "It is what it is."

What's that supposed to mean? she wondered. Liam got out of bed then, grabbed his clothes, and went into the bathroom.

"Here we go again," she muttered. Would he say, "See you later," or nothing at all? Oh no, not this time. There was no way she was going to let him walk out the door without acknowledging a few things first.

He came out of the bathroom, all buttoned up and tucked in, ready to leave. He seemed preoccupied. She suddenly became furious. All he had to do was leave a little money on her dresser to make her feel like a call girl. She grabbed her robe, put it on, and chased him into the living room. "Please don't leave just yet. I want to ask you a question."

She wasn't given time to ask it. Stamos was knocking on the door and calling Allison's name. She tightened her robe and opened the door a crack.

The doorman didn't ease into his news. "Those maniacs are downstairs again. They're very upset."

"Enough already. Wait ten minutes and then send them up, please."

Muttering to herself, she rushed into the bedroom to get dressed. "I'm through being patient. They aren't going to go away without a fight, and by God, I'm going to give them one." She called to Liam in the living room, "You should probably leave. Otherwise, you'll have to arrest me when I start punching them."

"I'm not going anywhere."

He would turn stubborn on her. "A few minutes ago you couldn't wait to get out of here. . . ."

"No, that's not true," he argued.

"Okay. Why do you want to stay?"

He looked sheepish. "I'm curious."

She slipped into her jeans and was buttoning her blouse when she returned to the living room. Liam put his hands on hers. "I'll do that."

"I've got it.

He smiled. "No, you don't."

She looked down and only then realized the buttons weren't lined up. Feeling foolish, she stood there and let Liam fix them. When he was finished, she tried to step back.

He followed, tilted her chin up, and kissed her. "Take a deep breath," he suggested.

"Why?"

"You're hyperventilating."

"I'm angry."

The relatives from hell were banging on her door. She did as Liam suggested, but a deep breath didn't help at all. She was still tense and livid.

Liam beat her to the door and opened it. Russell Trent came barreling in first. The smell of alcohol swirled around him like a rancid cloud. His wife, Jane, followed. Her shoulders were hunched and her deep-set eyes studied Liam suspiciously before turning to Allison.

"We didn't know you had company," Jane said.

"This is my friend," Allison said. Not wasting any time, she added, "You shouldn't have come here."

Jane tried to soften her expression, but the smile that curled her lips didn't reach her eyes. "We just wanted to see how you're doing. You know we worry about you."

Allison thought she was trying to act timid, which was laughable.

"May we sit down?" Jane asked.

Russell was already sprawled on her sofa, so the question didn't merit an answer.

"Why are you here?" Allison demanded. "I've already told you you're getting nothing more from me."

Jane glanced at Liam, who was standing by the door and watching her like a hawk. She hesitated before answering Allison, as though she was carefully measuring her words before speaking. "We received a summons of a sort just a few days ago, and we were shocked. Really shocked. It all happened so long ago."

"What happened so long ago?"

"Your dear parents died." Jane shook her head and pulled a tissue from her purse, trying her best to act sincere. "We still mourn them."

Allison thought her performance was nauseating. "No, you don't mourn them. My father didn't like either one of you, and for good reason."

Uncle Russell pushed himself upright. "No, no, that's not true. They loved us."

Allison wasn't going to argue. "You still haven't explained why you're here."

"We received a summons that says they want an account of every dollar we spent on you and Charlotte. That's simply impossible," Jane huffed. "Who saves every little receipt for all those years?"

"And you spent a lot of money on us, did you?" Allison asked, doing her best to hold her temper under control.

"Of course," Jane insisted. "It cost a lot of money to feed and clothe and educate you two girls."

"Five hundred thousand?" Allison asked.

Jane was taken aback. "What?"

"Did you and Uncle Russell spend all of the insurance money on Charlotte and me?"

"Of course we did," Jane countered.

"Stop," Allison demanded in a near shout. "Just stop. You didn't spend any of that money on us. We know where it all went. You purchased your house and the land around it. You paid off your bills. You—"

"All right," Jane cried out. "We were wrong, and we're very sorry."

"You were horrible to us. You know that, don't you? You kept threatening that you would put me in foster care without my sister if I acted up. And we had to work to pay for anything we wanted, even school. Remember? And God help me if I was ungrateful. Those terror tactics started when I was four years old."

Seeing her approach wasn't succeeding, Jane decided to double down. There was a sigh and a contrite lowering of her eyes when she said, "We realize now how insensitive we were. We really are ashamed of our behavior, and we're so very sorry."

It was the most insincere apology Allison had ever heard. "What is it you want?" she asked, her voice flat and emotionless. "Or did you come here just to apologize?"

"Actually . . . ," Jane began. She looked at her husband.

Russell teetered when he stood. "We want you to go to court with us and testify on our behalf," he said.

They had rendered Allison speechless. Several seconds passed before she responded. "You want me to lie for you."

"It wouldn't be a lie," Jane insisted. "No, no. We did give you a place to sleep, and we fed you."

"What happens if I don't go to court?"

Jane dabbed at the corners of her eyes, pretending to keep the tears at bay. "We could end up in prison."

"Think of the positive," Allison said. "You'd get to see Bill more often."

Liam coughed to cover his laughter. He had to admit

that the utter audacity of Jane and Russell's plea was impressive, but even more impressive was the way Allison stood up to them.

"You would let us go to prison?" Jane demanded.

The sneer that Allison was accustomed to seeing on her aunt's face was making its way to the surface once again. So much for acting timid, she thought. She went to the door and Liam opened it for her. "It's time for you to leave," she ordered. "Don't come here again. If you do, I'll get a restraining order and call the police. Now, get out."

There was fire in her uncle's bloodshot eyes. "You'll go to hell for this," he mumbled as he stormed past.

Aunt Jane made it to the doorway and then stopped. "Why are you doing this to us?"

"Why?" Allison smiled. "I guess I'm just ungrateful." She slammed the door shut and fell back against it, taking a long, deep breath. When she was calm enough to speak again, she looked at Liam. "I'm sorry you had to see that," she apologized.

"I'm not," he said. "I'm very proud of you."

"Proud?"

"Yes," he answered. "You stood up to them, and they deserved it. The way I figure it, there are three kinds of people. The first kind are the good people who mostly do good things with their lives. The second are good people who sometimes get off track and do bad things. And then the third kind are the bad people who do bad things. I'd put your aunt and uncle in that category. I don't think they'll ever see the error of their ways."

"You're right. I'm sure they still think they can badger me. I haven't heard the last of them." She straightened her shoulders. "But I can handle it," she said with assurance.

"Good girl," Liam said as he gave her a hug.

He went to the desk for his gun. As he was strapping it

on, a text came into his phone. He glanced at the screen. "I've got to go," he said without explanation. He slipped the phone back into his pocket and then walked over to give her a quick kiss. "Sorry. I've got to take care of something. You said you had a question. Can it wait?" he asked.

"Sure," Allison said, resignedly.

And once again she watched him leave.

*HER JOB SAVED HER FROM DWELLING ON LIAM, AND FORTU-*nately, at night, once she turned on her new laptop, she could still escape into her work, and the world swirling around her ceased to exist.

She was back to two agents driving her to and from work, but now she knew most of them and enjoyed their company. Her assignments had become intense, many involving missing funds, and she had to stay late nearly every night.

Jordan had seen the photo of Allison's crunched car—Noah got it from Alec, who had gotten it from Liam. She called to commiserate.

Allison's greeting wasn't the usual. "Men still suck."

"Uh-oh. Should I come over?"

"No. I was just making a statement of fact. What's going on?"

"Your car. Tell me what happened."

"You already know what happened. I told you about it."

"Yes, but I just now saw the photo. I can't believe you walked away from that crash. My God, you hit a tree stump and then flipped and flipped. . . ."

Allison laughed. "I know. I was there."

They spent a half hour discussing the horrible crash. Then Allison said, "I've got to get going. I'll talk to you soon."

"Wait. Did you want to embellish on your opening remark?" Jordan asked, trying to be diplomatic.

"No, not now."

Allison worked another hour and then went to bed. She was thankful Jordan hadn't asked any questions about Liam. Maybe she already knew that the nonrelationship was over. Regardless, Allison wasn't ready to talk about him. Her emotions were still too raw.

Just as she was drifting off to sleep, her phone rang. Her uncle Russell was on the line and was so drunk his words were slurred. He wanted her to know what an ungrateful bitch she was. All of his misery was her fault. She agreed just to get him to stop, but that didn't work. She could hear her aunt Jane screeching like a colony of bats in the background. The sound was ear-piercing. Allison ended the call in the middle of one of his colorful threats.

"Bitch" seemed to be the word of the day, for, not five minutes later, Brett Keaton called to scream that very word at her over and over again. He told her he knew she had taken his work and made it her own. Great, now he believed his own lies. "You should be afraid," he threatened. "Bad things can happen."

She sighed. She was so sick of it all. "Bring it on," she said, and then she ended the call.

All she needed now was for Brett's partner, Fred Stiles, to call and threaten her. Then she'd have the devil's trifecta.

Disheartened and feeling all alone, she muted her phone, turned the lights off, and crashed.

TWENTY-SIX

ON FRIDAY, PHILLIPS CALLED ALLISON INTO HIS OFFICE. SHE assumed he was going to give her another one of his enthusiastic pep talks as to why she should continue to work for him. She knew how much he enjoyed their talks, and for that reason she decided not to tell him she wanted to stay on at the FBI. In fact, she planned to wait until the last possible minute before giving him a reason to gloat.

Phillips was waiting for her in the doorway, and there, standing next to him, was Curtis Bale. Before she walked into the office, she braced herself for another yelling fit about how she'd ruined his life. Phillips pointed to her chair. She didn't want to sit, but she thought she probably should. Phillips was giving her the nod, whatever that was supposed to mean.

"Okay, I'm ready," she said, staring at Bale. "Let me have it."

He smiled. "I want to apologize to you."

She was hesitant to believe him. "Okay . . ."

"I finally realized I needed to get my head out of the sand

and look at the evidence. You found the leak, and it was in my department, and I missed it." He sounded sincere.

"He was very clever the way he hid what he was doing," she said, offering a bit of empathy.

"Still, it was my responsibility. I lost touch with the people in my division. I should have been more vigilant."

She liked that he was owning it. "What happens now?"

"I'm taking some time off," he said.

"Then he and I will talk again," Phillips supplied.

She extended her hand to Bale. "I wish you good luck."

Bale shook her hand. As she watched him walk out of the office, she thought about the irony of it all. If Bale had been a better manager, if he had rid his division of bad employees, there wouldn't have been a leak, and her life would have been very different. It was the leak that had brought Liam to her. At the moment she wasn't sure if that was a good thing or a bad thing.

Phillips waited until they were alone, and then said, "I'm not usually wrong, but I admit I made a mistake with Bale. He was so irrational when it came to blaming you for the mess he was in, I actually thought he might be responsible for running you off the road."

"What made you change your mind?" she asked.

"We discovered he had left Boston and driven out to visit his sister in Ohio. He just returned a couple of days ago. There's nothing to link him to your crash."

"That's good to know. I guess you don't need to send guards wherever I go now," she said hopefully.

"I'm afraid that's not going to change," he said. "Bale wasn't responsible, but someone was, and he's still out there. Until we find him, you'll have protection."

She was just about to return to her station when Phillips surprised her by asking if she was still going to be modeling for a benefit at the Hamilton Saturday night.

"Yes," she answered. "And it's important, so please don't drag me back in here."

He promised not to bother her, and in the spirit of good-will, since he'd been working her like a dog, he announced she could leave at noon today.

Two agents accompanied her to the spa and salon where Giovanni had booked appointments. She promised to text them when she was finished, but they refused to leave. After a long negotiation, she finally convinced them that two men standing watch might be a tad unsettling for the women patrons of the salon, and they reluctantly agreed to wait out-side. She then spent three hours getting waxed and lotioned, pedicured and manicured, and an extra hour listening to her favorite hairdresser, a most unusual young lady named Penny, who had more piercings and tattoos than an entire biker gang. Penny caught Allison up on her exciting life. She always had at least three boyfriends—at the same time, of course—because otherwise, she explained, she would be bored. Penny believed her life was complicated, but com-pared to Allison's, it was a walk in the park. Allison couldn't tell anything about her own life, not that she wanted to, so she sat quietly and listened, letting Penny think she was one dull bookworm.

"I don't get it," Penny said. "With your body and your looks, you should have men falling all over you."

Allison wanted to change the subject, but Penny wasn't ready to talk about anything other than Allison's miserable dating history. She gave her tips on how to attract a man while she trimmed her hair, and when she was done, she air-kissed Allison on both cheeks and sent her on her way. Penny didn't notice the two men waiting in the parking lot.

The agents dropped Allison off at her apartment, and she decided to give herself some time to decompress. She was tired of worrying. She had spent far too much energy stressing over Bale and Bill and Brett and Stiles and her aunt and uncle. She wasn't going to worry about Liam, either, although that was easier said than done. She prided herself on not breaking down and crying, and once she was back in her living room she reached for her new laptop. There was only one problem. It was becoming more and more difficult to escape into her work. Liam kept getting in her way, and that infuriated her.

A day later Giovanni lifted her out of her pitiful mood. She couldn't feel sorry for herself when she was with him. Even when he was barking orders, he was fun to be around. She loved him for a lot of reasons. He was kind and generous and honorable, and most of all she loved him because he really cared and watched out for her.

He was also quite a taskmaster. She was told to be in the suite at the Hamilton at exactly four o'clock, and she didn't dare come late. Giovanni was fanatical about punctuality. Three designers were showing their work and donating substantial amounts to a children's fund. Allison was one of five models for Giovanni.

The setup for the show had been carefully thought out. Each designer was assigned a section of a large ballroom with double doors that opened outside to a magnificent garden. The walkway had been built up a few feet above the audience and ran the length of the garden. There were rows of chairs on either side with cameras and lights positioned everywhere. Fortunately the weather was cooperating. It was going to be a beautiful, though somewhat humid, evening.

Giovanni had been alerted that Allison had arrived and rushed to greet her. Impeccably dressed in a dark suit, he looked more like a movie star than a designer. Tall and lean with an Adonis face and dark curly hair, he could have passed for thirty but was actually in his middle fifties. She kissed him on both cheeks and then hugged him.

He held both of her hands and looked deeply into her eyes. "How are you doing?" he asked.

"I'm good," she assured him.

"Are those ghouls leaving you alone?"

"I'm ignoring them."

"You'd tell me if there were any more problems, wouldn't you?"

"Yes, I would."

"I love you like a daughter. You know that, don't you?"

"I love you, too."

He let go of her and began giving orders. Allison changed into a wrap, sat in one of the makeup chairs, and waited while everyone scurried around her in a controlled panic. A curtain separated the different designers who were showing previews of next summer's collections, and Giovanni's assistant, Peter, was making certain no one got a peek at his creations.

Giovanni had requested to be last. Allison was scheduled to model three different outfits. According to Giovanni, the showstopper was the evening gown she would wear for the finale.

The show went off without a hitch. After walking the runway twice, oblivious of the crowd and the flashing lights, Allison returned to get ready for her last appearance. She sat in the chair, her posture ramrod straight, as Giovanni's team worked their magic and transformed her into what they declared was their greatest achievement, a compliment that didn't hold much weight since they told her that very thing every time they got her ready for a show. Her eye makeup was a smoky gray, and her hair was down, swaying below her shoulders except for one strand that had been twisted into a thin braid and pinned into a crown on top of her head.

Once she was made up, Peter slipped the gown over her head. It was virginal white with a beaded low V-neck top.

The beading cascaded down onto the gathered diaphanous silk skirt. When she walked, the fabric flowed as though she were a Greek goddess floating on air. Her curves made the gown all the more provocative with each step she took.

At last she was ready for Giovanni's approval. He finally appeared from behind the curtain and gave her the once-over. He seemed to be taken aback by the sight of her, and then he nodded.

She stood near the double doors ready to make her entrance. Instead of blocking out the audience, this time she peeked around to look over the crowd. She was surprised by the number. Only those benefactors who had paid a steep price for a ticket were allowed to attend, but obviously crashers had gotten in somehow. They were five deep behind the last rows.

There was a subtle change in the lighting and the music. The pulsing sound was deeper, building anticipation. Allison stood still, waiting for the tap on her shoulder telling her to walk, her mind racing. She did try, but she couldn't disappear now. Her mind went to Liam. Could he be there in the crowd? It was a crazy thought, yet nothing would have surprised her. He'd shown up on the street when Bill confronted her. He had been there when her car crashed down the hill. He might even have been at her graduation. He seemed to show up at the oddest times.

At every show she'd ever done for Giovanni, his assistant would whisper something outrageous right before she started down the runway to help her relax. She thought he'd forgotten, but as it turned out, tonight was no exception.

"Remember the three rules, Allison. No tripping, no smiling, and no puking on the guests."

She almost burst into laughter. No puking on guests? She wouldn't be able to get that visual out of her mind anytime soon.

Peter stood behind her, and when the music reached a crescendo, he touched Allison's shoulder. "Go," he whispered.

She stepped around the corner. Her body went on autopilot, and she walked just the way she was supposed to, long-legged strides, head held high, devoid of any expression on her face. At the end of the runway, she assumed the pose for a second or two, then pivoted and headed back. Thunderous applause followed her.

WHILE ALLISON WAS BEING TRANSFORMED BY GIOVANNI'S team, Jud Bronsky was waiting to be interviewed.

An extremely unattractive man with a personality to match, Jud was built like a gorilla, a fact he was proud of because he believed his size and shape made him look more threatening, and in his line of work, that was an important requirement. Jud had long arms and legs and hair growing out of his knuckles and his ears. He wasn't much for grooming. He did shave because he thought he looked younger than his thirty-two years without a beard, but that was as far as it went. Showering was only done when he was in the mood, which wasn't all that often, but he believed his cologne was better than soap any day. His friends, what few he had, called him Tarzan, and Jud liked the nickname because it made him feel cocky.

He wasn't feeling cocky now. He was sitting in an interrogation room sweating bullets while he waited for the FBI agent to tell him why he was being detained. He was going to demand an attorney but wanted to wait until after he found out what he was going to be charged with. Maybe this was just a fishing expedition. Maybe he wasn't even a suspect, and they didn't know what he had done. That was it, he decided. They were just fishing for information.

Jud was certain they didn't have a shred of proof that

he'd done anything wrong. The car he'd used to run the woman off the road was in the junkyard now, in line to be stripped and crushed. His cousin Eddie, who ran the junk-yard, promised he'd get it done as soon as possible. As a precaution Jud had already wiped the car down. There wasn't a single fingerprint anywhere. He'd been meticulous about that, making sure he didn't miss any spots. No, the FBI didn't have anything on him, and the only reason he was sitting there waiting was that they wanted information.

He was a little apprehensive about the agent coming in to question him. He'd heard the other agents talking about him. They sounded respectful but also a little nervous. Jud decided it was all an act to scare him.

He was wrong about that. Exactly thirty seconds after Special Agent Liam Scott walked into the interrogation room, Jud was shaking in his boots.

Another agent walked in first. He took up a position by the observation window with his arms folded, silent and watchful. Then Liam Scott walked in. He dropped a file on the table and, towering over Jud, said, "You're being charged with attempted murder."

"What? No, I didn't try to murder anyone. I didn't."

Liam acted as though Jud hadn't protested and contin-ued. "I'd get a good attorney if I were you because, when I'm done with you, you could be going away for the rest of your life."

In all the times he'd been dragged into a police station, Jud had never been told to get an attorney. The detectives usually tried to discourage him. This agent was different.

"You don't have anything on me," he stammered. "I don't need an attorney because I didn't do anything wrong."

The bluff didn't work. "There are highway surveillance cameras showing you tailing Allison Trent. We found your car, you prick. You tried to kill the woman I love. I just may kill you myself, right here and now."

The look in the agent's eyes sent chills down Jud's spine. "I didn't even know the woman. Why would I want to kill her?" he asked, trying to sound sincere.

"We'll ask your cousin Eddie when he testifies against you."

Jud knew he was cornered. He had been hoping the agent was lying about finding the car, but now Jud knew he was telling the truth. Damn his cousin. Eddie hadn't done what he'd been told. He'd promised to destroy the car, and Jud had given him a hundred dollars to do it quick. What a slacker, he thought.

Liam checked the time and turned to leave. Allison was at the Hamilton, and he needed to see her, to make certain she was all right. There were two agents with her, but he wouldn't stop worrying until she was by his side.

"Book him," he ordered as he reached for the door.

"Wait." In a panic, Jud blurted, "I want a deal. For a lesser charge I'll give you the name of the man who hired me. Just charge me with a misdemeanor."

Liam laughed. "For attempted murder?"

"I wasn't trying to kill her, I tell you. Going down the hill like that was an accident. I was only trying to get her to stop, but I hit her bumper too hard."

"Why were you trying to get her to stop?"

"I was supposed to steal her laptop."

Liam put his hands flat on the table and leaned over. "Who were you working for?"

"Do we have a deal?" He looked from Liam to the other agent expectantly.

"Depends," Liam said. "What can you give us?"

Jud persisted. "I want a deal first."

"You help us out, we'll help you," Liam offered.

Jud took a deep breath and said, "Fred Stiles."

"What about Stiles?" Liam asked.

"He's the guy who hired me. You see? I'm cooperating."

Liam knew Bronsky wasn't finished confessing. His body language said as much. He was squirming in his chair and couldn't look Liam in the eyes.

"It wasn't an attempted murder," Jud insisted. "I was just supposed to take her laptop and make her come with me." He dared a quick glance up and wished he hadn't. The agent looked as though his anger was ready to erupt.

"Where were you going to take her?" Liam asked.

"I didn't know. I was just supposed to get her and then call for a location to drop her off. The only thing I was told was that she was supposed to finish some program. I figured the less I knew, the better. I didn't want her to get hurt, and I would have gone down that hill to see if she was okay, honest, but I saw a car coming, and I had to get out of there."

"Where is Stiles now?"

"I don't know. I haven't seen him since he gave me the job. Stiles can be a real badass if you don't come through for him. He always gets what he wants. I figure if I lie low for a while, he'll calm down. My guess is he's already got somebody else to do the job. One thing I know for sure about him, he won't give up. He'll send . . ."

Liam was out the door before Jud finished his sentence.

TWENTY-SEVEN

ONCE BEHIND THE CURTAIN, ALLISON LET PETER CAREFULLY remove the gown. After dressing in her silk skirt and blouse, she sat in front of a mirror and unwound her braid. She brushed her hair and thought of Liam. She had actually expected to see him in the crowd. The longer he stayed on her mind, the angrier she became and the harder she brushed. A few minutes later, her hair was shiny and straight, and her anger had subsided. She finally came to the realization that she was being completely irrational. She just wanted to feel sorry for herself. How could she not? she justified. In the last few weeks she'd been told she'd ruined innumerable lives. She had ruined Bill's life because she hadn't kept him out of prison. She'd ruined her aunt's and uncle's lives because she wouldn't lie for them in court. And, oh yes, she had also ruined Brett's and Stiles's lives because she wouldn't let them steal her work.

Were they all crazy? Or was she? The question merited thought.

She took a cotton ball and some mineral oil and removed the eye shadow. She'd wash off the rest of the makeup when she got home, she decided. The FBI agents would be waiting for her.

The party had moved inside to the ballroom, where the air-conditioning cooled the guests, and food and beverages were in abundance. Giovanni was the star, as usual.

Allison was leaving the dressing room when Peter found her and handed her her purse. "Your boyfriend is here," he said. "He wanted me to remind you that you're supposed to wait for him in the garden."

She started to tell him she didn't have a boyfriend, then changed her mind. "What did he look like?"

"How many boyfriends do you have?"

"Too many to count," she answered. "Now, please tell me. What did he look like?"

"He's kind of tall, with blond tips in his hair, and to be honest, darling, I think you should tell him to stop using so much self-tanner."

She froze. Oh God, he was describing Brett. He might have been there to threaten her. Then again, he had it in him to be violent. She'd witnessed his temper tantrums. She wasn't going to panic.

"Are you all right?" Peter asked. "You've gone pale."

"I'm fine," she said. Peter turned to go back to the party, and she called after him, "Tell Giovanni I'll talk to him later. I'm leaving."

"No need to hurry, Allison. I'm here now." Brett spoke from right behind her.

She started to run for the doors, but Brett anticipated the move and latched onto her upper arm. He jerked her around to face him. They were the only two in the dressing room. Everyone else had gone to the party. There wasn't anyone to help her.

His eyes glowed with his hatred. "You're coming with me."

"Why?"

"You have to fix this mess you created. You stole everything from me. I want you to give it back."

"I stole from you?" She was so astonished by his absurd remark she had to pause for a second. "You tried to take my work and pass it off as your own."

He squeezed her arm even harder until she cried out. "I ordered a new car, and now I can't pay for it, and I bought a condo down in South Beach, but they want the money or the deal is off, and I don't have any money because of you. You took all that from me, and you're going to give it back."

She couldn't believe how he could justify his actions. "You think saying it's yours makes it yours? I'm not giving you my work."

"It's mine. I worked on that program for a long time, and you can't prove I didn't."

"You're delirious. You'll never get away with it."

She could see panic overtaking him. He shook her hard. She was surprised by his strength. "You humiliated me in front of my peers and my investor," he said.

"Do you mean Stiles?"

"Of course I mean Stiles. He's going to see I followed through on my promise to make us millions. I shouldn't have gone to him. . . . I shouldn't have asked him for money, but I didn't realize how dangerous he was, and now . . . Please, Allison." His bravado was beginning to vanish and now he just sounded pathetic.

"Let go of me," she demanded.

"All I need is the missing code, and you have to give it to me."

Brett was desperate. He'd gotten in over his head and now he was drowning. "No." She tried to peel his hand away, but he wouldn't let go.

"I already have buyers," he said. "I can make it worth

your while. Just let me have the whole program, and I'll give you a cut."

"No."

He looked desperate. "You're coming with me, and you're giving me the entire program. He'll kill me if I don't get it."

"You're going to have to drag me out of here, and there are two men outside who aren't going to let you do that."

"I've seen them. You don't think I haven't planned a way out?"

"In about five seconds I'm going to start screaming."

"I didn't want to do this," he said. He pulled a pistol out of his pocket and showed it to her before putting it back, with his hand on the trigger and the barrel pointing at her.

"Where did you get that gun?" She was so shocked she could barely think.

"Stiles gave it to me."

"My God, Brett. You aren't a killer. You need to get away from him," she said. "And get rid of that gun."

He acted as though he hadn't heard a word she'd said. "I swear I'm going to shoot you if you don't get moving. If I can't have that program, you're not going to be able to sell it, either. I don't have any problem killing you."

He pressed the gun into her side and pushed her toward the doors that led to the garden. She opened the doors, took a step through them, and stopped.

"Move," Brett ordered as he gave a shove to her ribs.

"I'm sorry, Brett," she said.

"For what?" he asked sarcastically. "Making my life miserable?"

"No, I'm sorry you're about to get shot. I imagine it's going to hurt like the blazes."

Brett took a step forward, and that was when he saw Liam standing outside the door with his gun drawn.

"Get out of my way," Brett shouted. "I'm not going to hurt her. We're just going to work on our program, and I'm driving her home." He was scrambling for words, his hand still on his gun.

"Let go of her and put your hands up," Liam ordered.

Brett shook his head and pulled Allison closer.

"He has a gun," she warned.

"I know." Liam's voice was calm and steady. "Put your hands up," he repeated.

Brett reacted. He yanked the gun from his pocket and was raising it when Liam fired. Before Brett finished his first howl of pain, Liam had grabbed the gun from his hand and pulled Allison away from him.

"You shot me," Brett cried. "You shot my arm."

Liam nodded. "Yes. Yes, I did."

The other two agents came running. Allison moved close to Liam and watched Brett being handcuffed. As one of the agents carted him away, Brett clutched his arm and demanded to be driven to a hospital. The second agent turned to Liam. "We'll take it from here," he said, and then turned to Allison. "I can send a car for you."

"I'll take you home, Allison," Liam stated in his no-non-sense, "don't argue with me" voice.

"Wait a minute. What are you doing here?" she asked. The fact that he had appeared out of nowhere had just hit her. "Did you know Brett was coming?"

Liam wanted to get out of there and tried to pull her along, but she wasn't cooperating. Seeing that she wasn't going to wait for an answer, he decided to give in. "I came here for you," he began, and before she could react, he continued. "I knew someone was going to come after you, and I wanted to get you out of here and make sure you were safe. If anything ever happened to you . . ."

He couldn't go on. The thought of losing Allison was

almost too much to bear. He pulled her into his arms and held her tight against him.

She could feel him shaking. "You were worried about me."

"Hell yes, I was worried." He kissed her forehead, then pulled away from her. "The man who ran you off the road works for Stiles. His name is Jud Bronsky, and he's going to turn state's evidence against the bastard. He's got a lot to tell."

Astonished by the lengths Stiles had been willing to go to, she whispered, "He gave Brett the gun. I don't know if he would have shot me or not."

"I'm certain Stiles or one of his men wouldn't have had any qualms about killing you. He not only wanted your laptop; he wanted you. He was sure he would be able to force you to give him the rest of the code for your software. You'd disappear and he'd sell your work and make a fortune."

She was having trouble taking it all in. "Where is Stiles now?"

"I just got a call. Bronsky was able to give enough information to track him down. He's in a gated enclave about a half hour out of Boston. Agents are picking him up right now."

She was weak with relief. "Brett told me he was afraid of Stiles. Now I understand why. I can't help feeling sorry for Brett."

"Oh, hell no."

"What?" she asked, confused by his reaction.

"You are not going to try to make a deal for Brett or plead on his behalf. He had a gun on you. I'm never going to forget that." He took her hand and started to walk toward the lobby. "I don't like you wearing all that makeup," he said, hoping to change the subject until he could get his nerves under control.

"And I don't like you looking half-dead."

"I don't like seeing anyone pointing a gun at you."

"I didn't particularly like it, either," she replied.

"It scared the hell out of me."

She glanced up at him. "Me, too."

They were in the middle of the lobby when he stopped and turned to her. "I'm never going to let anyone hurt you."

"I know."

He leaned down and kissed her. Now was neither the time nor the place, he told himself, but it didn't seem to matter. "I love you, Allison."

"I know you do."

She tried to keep walking, but he stopped her. "That's all you have to say to me?"

"I love you, too, Liam."

He kissed her then. His mouth covered hers in a kiss that held nothing back. They were both having difficulty catching their breath when he lifted his head. She tried to take a step back. He wouldn't let her.

"Isn't this where you tell me you have to leave tomorrow, and a life with me could never work because of your job and the demands on you?" she asked.

His arms were wrapped around her waist, and he stared into her eyes as he answered, "Yeah, that's pretty much what I used to believe . . . until now. I can't seem to stay away from you. Have you noticed?"

"I have noticed."

"What do you think we ought to do about it?" he asked.

She had a sly twinkle in her eyes, and he couldn't wait to hear what she would say.

"You're conflicted, Liam, but I'll be happy to clear it all up for you."

"Conflicted, huh?"

He didn't let her explain. He was suddenly eager to get

her back to her apartment so he could show her how much he loved her. He had quite a bit inside him to say to her, too. It wasn't until they were on their way that she finally got his full attention.

"I'm not going to stay around and watch you work yourself to death. I won't do it, Liam. I've been working eighty-hour weeks for Phillips because of that stupid contract, but as soon as the six months are up, things are going to change. I need a life outside of my computer."

He nodded, but neither one said another word until they were back in her apartment. His silence was making her extremely anxious.

"What do you think?" she finally asked.

"I need a life, too."

Tears came into her eyes. "You do?"

"Know what else I need?"

"What?" she whispered.

"I need you." He put his arms around her waist and pulled her close. "I love you." He paused for a second and then said, "I quit my job."

"What . . . You what?"

"I've been giving it a lot of thought the last couple of weeks. It took some hard-nosed soul-searching, but I finally figured out what I want. I told the bureau I was going to hand in my resignation Monday."

Flabbergasted, she stepped back so she could poke him in the chest. "But you love your job. And you quit? What is wrong with you? Don't you know how to do anything in moderation? Does it always have to be all or nothing with you? Stop grinning at me. I'm trying to make you think about your future."

"I am thinking about my future," he insisted.

She let him kiss her before she asked, "When you told them you were quitting, what was the reaction?"

"I got promoted."

"Promoted?" she repeated. "You got promoted?"

He shrugged. "Go figure."

"What does that mean?"

"Hell if I know."

He took her hand and led her into the bedroom. "I won't be traveling much with my new position. I've really grown to dislike it, anyway, and I've trained enough agents who can get the job done."

Astonished by what he was telling her, she turned to him, speechless.

"Sweetheart, if you don't take your clothes off, I can't ravish you."

He was desperate to touch her, but he let her wash off the makeup first. When she returned to the bedroom, they set a new record for disrobing. He wanted to go slow, but the passion was too strong. All the feelings he had been holding inside for so long exploded in a glorious moment of ecstasy.

Later, when she was lying next to him, Allison started laughing for no other reason than she was deliriously happy.

"Next time we'll take it slow, I promise," he said, and then he laughed because he knew with Allison, that wasn't possible.

He leaned up and took her hand in his. "I've been thinking. . . ."

She waited, and when he didn't continue, she said, "Yes?"

"What?"

He looked pensive. What was going on in his mind? "You said you've been thinking."

"That's right. I've been thinking you'll want me to come home to you every night."

She smiled. "Yes, as a matter of fact, I do expect you to come home to me."

He was searching for the right words, feeling awkward and unsure, which was completely foreign to him. But he wanted it to be right, and he had to get it said now.

"And I'm thinking you'll want to sleep in my bed every night, so it should probably be our bed."

"You're right again. Liam, what are you trying to say?"

He shrugged. "I'm thinking we should probably get married."

"Yes, we should."

He grinned. "Okay, since you asked, I'll marry you."

"I did not ask you—"

"Sure, you did. Just now."

"I should warn you, it's not going to be normal."

"Sex or our marriage?"

"Our marriage."

"I didn't expect it would be."

"I'm not normal," she whispered. "You need to know that."

"Sweetheart, I figured that out five minutes after I met you. You're far superior to normal."

Her eyes filled with tears. "That's the sweetest thing you could have said to me. What's the matter with you?"

"I love you. That's what's the matter."

She cuddled up against him and closed her eyes.

He gently stroked her hair with his fingertips. "I guess we should start looking for a town house somewhere in Silicon Valley."

"About that . . ."

"What?"

"I'm thinking we should live here in Boston."

"Yeah? With the new job, living here would be perfect for me," he admitted.

"I'll still take on the boys," she said. "As soon as I'm finished with my newest weapon, they'll all want it. The FBI gets it first, though."

"Will you set up your company in our home, then?"

"About that . . ."

She sounded so earnest he braced for the next announcement. "Yes?"

"I'd like to keep working for Phillips."

"You're serious?"

"Go ahead and laugh. I know you want to."

He did exactly that. Once he calmed down, she explained that she was still going to run her company with Jordan. "Please don't tell Phillips."

"He's going to notice when you keep coming to work."

"He's going to gloat."

"Yes, he will."

"The working conditions will have to change, of course. I'm only going to be available part-time. And I don't want him pointing to the chair any longer. It's just plain rude."

"He loves pointing. You're going to take that away from him?"

She sighed. "Okay, I'll let him point to the chair."

"You're such a pushover," he laughed.

"Hey!" She jabbed his shoulder with her finger.

Liam grabbed her hand and kissed it. "When will you tell Charlotte you're going to stay in Boston?"

"About that . . ."

"You want me to tell her."

"I'll tell her we're getting married first, and then I'll slip in that we're staying in Boston. I'll probably blame you."

"That's fine with me. Are you going to tell her you finally confronted your aunt and uncle and really let them have it?"

"Probably," she said. "Letting them have it didn't seem to do any good. They're both still calling. Uncle Russell is always drunk and always shouting."

"You've done enough," he said. "I'm begging you. Let me have a turn. I can get them to stop. I promise."

"Sure. Why not? Take a turn. Then they can start calling your number."

"No, they won't," he said with complete confidence.

"You mentioned with your promotion you can take a step back and let other agents you've trained handle more of the work."

"That's right."

She raised herself up on her elbow and propped her chin in her hand so she could stare into his amazing green eyes. "And exactly what is that work?"

He answered, "Maybe someday when we're old and gray, and we're rocking on the front porch watching our grandchildren, I'll tell you all about it."

She kissed him on the cheek and laid her head back down on his chest. For the first time in her life she knew how it felt to love and be loved.

"Sounds good to me," she whispered.

Ready to find
your next great read?

Let us help.

Visit prh.com/nextread

Penguin
Random
House